CONARD COUNTY: HARD PROOF

RACHEL LEE

HIS BRAND OF JUSTICE

DELORES FOSSEN

MIX
Paper from
responsible sources
FSC
FSC C007454

This book is produced from independently certified FSC
paper to ensure responsible forest management.

For more information visit: www.harpercollins.co.uk/green

Printed and bound in Spain
by CPI, Barcelona

MILLS & BOON

First Published in Great Britain 2020
by Mills & Boon, an imprint of HarperCollins*Publishers*
1 London Bridge Street, London, SE1 9GF

Conard County: Hard Proof © 2020 Susan Civil-Brown
His Brand of Justice © 2020 Delores Fossen

ISBN: 978-0-263-28045-6

0920

MIX

CONARD COUNTY: HARD PROOF

RACHEL LEE

Chapter One

Steve Hawks glanced impatiently at his watch. Time was getting on, Conard City was nowhere in view and he had an appointment to keep. He hated being late.

If it hadn't been for the obstacle in the road that had been too small to see, he wouldn't be this far behind. Damn tire change. At least the rental company had provided a full-size tire, not a doughnut, which would have slowed him even more.

Ah, well, he could try his cell again, if he could get a signal out here. Looking at the open expanse with mountains in the distance, he doubted he would.

Oh, hell. For once the world would have to wait for him.

He had a couple of weeks before his production crew arrived, but it was necessary to do groundwork for his TV show: *Ghostly Ties*. He had to know his clients, had to know the area and fill in some local history before filming.

Although he'd been at it for three years now, Steve sometimes found it difficult to say he hosted "one of those ghostie shows." A far cry from his former life as a detective. However, he figured it was just a different type of investigation. He looked for rational explanations and he delighted in local history and lore. All of which required a lot of detective work.

Quit it, he told himself. He didn't mind the work at all. In fact, he enjoyed it. Without it, he couldn't have sent his parents to a happy retirement in Costa Rica. Great side benefit.

So he drove down this aging state highway, amid ranches—was that what they were called or were these something else?—looking at endless square miles of browning autumn grasses and trees. And occasionally a bunch of cows. Or steers.

He laughed at himself. He had a lot to learn out here.

Then he saw a large flock of sheep. Okay, was that a *sheep* ranch? He shook his head and hoped he didn't make a total fool out of himself before he could ask the right questions. Not that it really mattered. He'd realized long ago that you made more friends if you could laugh at yourself.

At long last, he saw what appeared to be rectangular shapes rising in the distance. It sure wasn't the slowly rolling hills he'd been seeing most of the way. At least the mountains appeared to be growing. For the longest time, the mountains hadn't seemed to be coming closer. Now they did. Big and looming.

And that must be Conard City up ahead. A huge semi and trailer seemed to come out of nowhere over the lip of a rise and roared past him, buffeting his car a bit. So there *was* life out here.

He'd been to many places in his life, but he honestly couldn't remember one with such huge empty expanses.

DEPUTY CANDELA SERRANO, Candy for short, waited in the sheriff's office for the arrival of Steve Hawks. She'd drawn the "short straw" for who was going to babysit the guy, but it hadn't really been a drawing. She'd been here only six months, replacing Cat Henderson, who had apparently been quite popular among the deputies. Plus, being so new, Candy couldn't expect to do anything major until she'd been assessed.

Anyway, here she was, assigned to assist a ghost hunter,

of all things. To be a liaison. To smooth his way and maybe keep him out of trouble.

Not that she really minded. Ghost hunting seemed like a scam to her, but there was no reason helping couldn't be fun. As October settled in fully, with Halloween looming, the shorter days and the atmosphere might add to the spookiness. Or at least those were her arguments for making the assignment more palatable.

While she didn't like ghost-hunting TV, she *did* like spookiness and hat strange upside-down magic that held dark promise like a good thriller.

The streets around town were already succumbing. Uncut pumpkins decorated front porches. She looked forward to seeing their carved faces. A few trees dangled sturdy skeletons, and she saw more than one bedsheet ghost. And she always grinned.

A much pleasanter environment than the places she'd visited in the Army. Too often she had to shake herself out of a horrifying memory. A good ghost story might be a relief because she knew all about *real* ghosts.

Velma, the ancient dispatcher, sat on the far side of the room, her headset firmly planted under and around her thinning gray hair. There was a rumor that dispatch was going to be moved to a room in the back, but in six months Candy had come to like Velma and her colleagues right where they were. They were company, and their chatter was just as illuminating as the police band radio. Maybe more so because the dispatchers talked to individual patrols, giving Candy better detail. Plus, they could talk to cops who had for some reason moved to cell phones from their radios.

She supposed that in time she'd understand that, too.

Velma suddenly spoke. Her smoke-roughened voice emerged from the ever-present cloud of the cigarettes she frequently smoked right beneath the no-smoking sign.

"This might be your guy, Candy."

Candy turned her attention to the front door. Oh, yeah. The autumn clothes fit fairly well with the surrounding area, except they looked almost new. No years of wear.

Good-looking guy, too. A face for TV maybe, except not perfect. Those slight imperfections, a scar on his chin and a nose that wasn't perfectly straight, suggested a past that might be almost normal.

"Hi," he said. "I'm sorry I'm late. Had a little car trouble on the way. I'm looking for Deputy Serrano?"

Candy rose immediately from her desk. "Steve Hawks?"

"So they tell me." With an engaging smile, he offered his hand and shook hers. "I wouldn't blame you if you're irritated. I hate to be late, but damn, those mountains just wouldn't move any closer."

She chuckled, knowing exactly what he meant. "For the longest time they just seem to be pulling away. Have a seat, Mr. Hawks."

He sat in the chair beside her desk. Then he came straight to the point. "I imagine you didn't volunteer for this assignment."

She didn't know quite how to answer that. Nothing seemed politic.

"I like a link with the local police," he went on. "I want facts, not fiction, and a lot of what people think is true just isn't."

She had no trouble understanding that. Already she began to like him. Facts, not fiction, seemed like a good motto. "I prefer facts myself." She hoped that didn't sound like a challenge, but it probably did. Too bad.

The door swung open, admitting a uniformed deputy named Connie Parish. She flashed a grin as she headed toward the break room. "Seems like you're sitting right where Cat used to sit." Without a pause, she kept striding toward the back.

What did that mean? Candy wondered as she returned her attention to the puzzle named Steve.

"Do you know the Castelle family?" he asked. "I'm here to interview them."

"I know of them. I don't think I've talked to them except in passing." Were they subjects for his show? That was hard to believe considering she'd often seen the adults outside playing with a young daughter and a growing dog. A normal, happy family. Not one shadowed by uneasy things.

Now her interest was piqued. "Do they have a ghost problem?"

"That's what I'm here to find out. I'd love to debunk it for them." He glanced at his watch, then rose. "I need to check in at the motel. How about we have dinner somewhere so you can grill me along with a steak?"

He probably had an expense account, she decided. So yeah, she'd hit him up for a dinner. "You have two good choices in this town. The truck stop grill or Maude's place. Good food at both."

He arched a brow. "That's it?"

"The Mexican restaurant hasn't opened yet, but we do have a burger place and a pizzeria on the edge of town. The burgers are okay, Maude's are better. Pizza?" She shrugged, hardly a recommendation. "Both are popular hangouts for young people. Oh, yeah, how could I forget Mahoney's Bar? Great sandwiches and fried chicken."

Steve nodded, apparently accepting the limitations. "I'll meet you at Maude's at six, then. I can get directions at the motel."

She pointed straight out the window. "The café is tha-taway, a half block. The City Diner, the sign says, but everyone calls it Maude's."

"Been here forever, huh?"

"Maybe two forevers."

That elicited a bark of laughter from him as he headed toward the door.

"Seems like an okay guy," Velma remarked, then went back to her duties, acknowledging an officer on the radio who was making a traffic stop outside town.

An okay guy? Maybe. Since he was a television star, Candy withheld judgment and just hoped she didn't meet a soaring ego.

DESPITE HIS TARDINESS, Steve thought he had started on a decent path with Deputy Serrano. He'd sensed only a mild resistance, for which he couldn't blame her. Babysitting a reality TV personality wasn't on most people's top-ten list.

On the other hand, he really liked to get the police involved as much as he could. Even one on-screen interview of a cop providing information could prove extremely revealing, and it certainly lent credence to his investigation. If Serrano didn't want to do it, she might well know someone who would.

He'd like to get her, though. She was a pretty Latina he judged would photograph well.

What the hell did a guy wear to a dinner at a café in this town? Dress up seemed unlikely from his minor scoping as he drove in. He settled on jeans and a white dress shirt. Without a tie, and with sleeves rolled up, it became casual.

Dang, he could remember times when he never had to think of such things. As a plainclothes detective, he'd needed only a couple of suits and a whole bunch of clean shirts.

Big deal. The clock said he had a little time to unpack, not that there was much. During the next few weeks, he didn't need anything that couldn't be cleaned in a coin laundry. When his production team came, they'd bring more with them.

Then he sat in the chair beside the small table and looked

around at the room. Someone had tried to modernize it, but large-purchase bedding and lamps from a supply house didn't quite make it. Chosen to be inoffensive, they practically blended in with the motel-room background. The walls, however, were solid wood planks, not paneling.

Not that he minded. He'd slept in worse places because the show did have a budget. One hotel was expensive? Then find something cheaper at the next location. He didn't think the La-Z-Rest motel was going to break any bank.

And why didn't this motel give itself a face-lift with a new name? It was so 1950s. All it lacked was a sputtering neon sign. No sputtering here.

Sighing, eager to be doing something besides sitting on his can, especially after a long day in the car, he pulled out his slim leather portfolio and looked at the numbers he needed to call. The Castelles first. They were the ones who were worried enough to call him.

His major goal in this was to ease a little girl's mind. The seven-year-old had the problem and her parents didn't know how to handle it. They'd tried everything, they'd explained the first time he talked to them.

His secondary goal was to ensure no one was after the family, and that neither parent was frightening the daughter for some end of his or her own. He'd been a cop too long to overlook such possibilities.

He hoped they didn't necessarily want a paranormal explanation. He'd need actual proof before he could do that, and thus far he'd almost never needed those words: *I don't know what it is.*

Paranormal. Damn, this country had begun to fall into a state of belief.

HALF AN HOUR later he decided to stretch his legs by walking to the diner. He'd left a voice mail with the Castelles and said he'd call in the morning. Now he wanted to make the deputy a little less dubious about him. He didn't need her trust, but he *did* need her cooperation.

With night falling, the air had grown chillier. Fine by him. Except for catastrophic weather, the mostly steady climate of Southern California had become boring. Pleasant but boring. Every now and then he got a little jolt when he was reminded that other places rolled through seasons that were different.

Not that he wanted to be shoveling snow for months on end, but he enjoyed the changes when he ran into them.

When he reached the diner, he spied Deputy Serrano sitting at a table right in front of the window. She had twisted to look up at a man who stood beside her and spoke with expansive gestures. She was smiling.

All to the good, Steve thought as he moved between tables to reach her. The place was crowded, which spoke well of the food. His stomach rumbled, reminding him that he'd skipped lunch because he was late.

Delicious aromas filled the room. The clatter of utensils and plates joined with various conversations. The diner felt friendly.

By the time he reached Serrano, the man had moved on. When she saw Steve, she gave him a polite smile. Just that, nothing more. At the same time, she pointed to the chair across from her.

He slid in and leaned back, hoping not to make her feel crowded at this small table. "Hi," he said as she passed him a plastic-covered menu. Surprised fingers told him it was clean, not greasy or sticky as he would have expected.

The woman who brought him coffee, a rather large angry-looking person, slammed down cups and began filling them with coffee. "Back soon," she grumped and stalked away.

Steve couldn't help but raise a brow in Serrano's direction.

Her faint smile widened a bit. "Maude, the owner. Consider her to be part of the local color."

"Does she hate running this place that much?"

The deputy shook her head. "I don't think so. She's been here for nearly fifty years."

Well, that was a puzzle, he thought as he scanned the menu. Not a bad selection for a place so small. Most of it could be cooked on a grill, another time-saver.

"Any recommendations?" he asked Serrano.

"Just about anything. In fact, everything."

He looked at her and she shrugged.

"I've only been here six months," she said. "Long enough to say I've never had a bad meal. Long enough to add that eating here, while delicious, makes your arteries cringe."

That was okay by Steve. He usually ate healthy stuff, but he didn't mind going off the wagon occasionally. Else how could a man get a large rare steak? Or a really good pork chop?

Or even some fries. He had a weakness for them.

After they ordered, he eyed the deputy across the table. She didn't seem all that eager to indulge in casual conversation, which was fine. Her eyes, however, actively scanned the room. Alert.

When they were served, she with a burger, he with a steak sandwich, she sighed.

"I'm sorry, Mr. Hawks. I'm not freezing you, but I just don't know what to talk about. How about business?"

"Call me Steve."

One corner of her mouth tipped up. "I'm Candy. What are we supposed to do here?"

"Well, I'm here for the next few weeks ahead of my production crew. I need to speak with the Castelle family, find out their whole story and gain some rapport with their daughter."

"Meaning?" She held half the burger in her hand.

Steve took her cue and picked up part of his steak sandwich. "She's only seven, Candy. Talking with a stranger won't be easy for her. But I need *her* to tell me what's troubling her, not what her parents think is bothering her."

She nodded, taking a bite out of her burger and dabbing at some escaped juice.

"So that is one of my first goals. Second, I need to get in the weeds on any local lore that could possibly be related, and probably into some local history. I need to build a picture of what might be going on here."

She nodded, then snagged a fresh napkin to wipe her mouth again. "And what will you do with this picture?"

"It's my hope to find some banal answer to the problem. To be able to reassure that family and the little girl that nothing bad is happening and they can ignore all this."

She blinked. "You don't want a ghost?"

"I'd really rather not. I hate it when I can't come up with a better explanation."

"Wild."

For the first time he saw her face relax, as if she were letting go of an internal tension. *One hurdle cleared*, he thought.

"But how can you make a ghost show without finding a ghost?" she asked, a perfectly reasonable question.

He replied firmly: "My goal has never been to find ghosts. What I want to do is reassure terrified families who think they've reached the limit of plausible explanations. And if I can't debunk the ghost idea, then I want at the very least to be able to reassure them they have nothing to fear."

"But couldn't you just say that?"

He shook his head. "They've already been saying it to themselves. If nothing else, they can see me do a complete investigation to assure them there's nothing there."

"But how can you do a ghost show if that's your purpose?" She repeated her question, and he sensed she needed more.

He wiped his own mouth and leaned forward a bit. "Because I'm doing a show about people who *believe* they have ghosts. I take them seriously."

CANDY DECIDED HE might not be the con artist she expected. He had a different twist on the subject matter, or at least different from what she'd expected. Of course, if he was conning her, she probably wouldn't know at first. Time to keep the radar up. Trust him? Trust didn't come easily to her.

But if what he said was true, then he wasn't simply out to create a spectacle with a family and their problems.

"Why does it have to be done on TV, though?" She hoped that didn't offend him, because if it did the next few weeks were going to be tough.

"It's simple," he answered as he reached for a home fry. "When I was a cop, I noticed a continuing uptick in the number of calls that people blamed on the paranormal. I couldn't do anything except tell them they didn't have a prowler, nobody was in the house, maybe they needed a plumber, and then I'd have to move on. The people were still afraid, and sometimes they'd call several times with the same complaint."

She shook her head a little bit. "That must have been frustrating."

"To some. It troubled me. These people weren't getting any help from us, and we're supposed to be able to help."

"Good point." Partly, at least. There really wasn't something a cop could do sometimes.

He finished the fry and reached for another. "Anyway, after a while, on my off-duty time, I went back to talk to these folks and tried to work with them. What with one thing and another, this production company approached and offered me a series. I didn't want to do it at first, but they made it obvious that I could do a whole lot more helping if I had the money for it and didn't have another full-time job. I told them I would, but only if they weren't expecting paranormal answers."

"And they agreed to that?" The notion surprised her. She wouldn't have expected it.

He tipped his head to one side briefly, an almost shrug. "They thought it would be an original spin. Three seasons later, I have to think they were right."

"It seems so." Her appetite had returned in full force, and she looked down at the burger on her plate. It looked better now than when Maude had slammed it onto the table. Yup. She lifted it, ready to finish it.

Candy felt, too, a whole lot better about what was to come. They continued to eat for a while before she asked, "Have you ever found a ghost?"

"Not anything I'd take to the bank. I wouldn't exactly mind if I found some good evidence, except that it would turn my worldview upside down and give it a good shaking."

She laughed, liking that. "It would for me, too."

Considering this assignment was going to be close to a month long, any positive she could find would help. It might be fun in more ways than just watching this all unfurl. Steve Hawks seemed to have a sense of humor, which made almost anything easier to deal with.

She also had an inkling that the success of his show wasn't entirely dependent on what he found, or the stories he told. No, he had charisma, the kind that would draw viewers along the paths he wove with his storytelling.

A unique kind of storytelling, she suspected. Unlike some of the ghost shows she had watched briefly, where a dash of history and a lot of "Did you hear that?" failed to tell a tale of any kind. Lots of supposition, little substance.

"Are you a fan of paranormal shows?" he asked.

"I stuck my toes in for a while. Curiosity. But I haven't tuned in recently."

"You're not missing much," he admitted, then flashed the most charming grin.

Damn, she could understand why people kept watching. She suspected his fan mail was positively steamy. She certainly needed to avoid that reaction.

Pushing her plate to one side, Candy reached for her coffee. She was one of the lucky ones—or unlucky, depending—that caffeine didn't keep awake. Sometimes at one in the morning she had wished it would.

"WHAT ABOUT YOU?" Steve asked. "You said you've been here only six months?"

She nodded. "Army. Discharged over a year ago."

"Army, huh?" He felt surprised, though he couldn't say why. Maybe because he'd thought she'd been a cop for a long time, like him. "What did you do?"

Then he saw her face harden, her eyes grown distant. For several beats she didn't answer, and when she did her voice sounded tight.

"Too much."

He let it drop, intuiting that there were memories she didn't want to revive, and he didn't want to push her there.

His view of her altered, however. She had a background that only someone who'd been there could ever fully understand. His work as a cop didn't come close. How could it?

He wasn't an insensitive man. His ability to empathize had often caused him difficulty in his own work. Cops didn't like to talk about it, but most had strong feelings when it came to victims and their families. Some cases even became downright personal. First responders could rarely stay detached no matter how hard they tried.

To that extent, he understood how memories could ride

your thoughts or become buried until they surfaced suddenly in a nightmare or were resurrected by another situation.

He sought safer ground. "How do you like working here?"

Her faint smile returned as if she had swept something aside. "So far, so good. People are great, the job is mostly routine. I've still got a lot to learn, obviously, but everyone in the office is being really nice about my inexperience."

"Sounds like a good group of people."

"The best. I'm filling some big shoes, though."

He arched a brow and resisted the urge to eat another home fry. *But why?* he asked himself. *Why not have one?* He helped himself. "Whose shoes?"

"My predecessor. She was with the department for over two years, then left to follow her Army husband to his post."

"Not a very liberated thing to do."

Candy laughed. It had been the right note to hit.

Then she answered. "On the surface, maybe not. But she found another police job, and I can understand why she wants to be close. They hadn't been married for long."

"That does make a difference from what I've seen."

Now it was her turn to look quizzically at him. "Never tried it?"

"Me? Not yet. I'm like a ton of bricks. Someone will need to knock me over."

"Maybe with a feather?"

He liked that. "Absolutely with a feather. Make easy work of me."

He drew a chuckle from her and decided they were moving to comfortable ground.

"What do you need me for?" she asked.

"Any difficulties that might come up when we start filming. Not from people so much as the authorities around here. I need to know if we're getting out of line. Toes must not be stepped on."

Candy nodded. "Anything else?"

"Smoothing introductions so people don't see me as a suspicious stranger. Any advice you can give along the way about where I should look or who I should talk to."

"Reasonable."

Maude made another banging round and refreshed their coffee.

"Amazing," Steve murmured, looking down.

"Good food," Candy answered. "From what I understand she's always been like this, and her daughter Mavis is doing a good job as copycat. Anyway, I think folks have been used to it for a long time."

He could see that, but being an outsider he wondered if he'd ever get used to it. It was a slightly disturbing punctuation to a meal.

He'd been a people watcher for much of his adult life, though. A bit of a character collector. He added Maude to his mental file.

Candy cradled her coffee mug as if warming her hands. "What do you need a deputy for? Wouldn't someone else be in a better position?"

"Evidently not. We contacted county and city officials and they referred us to you."

Another smile flitted across her face. "Cowards."

He grinned again. "Most politicians are."

A while later, after Steve had overindulged with a piece of the best peach pie he'd ever tasted, they parted ways outside, agreeing to meet at the sheriff's office at nine the next morning.

He started walking back to the motel, then decided a little more local atmosphere would be good. It was almost Halloween, and the pumpkins and pretend ghosts drew him. Shoving his hands into the pockets of his jacket, he began a lazy stroll more to see the way the town looked than to admire uncarved pumpkins.

There were old enough neighborhoods where he came from, but they weren't entire towns like this one. He imagined roots around here, deep as the largest tree, tying everyone together.

Very cool. He liked it.

BEN WITTES SAW the stranger as he was walking past the Conard County Sheriff's Office. His interest perked immediately.

He wondered if this guy was the ghost show host who was rumored to be coming to town. Maybe so.

As a psychic, Ben thought he might be able to help the guy out. After all, he was able to communicate with spirits. He did it all the time.

Go for it, whispered one of the spirits. Maybe his guide.

Yeah, he'd go for it. He could provide information that they'd never find for the show.

Now all he had to do was wait for the opportunity.

Smiling, Ben continued his stroll, feeling pretty good. This was his opportunity to make a splash with his skills.

Chapter Two

In the morning, Candy looked out her window at a perfect autumn day. While she loved sunshine as much as anyone, the low scudding clouds, dark with their hint of a threat, were appealing given the season.

She laughed quietly at herself as she donned her uniform for another day on the job. She really did like it here, and the longer she stayed, the more she liked it.

Just last evening, after her dinner with Steve Hawks, she joined some women at the library for their book group. They met once a week for discussion, and those meetings turned into a lot more than book reports. Laughter filled their room, someone always brought baked goods, and they wound up talking about families and sometimes jobs.

She had started to make friends. A good feeling, especially when she was still easing her way into this new job and new town. Everyone at the office was friendly, but it wasn't the same, not when she felt she was under a microscope. Superficially that didn't seem true, but she couldn't help thinking it. It wasn't as if she had any prior experience in the police.

Candy was still surprised that she'd been hired. She'd been bouncing around since her discharge, aware that infantry training and combat experience weren't exactly marketable skills. Some private security firms had wanted her, but deep inside she'd felt, maybe mistakenly, that she would become a mercenary. A soldier for hire.

Then, taking a flier, she had applied for this job when she read about it in the classifieds online. Six weeks later, after an interview, she'd been hired.

Yep, that amazed her. When she expressed her astonishment to the sheriff, Gage Dalton, he'd laughed. "It's kind of a tradition around here. We already know you're brave, able to work in teams and trainable. We can do the training."

Maybe she'd found her place.

She popped out to walk to work. She liked the weather, she liked the nip in the air. Uncarved pumpkins didn't exactly look cheery in this light, nor did the lack of Halloween lights. For now, the street was not lined with bright pops of orange. A dismal but gorgeous day.

Candy closed her eyes momentarily and smelled the air, listening to the sounds as a breeze brushed more dying leaves around. Perfect.

Yeah, perfect for a ghost hunt. She grinned into the chilly breeze, wondering what the days ahead held. For the first time in years, anticipation didn't bring dread. Her internal pressure valve had begun to release.

She was still smiling when she reached the office. Guy Redwing, a friendly dude, sat behind the duty desk and greeted her pleasantly. "How's it going, Candy?"

"Just fine," she answered, then waved to Velma as she passed her. The coffee urn usually held battery acid, but there was a pot of hot water and plenty of tea bags. A foam cup filled with English breakfast tea was only a few minutes away.

The office appeared empty this morning, and she returned to Guy with her cup, asking, "Something going on?"

He shook his head. "No coffee klatch this morning. There was apparently a lot of vandalism last night."

"Really? There hasn't been much since I got here."

He snorted. "You haven't been here long enough. Halloween brings out something crazy in the kids. Anyway, the vandalism isn't usually earthshaking. Mostly egged cars, some spray painting of scary faces at the schools. So far I haven't heard that they've sprayed anybody's house."

"Well, that's good."

"If we catch some of them, they'll get a workout with deck brushes."

She thought that sounded like a great idea, better than fines or suspended sentences.

"Oh, yeah," Guy added. "Did I mention at least two houses have been toilet-papered?"

"At least?" Candy sat in the chair beside his desk, holding her tea in her hand.

"Yeah. At least. And there may be more before we move into Thanksgiving season. Anyway, I'm sure we haven't gotten all the reports yet."

"That toilet papering has to be miserable to clean up."

Guy flashed a wide grin and mimicked an evil laugh. "Not if we find the perps. The nice thing about kids this age? They don't know when to shut their mouths. I'm sure we'll start to find them bragging online before long."

Candy had to chuckle even though apprehension began to niggle at her. Steve Hawks would appear at any minute and, even after their dinner last night, she still wouldn't trust him any farther than she could throw him. He'd made a reasoned case for what he was doing, but he was still here and still about to put a family's fears on television. And to make money from it.

There was no escaping that.

Oh, well, she'd get through this as cheerfully as she could. Being a good soldier was one way to look at it. She'd do her duty, whether she liked it or not.

Then the man himself walked through the door with a rush of cold air. Today Steve wore his leather bomber jacket zipped up, and she couldn't help wondering how cold it would have to get before he decided he needed a jacket or coat that would cover his butt.

"Hi," he said with a smile. "Ready to go?"

"Where to?" Candy asked, rising from her chair and tossing her empty cup in a nearby trash can.

"To visit the Castelles. Ten o'clock appointment. But hey, is there anywhere convenient I can get a decent take-out coffee?"

That surprised her. "Haven't you eaten yet? Everyone serves coffee."

"Not enough for me. Maude's?"

"Absolutely."

"Come with?" he asked, raising a brow. "Or meet you back here."

She decided to go with him. Another chance to walk ahead of what she feared would become a problematic day. The wind hit her smack in the face when she stepped outside.

"Whew," she exclaimed. "When did that happen?"

"The wind or the cold?"

She glanced at him askance. "What do you think?"

"Ha. You want some coffee, too?"

After they got two tall cups full of steaming coffee, Candy asked, "Do you want me to follow in my patrol car, or do you want to ride along? Whichever you think would least worry the family."

He paused to look down at her. "Why would they worry? They know who I am."

She just shook her head, wondering if this was a taste of his ego. "The face recognized around the world?"

That darkened his expression just a bit. "They knew who I was when they contacted me. I've spent hours on the phone with them. I am not exactly a stranger."

She couldn't really argue with that. At this point, the

Castelles probably felt they knew him better than any local cop. Especially her. Waving from a patrol car as she drove by and exchanging a few words with them at the end of their driveway hardly constituted any kind of relationship.

"I'll follow," she answered briskly, warning herself not to make quick assumptions about any of this. That wasn't part of the job, nor was needlessly annoying him.

Outside the sheriff's office, she climbed into her official SUV and backed out. She didn't exactly need to follow him because she knew where the Castelles lived. He would, too, assuming his GPS navigator worked. Which was often hit-or-miss in some places around here.

The Castelles didn't live very far out of town. They had moved into an older house on some acreage. It had a barn, which could still be useful if they wanted to renovate it, and the house was only one story. Except this one had a steeply sloped, high roof with some windows that suggested the attic could be used as living space.

She wished she could find out. She'd always felt some appeal in finished attics, although she'd have been hard-pressed to explain it. She certainly had never lived in a house with one.

Sometimes her own brain made her wonder.

Steve arrived without a problem and pulled into the long asphalt driveway. Not sure what to do at this point, Candy parked on the shoulder near the mailbox. If anyone wanted or needed her, she'd be in plain view. Sipping her coffee, grateful for its warmth, she kept an eye on the house.

She saw Steve walk up to the front door, then disappear inside. This was *not* going to be an exciting morning for her.

STEVE GREETED ANABELLE CASTELLE with a warm smile. He hardly needed her to introduce herself since he'd already seen her on the video she'd provided. Dark hair, blue eyes, and a classic face with great bone structure that was looking a little frayed around the edges. She wore a blue flannel shirt over black slacks.

"Where are all the people?" Anabelle asked. "I was expecting an invasion."

"Sorry. Didn't I tell you? I come alone first. It makes it easier for us to talk. I need to meet the three of you, then start looking into some background."

She nodded, leading him toward a living room. "Have a seat. I'll get Todd." She paused as she turned, giving him a tired smile. "I always like the history part of your show best."

"Thanks." he replied. "You look tired. Do you want me to come back another time?"

She shook her head. "We had a rough night last night. There are quite a few of them these days."

Todd Castelle looked haggard, too, as he joined them. An average-size guy with the light brown hair that often indicated someone who had been blond once upon a time. His dark-haired wife had the blue eyes, though. He had the gray.

"Why is a cop parked out front?" Todd asked. "Is something wrong?"

Steve hastened to reassure them. "She's my minder. They call her a liaison." He gave a light laugh. "I don't know if she's supposed to help me as much as she's supposed to reassure the people I talk to."

"Well, she shouldn't have to sit out there," Annabelle said.

Todd agreed. "I'll go out and get her."

"And I'll make some coffee," his wife replied. "It's getting chilly in here. You sure that heat is working?"

"Honey, it's set to sixty-eight."

"Yeah, but I still get cold." She rose while Todd headed to the door and gave Steve a wry look. "We argue about this year-round. I'm either too hot or too cold, and he's always just right. Must be hormonal differences."

Steve wouldn't have stepped into that potential minefield for anything, not once hormones were mentioned. But he chuckled, the safe response.

He also wished they weren't bringing Candy into this. He needed the time getting to know his clients without their holding anything back because someone else was listening.

Oh, hell, he'd make up for this somehow. There'd be another interview, one without Candy, he hoped. Not that he didn't like her well enough, considering they'd just met, but she was still an official, a cop, and few people wanted to be wholly frank while a cop listened.

He ought to know. His years on the force weren't *that* far behind him.

Candy entered with Todd, gently refusing coffee, holding up her take-out cup as if in explanation. Soon Anabelle had them all seated in the living room, the aromas of fresh-brewed coffee filling the air.

Steve waited a minute, then said, "Would you mind walking me through everything again? I want to be sure I haven't missed something."

Annabelle looked surprised. "I thought we would do that on the show."

"You will, but we'll have to edit it for length. You won't be able to give me all the details then, but I need to be sure *I* don't miss something. With or without the show, I'll investigate fully. You can always back out anytime you want."

Todd and Annabelle exchanged looks. Todd nodded and spoke. "That's what we agreed to. And if we change our minds, you'll still investigate?"

"Thoroughly. That's how I got into this business in the first place."

Todd looked satisfied. "The intro to the show says you're a former homicide detective."

"That's right. Twelve years as a detective, and before that I was a patrol officer. I can tell you which was more interesting."

That drew a small laugh from Annabelle. "The intro also says that you got into this because of your policing."

"Not exactly. I was increasingly disturbed by the number of people who called in complaints of paranormal activity. And I was limited in what I could do. Check the premises, check the yard. It was no help at all. That's when I started going back when I was off duty to see if I could do more."

Annabelle tilted her head. "You really care that much?"

"That's how I wound up here. And that's why I'm willing to go ahead with this investigation even if you decide not to do the show."

For the first time, Candy spoke. "That's remarkable."

Steve noted there wasn't a touch of sarcasm in her comment. Maybe he was persuading her that he wasn't a con artist.

He wasn't sure about the Castelles, however. Yes, they'd called him. Yes, they'd said they would do this. But now they were looking down the barrel of having to appear on a nationally televised show. A lot of people didn't want to take their crazy stories public.

Then Todd surprised him. "I'm a graphic artist for comic books. Annabelle writes them. Any of our friends won't be surprised if we get wacky over this."

"It's true," Annabelle agreed. "We're already off-center, living in a world of superheroes and magic powers. Heck, this could be one of my scripts."

This time it was Steve who wondered about *them*. What if *they* weren't on the up-and-up? What if they saw some free publicity?

Oh, hell, a new wrinkle. But he didn't let those thoughts show on his face. One thing about being a homicide detective, you learned to control your face and emotions unless they'd be helpful.

"Anyway," Todd said, "I don't see any reason, at least not yet, why we'd back out of the show."

Steve returned to his original question. "Can you tell me all about it? Would you prefer to have Officer Serrano wait outside?"

"Why?" Todd asked bluntly. "We're proposing to take this to TV. Might as well get used to telling the world."

Annabelle sighed. "Where do you want me to start? Why we moved here?"

Steve nodded.

"Big space, cheaper cost of living. We wanted Viv and her dog to have a place to run that didn't involve a trip to a park. Cheaper because it's not the big city. In our job, we don't make a whole lot, so coming here let us have more room and still live within our budget. Maybe less crime. I suppose time will answer that question."

Steve spoke. "And now Viv's afraid."

Todd replied. "That's killing us. We brought her here to give her a freer life but she's scared all the time."

Then the story began to tumble out of them. He'd heard most of it on the phone, but he was looking for details that might have been overlooked.

A couple of months after they moved in, Viv started talking about an invisible man in her bedroom. She said she didn't like him and wanted him to go away. Naturally they tried sleeping in her room with her as opposed to taking her into their bed. They hadn't wanted to encourage fanciful tales that might simply arise from the big move they'd made.

It *had* been a huge change in her life, Annabelle said, and since moving was a great stressor even on adults, she had at first assumed that was what was going on.

But when they stayed in the room, they heard nothing and saw nothing. Things quieted down, and Viv seemed to go back to normal.

But then it started again. "The man keeps talking to me!" Followed by Todd and Annabelle taking turns sleeping in her room with her. Neither of them heard anything and tried to ease their way back to a more usual arrangement.

Once again everything quieted, until the night Viv refused to calm even when they stayed with her. She began screaming and crying for them to make the man go away. Whereas she'd been afraid only at night before, her terror seemed to grow until she refused to even play in her room.

Todd and Annabelle were totally perplexed. Viv was okay playing in the yard with her puppy, or playing in another room they had turned into a playroom, but she refused to go into her own bedroom. A handful of times she went back in there to get something she wanted, and entirely too often would come out and claim the man had talked to her again.

But Viv had no idea what he might be saying. None. She just didn't like his voice and especially didn't like him being invisible.

Eventually the Castelles had begun to wonder if their daughter had a serious problem. They took her to a highly recommended child psychologist.

That impressed Steve. In his experience, most parents didn't want to believe their children might have a psychological problem. The shame frightened them, as if they would turn out to be failures as parents. It often prevented action. But not for the Castelles.

After six weeks of making the lengthy trip to see the psychologist, they got an answer that wasn't entirely reassuring.

Annabelle continued with the story. "The psychologist said there was absolutely nothing wrong with Viv. That it was a phase, maybe precipitated by our move, but she'd grow out of it."

Steve felt a burst of sympathy. "Did that make you feel better?" He suspected it hadn't.

"No," Todd said bluntly. "He told us our kid isn't mentally ill, which is great, but that she was just acting out. And while I'm no psychologist, I heard a subtext."

"Which was?"

"Our daughter is having emotional problems, but temporary. That's not a lot of string to hang on to."

Steve set his coffee aside on an end table and leaned forward until his elbows rested on his knees. He clasped his hands, thinking and absorbing.

"Okay," he said presently. "That wasn't the end of it, though."

"Of course not," Todd said. "I'd already checked the basement for banging pipes, humming things, anything that might reach her room from below. Nothing. But I went and checked it all again. Useless. Hell, I even went up into the attic where there's no plumbing or wiring except for several bulbs at the top of the stairs."

Annabelle spoke again. "In one way I think that psychologist was all wet. Viv's not acting out. If she were doing that, she'd be acting out in every other room in this house. She'd even act out at school sometimes. She's not."

Todd nodded agreement. "That doesn't seem like a useful explanation."

"It's not," Annabelle said firmly. "What's more, the problem didn't go away."

Steve waited. "How did you know that?"

"Because Viv walked by her bedroom one evening and said she heard the man singing."

"Singing!" That startled Steve a bit. It was a new claim to him. Crying, yes. Shouting, yes. Talking, knocking, moving things, but this was the first he'd heard of singing.

"Yeah," said Todd almost wryly. "Weird. Weirder than the rest." He sighed, passing a hand over his face. "Then Annabelle…" He broke off. "I'll let her tell it."

"I heard it, too," she said quietly. "Just once. I'd gone into Viv's room to get some of her winter clothes, and I heard it. It *did* sound like a man talking, but from far away. He didn't sound as if he were in the room." She shook her head. "I felt like ice water ran down my spine. I raced to get Todd, but by the time we both came back, it had stopped. Then I noticed something else I hadn't really paid attention to before."

"That was?"

"Viv's dog was in there, and he was growling at the wall with his hackles up. I'd never seen him do that before. Or if he had, there in her room, I hadn't noticed. Then I noticed him doing it more often."

Steve had some familiarity as a cop with a dog's heightened senses. They could detect things that humans couldn't. But more than that, they usually knew when something was a threat. More trouble.

"Anyway," Todd continued, "we started paying attention to Buddy. Most of the time he didn't seem disturbed. He was happy, prancing around the house, playing with Viv. But every now and then he'd react to something in her bedroom. Not constantly, just sometimes."

Steve waited expectantly. He thought he knew the rest, but he wanted to hear it again. Much could be revealed by faces that wouldn't necessarily come across in a phone call. He was getting the close-up look he needed.

"Viv," said Annabelle. "It's getting worse, Steve. She doesn't want to even walk by her bedroom. She begged us to get rid of the man. Do you know what it's like to have your daughter desperately begging you for something you can't give her?"

While Steve had no children, he didn't have any trouble imagining how awful the Castelles must be feeling. "Are you still sleeping with her?"

"She's in our bed every night now, and some nights she doesn't sleep at all because she was terrified the man would come out of her room and find her."

It was definitely getting worse, Steve thought. For Viv, and for them.

Todd spoke. "Anyway, I decided I had to do something. Anything."

Annabelle jumped in. "Maybe we're being crazy. I don't know."

Steve replied, hoping he could reassure this couple. Their pain wrenched at his heart. "I'd be going crazy, too."

Annabelle gave him a faint smile. "We watched some ghost shows from time to time. We're not avid, but we think they're fun. Or we did until this. Anyway, EMF…"

Electromagnetic frequencies. They could affect the brain and cause weird experiences. He was familiar with them.

Todd joined in. "I got us an EMF meter just before we called you. We figured that since the voice was confined to Viv's room, there might be something like that going on. She might be extremely sensitive. The dog, too. It might also explain the voice Annabelle heard that once. But either way I didn't want Viv in there if some electrical frequency was messing with her brain. Or maybe causing some disease. I thought I'd checked all the wiring, but I didn't get inside the walls. We had to know."

"Good decision," Steve said. "*Excellent* decision and I'm not just saying that because I hunt this stuff. This is something important you need to clear up for Viv's sake."

"That's what we think," Annabelle said. "I sure wasn't about to consider an exorcism or something. Not then, not now, unless you find a reason. Calling it paranormal is the last thing we want to do."

Steve straightened. "You know I try to debunk. That's my main goal. What I want is for people not to be afraid."

"That's why we called you," Todd said. "If you can debunk this, we're going to find a better psychologist. Someone needs to help Viv, and she's become convinced there's ghost in her room."

Steve frowned. Kids. They were incredibly honest about many things, and he didn't think it was likely Viv was exaggerating her fear or making up the story. "Did you find any EMF?"

Todd answered. "Some but not above a normal level. And no more in Viv's bedroom than in the rest of the house."

Steve decided he had gleaned about all he could from this first interview. Maybe the most important thing had been observing the Castelles. They were genuinely concerned about their daughter. They weren't exaggerating their claims, nothing about dark figures and black mists. They weren't even claiming to be tormented themselves. A very focused investigation on their parts.

"You've done well," he told them. "I'm impressed."

Both parents looked mildly relieved.

"Okay," he said. "I may want to ask you more a little later, but I need to meet Viv. And the dog." He smiled. "If you don't mind, that is, but it'll help me to hear from her what she's experiencing and what she thinks is going on. To do that, I'm going to have to gain her trust so that she feels free to talk to me. Do you mind?"

"Of course not!" Annabelle exclaimed. "For heaven's sake, the entire reason we called you was for help. And one of the things we discussed was whether you could talk to Viv without encouraging her fears. We believe you can."

That was a big vote of confidence, Steve thought. A huge one. "When can I meet her?"

"How much time do you need?"

"As much as she'll give me at our first meeting. It has to be fluid. She sets the boundaries. And where is the dog?"

Todd smiled faintly. "Out in the back in his run."

"Can I meet him? Is he friendly?"

At that, Todd laughed. "He's so friendly he'd love a burglar to death inside our front door. Buddy would knock him over because he so big and kiss him until the burglar begged for mercy. We're still trying to teach the dog not to jump on people when he wants their attention."

Steve grinned. "What's the breed?"

"Half American Staffordshire, and about half blood-hound."

"Big, then. Interesting mix." But Steve glanced at his watch and realized the Castelles had been talking with him for the last three hours. "Listen, you two probably need some sleep, so I'll leave you to it. Tomorrow you can tell me what was so awful about the last few nights, introduce me to Buddy and tell me when's a good time meet Viv. Okay?"

Ten minutes later, he and Candy were outside.

Chapter Three

Outside, just as they reached Steve's car, Candy asked him if he needed her for anything else. She figured if he was off for the rest of the day, she could go back to the office and find something useful to do.

Man, she had felt like a fifth wheel in there. Nothing to contribute, just an observer. She was really surprised the Castelles had invited her inside. Surely they hadn't wanted an audience.

Steve spoke. "You don't have to stay with me every minute."

She shrugged. He might be right, but he also might be wrong. She hadn't received any other assignment. Unless he said he was going to work at the motel, she needed to stay. "You're my detail."

He grimaced. "I didn't want that. If I'd wanted a full-time assistant, I'd have brought one along. I'm sure you have a whole bunch of things to do that are more important than shepherding me around."

Candy felt a flicker of amusement. "I understand why you might not want that. But I'm equally certain the city fathers didn't toss this to the sheriff because they wanted you rolling through here like a loose cannon. I guess I'm the city protection squad. No bad publicity here."

That drew a grin from him. "You might be right. Most of

the places I've been to have been too big to worry about it. Not only is Conard City way smaller, but it's also pretty isolated."

"Yup. They'd like to draw more visitors, not drive them away. So please, Steve, make us look good."

The wind kicked up again and she felt her cheeks sting. The frigid warning breath of winter.

"I don't know about you, Candy, but I'm a Southern California guy, and I need to get indoors. I'm going for lunch. If you want to join me, feel free. Me, I'm going to see how many people I can talk to while I eat."

"If you want to talk to locals…"

"Got it. Maude's. See, I learn."

Her entire face relaxed into a smile that seemed to reach all the way through her. She guessed her tension over this guy was easing. She was a long way from trusting him, but she was beginning to believe he wasn't going to be a major headache.

"I'll see you at Maude's," she said, and walked back to her patrol vehicle.

While Candy hated to admit it, even in the privacy of her own mind, he'd impressed her while he was talking with the Castelles. Very sympathetic, supportive. She hadn't heard him trying to persuade them of anything. Not even being on his show.

But there was still a lot of crap. She mulled it over as she drove into town. He was still a ghost hunter. He said he didn't believe in the paranormal, but he was still making his living from it.

As she had seen today, the people who called him were desperate. Willing to consider, no matter how outlandish, anything that could help them.

That made them vulnerable. Exceedingly vulnerable.

She sighed as she finally pulled into a parking place at the station. For a few minutes, she sat drumming her fingers on the steering wheel as she thought.

She didn't like the whole premise of what Steve was doing, of what the other programs were doing, in fact of the whole field of paranormal investigation. That was a personal prejudice and she knew it.

People were entitled to their own beliefs, of course, but while she'd let them have at it, she didn't have to approve or fail to observe her own beliefs.

At this point, however, this wasn't about beliefs. She'd watched the Castelles talk to Steve. He hadn't fed their concerns. He wanted *their* story. In their own words.

But that didn't mean the Castelles weren't desperate, and desperate people were easy marks. They wanted their daughter to be okay, and at this point if it took someone running around with a recorder and camera, claiming to have heard something or felt some evil spirit, they might well buy it.

Which, as far as Candy could see, wouldn't really help anything.

Giving up trying to escape her own mental gyrations, she left her car and walked toward Maude's. She didn't like this whole idea, didn't like her inchoate position, but that didn't matter. As ill-defined as her assignment was, she still couldn't walk away from it.

And she sure as hell wouldn't walk away until she was sure that nobody was taking advantage of the Castelles' fears.

Maybe that was her real assignment. Maybe no one thought *Ghostly Ties* would be able to ding the town or county in any measurable way. Maybe they just didn't want a bad outcome for the family.

That wouldn't surprise her. Even in the short time she'd been here, she'd discovered this gossipy little town was very protective of its residents. Even the new ones.

WHEN SHE WALKED through the door of Maude's, the lunch crowd had mostly evaporated, transforming into quieter little groups of people who'd stopped for coffee and maybe a light snack. The usual clatter from the kitchen had quieted as the load lifted. Later this afternoon, activity would spike again.

Steve was seated at the same table they'd occupied last evening, facing the door, a tall coffee in front of him.

She came to join him, but then stopped. A prickle of anxiety hit her, snagging her attention. Then, taking a deep breath, she approached him.

"Hi," he said. "Take a seat."

She hesitated, nearly hating herself for what she was about to say. "Would you mind switching seats? I can't… I don't like to sit with my back to a door."

His brows lifted, then his face gentled. He rose at once. "No problem."

She despised herself for this weakness, but some things had lingered long after she'd come home from the war. This was hardly the worst of it. Unfortunately, it had a way of snapping at her heels when she least expected it.

She slid into the chair that he had just vacated and unzipped her jacket, letting it hang open.

Mavis, Maude's daughter, arrived, pad in hand, with her grumpy expression. "You want coffee? A big one like his?"

She glanced at Steve's take-out cup. More than a mug could hold, but that cup would keep the coffee warm for longer.

"Thanks, Mavis."

Without another word, Mavis trudged away. Unlike her mother, who had the dowdiest dresses in the world, Mavis preferred pants. Jeans, slacks, it didn't matter. Evidently no skirts for her.

"I don't know about you," Steve said, "but I need some lunch." He pushed one of the plastic menus her way. "In fact, I need more than a little lunch. Maybe a big one."

Neither of them said much until their food was delivered. Candy had wanted a salad, but when she considered going home later and cooking herself dinner, she opted for a grilled chicken sandwich. Steve ordered two BLTs.

Instead of separate servings, home fries arrived on a single large plate.

"Thank God," Steve said. "I have such a thing for fried potatoes, and now that they're here, I can't waste them."

Candy laughed, releasing the anxiety that had been dogging her since the moment she'd walked through the door.

"Save me from myself," he said, gesturing toward the potatoes. "Eat some."

He really did have a lot of charm. She also liked people who could make fun of themselves. But…he was still essentially an unknown.

"What did you think of the Castelles?" he asked, dabbing at his chin with a napkin.

"They seem like very nice people." She wouldn't say more than that. She wasn't about to sit in judgment.

"I thought so," he agreed after he swallowed. "I'm trying to eat my sandwiches and not the fries." Then he picked up a potato and popped it in his mouth. "Not the day for a New Year's resolution."

That drew another laugh from her. "You should do a stand-up routine."

"Not unless I can do it with a plate of fries in hand." He paused. "Seriously, what was your impression? I'm not asking you to judge their character."

She hesitated briefly, then offered what she thought was a safe answer. "They seem very upset."

He nodded. "That was my feeling, too. They weren't feigning their worry."

Her interest spiked. "Have you run into that?"

"Of course. For every ten thousand people who watch these shows, there are another thousand who want to be on them. To star in them. Mostly they're people desperate for attention, but sometimes they're just scammers. I don't know what your time in the Army was like, but I was a cop for a long time. Hell, you get people so desperate for attention that they'll confess to terrible crimes they haven't committed."

"I haven't run into that yet, meaning only that I haven't been a cop for long."

He ate for a little while, then spoke again, thoughtfully. "It's really sad to meet someone like that. I can't imagine feeling that invisible, that unwanted, that uncared-for."

"Is that always what it is?"

He shook his head. "There's a percentage of people who just need to be the center of attention. It doesn't matter how much attention they get otherwise, they're hungry for more. Anyway, that's not the Castelles."

She nibbled some more, then reached for one of the fries. "I can't resist either. And I can always bag my sandwich for home."

He smiled at her. "Dig in. Please."

"But how can you be *sure* that Castelles aren't attention-seeking?"

"My gut. As a detective I had to rely on it, and most of the time I was right. But… I could always be wrong." He also had other concerns, like the *real* family dynamics rather than their public face. Or the possibility that they'd been fleeing, rather than moving. Tonight he'd call a woman who sometimes did research for him, a former cop herself.

"Well," she said, "I thought their concern was genuine. If it wasn't, they deserve an award. They really seem upset about their daughter."

"That caught my attention," he remarked, seeking another potato wedge with his fingers. "I most often hear stories about the entire family being affected. If not the whole family, then most of them. Sometimes it makes me wonder if the ones claiming the experiences are kind of having a bit of group hysteria. As if they've ginned each other up, feeding more and more into the mass experience until it becomes huge. On the other hand, it raises more questions, for me at least, when there's one or two who claim to have experienced nothing."

He shrugged one shoulder. "That's not a metric, of course. The theory is that some people are sensitive and others are not. What I'm getting at is that the Castelles are very focused on what Viv is experiencing, and only Annabelle claims to have had her own experience, just that once. That's unusual."

"I can see that." Which she could even though she hadn't watched any of these programs in quite a while.

"Anyway, I'm inclined to believe kids, even though they can be wonderful liars."

She tilted her head. "Why's that?"

"Because they're almost never *good* liars."

She grinned. "It's true, isn't it? I haven't had a whole lot of time with youngsters recently, but I can still remember how rarely my brother and I could get away with anything."

"That's it. It usually doesn't take long to suss out the truth."

She remembered what Guy Redwing had said just that morning about how the vandals would start talking or bragging online. Even older kids could set a trap for themselves.

Candy couldn't eat another bite, so when Mavis came around to see if they wanted more coffee, she asked for a take-out box.

"What's your plan?" she asked after Steve, too, asked for a box for his remaining sandwich. He just kept plugging at the fries, though, causing her inward amusement.

"Well, I'm going to call the Castelles later to set up a time to talk to their daughter and meet the dog. And I need to start my local research. Who can I talk to who might give me some interesting data, particularly about that house?"

"I haven't been here very long, but I'd suggest the head librarian, Emmaline Dalton. Everyone refers to her as Miss Emma, though, and I don't know why. I guess I could ask someone. Anyway, her family has been here forever, and she'd probably be a good person to talk to first."

"Okay, then, I'll head on over. Do you need to watch me?"

She laughed. "I'm not sure exactly what I'm supposed to be doing, but yeah, I guess I should."

He winked. "I could imagine far worse people attached to my hip. And I do want your help with local legends and stuff."

"Miss Emma will know far more than me."

"Candy, that's exactly what *I* want from you. Guidance to local fonts of information. Maybe a little research into various crimes. But first I need direction."

FAR FROM BEING annoyed with Candy's determination to follow him, Steve didn't mind it at all. Whether the town had realized it when they made her his liaison, she leant an aura of authority. With her present, people were more likely to trust him.

The only conversation he had worried she might stymie with her presence was his conversation with the Castelles. For everyone else, she was like a seal of approval. Plus, she really might be able to help him with records searches.

If she was willing, of course.

But he also felt some sympathy for her. She may not have been a cop for long but, especially with her military background, she probably wanted clearer orders and a better view of her mission here. Instead she was basically flying blind.

He'd caught that thing at the diner, however. Her distaste for sitting with her back to the door. That must result from her Army experience, waving like a quiet reminder that this woman had been through a helluva lot. He wondered if she had a bit of PTSD as a result…or more than a bit. Depending on her military postings, she might have a whole lot.

He didn't need to get personal with her in order to do his job, though. The cop in him picked up enough clues to sense the ground ahead, and whether it would be good or bad. The joys of being an experienced detective: his critical mind never shut down. The hail-fellow-well-met surface he wore concealed his lifetime of suspicion.

The library proved to be one of those built by funds from Andrew Carnegie back around the turn of the last century. It wasn't huge, but it stood sturdily against the tests of time with its red brick structure and the concrete lintel engraved with Carnegie's name and the year.

He'd heard that Carnegie had become a philanthropist after he learned what his business partner had done to labor protesters. One could argue that Carnegie, even though he'd been in England at the time, hadn't been unaware. Whatever was true, well over two thousand libraries had been built, and had fed the minds of generations. Not a bad legacy.

He climbed out of his rental, feeling the cold wind grab at him again. Overhead, dark clouds still dragged through the sky like portents. He smiled at himself. He wasn't one to be given to fanciful thoughts. Or maybe he could be at times.

He waited until Candy had parked, then joined him on the front steps.

"I need to get out my warmer jacket," he remarked. "Can you introduce me to Miss Emma?"

Her expression turned wry. "Are you sure you want to put your reputation in my hands?"

"Cute. Let's go."

The library was warmer inside, not surprising, but it wasn't exactly *warm*. Maybe to help preserve the books, maybe to save on energy or maybe because the locals were used to cooler temperatures and nobody wanted to bake.

Candy led the way to the round center desk, the hallmark of an era. From one of the side rooms he heard voices, young voices who seemed to be discussing games. Off in one corner, a woman was reading a storybook to a bunch of very young kids, too young for kindergarten, he surmised.

The middle-aged woman behind the desk was a study in graceful aging. She had the kind of bone structure in her face that would keep her beautiful for decades to come. Her reddish-and-gray hair was caught up in a bun. With those green eyes, he'd have bet she had once been an eye-catching redhead.

"Hi, Candy," she said, looking over the top of the wooden counter. In front of her sat an older computer that probably meant the library had switched to digital cataloging but, nearby, a wooden card catalog still remained. He was old enough to remember searching through one of them to do research when he was in elementary school. Nostalgia breathed through him. Of course, once upon a time he'd believed he'd never give up print books. He liked the smell of them, the weight of a volume in his hands.

He'd lost the battle. His laptop had two e-readers on it.

"Miss Emma," Candy said, "I'd like you to meet Steve Hawks. He's in town to do a ghost-hunting show."

"Yes, I heard." Miss Emma rose, still smiling, and extended a hand across the counter. "We have your earlier programs available on DVDs here."

"I'm flattered." Not really. If his ego could be so easily flattered, self-disgust should overwhelm him. "I understand you have the best brain to pick around here when it comes to local history."

Emma laughed. "I've been here for much of it. My dad was once a judge here, and my family helped found this town. You could say I'm steeped in the history. Always my avocation. Let's go into my office."

Another woman appeared in answer to Emma's call. She came out of the room that was full of young voices.

"Can you take over for me out here, Nora?" Emma asked her.

"Absolutely. My sons will probably enjoy my absence more than my presence."

Emma had a spacious office. Apparently, space strictures didn't apply here. Shelves were filled with books, a few stacks of them decorated a corner, and her desk had very nearly disappeared beneath another computer and a scattering of papers.

"Pardon my desk," she said. "We're still trying to get all the books into the digital catalog."

"Probably one heck of a job," Steve offered.

Emma nodded. "And way past due. Have a seat, both of you."

CANDY TOOK A chair that was farther from the desk than the one Steve chose. She was prepared to listen with half an ear to a subject that didn't especially appeal to her. A little local history? Great. A detailed one? Not necessary for her.

This was a go-nowhere task. She had to suppress a sigh. She wasn't at all sure what Steve needed from her, and not sure what her bosses expected of her, and she wondered if this was going to be much fun at all. She sure as heck didn't feel like she was accomplishing much.

Maybe she ought to just go back to the office, find some work to do and wait for Steve to call her if he needed something. Whatever the town wanted from her, she doubted this was it. Making his path easier? Hey, didn't they have a PR person they could have asked to take on this job?

Impatience was beginning to irritate her. Sure, it had

been interesting to hear him interview the Castelles, and their story had been fascinating. But.

Yeah, *but*. Here she sat listening to an innocuous conversation about the history of this town. How could most of that be involved in a ghost hunt?

Then her interest awoke again.

Steve asked, "Do you know anything about the house at the edge of the town that the Castelles have bought?"

Miss Emma frowned. "I heard a family had moved in, if you mean that farmhouse to the east of here."

"That's it."

"Off Granger Road," Candy elucidated.

Emma nodded thoughtfully. "I'm not specifically aware of the history. I know when I was young it had become the subject of campfire stories. But an empty house is a perfect stage for that."

Steve leaned forward a bit. "It was empty for a long time?"

"Yes, it was," Emma answered. "You'd have to go to the recorder's office to get any details, though. It hasn't been high on my list of things to learn." She smiled slightly. "As a historian, I prefer the broader sweep in the local area. You can get details from the recorder."

"I'll do that. Thank you very much."

Steve was standing when Emma said, "You know who might have more personal information? The previous sheriff, Nate Tate." She looked at Candy. "Have you met him?"

"Not yet, but I've heard plenty about him."

Emma's smile broadened. "He's local icon. You don't want to miss the chance. I'm sure Gage can set it up."

"Gage?" Steve enquired.

"My husband, a.k.a. the current sheriff."

"Wow," Steve said to Candy as they stepped outside. "The previous sheriff. And her husband. Is this place incestuous or what?"

Candy laughed. "Not really, but it's small. The other woman you glimpsed? Nora Madison, the current police chief's wife."

"Okay, then. Don't steal a book."

"Might be wise."

He stopped on the sidewalk. "You know, if I was a historian, I'd want to spend weeks, if not months, interviewing Miss Emma. She sounds like a font of local information. Unfortunately, I have to be more directed."

"I can see that. First, you don't have months. Second, you need to do a TV show."

"Yep. So about this former sheriff…"

She forestalled him. "I'll get in touch for you, set something up if he's willing."

"Thank you."

"What about the Castelles, though? I don't want to make the appointment if you're going to be tied up."

"No," Steve answered. "I wouldn't want that either. I'm going to call the Castelles this evening and set a time. I'll let you know."

Evening. Evening had crept in while they were in the library, and it was dragging into night. Clouds still sailed through the twilight overhead. She wondered if they'd last another day.

Candy watched Steve drive away and felt a bit of relief. It had been a long day for her, never alone, always alert to matters that didn't especially interest her. Guard duty.

Well, not exactly that, but close enough. She reached to snap her jacket, then to head back to the office. The former sheriff had to be next in her sights.

FOR STEVE IT had been a productive day. He'd met his clients face-to-face and had been favorably impressed. He'd also gotten a good lead to that guy, Tate, who might be exactly what he needed for his show.

And Emma herself had provided more information: the house had generated tales of haunting. Now he had to find out how long the house had remained empty or if it had ever been renovated, and if so, had the Castelles done it.

While he might not agree with a lot of the explanations in his field, he knew he had to answer for them. It was widely believed that renovating a house could disturb spirits.

He wasn't inclined to believe it. He had a general problem with the whole idea of people hanging around after death. But if they did, why should they get exercised because a house had been altered? Especially since that house had probably been altered more than once over time?

The other problem he had was a simple one: too many ghost hunters spoke for the dead. Unless there was some communication with the so-called spirits, how could anyone know what they were thinking? Assuming they could think at all.

He was a skeptic by nature, but he also accepted his own curiosity about the subject. He'd like to know. Really. He'd like to settle all this in his own mind somehow. So far he hadn't been able to.

That left him with doing his best to reassure frightened people. After he met Viv, and started to build a relationship with her, he was going to go all over that house and property, looking for a rational explanation.

And he was going to explore the family's background. He picked up the phone to call his researcher, Dena.

One thing he knew for sure: if that child was genuinely hearing a man's voice in her room, he was going to get to the bottom of it.

Chapter Four

The next day, Steve awoke refreshed and ready to begin. His hope for conversations with more locals had begun to get answered the evening before at the diner.

Apparently, word was getting around that he was in town to do a TV show. Some folks even recognized him. A few actually stayed to talk after a greeting.

He hadn't gotten any truly useful information, but he felt that might come eventually. It was difficult right now because he didn't want the whole community to know whose house he was investigating. That might hamper his work, but worse, it might upset the Castelles to become front-page news before there'd been a solution.

He got it. They didn't want people all over town discussing whether their daughter had a mental problem or whether they sucked as parents. Who would?

He didn't yet have anything to legitimize their experiences. That was a bad way to go public. The Castelles had every right to expect better of him. It would be different once he had some answers for them, but he didn't need a warning announcement that they wouldn't be happy if they ended up with neighbors camping outside because of curiosity. Or teens being drawn because it was cool there might be a ghost.

Or Viv facing teasing from classmates.

It wouldn't take long for one nightmare to become a second.

He ate breakfast at the truck stop because it was conveniently across the road from the motel. And maybe because it gave him some thinking space to be in a place populated mostly by transients. Nobody here was likely to want to talk to him about much, if anything.

BEN WITTES LEARNED that the guy he'd seen was the ghost hunter. He was delighted with the possibilities. He could speak for the spirits who lingered so unhappily. He called the show's producers to see if they would use him.

The spirits had been clamoring for attention for weeks now, as if they knew who was coming. They surely wanted Ben to speak for them, the voiceless who couldn't begin to speak for themselves.

Ben was the only voice they had, and it made the inside of his head awfully noisy. It's not like he could simply turn them off. Yeah, he could get them to tone it down, but he knew they were desperate. He felt guilty sometimes for not listening more or better.

Lately one voice had become louder than the rest. He wasn't sure who exactly it was, but he kept listening for information.

In the meantime, Ben had a bigger worry. He often woke in the morning with dirt on him, under his nails and on his clothes. Why was he dressed and what was he doing at night? He had no idea, and that frightened him. What if one of the spirits was taking him over?

They had no limits on what they could do, not anymore. Heaven and hell no longer bound them.

Chapter Five

Steve went over to the Castelles' in the morning to meet Vivian. He left a message on Candy's phone about where he was going and why, but he couldn't imagine any reason for her to want to follow him.

She was a liaison, not a guard, and while he liked to have a connection with the local cops, he didn't need to be constantly watched. It wasn't as if he were any kind of threat to the community.

He met Buddy first. Last night he'd spent some time on-line looking up the two breeds the Castelles had indicated, wanting to know what he might be getting into with this "big" dog. If they didn't get along, he'd ask to get to know Vivian without her pet. It would be better, however, if she had Buddy with her to relax her and give her a friend at her side.

The dog resembled the American Staffordshire breed more than he looked like a bloodhound, but he had some cute wrinkles on his forehead that seemed to give him character. He was also taller than an Am Staff, closer in size to a bloodhound.

Steve also quickly discovered that Buddy had the bloodhound personality: gentle, sweet, affectionate. It didn't take them long to become fast friends, and Buddy showed absolutely no hesitation about welcoming Steve. The Castelles had been right about him—he was more likely to knock you over and love you to death.

Buddy also had a bloodhound's nose. When he fixated on an odor, he forgot everything else until he was satisfied.

Which got Steve to thinking about the dog staring at the wall like that. Maybe he hadn't been sensing danger. Maybe there was a smell that had caught his attention.

An interesting change in perspective.

As Steve sat on the grass with the large dog stretched out beside him, content to be scratched until Steve thought his arm might fall off, he thought about Buddy staring fixated at the wall.

There had to be some kind of odor, he decided. Buddy wouldn't stare fixedly at a sound. But what? It could be almost anything. Maybe there was a smell in the wall itself or coming up from the basement. He'd have to check it out.

A good lead for a start. Something other than the obvious paranormal.

Although that didn't do a damn thing to explain the voices Vivian was hearing, or the talking that Annabelle had briefly heard.

Lying back on the cold, hard ground, he stared up at the gray sky while Buddy sniffed him. Okay, maybe it hadn't been an odor that had caught Buddy's attention. He'd heard of dogs reacting to the paranormal, although that was another idea he needed to check out for himself. Maybe Buddy would wind up helping him with that.

At last he sat up, convinced that the dog wouldn't be a problem, and headed into the house to meet with Vivian. While he didn't want anyone to disturb his conversation with the girl, and it would be totally innocuous to start, he didn't want to take the child away with him, not even as far as the backyard, on their first meeting.

He was sure Vivian had been given all the stranger warnings, especially in the big city.

Annabelle and Vivian were sitting in the kitchen. Steve smelled hot chocolate and Vivian had some of it smeared around her mouth. She looked at him rather suspiciously.

Central casting couldn't have sent him a more photogenic child. Long blond wavy hair, bright blue eyes. A pretty child's face.

"Viv," Annabelle said, "this is Mr. Hawks. He's going to try to find out about the voice you keep hearing."

Viv's expression didn't relax very much. He guessed it was a topic she didn't want to visit.

He queried Annabelle with his eyes and joined the two of them at the kitchen table. "You can call me Steve, Vivian," he said pleasantly. "If I get to use your first name, you get to use mine."

That brought a slight smile to Vivian's lips. Annabelle handed her a napkin, and Viv wiped her mouth with it.

Buddy had followed Steve in, and now he sat beside Vivian, looking even larger when measured against the girl's size. That dog had to seriously outweigh her.

"Buddy's a great dog," Steve said. "I like him a whole lot. But he's so big. Does he listen to you?"

Viv nodded, set down her mug, then leaned over to hug Buddy right around his neck. The dog started grinning.

Okay, Steve thought. That relationship had been established.

"Did you get Buddy when he was a small puppy?"

Vivian answered for the first time. "He's still a puppy."

Annabelle spoke. "I think Steve is asking about when we first got him, when he was still a baby."

And that was why he needed to gain Vivian's trust so he could talk to her alone. Annabelle would mean well, but she'd insert as she thought necessary for clarity. Not what Steve wanted at all.

Vivian was okay with it, however. She let go of Buddy's neck and spread her arms, palms turned inward. "He was this big."

"Not very big at all."

"Smaller than me," Vivian asserted. "He slept in my bed."

"Does he still? I mean, if he sleeps in your bed, where do you sleep?"

That drew a giggle out of the girl. "I make myself tiny."

"I bet you do. Very tiny."

And this added yet another wrinkle. If the dog was sleeping in her room, why was she so scared? Maybe because Buddy wasn't protective? Or did she think Buddy didn't hear the sounds because her parents didn't?

Or, if she thought it was a ghost, nobody else needed to hear it at all?

Or even, from his perspective, voices didn't bother that dog at all. Given how friendly he was, maybe it was just another background noise to him.

A little over an hour later, Steve departed, promising to return the next day. He'd played card games with Viv, who was on her way to becoming a card sharp. He'd never done so badly with a simple game of War. She had the devil's own luck on a deal.

Vivian's acceptance of him had begun. Good.

Now he needed to find a way to look into the history of the Castelle house. Was there lore associated with it? Was there some kind of notable history?

First place to start was the recorder's office. All the details about who had owned and sold the land back to whenever they started keeping records of such things. Probably pretty decent records since he was sure that the Castelles couldn't have gotten a mortgage without a clear title. The title company would have taken care of that.

When he checked his phone, however, he discovered the nearest title company was ninety miles away…and he couldn't even be sure it was the right one. Chances were the Castelles wouldn't know either. Mortgage companies tended to deal with title companies themselves, keeping the certificate on hand. And charging the client for it, of course.

Sometimes he walked the edge of being cynical. He supposed he was fortunate that after all those years of being a cop he hadn't become hardened and jaded.

He wondered, too, when Candy would get back to him about meeting that retired sheriff. He was already champing at the bit for that interview.

As well as one with Vivian. That child was as smart as a whip, sharp as a tack or whatever overused simile you wanted. He anticipated she'd give him a view that her parents couldn't begin to.

CANDY SPENT MOST of her day trying to track down Nathan Tate for Steve. No answer on the phone, not even his cell, and when she went by the Tate house, no one was home.

Well, people had lives. They weren't all sitting around waiting for a chance to talk to Steve Hawks. Steve was just going to have to do the waiting, and she wasn't about to knock on neighboring doors to find out where the Tates were. Man, imagine the uproar she'd cause. No explanation could ease the fears that would arise from a deputy asking those questions.

Giving up for now, she headed back to the office, believing there had to be something truly useful to do. Not that this department seemed to be overburdened most of the time. If you wanted excitement on a regular basis, this wasn't the place to get it.

Just as she was about to enter, she saw Steve climbing the courthouse steps. The courthouse was located in a large area between four streets that contained a park, as well. It was aptly named Courthouse Square, surrounded on four sides by shops, a bakery and an ice cream parlor. Behind the sheriff's office, facing the square, was a decently sized phone service to help people experiencing everything from abuse to suicidal thoughts.

People everywhere needed someone they could privately talk with, with someone who was objective and could give them advice or get them help.

Diners, like Maude's, weren't the best place to have a personal conversation. Too many ears might overhear.

Instead of going inside, she followed Steve to the courthouse in case she could help. She suspected he was headed for the recorder's office, and she shortly was proved right.

She found him talking to one of the clerks and learning the reality of a truly small town.

"Well, Mr. Hawks, we may have nearly fifty years of records on microfilm and microfiche. I'm not sure about earlier records, or whether any were hit-and-miss. We've got other records over at storage, if you need us to hunt them up."

"I hope I won't," he answered.

The clerk laughed. "I hope so, too. We're a very small department because of budgets, and because we're not all that busy." She lifted an eyebrow. "I think you can tell we aren't having a boom on sales of property, or purchases for that matter."

It was his turn to laugh. "I hope you aren't. A boom would disrupt your town, wouldn't it? It seems so peaceful."

She leaned forward a bit and lowered her voice. "This place is eternally hoping for a boom. At least we got the junior college."

She promised to find the records she could on fiche and film. He thanked her and turned away, spying Candy immediately.

"Riding herd on me?"

She shook her head. "I just couldn't resist seeing how you responded to this reality. We've got the same thing going on over at the sheriff's. Recent records are digitized. Everything's still on paper, though, because we don't want any computer mess-ups."

He laughed. "Gotcha. I hope I won't have to ask anyone to dig into archives."

"It would be greatly appreciated by the men and women who work over at the archive building."

He glanced at the wall clock hanging just behind the recorder's window. "Dang, I knew I was getting hungry. No lunch and it's almost dinnertime. You said Mahoney's is good?"

"Very good with a limited menu. There might even be some people there who'd be willing to talk to you about the Castelle place."

He looked mildly surprised. "But not at Maude's?"

"You might still be under suspicion over there. New fella."

"Why is Mahoney's different?"

"Give anyone a few beers and they're much more likely to talk."

He laughed again. "Come with me?"

He watched her hesitate, then she nodded. "Sure. Maybe my uniform will vouch for you more than a few beers. Of course, it could have a very different effect."

He knew exactly what she meant. When he'd been in uniform, he'd noticed how quiet even a rowdy place could get when he entered.

As they walked down the street, taking in some of the spurt of Halloween decorations in the shop windows, he asked, "People around here don't like to see uniforms?"

"I wouldn't say that. I'm new, too. When some of the other deputies and I drop in after a shift, there's usually a lot of friendliness. I don't see as much if I go in alone."

For the first time he considered how new she was here,

and how that could affect most of her daily life. "It takes a while to get rooted?"

"Probably an entire lifetime." She paused. "I never forget that at least ninety percent of the people here grew up together. This town, this county, is rare."

"These days, yeah. People in other places are a lot more physically mobile."

"I was an Army brat. Funny how close people in the military can get over time. We might change postings, but eventually you run into people you knew from a previous posting. Made it kind of difficult on kids, though."

She paused as they reached the door of Mahoney's. "When my dad was in, changes in postings occurred more frequently than now. Each move was wrenching, mainly because we were kids. You'd make a friend, then move. Next time you ran into them, they'd have changed and I would have changed, too. That meant starting all over again."

She came by her interest in the military honestly. He tucked that away in his mental file. Then he reached for the handle and opened the door. "I hadn't thought about that."

"No reason you should."

Inside the bar was warming up for the evening. Some of the tables were already full. Country music played in the background. There were only a few stools at the bar that remained empty. Steve liked the atmosphere. He wouldn't have been surprised to learn that this bar dated back to the days of the Wild West.

They settled at a table against a wall, and Candy sat facing the door.

A cheerful waitress came over to take their orders, quite a difference from Maude. Both ordered fried chicken, and Steve asked for a beer while Candy chose club soda with lime.

"Aren't you off duty?" he asked.

"Not right now."

Steve leaned back, wondering if she considered herself on duty because of him, or if she just didn't like to drink. The latter was always possible. It made no difference to him as long as he wasn't hampering her. He didn't know how to ask because it really wasn't his business. Her choice.

He noted again how attractive she was. A beautiful face surrounded by short, dark hair and decorated with warm brown eyes. Eyes that he had seen grow chilly.

Their drinks arrived quickly and were followed soon by the chicken. He suspected this bar turned over chicken swiftly. A quick scan of the people around them suggested he was right. Lots of plates of chicken out there. Well, that boded well.

At least there was no plate of fries to tempt him. He smiled.

"Something funny?" she asked.

"Only me. I was feeling grateful there are no fries."

At last she laughed. "Good point. You're killing my diet."

"Mine, too. Oh, well. A couple of weeks of self-indulgence won't kill me."

"You ever heard that old joke? If I'd known I was going to live this long, I would have taken better care of myself."

"Ha! No, that's the first time. I like it."

A thaw had begun. He felt Candy had let go of a little of her suspicion.

Well, he'd grown used to that ever since he started doing his show. Back when he'd been a cop trying to help frightened families, he'd been more warmly welcomed. It was reasonable for people to question his motives now, although he found it a bit tiresome to keep dealing with it. Maybe someday he'd be treated less like a con man. Although that was improving as his show became better known.

He just wanted people to realize he was honest. Maybe that was the thing that bothered him most. Oh, well, he'd chosen this path and he very much believed in personal responsibility for choices.

Which didn't always make them easier to endure.

They ate silently for a while, and he wondered what he should be talking about. "You get anywhere with the old sheriff?"

Yeah, dude, bright. Bring up work when she should be enjoying dinner. With him, however, questions seldom stopped.

"No luck so far," she answered, looking up from her two pieces of fried chicken. "He's out of town, and I'm damned if I'm going to question neighbors about when he'll be back."

"Afraid of worrying people?"

"Of course I am. How many times did you flash a badge without creating a stir?"

"Rarely," he admitted. "I met Vivian Castelle today."

She nodded and wiped her fingers with a napkin. "How did that go?"

"Pretty well, actually. Bright kid, she opened up some with me after numerous games of War."

"War?"

"A card game that even younger kids can play. She beat me soundly. I wouldn't want to argue with that child's luck."

That drew a wide smile from her. "Like that?"

"It didn't matter which of us dealt. Anyway, I'll probably need some more time with her before she's ready to talk about her experiences."

"How come?"

"Because I need her to speak for herself without Mom or Dad correcting her or adding things to clarify. I want *her* story."

"Makes sense."

Well, she'd talk about the case, but not about herself it seemed. Silence until that came up. Past bad experience?

Or her nature? Whatever the cause, he wanted to find a way around it. To discover something about her.

And maybe that was just a man's response to a woman he found to be beautiful. Or maybe not. Crap. He'd heard women complain that men wanted to talk only about themselves. He didn't want to be that guy. Yet here he was, talking about his job. Every single minute.

So he attacked the problem indirectly. "Still worried I'm taking advantage of people's desperation?"

She paused, halfway through her second chicken thigh. A dark meat lover. "Maybe less than I was since I heard your interview with the Castelles."

"Why's that?"

"Because you never once led them or prompted them. It was all about what they thought and felt."

She'd noticed that. Good. He tried hard not to lead his clients. Another skill of a good detective. Let the witness or suspect tell it. Ask questions, but don't suggest. Suggesting often led to lies that later wouldn't stand up.

She spoke again as she finished her chicken and tried to wipe her fingers and mouth with yet another napkin.

Steve said, "Don't you wish restaurants served those heated finger towels? Or the little bowls of hot water with lemon in them?"

"Oh, yeah, it would be nice. I'll go to the ladies' in a few to wash up. What about your cases?"

No diverting her. Easier than talking about Candy, apparently, he thought as he finished his own meal. "I told you about the cases with people who feared noises in their house, or the feeling that someone was looking in their windows. Or the figures they believed they saw."

She nodded and crumpled the napkin on her plate. The waitress whisked it away and gave her another club soda. "That's a general description."

"It's hard to cover one particularly. Lemme think for a

minute or two. See if a case stands out. Do they serve Corona here?"

"They might. Most people just get draft beer."

"I'm fond of Corona." He lifted a finger and the cheerful waitress returned. He wondered if she'd be feeling this perky at closing time. There was little question this bar was going to get rowdier. "Do you have Corona?"

"Oh, yeah. It's become really popular among our younger customers."

"Thanks. Candy, do you want anything?"

"A nice cup of hot chocolate, Mary. Please."

Steve looked wryly at Candy as Mary weaved her way back toward the bar. "I should have asked about the Corona when I first ordered. But the draft on tap is good."

"I can't tell the difference between one beer and another. Maybe because I drink it so rarely."

"That would matter. Now about my cases when I was still a cop..."

CANDY WAITED PATIENTLY even after her hot chocolate and Steve's longneck arrived. She wanted to hear this, hear what had been important enough to pick up an off-duty avocation. She had begun to think that he was truly concerned about people, but she needed more convincing.

"Well, I remember a case about an elderly lady living alone in a large house. She was *very* old, maybe close to ninety, and frail. Honestly, I couldn't believe she was rattling around in that place all by herself. Still cooking for herself, still cleaning the areas she used. I was impressed, but what if she hurt herself? She didn't even have one of those buttons to call for help, you know the ones that hang around the neck?"

She nodded. "I hear they're not cheap."

"That may have been part of the problem. Social Security doesn't go very far, and she owned the house. That meant upkeep, of course, but I'd have bet she'd socked something away against that. In the meantime, she didn't have rent to pay, and these days that's as expensive as a mortgage."

"Maybe so." Candy could see that. "She was probably very independent, too."

"She also didn't want to leave because that house held more than sixty good years of memories for her. She talked about her husband, about her children and grandchildren. Even great-grandchildren. It was a short litany, waving at framed photos, but I stood there listening and wondering where all those people were. None of them might be able to talk her out of that house, but surely there was someone who could come stay with her?"

Candy shook her head.

"I know. I don't know where they all were. Families often move away pursuing jobs. I get it. You joined the Army. I'll bet your dad had been out for a while."

"Well, yeah."

"So okay. My parents are retired in Costa Rica. I can't just bop down every weekend to visit. Or every month for that matter. But I *can* hire someone to help them out and check on them."

"Good point." She so far liked the way he thought. Concern for an old woman he didn't really know. Thinking of ways to help his parents. "Anyway…" She pressed him.

"Anyway. I was doing a wellness check, not just answering her call. Back then I was a uniform, so I was pretty sure she felt better having me there. Having my partner, too, although he was outside checking around the house. Which was isolated. Still farmland, although run over by that time. Plenty of brush and woods to hide in, so he had his job cut out for him."

"I can imagine. But one question?"

"Yeah?"

"Were all these places you checked isolated?"

"Nope." He shook his head a little. "Some were in busy neighborhoods. Some people had neighbors who'd had experiences in their houses."

Uneasiness trickled down Candy's spine. Did she really want to hear this? Everyone carried a bit of superstition, even if it was as mild as knocking on wood. Was she about to run into hers?

This time he corralled himself. "Back to my elderly lady. Anyway, she was alone, isolated. Yeah, I was worried about her. I couldn't mistake how frightened she was. I was even concerned that that kind of fear might kill her."

"I didn't think of that, but you're right." Candy frowned. His imagery was vivid.

"If you'd seen her, you'd have shared the same concerns. But back to the rest of it. She kept seeing this black shadow of a man. He'd just suddenly be there, in a doorway or beside her bed. Then he was gone, and she told herself she was imagining it. But when it kept happening, she wondered if she was losing her mind, so she didn't call anyone about it. And then she heard banging and footsteps upstairs. Night after night. She was convinced someone had broken in, and after a week of that, she called us."

"She took it for that long?" Candy was amazed.

"Yeah, I know. But she was afraid for her mind. Afraid someone would come and put her in an institution."

"Rock and a hard place," she murmured. She was building one hell of a picture in her mind and could well understand why Steve would hate leaving her alone. "You didn't call anyone?"

"How could I? She'd made it clear that leaving that house would likely be the death of her. I didn't want to be responsible for that."

Candy put her chin in her hand, forgetting the large mug of hot chocolate that still steamed in front of her. "Wow."

"Yeah. Anyway, I searched the entire house for intruders. Top to bottom, including a dusty attic. Windows all locked, no sign of forced entry. I had to go back and tell her there was no one in her house. Then my partner came in and said he hadn't been able to find signs of anyone outside, although he did say kids might have run away too quick to be seen."

"That didn't help, did it?"

Steve sighed. "Not on two levels. First, she hadn't complained about anyone being outside. Second, even though everything that was troubling her was indoors, I couldn't find a damn thing. I told her if she heard or saw anything more, she must definitely call the emergency line. I told her I'd make sure someone came right away. I made her promise to call."

His gaze grew distant. "I left feeling like crap, feeling helpless. I got annoyed with my partner for dismissing it as an old lady all alone and wanting attention. He even called her batty. I couldn't dismiss it."

He drank some of his beer, then focused on her again. "I couldn't just toss it for a lot of reasons, and one of them was I'd been hearing other complaints just like it. This whole haunting thing was beginning to trouble me. And that's when it really began."

She remembered her hot chocolate and lifted the mug. Mahoney's made the best. Rich and creamy. "Did the woman call again?"

"Two days later. A patrol headed out there as quickly as they could and found nothing. Again. When I heard some officers talking about it being a waste of time and that the woman needed an ambulance, not a cop, I made up my mind I was going out there."

"I would have, too," Candy agreed. "Good for you."

He smiled faintly. "Not within my purview as a cop, but

within it off duty. She recognized me and we got going on a complete investigation."

Dang, Candy thought, it was becoming increasingly difficult to distrust this man. He was really too handsome for one thing. Not storybook handsome, but appealing. Now she had to deal with her hormones, as well. Great. Just great.

She thought about the scene he had painted so effectively, mostly thinking about that poor old woman stubbornly living in a house she had loved for many decades, only to find herself terrified inside it. "Did you help her?"

"I don't think so. I went out at night to her house to investigate. I stayed all night as often as my schedule would allow. Several times a week for a few weeks. Never heard anything, never saw anything. Nor did she."

Candy nodded. "So you had to give up?"

"Sort of." He shook his head, looking sad. "I installed cameras in every place she'd had an experience. I put sound-activated recorders in every room. I think they made her feel better, knowing I'd be watching and listening by long distance."

He sighed and put his beer bottle to one side. "Never recorded anything. Then she died a few months later. It'll always be a mystery."

"You don't like that."

"Hell no. Sometimes there's a rational explanation. Sometimes I can at least provide comfort, and sometimes I doubt I give people anything at all. I can only try."

He leaned toward her. "You know what a psychologist told me?"

"What?" She wanted to hear this.

"A lot of his colleagues are seeing a large uptick in patients who come to them with complaints of anxiety, fear and depression. The patients are blaming it on the paranormal. The psychologists are blaming it on the huge number of ghost-hunting shows, and say they spend a lot of time trying to deprogram people."

She felt her eyes widen. "My God. How did that make you feel?"

"Not good. On the other hand, I try to find reasonable explanations, and failing that I try to make people comfortable with what they're experiencing. It's all I can do. Considering the number of people who call for help, I can't ignore the problem."

Candy experienced her first sympathy for him. "Have you ever sent anyone to a psychologist?"

"Hell yeah. I just don't usually do it on screen. Some things need to be kept private. Can we go?"

BEN WITTES WALKED into Mahoney's in time to see that deputy and the ghost hunter leaving. Interesting combination.

One of the damn spirit voices emerged loudly into his head.

Get on with it!

Sure, as if he could just insert himself into that investigation. Just walk up and demand it.

Shut up! he shouted inside his head. *Damn it, just shut up.* He ought to be able to enjoy a sandwich and a beer without being pummeled by annoying spirits.

The voice that had been growing louder and more demanding quieted down, but the voices in the background became annoying mumbles, mainly because he couldn't make out what they were saying.

He ignored them as best he could. There were a couple of empty stools at the bar and he slid into one. Nobody greeted him, but he was used to that. His entire life in this town people had ignored him. Except for the bullies in school, but even then he'd realized he wasn't the only one being bullied. *Nothing personal in it*, his mother had always said.

However, that one spirit was right. If he could get himself on that ghost-hunting show, he wouldn't be ignored any longer. He *had* to manage it.

For a while it would even make him a big man around here.

That thought was satisfying enough that he smiled at his tuna salad sandwich and tried to figure it out. If the show's producers didn't call him back soon, he'd find another way.

Chapter Six

Candy had plenty to think about that evening. Outside, Halloween was approaching with snow flurries and more carved and lighted pumpkins.

Inside her snug little rental house—*snug* being another word for *tiny*—bright colors greeted her. Given her heritage, she preferred them to the understated, and she wasn't afraid to splash around reds, yellows, greens and electric blues.

She lit her fireplace for the first time since she'd moved here. She didn't want to use it much, being conscious of its inefficiency and the pollutants it emitted, but this one night it didn't seem like a major sin.

And tonight it was comforting, the dance of flickering orange-and-yellow light around her small living room. The warmth, unregulated, sometimes made her hot. Right then, hot felt good.

Steve had given her much to consider, especially that part about what the psychologist told him. She sipped hot cider spiced with a cinnamon stick and turned everything around in her head.

The statement from the psychologist had surprised her, although in retrospect it shouldn't have. Even though she wasn't a fan, she'd been aware of the increasing number of ghost shows on cable channels. Sometimes she had to look hard for something else.

There *did* seem to be a growing interest in conspiracy theories, too. She wondered if the inclination had always been there and was now coming to the forefront. Probably.

She was no fun, she supposed, but she didn't buy into ghosts, aliens, or UFOs. There were enough real threats to worry about. On the other hand, she guessed it might be enjoyable to fall in with a group of similar believers and carry imagination to its wild conclusions.

But ghosts and the paranormal were different. Those ideas actually scared people, and anxiety and fear could make them sick, whether physically or emotionally.

Cripes, there was no real way to think herself through this. She'd simply have to watch and wait for whatever Steve came up with. She just hoped it helped the Castelles.

Sighing, she got herself another mug of hot cider, then settled in to enjoy the fire, the chilly evening and the comforts of home.

For a long time, her only home had been the people in her squad. Friends. Closer than friends, like family. Except nothing could ever enfold her the way her large family's love had. A boisterous crew of immediate family and extended family, aunts, uncles, cousins.

She had walked away to join the Army, an attempt to find herself. A youthful notion, an identity crisis, maybe a need to follow in her deceased father's footsteps. Whatever. But that had carried her to places that had made her unwilling to go home. Changed forever, not wanting her family to know this new person. Maybe not wise, but the feeling ran deep anyway.

Worse, her younger brother had followed her into the Army, and he'd been killed in action. The guilt dogged her constantly. She felt responsible, and she couldn't believe the rest of her family didn't feel the same, at some level. They'd deny it, but she would still know it was true.

With difficulty, she yanked herself away from that

yawning cavern before it consumed her. These days it was easy to trip into places inside herself that were hideous.

She sighed again and began listening to some of her favorite songs in her head. It was a skill she'd chosen to develop during many long, tense nights. It was almost as good as having a CD player in her pocket, except it didn't get in the way of her hearing.

Part of her wanted to close her eyes and just let the warmth flow over her. Another part wanted to enjoy the dancing of the firelight.

She kept her eyes open as long as she could and thought about the coming day. This might get exciting.

ON THE OTHER side of town, Steve made some calls to his production crew from his motel room. They'd found a psychic for him, he was told. One right there in Conard City.

Great, he thought, but held his tongue. He'd argued with them about this before and was always told that the fans liked it.

Just because the fans liked it didn't mean he had to. They'd probably like it even more if he ever found proof of a ghost, but it sure as hell was going to take more to convince him than a psychic wandering around claiming to *feel* things. From his perspective, his clients were already feeling enough.

They could do the job themselves. *In this room we feel like something evil is watching. Over there we've seen a black shadow figure. This is horrifying. I believe he wants to hurt my family.*

Well, all the psychic usually did was say the same thing from a different perspective. Which was not to say he was convinced real psychics didn't exist. There'd been a few who'd made the hair on the back of his neck stand up.

But most of them just made him want to roll his eyes.

Having a psychic from right around here was especially

problematic. They'd be clued in to the local history, able to repeat stories and anecdotes that would appear to stand up under scrutiny. Except because of Steve's investigation, they rarely would.

He'd seen a few, though, who came in from elsewhere and had no obvious connections with the things they told him, things he had found out independently, and only with a great deal of research. Some of those things weren't available by any means except talking to a local historian. Like Miss Emma.

Come to think of it, he needed to get back to her. Memories might have been spurred by his questions. She might even have done some research of her own to see if she could find something useful.

She'd definitely impressed him. There was an air about her that made her seem both wise and intelligent. He suspected her dismissal of her knowledge of local history had been self-deprecating. She hadn't learned it from growing up surrounded by it. Saying it was her avocation had probably been closer to the truth. A woman like that had to be doing more with her days than simply entering books in a card catalog or checking books out.

Which inevitably led him back to Candy Serrano. She must be bored with this assignment. She was, after all, a woman who'd joined the Army, evidently had seen combat, then had joined a police department. Being a babysitter probably chafed the hell out of her.

He'd heard from a guy at the gas station that Candy's predecessor had been tasked to keep an eye on an angry special ops guy. A paratrooper who was after his brother's killer.

Now here was Candy essentially tasked with the same type of job, only with a much less interesting character. Hell, he was far from being a time bomb ready to blow up.

Nah, he hadn't even been exciting as a detective. Some of his cases, yeah, but not him. It still astonished him to be recognized on the street or in an airport. The low profile he'd once nurtured was in the distant past now.

Well, there didn't seem to be anything to do except embrace it. He'd stepped into this job to help people. He was even able to help people who were never on the show. That was what his spare time was for.

But Candy must be wondering why she'd ever wanted to be a police officer. That was another question he would like her to answer. After a life of such extreme excitement, what was she doing *here*? A charming town to be sure, but maybe too peaceful?

Damn, he wished he could get her to talk about herself. In that regard, she was totally buttoned up.

Then he had a thought. This local psychic. Maybe she'd have some information about him. Scuttlebutt if nothing else.

He reached for his cell phone and dialed her, wondering if he was going to ruin her evening the way he seemed to be ruining her days.

But he couldn't tolerate inactivity and so far he hadn't accomplished very much. Anything that felt like forward movement would be good.

CANDY HAD DOZED off in her chair but awoke immediately when her phone rang. The fire had died down quite a bit, the room was slowly cooling, but it still felt good. The dancing light had settled to a dull red glow. Nice.

But maybe the phone brought some excitement. She could still use that.

It was Steve, wanting to talk to her about some psychic. She seemed to have a vague memory that there was a guy in town, but she'd had no reason to pursue it. Was he actually going to use a psychic? Her impression of him sank a notch.

She told him to come over and gave him her address. "I've got a fire on the hearth and I don't want to leave it unattended."

"I'll be there shortly."

Whatever it was, she doubted it would be boring. She shook herself out, working out some of the stiffness from sleeping on a recliner, and went to her kitchen to warm up the cider. No beer here. She hoped he'd survive.

BEN WITTES AWOKE in the middle of the night with dirt on his clothes and pine tar sticky on his hands.

What the hell?

He searched his memory and had only a few snatches of having been in the forest. Late evening? He didn't have enough memory to know. Why would he have gone onto the mountainside anyway?

You've got to make it real.

There was that one voice again, louder than the rest. He wished he could silence it by putting the pillow over his ears, but spirits couldn't be shut out by such things.

Staggering wearily, he went to his bathroom and stripped off his dirty clothes. He knew the shower wouldn't get rid of the pine tar, but it would get rid of the dirt he seemed to be wearing all over his hands, and even his legs. Had he been crawling?

As he scrubbed, he noticed pine needles were already beginning to clog the drain. Damn. He wished he knew what was going on.

Stop the deputy.

Stop the deputy from what? Which deputy? The one who was babysitting that ghost hunter? Why would he do that?

Fear had begun to stalk him as he slowly lost control of his nights. What might happen to his days as well if this kept occurring?

Why did he have holes in his memory?

Was he possessed?

The idea of going to the church to ask to be exorcised floated into his brain.

Don't be stupid. The pastor will never believe you. He'll think you're mad.

Ben scraped the pine tar off his hands as best he could, but stronger steps would be needed. He didn't reach for a towel, for fear of ruining it. Instead he padded naked and dripping toward his garage.

You're not possessed.

Maybe not yet. And maybe he was well on his way.

His fear deepened. He'd never imagined this.

Possessed.

IT WAS NEARLY midnight when Steve arrived. Candy smothered a yawn and went to invite him in. Cold arrived with him, and she regretted not wearing her sweater.

"Hot cider with cinnamon?" she asked him as he closed the door behind him.

"You have no idea how good that sounds."

Yeah, she did. That's why she'd been drinking it herself. "I'll go get it. Have a seat in the living room. What's left of the fire is warming the space."

"Gladly."

She listened to him walk away as she turned into her kitchen. Like everything in this house, it was small. She often wished for more counter space when she got into a baking or cooking mood. It was, however, bright with sunflower-yellow paint and blue canisters.

A copper-clad pot on the stove still held warm cider, and she turned on the gas to heat it up to a better temperature. She wasn't going to look for anything to eat, though. This wasn't a social visit and Steve wasn't an invited guest.

It wasn't her mother's way, nor the one she'd been taught, but Steve didn't qualify even as a friend dropping in. Nope. Her spine had stiffened since leaving home.

She carried a mug for him and a fresh one for herself back to the living room. He'd chosen to sit on the sofa rather than her recliner. Maybe because all the stuff on the table beside the recliner labeled it "her" chair.

Mildly amused, she handed him his mug, then sat facing him. "What's up?"

"This cider is really good. And you don't have a TV?"

Strange question. "Not in here. If I watch, it's usually in my bedroom while I'm falling asleep."

"That's so flattering."

She had to grin, deciding she might even enjoy this visit. "Hey, you're not the only one I'm boycotting."

He snorted. "That would make me too important. Anyway, the reason for this terribly rude late-night visit is that my producers have found me a psychic. Not that I want one. I'd rather skip it entirely."

She leaned a little toward him, revising her opinion of him once again. Just a little. "Why? I thought that was part of your genre."

He winced. "For some. I hate it, but the feeling is the fans like it. I don't agree. I mean, I'm running a counterflow show. Not following the accepted routines or supposed discoveries. I like to think we have a somewhat different fan base. Then the producers pull this."

She nodded. "But doesn't your opinion matter? You're the star."

"It matters less than you'd think. They took a flier on me. Evidently it's working well enough that they keep renewing me. That could end. Or I could quit, I suppose, but that would leave me without a job, and going back to police work wouldn't help me keep my parents in Costa Rica."

She hadn't thought of that. Feeling a bit startled, for the first time she considered that he was very much in a bind, too.

She asked, "You ever wonder what you'll do if they push you too far in a direction you don't want to go?"

"All the time. Maybe the most important thing to me is my parents. They've dreamed about retiring in Costa Rica since I was in high school. It was less expensive then, and they thought they could make it on Social Security. But over the years, it all grew more expensive, including the income requirements for moving there, and I watched the dream start dying. I was happy as hell to make it possible for them. I absolutely don't want to be the cause of taking it away."

She honestly ached for him. What a tough place to be, with his parents' happiness hanging in the balance. He had to keep his show, and if that meant dealing with psychics, he'd deal.

"Now what about this psychic in town? Do you know anything about him?"

"Just an occasional mention on the grapevine. Nobody seems especially interested, or at least not interested enough to really talk about him."

"Not a superstitious town, huh?"

"I'm not sure I'd say that. Who doesn't knock on wood? Even I do that." She didn't feel sheepish about it either. "Everyone's leery of tempting fate."

"No kidding." Steve sighed. "Nothing? I've wasted your time and kept you awake."

"Not really." Candy sipped more of her cider and considered setting her mug on the hearth to warm it more. It had cooled down fast—everything in a mug did—but she liked it hotter than room temperature. "Anyway, like I was saying, I'm not sure it says anything about superstition. It may just be that this psychic makes them uneasy. I don't know many people who are comfortable with the whole idea of talking to the dead."

"Used to be a big fad, spiritualism." He drained his cup. "Man, that was good. Thanks."

"You're welcome. Anyway, spiritualism. I don't think we've got any table tippers around here. I'd have heard about that by now. No, it just seems to be the one guy, without a following."

"Better for me."

"How's that?"

He smiled crookedly. "I don't have to deal with a bunch of true believers. Which I would, otherwise."

Her turn to smile. Her ignorance about this whole thing was astonishing. Or maybe not, when she'd never been very interested. "I'm taking it that you'd like me to look into this guy? If I can?"

"If he doesn't have some kind of criminal record, I don't know how you could."

"I can ask some of the other deputies what they might have heard. Or my book group at the library. We're meeting next Tuesday."

"That would be a great help. I don't want to go into this blind with this guy if I can manage it."

She had begun to feel kind of achy and breathless. It was as if he had brought an attractant through the door along with the cold air. It seemed to waft around her, drawing her closer to thoughts she didn't want to have.

"I guess I should go and let you get some sleep," Steve said, rising. "Where can I wash this cup?"

"Just leave it. I'll take care of it." She had an urgent need for him to leave before she started down a path that could only get her into trouble. She needed her objectivity, and he was leaving town in a few weeks anyway.

She didn't even walk him to the door. Once he left and she felt as if she could breathe again, she went to lock it.

Now she had to find out about a psychic? Seriously? She hadn't imagined her job this way.

This would mean looking into gossip, too. Oh, well, that could probably be called an official part of her duties. If she didn't listen to the grapevine, she might miss something useful in solving a case.

But a psychic?

Sheesh!

Chapter Seven

Candy walked into the office in the morning. Once again it was unusually silent.

"What's going on?" she asked Sarah Ironheart, who apparently was on the desk today. "Too quiet."

"Yeah. We got a call about a couple of missing teens first thing. Parents say they've been gone since yesterday afternoon, and neither of them is answering their phones. Which isn't necessarily surprising, given how many dead zones we have out here. Probably nothing, but no one's going to take the chance."

"I wouldn't either," Candy agreed. "Want me to run over and get you some coffee? I could do with one. Sleep is still in my eyes."

Sarah smiled almost puckishly. "That would be great. And Velma's not here this morning to be offended."

Candy laughed. "Where is she?"

"Even Velma must occasionally take a day off, like it or not."

"Latte?"

"Oh, that sounds so good!"

Candy strolled down the street to Maude's invigorated by the snap of the clear morning air, enjoying the cardboard Halloween decorations that leered from shop windows.

A couple of teens missing since yesterday afternoon

didn't seem like a total all-out emergency. Typical kind of kid stuff, like that vandalism and the toilet papering.

Know where your kids are? Great advice. Try it with teens. They had all kinds of ways to escape parental supervision. Candy knew something about that herself. She had some memories she'd never have shared with her parents on the rare occasion she escaped their constant supervision.

She gave Maude a cheery greeting but had no idea whether it was well received. A couple of minutes later she was headed back to the office with two large take-out cups filled with lattes.

When she arrived to give Sarah her coffee, another deputy was walking around. Micah Parish, a guy who was rumored to be past retirement. He sure didn't look like it. A powerful, Native American man with long, inky hair streaked with silver.

He intimidated her. It was his size that made her wary, even though he'd always been pleasant. A stupid reaction considering where she had been.

"Okay, Sarah," he said, his voice deep, "Where did those extra sat phones go?"

"Gage didn't take them when he left?"

"He wouldn't be asking for them if he had."

"Oh, hell," said Sarah, rising to leave her coffee behind. "Do you suppose grown people ever learn to put things back where they belong?"

Sarah and Micah disappeared to the back, then a short while later she heard Sarah exclaim, "Oh, for heaven's sake!"

"Thanks," Micah answered. "As if I'd ever have looked there!"

"You with all those kids? You'd have gotten around to it."

"Faith saves me the treasure hunts. And those days are pretty much past."

"Not around here."

"Evidently."

A minute later they both reappeared, Micah with a duffel bag that presumably held the missing phones.

Sarah dropped down in her chair, reaching for the coffee and calling out, "See you, Micah."

"Saturday night, right?"

"You betcha."

Candy looked at Sarah. "Saturday?" She knew she had no business asking, but for some reason she couldn't resist.

"Family gathering. I guess you haven't heard, but I'm married to Micah's brother."

That man had a brother? She wondered if the guy was a mountain, too.

Sarah ticked her fingers. "Let's see. My husband, Gideon, is Micah's brother. Connie Parish, whom you know from here, is married to Micah's eldest son, Ethan. There are assorted other Parishes of nearly every age, a few embedded here in this office." Sarah grinned. "Hard to believe that before Micah moved here there were no Parishes at all!"

"But your last name isn't Parish," Candy remarked, completely interested in the abbreviated family tree.

"Ah, well. Gideon's last name is Ironheart. He chose it for himself."

"Is it okay to ask why?"

Sarah shrugged. "No big secret. Gideon and Micah are brothers, but their parents split when they were young. Micah went with his father, and Gideon went with his mother. He's frank about having felt his father abandoned him. They had no contact at all. Then Gideon went to live with his maternal grandfather, where he dug into his mother's Indigenous roots. And there you have it. Ironheart."

Ironheart? It sounded like a good choice for someone who had felt deeply wounded. Almost an aspiration. "That's fascinating, Sarah. Thanks for telling me."

"Why not? Everybody else knows the story. No secrets around here. Anyway, it's a small town and everything gets tangled together sooner or later."

Candy hesitated a moment. "Listen. That ghost-hunter guy I'm tagging after?

"Steve Hawks. Yeah. What's up?"

"Well, for one thing, he wants to talk with Nathan Tate. Gage gave me the number but I haven't been able to reach Tate."

Sarah nodded. "Hard to do when he and Marge are off visiting their daughter in Los Angeles. He usually turns off his cell."

"Apparently so. A getaway, huh? I'm not in the loop."

Sarah laughed. "You'll be surrounded by the loop soon enough. Give them time. Anyway, Nate should be back in a few days. Anything else?"

"Apparently there's a local psychic."

Sarah frowned faintly. "I've heard a little about him. Ben Wittes. He claims to talk to spirits, I think. True or not, I don't know. What I do know is that most people roll their eyes, which means nothing at all one way or the other. Many of us are dubious."

"I'm not surprised. Steve said he isn't especially thrilled that his producers are thinking about calling the guy in."

At that, Sarah laughed. "I'm not shocked, although I would have expected him to go along."

"He's unexpected in a lot of ways. At the very least, he's not predisposed to believe in the paranormal."

"Now that *is* shocking."

"I thought so, too. Miss Emma said she has his show on DVD. Maybe I should check it out and watch some of it." Candy really didn't want to do that. She wanted her mind clear of any edited preconceptions, and she had no doubt those shows were edited in major ways.

She sighed. "The only other thing I can think of doing

is to wait until we talk to Tate, see what he knows about the Castelles' house."

"I agree. If he doesn't know much, I can't imagine where you'd go after that."

Candy rose, tossing her cup into a waste basket. "I'm sure Nate'll have some ideas. Or maybe Steve will."

"Nate likes puzzles, all right. And Hawks has experience. Don't fuss too much, Candy. It's Hawks's problem, not yours."

Good advice, Candy thought as she strolled out onto the street. Excellent advice. Her job was to help and keep him from turning Conard County into a three-ring circus.

Well, the latter was implied, but she figured it was the main reason. She'd been designated the town's protector. Except how she was to do that when she had no control over Steve and his crew? But she absolutely wasn't going to watch his show unless there seemed to be no alternative.

She had her limits, she thought wryly, although she hadn't quite found them yet. Ever.

Steve emerged from the truck stop diner, full of pancakes, syrup and bacon. Another sin. Man, he was going to have to make up for a lot when he got home. He was feeling pretty good even so.

Now to hunt up Candy before he went out to talk to Vivian. He believed the Castelles would be more comfortable with Candy there, even though he'd be talking to their daughter alone. They were protective parents, as they should be. He didn't mind that at all. He hoped it wasn't a facade that covered something dark in their background.

He called Candy on her cell. She answered promptly.

"Hey," he said. "Wanna come to the Castelles with me? I think you being there would make them a little more comfortable with me talking to their daughter."

"I guess so," she answered. "Meet you out there."

He'd appreciate it if she didn't sound quite so enthusiastic. On the other hand, he admitted, he wouldn't have been terribly happy in her shoes either.

Well, just get to it. It wasn't as if he'd called on Candy over a stupid matter. Nope. He wouldn't get much out of this town at all if he had to do all this by himself. He knew what he needed, and so far he'd had few enough pointers to the right places and sources. He was, right now, working blind, and he wasn't going to leave that child in a lurch.

So STEVE WANTED her to lend credibility. Candy felt a bit uneasy about that when she didn't know him very well. She had seen him be recognized a couple of times, but that didn't help her at all. A TV star hunting for ghosts?

Right. All that meant was that he was who he said he was.

Regardless, she did her duty, arriving at the Castelle house shortly after him. Evidently he'd already gone inside, so she went up and knocked on the door. Annabelle immediately invited her in.

"Good to see you again," Annabelle said with a smile. "Everyone's in the kitchen. Come on and have a hot drink. Coffee, cocoa and tea on tap."

"A warm drink sounds good." It did. It would be a while before she adapted enough to the cold not to want something hot because of the weather.

No sooner had she reached the kitchen and greeted everyone, including a darling girl of about seven, when her radio interrupted.

"Back in a minute," she told the Castelles and Steve. "Gotta take this."

Outside, she keyed in her connection to the office. Sarah answered.

"What's up?" Candy asked.

"We need all hands on deck. We found those kids and it's not good."

Candy raced back into the house and announced briefly, "I have to run. I hope I see you all later."

Then she dashed out again, her stomach knotting, her heart pounding. She couldn't deal with this if it involved a violent crime. She couldn't.

Memories from Afghanistan forced their way up, blistering, searing. Some events had burned their way into her brain, and the scar tissue hadn't thickened.

No, never again.

When she reached the office, deputies swirled around discussing the event and who was going to do what. Gage Dalton commanded.

Sarah motioned her over.

"How bad is it?" Candy asked.

Sarah's face seemed to have frozen in a frown. "They're dead, and from what I've heard, it isn't pretty. We need you here to coordinate traffic. Our dispatcher is going to be overwhelmed for a while."

Candy nodded, feeling relief that she was not being asked to go out to the site. Apparently, someone trusted her to handle communications, new or not. She could do that much and it probably wouldn't rake up any more horrific memories.

Yeah, right. She'd already learned she didn't need imagination to paint savage scenes: the knowledge was already imprinted.

But even though she didn't need to go to the scene, her stomach remained twisted into a painful knot and she began to shake, although not badly. Her heart refused to settle.

It was bad. Already she had too much information.

God, those poor kids, their poor families.

Vivian and her dog seemed comfortable enough. Steve chatted with the Castelles, asking if anything had happened last night.

"Not a thing," Todd answered. "Which isn't helping Viv at all."

Vivian looked up from where she was hugging Buddy.

Steve nodded and smiled at Viv. "I didn't think it would. I just wanted to know. Are you doing okay, Viv?"

"Not in my bedroom," the girl answered firmly. "I feel safe with Mommy and Daddy, though."

Quite a clear answer. Talking with her should be good. He looked at the Castelles. "Mind if I take Vivian into another room if she's willing?"

Annabelle was the one who bristled a bit. "Why?"

"Because, if she's agreeable, I want to hear the story directly from her. No attempts to clarify, which I can understand you wanting to do. Just let her tell it in her own way."

Todd was standing behind Annabelle and reached out to squeeze her shoulder. "He's right, honey. Her own way in her own time. We'll be nearby."

Annabelle nodded reluctantly.

Steve turned to Vivian. "Viv? You want to talk to me in another room? With Buddy, of course." The dog couldn't amend anything Vivian would say.

"Yes," Viv answered. "Can we play cards, too?"

"Oh, yeah. I've got a deck with me."

Viv smiled. "Okay!"

Then Steve had another question for the Castelles. "I know this isn't a big house, but can we have some privacy?"

Annabelle still looked reluctant, but Todd spoke. "Sure. You don't want her holding back because it's something we don't want to hear. We've got an office. Not much space left after all the stuff we've had to cram in there, but there are two good chairs. Oh, and a tabletop for playing cards."

"Ooh, the office," Vivian said, her blue eyes brightening. She grinned at Steve. "I'm not supposed to go in there."

"Well, this time you can," her father answered. "Just this once. Clear?"

Vivian giggled and jumped off her chair. "Come on, Buddy. Let's show Mr. Steve the office."

The office was pretty much as Todd had described. It was still amazing. He didn't know computer screens came big enough to be large-screen TVs. Large tablets occupied some space and Viv pointed them out proudly. "Daddy sometimes draws me pictures on these and then they're on the TV."

"Wow!"

He saw large posters tacked to the walls that looked like superhero stuff. Keyboards, mice, papers, pencil holders full of colorful pens... The scope of this work must be something else.

Vivian, taking on the role of hostess, placed the two office chairs, one on each side of an empty worktable. Buddy lay down nearby with a small huff. Clearly this wasn't his idea of playtime.

"So why can't you come in here often?" Steve asked casually, although from all the expensive equipment in here he could guess the answer.

"Mommy and Daddy told me I can mess up their work. They said the 'puters are always working even when they're not here. So if I bump something, I could stop the work."

"Makes sense." Her words drew his attention to the background sound of quiet fans blowing. "It's never quiet in here, is it?" Not if these machines never stopped working.

Vivian shook her head and reached for cards as Steve began dealing them. "I like this game."

"I can see why. You always win."

She giggled again. "Mommy says you want to know about my room."

That was direct and to the point. He'd expected to have to draw her slowly into the subject. Cripes, it made her scared enough that she wouldn't go in there anymore, not even to get her toys.

"I do," he answered as they both stacked their cards into neat piles. "What do you most want to tell me?"

"About the man." She kept looking at her cards, her hands steady, but she didn't flip a single card over. She wasn't thinking about them at all. Fear had taken over.

He could have tried to reassure her, but how could he do so truthfully when he didn't know what the hell was happening here?

"The man?" he prompted gently. "Someone you know?"

She shook her head violently. "Bad man. Bad man!"

"That's not good. Tell me what he looks like so I can hunt for him?"

She shook her head. "No. No."

He had to think his way around that. A lot of ways he could respond, none that wouldn't lead her. Damn, he needed to know exactly what *she* experienced.

Then her voice turned almost quiet, even a little sing-songy. "I can't talk about him. He might hurt me."

The back of his neck prickled. A break? God, he hoped not. "Viv…"

She lifted her head and her gaze focused on him. Thank God. "Can't see him."

"I can't see him?"

"Nobody can. Not even me."

"Well, that makes it tough. How do you feel about that?"

Vivian swiped the stack of cards away, some of them scattering to the rug. "I don't like it! If Buddy could see him, he'd save me."

Steve looked down at the superfriendly dog and wondered if Viv's certainty about his protectiveness was true. Regardless, he had no doubt that dog could knock a full-grown man off his feet with his relentless friendliness. "Buddy makes you feel safer."

"He used to."

"Used to?"

"He won't come in my room anymore. He used to always sleep with me."

Well, that was downright heartbreaking. "Do you know why he won't come in?"

"The man talks to me. I hate it! But I think Buddy hears it, too, and he hates it, too!" Buddy rose and came to sit right beside her. Some protectiveness there after all. Or concern for Viv's upset.

"It's scarier because you can't see the man?" *Leading. Watch it, Steve.*

"Yeah." Viv quieted and leaned over to wrap her arms around Buddy's neck. The dog visibly leaned into her. "Buddy growled at the wall. Mommy said maybe it was a bug."

"Does he do that often? Growl at the wall?"

Viv held up three fingers as she pressed her face against Buddy.

"Three times, huh?" More than the Castelles had mentioned. But maybe that was three more times when only Vivian had seen it. God. He rubbed his hands over his face. This was going to be a tough one unless he could figure out where that sound was coming from. A radio, a pipe, something being transmitted up through the wall.

But it *could* be as simple as that, so he'd better start hoofing it. He wasn't willing to wait until his crew arrived if he could solve this *now*.

But first, he needed to ask one more question before he let Vivian flee back to her parents.

"Do you know what the man is saying?"

Viv lifted her face and shook her head. "I tried. I told him to shut up."

"Loudly?"

She let go of Buddy. "I screamed it."

"Did it stop?"

"Once."

Steve tucked that one away. He didn't like the pallor that had washed Viv's face while talking about her experience and decided to postpone further questioning. "Come on, let's go back to Mommy and Daddy, okay?"

Viv leaped up as if shot out of her chair and ran back to the kitchen.

Steve wasn't sure how much he had to work with, but he knew one thing for certain: that child wasn't lying. Well, two things. She was also truly terrified.

AT THE SHERIFF'S OFFICE, Candy found little enough to do. The dispatcher, a middle-aged woman named Neesa, handled most of it with the ease of experience. Candy needed to offer her aid only occasionally, mostly to handle standard calls and pass them to deputies and city cops still on patrol.

But then the camera footage began to arrive. Black-and-white, it was being broadcast in as part of the forensics records. Black-and-white or not, Candy mentally filled in the colors and felt her gorge rise.

She didn't want to look, but understood it was expected of her, especially after Gage radioed and told her to keep an eye out for things they might miss, areas that were overlooked.

So she was glued to a view of two older teenagers, one male, one female. Left to die in the night's cold, then presumably savaged by wild animals. She prayed the savaging hadn't come first.

Cruel beyond words. What could those kids possibly have done to deserve this? Nothing. Nobody deserved this. Nobody.

She forced herself to sit in front of the large monitor, doing as she'd been told. Keeping an eye out for blind spots in the camera coverage. Which meant she had to look intently at everything.

"This camera thing is new," Neesa said. "I don't think

I like it. Anyway, it's supposed to make sure we don't lose film at the site. Everything gets sent back here and if anything goes black we'll know it before the scene is cleared."

Made sense. Except for people like her who had to sit here and look at the images and couldn't do a damn thing to help.

Then the camera homed in on various wounds. Detailed photos.

Nothing Candy hadn't seen before, but that didn't prevent nausea.

She clicked on the radio and spoke. "So far nothing that remotely resembles knife wounds or gunshot wounds. Mostly tearing wounds."

"Thanks," Gage's gravelly voice came back. "Thought so."

"Well, I'm not a medical examiner."

"None of us are either. I guess we should scan for a weapon anyway. You're going to get close-in shots of the places we look. Have Neesa put it on a split screen. But first I'm going to send you a three-sixty. You catch any jumps, let me know."

"Man, things have changed," Candy muttered. It reminded her of military operations.

"You can thank the commissioners. Gage wanted some more space, to get dispatch into another room because it's hectic and can interfere with comms in both directions."

"Makes sense."

Neesa's response was dry. "Sure. Not to the commissioners. Evidently some new tech caught their eyes. This is what that brings."

"Good backup?" Candy suggested as she watched the screen closely.

"Maybe for the military." Neesa sighed. "Gage is still trying to figure out all the advantages."

"Seems like he's found one."

"Possibly. We'd have gotten all this back on the helmet cams, and from forensics, who are probably already taking over."

Which would be a very good thing, little as she knew about the subject. She almost joined Neesa in a sigh but swallowed it. Bad enough she had to look at this horror.

"Candy?" Gage's voice came through the headset. "You get the full three-sixty?"

"I believe so."

"Okay, we'll let forensics place the markers close to the bodies. We're drawing back to look for anything we might find. Although at this point I think we've scuffed the ground quite a bit."

There was that, she acknowledged. And when this was over, she was probably going to go back to her house and vomit, right up and into dry heaves. Troops on the battlefield often did that, much as civilians might not want to hear it. Few grew hardened enough not to react.

Then there was the so-called thousand-yard stare. The empty, blank look in the eyes when the mind could handle no more. She'd seen that often. Sometimes she'd had it, too. Maybe still did at times.

She wasn't certain she wasn't experiencing it right now, that total shutdown. And she was supposed to go from this back to aiding Steve Hawks. Sure.

STEVE LEFT THE CASTELLES, determined to make a plan of some kind. He needed more info about the house, of course. As he emerged, and was about to climb into his car, he saw a truck pull up at the end of the driveway, blocking it. It might be a friend of the Castelles or someone else, but for a fact he wasn't going anywhere until that truck moved.

He waited, saw the driver climb out. Oh, well, he'd just walk out to meet the guy and ask him to move. He strolled down the drive, his hands tucked in his pockets against the chill. The man, better dressed for the weather but still ragged in appearance, strode toward him, his step a little hesitant.

What was going on here? Someone who didn't know the Castelles after all? Steve felt instantly protective, mainly because of that little girl inside. "Can I help you, stranger?" he asked when they were about six feet apart.

The man paused, stopped walking. "You Steve Hawks? From that ghost show?"

At that moment Steve would have preferred to deny it, but there might be information he needed. "I am."

The man nodded, his gaze growing distant. "I'm Ben Wittes. It's going to happen again."

Steve's attention sharpened. "What is?"

"The murders. Like when Samuel Bride lived here."

Steve felt his insides congeal. "What do you mean?"

"My spirits told me. People will die. The same thing is happening." Wittes looked at him again. "It'll happen again. Don't say I didn't warn you."

Steve, a man who didn't believe in psychics, nonetheless stood frozen as the guy returned to his truck and drove away.

He needed to get to Candy. Maybe that had been a threat.

Or maybe, Steve thought, looking back at the house, this Wittes guy knew something about the Castelles. He still wasn't ready to jump into the perfect-family scenario they painted.

Nobody was that perfect.

Chapter Eight

Candy made it home without puking. It wasn't easy. Her gorge kept trying to rise, but she battled it down and finally reached her kitchen table with a cup of tea, the gentlest thing she could think of. It'd either settle her or get rid of her stomach contents. At this point, even the latter would be a relief. She hadn't even changed out of her uniform, except for ditching her utility belt.

She put her hands on her head and tried not to cry. She had years of experience at holding back tears even though she'd seen plenty of tough guys give in to them occasionally. Still, she had tried not to. Tears might unnerve others who were holding up better.

But there was no one to see her right now, and nothing left to prove. She'd already proved she was as tough as anyone who went into battle. And her life had changed forever.

She couldn't leave it all behind. No way. But with each passing day, she shoved it back deeper into the mental locker.

Until today. She'd seen even more gruesome things, but those kids…

What had they done? Nothing. Nothing at all. Nothing to deserve that. And she hadn't expected to see such graphic video.

That had been a sideways punch to the gut. Maybe she

ought to quit and find a different job. Except she'd tried that without success. Unless she wanted to be a mercenary.

Never.

Tears finally started rolling down her cheeks as memories of her time in the Army rolled through her mind. The sound, the smells, the screams. Oh, God, the screams. People she knew torn up, burned, dead. Faces she would never forget, not until the day she died.

Initially, she didn't hear the knock on the door. Eventually it penetrated as it grew louder.

She shook her head, dashed away her tears on her shirtsleeve, hoping there hadn't been another emergency. She'd turned off her radio. She was off duty now, her cell phone was off, and she sure as hell didn't want to be bothered by anything less than a mass shooting in town.

So much for her idea that a small town would be calmer. Less violent. Stupid idea. People were the same everywhere.

She opened the door reluctantly and saw Steve Hawks. "Now's not a good time," she told him. Rudely, but it was the truth.

"I heard," he said. "I heard something."

For some reason that made her step back and let him in. He'd heard what? From where? She doubted the news was making the rounds in town yet. The sheriff had locked down all information. Did that matter? Maybe not, but Steve sure hadn't seen what she'd seen.

"You don't look good," he said as soon as he was inside.

"Tough."

"I'd have brought a bottle if I'd known. You're white. Your eyes are red and swollen. Get your butt into the kitchen and tell me what you can stomach."

He surprised her by reaching out to touch her cheek. "Cold as ice. Where's a blanket?"

What did she care?

Then he spied the throw over the back of the couch in the next room. "Here or the kitchen?"

She moved toward the kitchen. It wasn't as comfortable, but she didn't care about comfort.

When she sat at the table, he spread the throw over her and tucked it around her. Vaguely she sensed the warmth.

"What have you got? Anything you prefer?"

Her lips felt frozen.

"Alrighty, then. I'll look." Followed by, "Damn, I can tell you were in the Army. Remind me to ask you to organize me someday."

Distantly she felt as if that might be amusing. At another time. Right now it seemed pointless. Empty conversation.

Clatters. Cupboard doors closing. Even in this state, situational awareness never deserted her.

"Here." A cup appeared before her. Steam rose from it. She saw it and didn't care.

"Drink," he ordered. "Hot milk."

Hot milk? Her mother had made that for her. "I don't like it."

"Who cares. It'll warm you, maybe help you relax a bit."

Obediently, because she always followed orders, she reached for the mug with trembling hands. Hands that felt as if they belonged to someone else.

She hadn't raised it more than an inch when it slipped from her grip and spilled everywhere. She stared at the milk running across the table, some of it down her front. What did it matter?

She watched Steve's hands and arms as he wiped up the mess, including the milk that had run down her front.

"Okay, that's not going to work. Not until your fingers warm up."

He pulled a chair close and reached for her hands, chafing them with his bigger, warmer ones.

"Come back to me, Candy," he said quietly. "You've come back from far worse."

Had she? Apparently not. Like a tar pit, it just kept bubbling up and dragging her in.

But as he rubbed her hands, she began to return from the nightmare. His gentleness called to her. Drew her back from the brink. Offered her a touch of emotional safety. No one had ever treated her so kindly when the ugliness rose from the pit.

His touch reached her in a way that little enough had. Slowly she drew her hands back and tugged the throw tighter around her.

And gradually her vision returned from the tunnel. She saw Steve, saw her kitchen, saw the rag he'd used to wipe up her mess. Sour milk, she thought irrelevantly. She needed to wash it soon.

"Candy?"

Her gaze trailed back to Steve. "I'm here."

"That was rough for you. Take your time. About that hot drink?"

Her stomach had settled, she realized. "Cider. Please."

"Coming up. I think I'll join you. I'm wondering how any little kids could possibly want to trick-or-treat around here, as cold as it's getting."

"There's an annual Halloween party over at the high school. Or so I've heard."

"Good idea."

More clattering of pans followed by the *glug* of cider pouring from the gallon jug. A short while later, the aroma of hot cider and cinnamon. This time when he put a mug in front of her, she was able to reach with a steadier hand and stir it with the cinnamon stick.

Steve returned to his seat, moving it back to a more respectful distance. He had a mug of his own.

"Whatever you did after you left the Castelles was awful, wasn't it?"

She responded with a jerky nod. "I…didn't have to go to the scene, but the video was being broadcast into the office, and Gage asked me to watch it in case I noticed anything."

"What happened?"

She looked down. "An ugly violent crime." She couldn't say more, not yet.

"God!"

She felt the cider had cooled enough to drink safely, and lifted the mug to her lips, glad to see her hands were steady and her fingers were feeling again. Hot and good. Very good.

She sensed he was withholding something, but she didn't want to deal with it yet. She needed time to put all the tumbled blocks inside her head back into order. Whatever order they might find again.

Steve spoke. "I'm so sorry you had to see that."

"I've seen worse." Which was true. "It's just so pointless. Not combatants. No threat to anyone."

He nodded and reached out to touch her hand briefly. "Take your time. No rush."

But another thought began to penetrate the fog in her head. "You must have come here for a reason."

"Nothing that can't wait until later."

But she could tell he was troubled. For a detective who must have had a poker face at one time, he could be quite transparent. "What's wrong?"

"Nothing exactly. Nothing that can't wait. Not urgent."

She had to live with that, she supposed, at least for a little longer. Steve had a mulish look for the first time since she'd met him. Probably little budged him until he was ready.

A good trait for a detective? Another thing that didn't matter.

She was searching for inanities, she realized. Anything

to redirect her own mind. An escape hatch, or a temporary break. Anything that would help her finish moving from the past to the present—and the present wasn't looking especially good right now.

She continued drinking the cider, beginning to wonder if she needed something sweeter. She might be having delayed shock, a mix of today's events with memories.

Something sweet truly sounded good, and for once in her life she didn't mind asking for some help. "On the counter there's a bakery box. Cinnamon rolls. I need one. Please."

"Coming right up. I may join you. Dinner wasn't on my list this afternoon."

"Help yourself."

He found two small plates and brought the rolls to the table. "Maybe someone will eventually explain to me why cinnamon rolls are good for breakfast but not for dinner. Cake is for a dinner dessert, but not for breakfast. Why?"

That cracked the ice that encased her and drew forth a small laugh. "I never thought about it."

"I mean, really, a sweet is a sweet and it shouldn't be rigidly prescribed for a certain meal. I like pie. I'd eat apple pie and peach cobbler for breakfast. But no. I'm welcome to pancakes covered in maple syrup."

"But not for dinner."

"In theory, although I think some restaurants make a good living by providing them round the clock."

"Which ought to tell us something." She had begun to feel grounded again, firmly planted in the present, although that did not banish the murders of those teens. Nothing ever would. Her mind was like that camera she'd spent hours looking at. Odd how you'd forget things you didn't want to and couldn't forget things you wished you could erase forever.

But as she ate the roll and calories began to rush through

her system, she remembered something else. "What did you mean, when you said you'd heard something?"

"I was given a vague prediction by this guy claiming to be a psychic. He came to the Castelles', looking for me I think, and told me his spirits had told him that murders were going to happen again. He said it would happen the same way it had when some guy named Bride lived there."

"God!" She dropped the remains of the roll and clenched her hands into fists. "God, Steve! You're a detective. How could you have thought this could wait?"

"Because I didn't know it had happened! I took it as a prediction, probably worthless, and came to you."

But Candy was having none of it. She grabbed the landline phone off the wall and dialed the sheriff's home number.

"Gage, Ben Wittes told Steve Hawks today that people might be murdered."

TWENTY MINUTES LATER, Gage Dalton arrived at Candy's house. He looked slightly rumpled, especially his shirt, as if he had grabbed one from the laundry where he had tossed it.

Steve noticed his appearance. It was hard not to. One side of his face was scarred with burns, and his voice was roughened. There was a story there that Steve decided to ask about later. That detective that Candy had criticized as falling down on the job? He was still detective enough to want to know the stories of people he met.

"Okay," Gage said. "Explain what Ben Wittes said."

Candy waved at him and Steve took over. "It's not much. Ben Wittes showed up at the house I'm investigating. He wanted to tell me one thing. He said his spirits were warning him that the murders were going to begin again, just like they had when a guy named Bride owned the house. I still haven't heard anything about this Bride guy."

Gage frowned. "I seem to vaguely remember something about a guy with that name after I started working for the department. Nothing important, some kind of local story or other. Since it didn't involve me or the department, and was kind of vague anyway, I didn't pay any attention."

"Understandable," Steve replied. "But Candy thought I was a jerk for not reporting it immediately. Former detective and all that."

Gage smiled faintly. "You didn't know what we found today, and the info you got was kind of squirrely anyway."

Steve grinned back. "Hey, I like squirrels. Some of the most intelligent and cute members of the animal kingdom."

Gage shook his head. "Tell that to the folks who spend a lot of time growing gardens only to see them ravaged by these so-called vermin. I think they're a little upset they can't shoot a gun anywhere in town, and they're not allowed to poison anything. Kids and dogs, you know. Or cats."

"I get it," Steve answered. He also liked Gage's answer. People in a tug-of-war against animals just trying to survive. A perennial problem.

But Gage was already rising. "I'm going to bring Wittes in for questioning. You want to be there, Candy?"

"Not tonight."

Gage nodded. "After today I'm not surprised. Must have been hard on you. I wouldn't have asked if I didn't think it was important."

"If you never ask anything of me, you might as well fire me."

Gage paused to pat her shoulder. "You're doing great. With time you'll like the work even more. It's not like we have problems like this very often. Anyway, I'll bring Wittes in tomorrow morning. I'd like you to see his reaction."

Candy nodded. "I'm sure I can do that."

"No rush anyway since this guy claims he's talking to

spirits. He won't ßexpect that to change matters so quickly for him, not even if he really knows something."

Then Gage left. Steve didn't move. He wasn't going to leave Candy alone while she was still so fragile emotionally.

She didn't speak for a while, intently staring at the table. He could only imagine the memories this had reawakened in her, but he had some experiences of his own. Well, more than a few. He didn't miss that about his former job. Not one bit.

He rose eventually, deciding she probably needed more calories. He guessed she hadn't been able to eat a thing since she'd been called in to monitor the video.

Overall, a good thing for the sheriff to have. He himself had seen too many blanks from crime scene techs' cameras, from body cams. Everyone seemed to have their own point of view about what was important at the scene.

This time he looked for something in her refrigerator and cupboards that would give her more than a cinnamon roll.

He discovered chicken soup, one of the richer brands, and started with that. If she could get that down, he'd try a sandwich. She had peanut butter on the shelf. He believed he had spied some cold cuts in the lowest drawer of the fridge. Sandwich makings.

He heated the soup in her microwave, then set it before her on the table with a spoon. "Eat."

She hesitated only a few moments before picking up the spoon. "You don't have to babysit me."

"I'm sure. I'm also equally certain that I want to. Quit objecting and get some more food in you."

"What about you?"

"I'll find something after you eat that soup."

He sat waiting, and finally the spoon started making its way between the bowl and her mouth. She reached for a napkin from the basket on the far end of the table and wiped her chin, and he laughed.

"What's so funny?" She looked right at him, a good sign.

"I see we both have a soup-drinking problem. I swear there's a hole in my bottom lip."

She managed a chuckle and went back to her soup. It must have agreed with her because she began to eat faster. That made him feel a whole lot better.

"It's stupid," she said as she finished the soup.

"What is?"

"I've seen things so much worse than those victims. Far worse. I shouldn't have reacted so strongly."

"I don't know about that. Sometimes small things can be enough. A sight, a sound, a smell."

She raised her head from the bowl. "You have it, too?"

"Believe it. While I'm sure my police experiences couldn't be as bad as yours, cases still haunt me."

She clearly pondered that. He rose. "What else can I feed you? Chicken soup may be great for viral infections, but not so much for shock. Sandwich?"

"There's some sliced ham and some salami in the refrigerator meat drawer. And some Jarlsburg cheese on the next drawer up. Help yourself."

Steve opened the refrigerator again and spied a bottle on the door. "Ooh, you like spicy mustard. A woman after my own heart."

"No other kind," she agreed listlessly.

She was sinking again. Steve found two plates and made some simple ham sandwiches on rye, faster than he'd ever made them before. He needed to get back quickly before the depression snagged her again.

"Here," he said, sitting across from her and placing two plates on the table. "Have at it."

"Thank you."

She still sounded too quiet, too slow. He wondered

whether he should bring the subject up now or wait until she'd eaten. Afterward, he decided.

She ate at least. No hesitation this time. Even if her mind was trying to wander elsewhere, her physical needs were taking priority.

When they were both done, he pushed the plates aside. "I want to talk."

She had a distant look in her eyes. He recognized it. "Say, try to come back for just a minute. You don't want to go there."

"No." She drew a deep breath. "Sometimes it's hard."

"I know it is. Are you getting any help with your PTSD?"

Her head jerked. "Why would I? Everyone has bad memories."

"Not the same. Not when they take over like this and give you a thousand-yard stare. Talk to me, Candy. Talk us both through this."

She sighed, picking up her napkin and folding it repeatedly, ignoring the yellow spot of mustard. As if she didn't care about it getting onto her fingers. Right then, she probably didn't.

"Candy? Look at me. Talk to me. Please."

"I'm sorry. I'm not a good conversationalist right now."

"I'm not asking you to make conversation. Just ramble." He was starting to get seriously concerned about her. Maybe it was ER time.

After a minute or so, she sighed. "I ought to be in control."

He waited to see if she would say more. When she didn't, he asked, "In control of what?"

"These memories. The way they take over. When it starts, they just take over. I try to cram them away, but they don't want to stop."

He nodded understanding. "That happens to me occasionally. And you had a massive trigger today. I believe if I'd seen what you watched, I'd probably be having some awful memories, too."

She sighed again and looked up from the napkin, which right now was about an inch square. "Sorry."

"For what? Don't apologize. This is a very difficult thing to deal with. Hell, I don't like to admit I have a problem and I seriously believe mine couldn't possibly be as bad as yours. You've seen a lot more of hell than I have."

She looked away briefly. "Don't minimize your experience, Steve."

"Why the devil not? You're busy minimizing yours. Guess you gotta be tough, huh?"

She looked so sad in that moment that he feared she was about to withdraw. His chest was already so tight with worry and concern that he doubted he could handle that. He was sure she wouldn't like being bundled into the car and taken against her will to the ER. He knew he wouldn't like it.

But then she spoke. "You're right. Be tough. I had to be for so long. I hate to admit any weakness."

"The good old Army. Well, cops have a bit of that, too. To some degree. And sometimes it makes us stupid."

Her gaze snapped right back. Oh, she was here now. Relief nearly swamped him. "Stupid. Are you saying I need treatment?"

"It might help, but that's not my decision. Anyway, I'll sit here all night driving you nuts until you get past this. Wanna play Hearts? Or Spades?"

She shook her head, but a faint smile dawned on her lips. "I never thought you'd become a friend. Is this what you do with your clients?"

"I'm not doing anything except being myself."

Candy chewed her lower lip, then said, "I believe that."

Well, that was good, because he sure as heck wasn't trying to shine her on.

"I think I can go to bed now," she said soon.

"Good. Point me to the couch, because I'm not going anywhere."

At least she didn't argue. She told him where to find spare blankets and a pillow. "You're not going to be comfortable. You're kinda long."

He flashed a smile. "I'll be fine. You get to bed. Morning at the office, yeah?"

"Yeah." Then she rose and walked away.

It still wasn't good, but it was better. At least he knew he'd hear her if she stirred during the night. He'd always slept like a cat.

Chapter Nine

In the morning, Candy felt a whole lot better. She was even eager to talk with Gage. Plus, she'd found a text message from the old sheriff. She told Steve.

"Nate Tate will be back today. He said he'd be glad to see you this evening."

"Well, super!" Steve looked cheerful this morning, as if he was glad to see her back to stability.

She felt embarrassed about last night, but she also felt grateful to him for sticking this out. Maybe she ought to join that veterans group that met on Saturday mornings. As her job would allow. Since those vets kept attending, there must be something useful in it, other than raking up bad memories. She could at least try.

Another beautiful, sunny day greeted her, but it had grown significantly colder. Steve was right. If this kept up, most parents were going to be dragging kids to the Halloween party. Not even that momentous day deserved frostbitten fingertips and noses.

The light snowfall they'd had had disappeared in yesterday's sunshine. Everything was starting to look brown, and the remaining colorful leaves had fallen from the trees.

She still enjoyed the dry air, though, and the sun warmed her anyway. Halloween decorations were blooming like autumn flowers as people added more to their yards and windows. She was feeling pretty good by the time she reached the office. Last night had been firmly shoved into its box, deep in the depths of her brain.

Steve had been wonderful, she thought as she rounded the courthouse square to the office door. Patient, kind, understanding. He was right about her getting some help. If there was anything that could reduce her memories of the nightmare that had been her life for too long, she was willing.

Her fault, however, for not realizing the totality of the problem. Nearly every veteran had some of these experiences, and she'd probably been foolish to believe almost everyone just dealt with it. Foolish to believe her situation was not that bad.

Yesterday had certainly taught her otherwise. She couldn't keep responding so dramatically to these things, not if she wanted to continue life as a cop.

And she did want to continue. She'd been feeling that she'd found a useful purpose at last, one that made her feel good about herself. Yeah, she had to do whatever she could to hang on to this.

Besides, she was growing to love this area, this town.

Feeling reasonably cheerful, she entered the office to face questioning Ben Wittes. That wouldn't be so bad, even if they had reason to believe he might have perpetrated the horrific crime against those teens.

Velma was back at her post at the dispatch desk, smoking her illegal cloud as if laws weren't made for her. Even Gage didn't think it was all that awful, but what was he going to do? Fire a woman who had been part of this department for more years than Candy had been alive? She could easily imagine department staff, including deputies, holding an insurrection.

Velma spoke even before the other deputies greeted her. Sarah Ironheart, Guy Redwing, Beau Beauregard. Friendly, familiar faces now.

But Velma had a message. "Gage wants you to meet him in the interrogation room."

Candy felt a moment of tension. Maybe she wasn't ready for this yet? It didn't matter. She needed to do this.

It had initially surprised her how much the corridors and offices wended through the large building in which they were housed. Apparently the office had snagged a whole bunch of space in the interior, behind the storefronts that ringed the block. From the street you'd never guess just how much resided inside.

Gage was waiting in the interrogation room, behind a steel table that supported shackle attachment rings on the other side from him. Two chairs sat on each side of the table.

"Ben Wittes should be here soon," he remarked as he motioned her to the chair beside him. "You don't have to question him unless something occurs to you. Just watch his reactions. It's always good to have a second pair of eyes."

"It sure is," she agreed as she took her seat.

"You had any coffee this morning?"

"Only a cup of what I made at home."

He flashed a grin. "I'll get someone else to risk Velma's wrath. Yeah, I'm a chicken when it comes to her. If you haven't noticed, she can breathe fire. You know. Like a dragon."

She laughed. "I've begun to discover that."

"So what'll it be? Black? Strong?"

"Latte, if you don't mind. Maude makes a darn good one."

Gage nodded. "When it comes to cooking, Maude never settles for second best."

He rose and went to open the door. "Hey, Guy? Two coffees. One a tall and black, the other a tall latte."

"Got it, boss." Redwing's voice floated from the front.

"Now," Gage said as he returned to his seat, "if Velma has a problem with that, she can squawk at Guy."

Another bubble of amusement rose in Candy. "What's with this coffee thing? I keep getting the feeling there's some kind of tradition?"

"There is. Velma makes a huge urn full of coffee every time she comes to work. It's famously bad. Only desperation on a busy shift causes anyone to drink it. You must have noticed all the bottles of antacids sitting out near the mugs. That's why."

"But she doesn't notice?"

"If she has, she probably thinks it isn't related to the coffee. It's one of her ways of taking care of us. She has a lot of those, you'll find with time. The department's mom. Who the hell is going to tell her that her coffee sucks?"

Candy understood perfectly. It was just another one of those things that was causing her to like this town.

Guy delivered the coffee just before Ben Wittes walked in, a deputy accompanying him. He looked a little surprised to be there, but not at all worried about it.

Candy studied the rather seedy-looking man. Nothing about him appeared to want to draw attention.

Gage greeted him pleasantly and invited him to sit. Ben did, then looked around before shrugging. "I never expected to be here."

"I'm sure you never did," Gage answered. "Nothing to worry about. We just need to ask a couple of questions."

Ben nodded. "What can I do?"

Gage gestured and the other deputy left the room. Candy never doubted that the cameras in the four high corners were recording this interview.

"I was wondering," Gage said, "if you'd heard anything about the murders of two teens on the mountain. You hear a lot."

Not even an Oscar-winning performance could have drained that guy's face so instantly white. He was shocked.

It took Ben a full minute to reply, and by then he had

started shaking. "No," he answered unsteadily. "Oh, God, no. I tried to warn that Hawks guy. My spirits said it was going to happen. I never thought…" He trailed off, still visibly shaken. "Oh, my God."

"Your spirits told you?"

Ben nodded. "They never shut up, but lately one voice is getting stronger. My guide, I think. But I never imagined his warning was late."

"So why'd you tell Hawks?"

There was a cup of water on the table, and Ben reached for it, looking at Gage. Receiving a nod, he gulped it all down.

Another few seconds before Ben replied. "I don't always trust my voices. Because nobody believes me when I tell them what I hear. Because Hawks hunts ghosts. I thought he might listen."

For the first time Ben's color changed, growing faintly red. "Because I'm trying to get on his show."

"Ah," Gage replied.

"Is that so awful?"

"Of course not," Candy said soothingly. "A lot of people want to do that." But by now she was convinced this man had no part in the murders. That initial shock could not have been feigned.

Gage spoke. "I guess maybe we should listen to what you have to say more often. Did the spirit tell you anything else?"

"Only that it was beginning again. Like back when Bride owned the house. A long, long time ago."

"Will there be more?"

"I don't know." Ben was beginning to sound almost desperate. "He hasn't said. But if he does, should I tell you?"

"Please," Gage said. "I'll listen. Promise."

Ben left a minute later, clearly immensely relieved. Gage looked at Candy.

"What do you think?"

Candy never hesitated. "Have you ever seen a man turn that white when he heard what had happened? I don't think he did it."

"I'm inclined to agree. That's a color I only see on family members when I bring the bad news. Interesting about his spirit, though."

Candy shifted uncomfortably. "I'm not a believer."

"I haven't been, but maybe I should at least listen."

"Steve was right, though. In and of itself, it didn't matter. And given that neither of them knew about the murders at the time, it makes even more sense not to take it seriously."

"I certainly wouldn't make too much of it. Well, get back to the task I'm sure you love." He winked. "Someone has to be on the bottom rung."

A good way of putting it, Candy thought as she exited the office with most of her latte. Dang that coffee was a perk and it was still hot enough.

She decided, however, in the pursuit of her duties, to follow Steve to the library. It'd be interesting to learn if Miss Emma had come up with anything. Right now, from his perspective, other than the little girl's complaints, the house must seem sterile.

She still wasn't ready to deal with the Ben Wittes thing, however. Gage was right to be willing to listen to him, but the whole idea that this guy was hearing voices in his head and that they might be right gave her the creeps.

Another thing to stash in her hurt locker unless it became important.

She dumped her cup in the bin out front of the library, which clearly stated that no drinks or food were allowed inside.

Steve was inside Emma's office with the door open. Emma spied her and waved her inside.

"We were just talking about the only Bride I can find,"

Emma said as Candy sat. "Very little in the library about him. A death notice, heart attack. No one at his funeral. His wife had left him twenty years before. In all, sad but unexceptional at this point. I can keep digging, though. You'd be surprised how many things get cross-referenced in the strangest ways."

Outside, Candy and Steve stood on the steps while October's gentle winds chilled them more.

Steve spoke into the biting air. "I said I'd come to the Castelles' house at about two. That leaves some time for Maude's."

She thought about it. Lunch was going to sound good before long and she'd have to take him over to see Nathan Tate this evening. "Let's do it," she answered. "But I pay for my own."

He grinned. "Lunch at Maude's as bribery? It doesn't cost that much."

"Around here, most folks *would* consider it bribery. I left my patrol car at the station, so I'll meet you there."

"You can ride with me, you know. It's part of your job."

She decided he was right. And rarely was there a time when Maude's didn't sound good.

When they walked inside, some of the breakfast crowd were still lingering over their bottomless coffee, but some of the local lunch crowd had begun to arrive. The place was beginning to buzz, and faces were a little friendlier. Steve had crossed the first frontier: he was now known.

Candy felt in luck. Maude had added potato and leek soup to her menu and had apparently gotten into the mood to fry a bunch of chicken. She and Steve ordered both.

"Was Miss Emma a lot of help?" Candy asked.

"She was, considering how long ago this was and how few public records seem to exist."

"We weren't far away from the Wild West then, from what I understand. Records may have been sketchy."

"Miss Emma thinks so. Man, this soup is wonderful."

Candy returned to business. Safer ground than getting personal again with Steve. "Still, there must be something in court records. That property must have sold after Bride died. He must have had some kind of will. Or maybe probate took care of it."

"I'm also waiting for info from a title company. I don't know how far back they have to search but it's gotta be long enough to please a bank."

She nodded, grooving on the hot soup. It was so rich and creamy, she had a feeling most of her chicken would come home with her.

"What are you going to the Castelle place for?" she asked.

"I want to explore the basement, see if noises could be rising from there up Vivian's wall. Then, tomorrow, the attic. Your help would be great."

"How so?"

"Somebody to listen in Viv's room."

Candy shook her head a little. "What about the parents?"

"I want someone totally objective in there. Not someone who's seen the dog react or heard some sounds herself."

Made sense. "You could solve this entire problem before your crew arrives."

"I hope. It'd be better for the family."

Again her approval of him rose another notch. Family before show. He wasn't kidding. "What happens if you can't do this program?"

He shrugged a shoulder and reached for his plate of chicken. "We'll do another. We're filming well in advance of air dates, so there's always something to plug in."

That made sense. "Do you always do these investigations by yourself, beforehand?"

"Mostly, except for a researcher off-site. I don't mind. I trust myself. If we find useful material, I can run through it as if it's the first time and it can be edited into a good story. Research *always* comes first. Period."

He'd told her that, but now she was beginning to believe him. A triumph for him, she supposed. Hostile deputy comes around.

STEVE WAS ACTUALLY looking forward to this part of his job. He had meters to take into the basement with him and find out if there were any anomalous readings down there. A high EMF could cause hallucinations in some people. Sometimes recorders picked up voices without an obvious source. Motion detectors could tell if something moved. Oh, yeah, lots of tech that he always worked in somehow, to reassure clients, to keep viewers watching.

The thing he was proudest of, though, was the lack of scam in what he did. Unless his producers called in a psychic. Those were the times he questioned what they were up to.

The Castelles greeted them warmly and Viv was excited to play a game of cards. He glanced at the parents and Candy.

"GO AHEAD," ALL OF them said, then the Castelles took Candy to their kitchen and offered her a drink.

"Water will be fine for me," Candy answered. She pulled her jacket off and slung it over the back of a chair. Annabelle gave her a tall glass of water.

"See?" said Todd, pointing to Candy's jacket hanging on the chair. "She's warm enough."

"Everyone's different," Annabelle replied. She was wearing a heavy fleece sweatshirt and pants, and another sweater was hanging over her shoulders. "Steve said he wants to check out the basement today and the attic tomorrow."

Todd sounded slightly irritated. "I already did that."

Annabelle frowned. "Yeah, but he's the expert, as you keep reminding me." She turned her attention to Candy. "Are you going to help?"

"Apparently. I get to stand in Vivian's room and listen to the sounds he makes."

"I did that," said Annabelle. "But it wasn't good enough. I only heard the sound that one time and Vivian wouldn't come in to listen."

Candy considered that problem. "Well, Viv's hearing voices, right? Maybe I'll hear something like that. Plus, he has all kinds of instruments he said he'll use."

Both parents relaxed a bit upon hearing that. More instruments meant more security, she guessed.

"I hope Viv can tell him some more," Todd said. "She's the only real witness."

Annabelle looked down, and for the first time Candy saw her shed a few tears. "We've *got* to help her."

"If this doesn't work, we're moving out," Todd announced firmly.

"But how? We sank everything into this house. Where would we go?"

"Anywhere else. I'll figure out something, I swear."

From the determination on his face, Candy believed he would. Good dad. Throw away everything they'd worked for so their daughter could have a better life and a dog. Just toss it on the trash heap to try again against all odds.

Steve returned with a grinning Vivian. "She beat me again. The odds favor her. We're going to have to try something a little harder soon. What do you think, Viv?"

"Oh, yes," said the little girl, sliding onto one of the chairs. "Can I have some chocolate?"

"Hot variety I hope?" Annabelle answered.

"Mmm. That's best."

"It certainly is for the amount of milk it gets into you." Viv wrinkled her nose. "I don't like milk."

"Clearly," her mother answered drily.

Candy leaned toward her. "I don't like milk either," she confided. "Especially warm milk. So I drink a lot of cocoa."

"Me, too." Viv grinned. "And cheese. I love cheese."

"Now *that's* good," Candy agreed. "My favorites are Swiss cheese and white cheddar."

Viv pondered that. "I like lots of cheeses. Except American."

Annabelle laughed. "Too sweet for my taste."

Viv screwed up her face. "Some kids like it a lot. Just not me." Then she looked at Steve. "You're going to make the bad man go away?"

"I sure plan to try."

"That's good." She turned to her parents. "Can I take Buddy out to play?"

"Just bundle up," her mother answered. "We wouldn't want anything to happen to that cute nose."

Viv turned to look at Candy and Steve. "Can my nose really fall off?"

Steve laughed. "Only if it gets too cold. So listen to your mother."

Viv seemed okay with that, and Buddy was already getting excited, as if he understood what was coming. Even better, neither of the Castelles appeared troubled by Viv turning to someone else, in effect questioning them.

"Smart dog," Candy remarked.

"Almost as smart as Viv," Steve replied. "Ready to get started as soon as Viv's outside?"

"Absolutely." Although she had no idea of what she might hear, or how she had become involved in his experiment. Oh, well. After last night, she owed him this at least.

But it was interesting to watch him attack this problem alone. None of the showiness she would have expected. As if he wanted to solve all this as fast as he could for Viv's sake.

Oh, hell, she'd never wanted to like him. This wasn't going according to plan. But whatever did? She'd certainly learned in the Army that plans were great, but never worked as well as they sounded. Never. Too many unpredictable things in the mix.

After Viv and Buddy disappeared out the back door, Steve stationed Candy near the wall where Buddy had alerted. Seemed like a good starting place, even to Candy. Then he handed her a radio.

"Another one?" she joked.

"Just for you and me. Tell me anything you hear. I'm not going to let you know what I'm doing."

She nodded and watched him leave the room. Maybe this was the wrong time of day to do this. She'd ask him later since Viv seemed to be hearing the voices at night.

She waited patiently as she heard him speak from the kitchen. Probably getting information about the basement.

Nope, not what she'd been expecting to do at all.

Then she thought of Viv. That little girl shouldn't have to live with terror. No way.

DOWN BELOW, STEVE wended his way among boxes and furniture that looked at if it might have been in the house when they bought it. Maybe they thought they could use some of it. The odor down there was musty, exactly like most basements.

When he reached the back of the basement, near Viv's room, he immediately noticed that in order to be right under the child's room, the basement needed to extend farther. He'd ask about that when he was done.

In the meantime, he had other things to take care of. He imagined this was the area Todd had checked out. There didn't seem to be any other place to go.

He set up his EMF detectors around the basement. If electromagnetic fields were involved, he wanted to know where they were strongest. Plus, not everyone had a problem with them. At least not the kind that would cause hallucinations of any sort.

But Viv might be sensitive to them, and this was an old house. It might have hidden wiring problems.

He positioned motion detectors as well, although they'd be little use while he was down here. But later he'd ask the parents to listen for their going off. Or maybe he could just get back here to pay attention himself. He still really needed some local lore and a way to fact-check it. If Candy was willing, she'd probably be an invaluable resource.

He found a sawed-off two-by-four and used it to bang on a pipe. He couldn't imagine that sounding like anything other than it was. Then he checked the heating ducts to see if any part was even a tiny bit loose.

He called Candy on the radio. "Anything?"

"Banging pipes," she answered drily.

He grinned into the radio although she couldn't see it. "About what I expected. A bit longer, if you don't mind."

"We aim to please."

Ouch, he thought. She really wasn't happy about this. Not that he could blame her. A deputy turned into an unwilling ghost hunter? Ha. Yeah, she'd love that.

He walked around checking the EMF meters. Only one place showed an elevated reading, right by the breaker box. Not unusual, and not high enough to cause concern for Viv.

Damn, he needed to find a way to help that child. A good reason that would help her and calm her parents. He hadn't the least doubt that no matter their outward calm around Viv, she could still sense their response to what she was experiencing.

Kids were gifted that way, with innate sensitivity to stress around them. Hard to fool. He wished parents would be more truthful with their children when they were upset.

Anyway, none of his business. He had a more immediate

concern, a little girl he needed to help. And the potential for some outside threat against the family. That still concerned him, that the Castelles might have fled some threat at their previous home. Or that something unpleasant was going on in their marriage and a child was being used as a weapon.

There was one thing he could say about his current occupation. As a detective, he too often arrived in the wake of a tragedy that had broken lives. In this job, he could arrive beforehand and try to help. Depending. Always depending on what was going on.

His recorder had been running all the time, collecting any unheard or unnoticed sounds in this basement. Now it would collect him, too. Ugh.

Then he cleared his throat and began talking to himself in an ordinary conversational voice. Man, he hated this. He always felt like a fool talking aloud with no one there. But he'd known people who did it all the time.

Like his great-grandmother. He'd asked her when he was a child why she did that. Her answer was both excellent and a lesson he'd remembered his whole life:

"Sonny, when I talk to myself I keep my secrets."

An interesting way to think about it, but it wasn't feeling like that right then. Nope, it just felt silly.

After about ten minutes, he quit, glad to be done with it. Then he radioed Candy. "Anything?"

"Not a thing," she answered. "What was I supposed to hear?"

"Nothing. I'm going to keep on for a few more minutes."

"Roger that."

He cleared his throat. He wasn't the world's best singer by any means, but he chose a favorite hymn that didn't require him to be a Pavarotti, or even a recording artist. It was also one that he knew the words to: "Amazing Grace."

Amazing grace! How sweet the sound,
That saved a wretch like me!

I once was lost, but now am found,
Was blind, but now I see.

HE FELL SILENT, listening to the quiet of the basement, then keyed the radio. "Anything?" he asked.

Candy replied. "I thought maybe I heard some very faint singing. Did I?"

Well, a step forward. "Be glad you didn't have to listen full volume. It's probably the only song I could sing without sounding like a dying animal. I'm on my way up."

He retrieved his recorder, turning it off, and headed upstairs, where he found Candy waiting in the bedroom. "So singing was it? Believe me, the conversation I had with myself wasn't a comedy routine. I just felt stupid. You ever do that?"

She smiled widely. "Not too often. And I feel silly when I do. But no, I didn't hear anyone talking. Just a very, very faint singing."

"Okay, then. More equipment in an empty basement tonight."

"Like what?"

"Cameras. A couple of digital recorders. I think I'll put them in Viv's room, as well."

"Sounds like a plan."

He gave her credit for not acting as if he'd lost his mind. She'd made it clear enough what she thought of this shtick.

They went out to talk to Annabelle and Todd. Viv was in another room with Buddy, whose tail thumped like a loud metronome.

"I'm going to bring back some equipment tonight to set up in the basement and in Viv's room. Just leave it all running and stay out of the basement."

Both Castelles sounded okay with that. In fact they sounded relieved that something was actually being done about their problem.

OUTSIDE, CANDY LOOKED at Steve. "You didn't mention that I heard you singing."

"On purpose. That's nothing to go on yet. All they'll know is that I made some noise. That won't help Viv's problem."

Candy frowned. "You're right."

"Besides, it was me down there. I'm sure they've gone down there when Viv heard the voices. I doubt they found anyone, or the problem would have been over before I got here."

He had a good point. That was when her stomach made an embarrassingly loud growl.

Steve laughed. "You need to eat."

"It sounds that way. I'm going to the market for a sub. They make decent ones."

"And here I thought I was becoming a fixture at Maude's."

She shook her head. "If that's what you want to do, go ahead. Maybe someone will talk to you seriously if I'm not there."

He paused. "What time do we go to Tate's?"

"He said eight."

"Okay. Where do we meet?"

"My place, seven thirty."

"You're on. And thank you."

Candy drove away wondering if he'd found anything useful or not. Apparently not, considering how much equipment he was planning to set up.

But while it had been very faint, she'd heard him singing. Not half-bad.

And an interesting choice of song.

Chapter Ten

"So Ben Wittes isn't a suspect?" was the first question Steve asked when he entered Candy's house.

"We sure don't think so. But nobody's ruled out yet. If we can find someone else, of course." Candy caught herself. He was familiar with how this worked. Sometimes she forgot his background. Well, he knew the procedure better than she did.

He just nodded, seeming unoffended by the rookie explaining the obvious to the pro.

"Tell me about the former sheriff," he asked as they drove toward Nate's house.

"His name is Nathan Tate, known everywhere as Nate. Regardless, I understand he came from the wrong side of the tracks, as they say. Went to Vietnam at eighteen, served in the Green Berets."

"That's impressive."

"It is," she agreed. "Anyway, a few years after he came back from the war, after serving with the sheriff's department, he was elected sheriff and remained in the job until he retired. After that his forensics expert succeeded him. Gage Dalton."

She snorted, feeling a sudden amusement.

"What?" he asked.

"Gage doesn't seem like a man people around here once called *hell's own archangel*."

"Seriously?" He twisted on his seat. "I've been wondering about his story since I met him."

"A helluva story. He was DEA. Undercover. His cover was blown. He was targeted with a car bomb that killed his wife and kids and he was badly burned. Someone told me he screamed so much after learning they were gone that he permanently ruined his voice."

"My God!" Steve fell silent.

"Yeah. The tragedy is damn near incomprehensible." Except she'd seen variants of it before, in war. War was an atrocity-making situation, something that was hard to live with afterward.

She shoved those thoughts back. Not now. She was as interested as Steve in what Nate Tate might know about the history of the Castelle house. God knew he'd been here long enough to have heard *something*.

But then so had Miss Emma. Surprising, the silence surrounding the Castelle house. Candy had begun to think everyone around here knew nearly everything there was to know about this area.

"Heard anything from the recorder's?" she asked as they pulled up before the Tate house.

"Not yet. Maybe another couple of days. I suspect someone is spending a whole lot of time sneezing from dust."

She laughed. He could be funny at times.

Together they walked to the door and were soon greeted by the former sheriff himself. He wore his years exceptionally well, only a dusting of gray in his dark hair, with the lines of a face marked by years of wind and sun. His voice was deep, a bit gravely, and even at his advanced age he still managed to be an imposing figure.

He invited them in, saying, "Let's go to the family room. Marge is out, but I like that room even if it's big for one person. This house rambles every which way, which is why you'll notice we're walking past bedrooms, offices and so on. It's practically a warren. We had six daughters and were constantly expanding. Anyway, I like it because of the memories. No kids hanging around with their friends anymore, and we rattle around in here like dried peas. We're thinking about selling."

Interesting view of the man, Steve thought. Six daughters? It must have been overwhelming at times. But he also liked a guy who'd choose a room because of the memories it contained.

The family room was large and warmly decorated. There were even some colorful beanbag chairs left over from an earlier time.

"Sit wherever you like," Nate said with a wave of his hand, then settled into a Boston rocker.

There were two sofas and an assortment of upholstered chairs. Candy picked a blue one, and Steve a green one. When she was seated, she pulled out her small notebook and a pen to write information down if need be.

Nate spoke. "I hear you're wanting to pick my memory. It's a long one, all right."

Steve leaned forward, resting his elbows on his knees and clasping his hands. "I want to do exactly that. Are you aware of the house the Castelle family moved into?"

Nate rocked slowly. "I know the house. Saw a young family moved in. It'll do that place and this town some good. Need more young folks like Candy here."

Steve smiled and Candy felt her cheeks color a little. That was a sideways compliment, she thought. It touched her.

"Anyway," Steve continued, "it's like a cone of silence has dropped over that house. I'm having a devil of a time trying to learn its history. Who owned it before, are there any stories about it?"

"Now that's a place." Nate nodded as he continued to rock. "Became quite something when I was in high school, just before I shipped out. Old man lived there. His name will come back in a moment, but it's been decades since I really thought about it."

Candy's interest quickened. It was amazing how she was getting drawn into this story, her curiosity growing more with each day. That was a good description from Steve: a cone of silence. This in a town where it seemed that if you wanted to know what you were doing, you just had to ask a neighbor.

Nate spoke. "Let me go back to the beginning, as much of it as I know. During my misspent teen years, it was occupied by a man who lived alone. A hermit, in the truest sense. People hardly saw him. He chased away kids who turned up to have a good time. Antisocial, but some of that was understandable, mainly because he'd lost his wife and no one knew where she went."

Nate shook his head a bit. "Sad how people can seize on something like that. The guy just wanted to be left alone. Instead, some folks created stories that he'd killed his wife and she was haunting the property. I heard it became a thing for youngsters to go out there at night on ghost hunts. The old guy chased them off, sometimes with a shotgun."

Nate suddenly leaned forward, his gaze becoming intense. "I was young and foolish. Everyone that age is. But I wasn't foolish enough to buy that crap or think those thrill-seekers had any right to bother a grieving man."

Steve spoke. "I couldn't agree more."

Nate's gaze went from intent to piercing. "Isn't that what you're doing over there? Thrill-seeking for millions who want to get scared in the security of their own homes?"

Man, Candy thought. *Full-frontal attack.* And clearly Tate was still as plugged into this county as he'd always been. She'd heard there wasn't a person or a secret that Nate didn't know. He was certainly up to date.

"What I'm here for," Steve said firmly, "is to help a

seven-year-old girl who's scared to be in her own bedroom. She thinks a man is talking to her, one she can't see. And in case you're curious, her parents have even taken her to a child psychologist. Anyway, helping that child is my priority, and if I can get it done before we start filming and unless that family still wants to do the show, we won't. Plain and simple."

Tate's eyes narrowed, as he digested what Steve said.

"I also have a reputation to preserve," Steve continued. "I'm hunting for reasonable, logical explanations. I am not hunting for a ghost, and frankly I haven't met one yet."

For the first time since their arrival, Nate smiled faintly. He nodded, then rocked for a few minutes.

"All right, then," he said presently. "Let's talk about the house. The stories kept growing while I was overseas. It wasn't enough that the wife had disappeared. Nope. Then it was claimed the old man had killed some teens who had trespassed. For some reason, by the time I got back, the tales had stopped in their tracks. I heard some talk about it all becoming campfire stories after that. Maybe the talk of murders shut it down."

"That's interesting," Steve remarked. "Were there murders?"

"I don't know. Seems like that might have turned this entire county upside down, and the old man would have died of something other than natural causes. I never looked into it. Wasn't part of my job, not an open case, and I wasn't especially tuned in to what teens were telling themselves sitting around a fire. I'd been away for eight years, didn't come back but once for a lot of reasons. Dead history by then."

Steve looked at Candy. "Would you be willing to look into this? Murders? Did the wife just run away?"

Candy nodded. She felt a strong need to know if this county had swallowed murders quietly and if so why. As for the wife? If there was an explanation, she'd find it, not that it would change much of anything. What people said to each other couldn't be silenced by an official explanation. But then, people liked a good conspiracy theory. If anyone years ago had claimed to have found the wife in Denver or New York, some would have insisted it was a cover-up. "I'll check it all out."

"Good," said Nate, leaning back again. "If this is going on, then it's not dead history after all. At best it could help a kid. At worst it could fire up all the legends again. As if folks don't already have enough to talk about." He cocked his head a bit to one side. "Well, around here I guess there's never enough for people to talk about."

Steve flashed a smile. "I've already begun to notice that."

"As for since then, there've been a couple of absentee owners. Probably thinking the land would be a good investment, which it might be if ever this town got back on its feet economically. There's hardly a building boom. At least they kept the place from going to ruin. Put some people to work with their money fixing things up, then eventually it went back on the market. This new family is the first to actually move in."

"Now that's definitely interesting," Steve said.

"I always thought so when I thought about it at all. Empty houses don't create a lot of police work unless they're vandalized."

Steve nodded. "No kids breaking in?"

Nate snorted. "Probably too afraid of a ghost with a shotgun. Yeah, I imagine old man Bride became part of the lore, too. Just too good to pass up."

Nate drummed his fingers briefly on the arm of his chair, then said, "I hear you were a cop once, Steve."

"Yes, sir. Detective after six years on the street."

"Good job. Anything else?"

"If I think of questions, can I call you?"

Nate smiled. "Hell yeah. I got plenty of time to reminisce these days. Candy has my number, obviously."

Candy laughed. "I've plagued you enough."

"Didn't mind at all. I hear there were two kids killed up near the old mining camp. Anything yet?"

Candy shook her head. "Early days."

"It would be. Sometimes I miss the harness. I generally behave myself and just bug Gage. He takes it well."

Candy grinned. "He'd have to. He's just the new sheriff after all."

It was Nate's turn to laugh. "Poor man. Well, hell, I get to be the old sheriff, so maybe *I* should complain."

Steve spoke. "You said the hermit's name was Bride. I've heard the last name before, just recently."

"It did come back to me, didn't it? Yeah. Samuel Bride. Wife was Ivy."

Candy jotted it down.

Nate turned back to Steve. "Let me know if I can do anything else."

Steve was nothing if not bold. "There is one thing. If we get to taping this show, would you mind doing an interview about the lore surrounding the house?"

"Why not? It's time that man's memory got laid to rest. And Candy?"

"Yes, sir?"

"You find out anything about what happened to that woman, let me know, too?"

She was happy to agree. "It would be nice to figure this one out."

OUTSIDE AGAIN, CANDY paused to look up into the night sky. "So many stars here. Like Afghanistan."

"Less city lighting," Steve answered, but he watched her closely. A beautiful woman who didn't deserve the memories she carried, and he hoped like hell that staring up at the stars didn't bring any of them rushing back.

She'd probably hate to realize that he was feeling protective toward her. A ridiculous thing to feel when she was evidently a very strong woman, and when there wasn't a damn thing he could do about her memories. He just hoped she made some new, good ones.

But the murders had really shaken her. He wondered how hard she was hanging on to her thoughts.

Then she lowered her face, smiled and started walking toward the car. "That was fascinating."

"I thought so. It sounds like most of the scary stuff was made up."

"That's what I thought, but I'll look into it."

"But, of course, none of this tells me why a little girl is hearing voices in her bedroom. And none of it tells me if this is threat to her or that family."

Candy paused with her hand on the car door. "You mean as in physical threat?"

Steve's insides tightened. He didn't like to think of these possibilities. Unfortunately… "I came here expecting to find something relatively innocuous to help the Castelles out. But if a real person is doing all this, then I need to wonder why. Anything I think of doesn't look good."

Candy looked poleaxed, but there was no point in pretending. He'd been ignoring the feeling that had been growing slowly in him since yesterday. A psychic, a spirit and two murders?

He'd been a cop too long to be a great believer in coincidence.

She looked at him over the top of the car. "But why? Who? My God, Steve, they just moved here."

"That doesn't necessarily mean a thing." He motioned her to get into the car, then slid in himself. With the doors closed, he felt more comfortable talking to her.

"It's like this," he said. "Any time I go into one of these cases, I'm looking for causes other than the paranormal. While it doesn't come out on TV, the fact is there are a lot of possibilities that are ugly. Lots. I'm a cop, I've seen too much to think that what looks like cotton candy on the outside doesn't have a cyanide pill at the center."

She stiffened at the wheel, and even in the dim light he saw her hands tighten around the steering wheel. "Damn," she breathed.

"Yeah, it's a terrible world. My thoughts run along ugly paths. But take the Castelles' situation. They moved to the middle of nowhere. Why? For a backyard? Or to leave something in the past? What if their relationship is rotten at the core? Or if one of them is? What if one of them is *using* Viv in some way."

He turned his head a little and saw her staring straight at him in the dark.

"That's just..." She seemed unable to find the words.

"I know. But you've been around, Candy. You know how horrible people can be. That child needs help. That means I look at every possibility, no matter how unthinkable it would be to most people. That's the part of this job that I don't talk about on screen or even in blurbs. It doesn't have to be ghosts. It doesn't have to be creaky plumbing or bad wiring. It can also be bad people. I don't skip looking into that."

He and Candy parted ways at her house. "I have to get my equipment out to the Castelle place for the night investigation. See you in the morning? I'll stop by with coffee."

"Sure."

He was aware of her eyes on him as he went to get into his rental.

And after listening to Nate Tate, the tension in him was growing stronger.

Maybe he'd been a cop too long. Or maybe he was right. If he was, he *had* to find out what was going on as quickly as possible.

BEN WITTES WISHED he could stuff cotton into his brain to shut the spirits up. They'd become excited about something and were yammering like a classroom full of kindergarteners.

Damn it. Imagine that the one strong voice in his head had been right about coming murders. The thought chilled him to the bone.

But the voice had been wrong about one thing. The murders weren't coming, they had already happened.

He clung to that, wanting no more even slightly accurate information about such things.

He wanted to give voice to the spirits lingering around that house, but not this kind of voice.

Although he didn't have much choice, like today.

Possession. The word floated into his head once more. What if Samuel Bride was trying to say something? What if this spirit had taken over someone else?

And if it were Samuel Bride, how could he have had anything to do with yesterday's murders?

But that one voice seemed to be slowly taking over, driving him to make that awful introduction of himself to the Hawks guy.

Closing his eyes, he began to pray for salvation.

Chapter Eleven

Steve set up his equipment that night, climbing into the attic to add more. The attic was huge, big enough to finish for a couple of bedrooms, but the only wiring visible led to lights at the head of the stairs and in the middle.

It was possible, however, that sounds might be transmitting from the attic down the wall to Vivian's bedroom. If he didn't pick up anything tonight, he'd bring the rest of his equipment up here for tomorrow night.

A good thing he had an unexpected tendency toward the technical, because one of the cameras wasn't working right, and he knew how to fix it.

In Viv's bedroom, he set up a wide-angle camera and a couple of voice recorders that would activate only if there was a sound. Best he could do unless he wanted to stay all night.

Not tonight. A scan of his earlier recordings had detected nothing but the heat turning on and the rattling of a duct that needed tightening. Not very useful since voices were the problem.

Downstairs again, he found the Castelles sitting in the kitchen over small snifters of brandy. A pleasant way to end the day. Vivian had apparently already gone to bed in her parents' room.

"How'd it go?" Todd asked.

"Pretty much blanketed. Hey, I needed to ask you a question."

"Sure, have a seat. Brandy?"

Steve smiled. "Don't get me started. I have to drive."

Annabelle laughed quietly. "Thus speaks the former cop."

But Todd took a different direction. "About your question?"

"Yeah. Brandy diverted me. So, about the basement."

Both Castelles leaned forward eagerly.

"I didn't catch anything today. That doesn't mean it isn't there, so after I do this part, I may need to get more intensive. More equipment maybe or spending the night in Viv's room. We'll see. But the basement."

"Yes?" Todd prompted.

"It's not big enough. As near as I can tell, it doesn't run under Vivian's room."

Annabelle spoke. "It doesn't. We noticed that, too, but the real estate agent explained it."

"Yeah," said Todd, jumping in. "He said that Viv's room was an add-on, and no basement was ever dug as far as he knew."

"Sitting on blocks." Annabelle nodded. "A good, firm base, the building inspector said, one that completely surrounds the room. No crawl space. We didn't worry about it after that."

A room with no basement. Steve wondered if he needed to deal with that somehow. If he could, short of tearing it all down. Hell. But if there was no basement, then how much could be down there? Some field mice? A rat or two? None of them would make voices.

He rose. "I'll leave you to your evening, then." On the way to the door, he paused. "Still hearing from old friends?" he asked casually.

"All the time," Todd answered. "Good friends are never left behind."

"Good." He smiled as he exited the house, thinking that problems never got left behind either. He hoped Dena, his researcher, would get back to him very soon. She was a wizard at getting public records that painted a background of his clients.

He drove past Candy's house on his way to the motel. Lights glowed from the windows, and he had the strongest urge to stop in. He wanted to learn more about her, beyond her Army career. Did she have family? If so, where? Were they close? What was the rest of her background?

This time it wasn't a cop's curiosity, it was a man's. Oh, trouble there, he warned himself. He didn't want to get attached to this place, especially a woman in this town. He traveled too much. His home was in Southern California and mostly he liked it. He doubted Candy would consider moving down there.

Hell.

He pulled up in front of her house and decided to knock even though it was nearing midnight. She could always tell him to drop dead. Besides, after last night, he was a little worried about her. What if her memories were still plaguing her?

Freaking excuse, that's what it was. Too bad. He got out of the car anyway, walked up to her door and knocked.

After a minute, she answered, looking surprised. "Steve!"

"Hey," he said with a pleasant smile. "I was thinking of going to Maude's before she closes to get a piece of pie. If you're interested, I'll bring you one."

Because he knew a cop never really felt off duty in a public place.

A slow smile grew on her face. "Apple, please, with a latte if you don't mind."

"I just hope she has some peach pie or cobbler left."

Well, that had gone well, he thought as he drove to Maude's. Now he only had to hope that the dragon would share some of the gold with him. Not that he really doubted it, but it was a fun thought about such a grumpy woman. He was beginning to wonder how she'd ever managed to have a kid.

Instead, Maude proved to be in a closing-shop mood.

"I got a piece of apple, and a couple of pieces of peach cobbler. You can have them just to clear out my display. No charge."

He beamed at her. "Very generous of you."

"Just don't like to throw away good food. I'll be baking fresh at four in the morning."

He watched her box the goodies. "How do you keep up this pace?"

She frowned. "It's the way of being in this business. Anything else?"

"Two of your biggest lattes, if it's not too late."

"For some folks, it's never too late to have coffee."

That was true. As a cop, he'd learned to depend on it for fuel.

Then he took a plunge, expecting to be rebuffed. "You hear anything about the incident on the mountain, I guess it was?"

Maude handed him the first latte, already capped. "Two murders, I'm hearing. Folks are getting uneasy. Maybe even a little afraid. They're also wondering why this happened right after you came to town."

Steve's stomach lurched. "They think I'm a killer?"

"Right now, new faces don't help the uneasy. They're wanting it to be a stranger, not a neighbor."

"Ugh," he answered even though he could understand. "And Ben Wittes?"

Maude snorted, giving him the second coffee. "Crazy

man. Most people just try to stay clear. Talking about spirits? I'm a religious woman, but I don't believe god loses souls, so what would they be doing hanging around to bother people?"

Good question, Steve thought. On the other hand, what if free will extended past death? It was a conundrum, if you thought about it. Occasionally he wondered.

But talk about garrulous. He wondered how he'd gotten so far into Maude's good graces. And he suspected he'd never know.

CANDY WAS KIND of glad Steve had stopped by. Her own ghosts were rattling the bars of their cage and threatening to escape. God, she needed to bury them for good, but she doubted she ever would.

Steve returned with two foam containers, and two coffees in one of those cardboard trays. "Grab a coffee before I drop it. These damn things barely support them."

She obliged, grabbing both of them. "Kitchen?"

"Best place to eat pie unless you want crumbs all over your living room."

He followed her.

"I want to vacuum as little as possible."

He laughed. "Every time I get back home, I hire a crew. I am definitely not the mopping or dusting type."

"I have to be. My mom always had a spotless house, aided by her kids. Then the Army took hold and taught me how to clean boot scuffs off a floor with a toothbrush."

"Seriously?"

She cocked an eye his way as she put the coffees on the table. "They had to keep us busy somehow when we didn't have other duties. But actually I think that was just another layer in teaching us who was boss, and to follow orders."

He could see that. But what a miserable job.

"White-glove inspections aren't just a myth. Try to survive one in bathroom facilities." She looked at him. "Plates and forks?"

"Please. Once in a while I need to pretend to be civilized."

That caused her to smile crookedly. She retrieved the plates and utensils, then sat facing him. He opened the containers and told her to help herself.

"That's a lot of pie and cobbler!"

"It is. Maude was cleaning out for the night and said she hated to throw away good food. No charge."

Candy lifted her eyebrows. "How'd you get on her good side?"

"Damned if I know." He watched Candy reach for the apple pie, then took a large square of peach cobbler for himself.

She indicated the pie. "That's two slices, I swear."

"So enjoy it." He ate a mouthful of cobbler, then said, "Maude told me something interesting."

"Yeah?"

"The town is uneasy about the murders. And they seem to be zeroing in on me. Stranger in town, arriving just before they happened."

"Oh, man." She paused with a piece of pie on her fork. "Another problem. I didn't expect that."

"Well, it makes sense under the circumstances. As Maude said, nobody wants to feel a neighbor could have done this. She also told me that Ben Wittes is crazy and people avoid him like the plague."

"I can believe that." She resumed eating. "It's not going to make your job easier if people are suspicious of you."

"I doubt it'll make it any harder. Trying to get information I can use in any way is like pulling teeth around here. Even public records. But you're going to look into the disappearance of Ivy Bride?"

"Absolutely. Nate piqued my curiosity."

They ate in quiet companionship, then Steve risked blowing the whole thing up. "Got any family?"

"Back in LA? Tons. A huge family."

"How are they doing?"

"Well, it seems."

But he'd noticed a tension coming over her and the remaining pie seemed to lose her interest. Maybe he should drop this right now. But he couldn't.

"You see them often?" he asked.

She shook her head.

"Family squabble?"

"Nothing like that." She dropped her fork onto her plate. "You want the truth? The war changed me in ways I don't like. I don't want to go back and face a hundred family members who'll all be wondering what happened to me. Who might start asking well-meaning questions. I don't want them to see the new me. Then there's my brother."

He waited, but nothing more seemed forthcoming. Her eyes were beginning to take on that absent look again. Oh, God, what had he precipitated with his endless curiosity? It was one thing to push a witness or a perp, another to press a friend.

But then she found voice again. "My brother followed me into the Army. I think it was because of me. Back then I was all excited about the possibilities. Then he got killed in the 'Stan. I wouldn't be surprised if they blame me for that. And maybe they should."

His heart had squeezed so tight that he doubted he'd ever draw breath again. God, the weight this woman bore on her shoulders. It had to be crushing her a piece at a time.

He wished he could hug her, but he wasn't sure it would be welcomed. He didn't even dare offer the trite advice *maybe you should call them*. That was something she needed to decide on her own.

He felt useless except to say, "Maybe he was following in your father's footsteps. The way you did."

"Sorry," she said presently. "I shouldn't dump on you."

"I don't mind. Really."

She picked up her fork again and began to eat pie with determination. "Thanks for the pie and coffee. It's delicious."

Locking away the entire conversation. He understood that, too. But this woman was a box of sealed secrets, and short of a pry bar he didn't know how to get her to open up. It would probably require the kind of trust they didn't have yet.

"Thank Maude," he answered, hoping to lighten the moment for her. "She totally floored me."

Again a small smile, as if it were almost painful. "I hear she can be surprising at times. Never happened to me, though."

"Maybe she has a thing for handsome men."

That startled a short laugh out of her, and she began to look more relaxed. "So you've got an ego?"

"Of course. I just hide it well."

Her smile widened a tiny bit. Maybe that's all he could hope for just then. The murders had been really hard on her, and it might be taking some time to come back from them. Maybe she never would.

People with caring hearts and strong consciences often carried guilt like hers, even when it wasn't justified. It was awful, though, that she felt responsible for her brother's death.

He supposed a psychologist would remind her that her brother had a mind of his own, that she was depriving him of his own autonomy to think he'd joined the Army solely because of her. Or maybe a psychologist wouldn't say that. He wasn't one himself and wasn't going to dip his toes into those waters.

A few minutes later, Candy spoke again. "You're seriously considering that the Castelles, or one of them at least, might be behind this?"

"No stone unturned," he tried to say lightly. Maybe it was the cop in him, but he'd found that if a guy narrowed his focus too much on a presumed idea, then he could miss important things.

"Doesn't seem possible," she answered. "Not from what I saw anyway."

"Nope. But the public face is often different from the private face. You wouldn't believe some of the criminals I've locked up that everyone thinks is nice, pleasant, wouldn't hurt a fly. Some things just can't be believed, at least not safely."

She nodded, putting down her fork, the pie only partly eaten. "I can see that. It still doesn't seem possible."

"Maybe it isn't. But what matters here is one small child, not anyone else."

At last her tension seemed to be fleeing, her shoulders growing more relaxed, a half smile coming to her face. "Maybe you're right. The family seems too pat."

"Exactly. As if they emerged from a TV show from fifty or sixty years ago. It's always possible that they're exactly what they look like."

But nothing left to chance.

Then his cell phone rang. Courtesy made him ask, "Okay if I take this?"

"Please."

He'd never understand how some people thought it was okay to answer a phone even if they were in the middle of a conversation. When had phones taken precedence over everything else?

Well, his just had, he decided. Even though he'd asked, which most people didn't. As if everyone was supposed to understand that a phone call was more important than they were.

He didn't bother leaving the table. His latte was there and, more important, he wasn't aware of any secrets that were likely to come across the phone. Candy was welcome to listen if she cared to.

It turned out to be his researcher. "Dena," he said cheerfully. "Got the dirt for me?"

"You bet," she answered. "You might want a pencil and some paper."

He paused. "That much?"

"Mostly basic details."

"Give me a minute." He lowered the phone and looked at Candy. "My researcher. You have any easy to access paper and pen?"

She rose and pulled the memo list off her refrigerator, and a pen out of a holder that was stuck there, as well.

"Thanks." He put the phone to his ear. "I'm ready, Dena."

He listened, scribbling down some high points. "You emailing that to me? Thanks a bunch."

"You owe me a scotch next time I see you."

Steve laughed. "You got it."

When he disconnected, he sat for a minute, thinking. Then he looked at Candy. "That perfect little family?"

She leaned forward. "Yes?"

"Todd's got a conviction for possession of drugs. They tried to nail him with trafficking."

Candy drew a sharp breath. "My God. You were right."

"Perfect on the outside, maybe not on the inside. How would you look at this?"

She hesitated visibly. "Nothing good springs to mind," she said eventually. "But you're the experienced detective."

"Well, what I see is trouble. Todd could indeed have been trafficking. The amount at arrest may have been too small to convince a judge or a jury. I need the details. In the meantime, who knows who he was dealing with."

She nodded. "Damn, Steve. You were right. Who knows what they were running from?"

"Or who might be scaring their little girl. Todd doesn't sound like the pillar of decency anymore."

Chapter Twelve

Steve drove back to the motel, glad he'd decided not to baby-sit equipment tonight. Tomorrow would be soon enough.

He fought an internal battle with himself, however. His thoughts kept turning toward Candy, as if she were a lode-stone and he was a piece of metal.

Damn, she was attractive. The urge to explore her every hill and hollow was beginning to preoccupy him entirely too much. The worst of it was, he didn't want to make her uneasy with some unwelcome advance. It had penetrated even his thick-skulled male brain that a lot of women hated it if they were made to feel like sex objects.

Not that he thought of Candy in only that way. Hell no. He liked plenty of the rest of her. She was smart and showed a restraint with him and his ghost hunting that he found admirable. So far she hadn't popped her cork and told him he was a conscienceless scam operator.

Nope. He even thought he might be winning her over to the possibility that he could be an honest man. Well, as honest as any person could be about themselves.

But the Castelles pulled him in a different direction. Todd had a drug conviction. He wanted to read his email from Dena to get all the details.

Because messing with drug gangs could get a whole lot more than messy. Because that marriage might not be as stable as it appeared on the outside. Because some unscrupulous sort thought he might torment Todd by tormenting his daughter.

Forget the psychic. There were bigger things afoot here than a self-deluded man who thought he was hearing voices.

He ran into the truck stop grill just long enough to get more coffee, then returned to his room, where he sat at the tiny table and opened his laptop.

He could read email on his phone, but he hated to unless the messages were short. *Old man*, he told himself. Not that he was that old, but he was way behind on this era of technology. Or at least in adopting it. People used to have face-to-face conversations, he thought. They'd sit down and talk to each other without reading their phones at the same time.

Then he almost laughed at himself. He wasn't old enough yet to turn into that guy screaming, "Get off my lawn!"

At least he hoped he wasn't.

Once again his mind tried to head back to Candy, but he yanked it away. Too many pitfalls, then add that to the likelihood that Candy wouldn't consider moving back to California—at least that's where he assumed she came from. She'd made her reasons clear for not wanting to go home again.

He hoped she'd get past that, but it was unlikely it would happen anytime soon. So what would he offer her?

A one-night stand, that's what.

Self-disgust filled him and he diverted back to the Castelles. As he read Dena's email, his concern about them grew.

Todd had been arrested, all right. For trafficking in drugs. The conviction for personal use had been granted by a judge who was evidently sympathetic to guys who were employed and had families. Or maybe because he was a handsome white guy.

An unbiased view of the criminal justice system said so. He'd seen enough cases to believe it, and much as he wanted to change that, he wasn't in the position. Charging was in the hands of the prosecutors. Convictions were in the hands of judges and juries, neither of which were totally impartial.

He sighed and continued reading. Todd had been sentenced to drug rehab, followed by community service for another year. He'd completed it all.

But that didn't mean it hadn't created stresses in that marriage. Maybe the family had moved out here to sever Todd's relationships with the wrong sort of people.

Or maybe they'd moved out here to get him away from drugs. Not a bad idea if it worked.

Or maybe they'd moved out here because he owed money to the wrong people.

The last one was the idea that concerned him most. There were some people on this planet whom you *never* wanted to owe money. People who weren't above killing you.

People who weren't above threatening you by showing how defenseless your kid really was.

Annabelle had mentioned they needed a bigger place to live that didn't exceed the constraints of their budget. He wondered if that was because they really didn't make a lot of money, or because they were trying to pay off someone.

Hell. This case had just grown complicated. It might not be about calming that family. It might be about protecting that little girl from very real danger.

Time to put on his detective's hat again. Time to get into that mind-set. He could do that without sacrificing his paranormal investigation. That much he still had to do.

Although ghost hunting had just taken a huge back seat to reality.

IN THE MORNING, just as the sun had begun to find its way into Conard City, he got a phone call from his producer, Etta Miller.

No holds barred on either side.

"Etta, this whole thing got complicated by a criminal past. I don't know if that's involved in this, but we may not have a show."

She sighed. "Steve, Steve, Steve."

"You know I don't lie to audiences."

"Yeah. I know."

"It was our agreement for me to do this program, so live with it. There are things I will not expose."

"I get it. But you'd better get on the stick with that psychic. He could be useful if this turns out to be on the up-and-up. Introduce him to the family to see how it works out."

Double damn, he thought as he ended the call.

But another thought wormed into his mind. What if the Castelles had been in hiding? Now that they'd been discovered, they might have thought that putting themselves on a nationally broadcast TV show could offer protection. With their identities out there, maybe no one would dare touch them.

He'd seen too much of this stuff when he'd been in law enforcement. He'd thought he might never see it again.

So much for pipe dreams.

CANDY HAD FALLEN asleep the night before thinking about what Steve had learned about the Castelles. If that were true, then this county might get a national shakeup whether people wanted it or not. Drug rings? What if that was ongoing?

She was supposed to be preventing that kind of stuff. Ha! Fat chance on this one.

But she woke in the morning from a much more pleasant dream. About Steve having remained last night. About the two of them making love.

As her eyes opened, her body felt flushed but she also felt like warm honey from head to toe. Softened. Pliant.

Abruptly she threw back the covers and welcomed the chilly air in the bedroom. Crazy. Just crazy.

Any relationship with Steve would be abbreviated in a few short weeks. Hardly more than a one-night stand. She'd had that kind of relationship only once before in her life and had vowed never to repeat it. It hurt too much. It had somehow made her feel dirty, used.

Nope. Not gonna happen.

A hot shower helped a little, especially when she stepped out into the cold air onto the bathmat. All wet, she began to shiver. That'd quell any errant desires, she told herself.

Later, her stomach full of warm grits and cheese, she donned her uniform and headed to the office. Now she felt an itch to research the Castelles herself and she still had to search for Ivy Bride. She hoped she'd find the woman had moved to somewhere far away.

As for the Castelles, it felt counterintuitive to her for them to want to be on TV if they were running from anything at all, most especially bad people. Steve held a different opinion, and she wanted to hear more of his thoughts on that.

She'd seen a different look about him last night. Something darker, less lighthearted. Something so focused she wouldn't want to be the object of that gaze.

The detective, she supposed. That part she might not mind watching in action. She had plenty to learn.

But research was next on her agenda, and as she drove the official SUV that she'd parked at her house last night, she thought about which case should be her starting point.

Finding Ivy Bride struck her as important. Nate had been right. It was time to lay the man to rest, if she could.

The Castelles… Well, she didn't doubt that Steve would

be hot on that case. He'd probably share with her, too, as he had last night.

This whole thing was getting a lot messier than she'd anticipated when she'd been assigned to liaise with a ghost hunter.

On the other hand, it had grown a lot more fascinating.

Once at the office, after greeting the others, she took a desk in the back of the wide-open duty area, away from conversations and distractions, and set to work.

Ivy Bride first. It proved easy enough to come up with the woman's maiden name, Haskell. She started the databases running, looking for obits for Ivy Bride, Ivy Haskell Bride and Ivy Haskell. Responses came slowly.

Well, yeah, she was searching a period sixty years ago. Many items hadn't been digitized, and when public records had made their way into databases, they were huge ones.

Taking advantage of the lost time, she went to Maude's to get coffee. If Velma scowled at her when she brought it back, Candy never noticed. It wouldn't surprise her if Velma was in on the joke and just never let anyone know. As she'd begun to discover, the woman could have a wicked sense of humor.

Velma was certainly too smart not to have noticed the collection of antacids against the wall behind the coffee mugs. Or maybe she was just stubborn.

In Velma's shoes, Candy would have tipped over the coffee urn and told everyone to get their own coffee. A big difference in temperament, which might be part of the reason Velma had kept her job for so long. Candy imagined that dealing with all these deputies, all the comms and all the crimes required a pretty calm personality.

When she returned to the desk, the computer search had started to turn up names. Sheesh, who would have thought there were so many women named Ivy Haskell. She was able to eliminate all of them by time frame. Born too late, couldn't possibly have lived to be one hundred and twenty. Not likely at any rate. Way too young to have been a married woman all those decades ago.

She worked at finding a way to narrow the search parameters even more by dates to reduce the number of results. She figured it out and put the computer to work again.

She also needed to hunt for name changes, she decided. Ivy Haskell Bride would have had to use her full name in order to change it by court order. Then there was always the possibility of a marriage. Just because Bride hadn't ever mentioned a divorce didn't mean there wasn't one. Plus, dissolution of marriage often gave a person a built-in way to change their name to anything they wanted.

So next, marriages and divorces. Then name changes. All public documents. But man, waiting for a computer to check public databases from all over the country was going to drive her nuts. She might as well go for a stroll, tap dance in the park or spend time at Maude's listening to the casual conversation as it wrapped around her.

Or she could just sit here with her coffee and practice the patience she had learned while standing post.

A while later, census reports started popping up. She found one for Ivy Haskell Bride, wife of Samuel Bride, all the way back at 1960, residence listed only as Wyoming. Ivy vanished before the 1970 census. Maybe the census had stopped providing public data on living individuals. If so, it must be causing headaches to genealogical researchers.

Well, that was another bracket. Name changes after 1960.

Death notices after 1960. She queried the Social Security database and found nothing. No death report filed there, probably because Ivy had never received Social Security.

The invisible, missing woman.

Several frustrated words ran though Candy's thoughts, but she knew she could dig even deeper if this didn't turn up more information. There were other databases available, mostly criminal and military. Neither one seemed likely for a farmwife of that era, but she couldn't skip them.

And, of course, she needed to check the sheriff's records to find out when the woman had been reported missing. If she even had.

The molehill was rapidly turning into a mountain.

It was also part of her job, whether for this Steve Hawks thing or some other reason. Being a cop wasn't always romantic or even interesting. Still, given how hard-won this position was, she wouldn't trade it in for anything.

STEVE HAD OTHER matters on his mind. Candy was dealing with Samuel and Ivy Bride. He needed more info on the Castelles before he went back out there.

Years as a detective had taught him that he could conceal his suspicions, and right now they were running high. He called Dena again.

"What, man?" she asked when she answered. "I gave you a bucketload."

"I know. But I wonder if you know any more."

"As if other stuff would be public record. I've got informants on the street, but if I target someone too closely, one of my people could get killed. I'll ask generally, but that may take a while. Basically, you're on your own."

He'd figured, but it never hurt to ask, especially when Dena's sources had proved fruitful in the past.

He thanked her and disconnected, then decided to wander over to the sheriff's before heading out to the Castelle place. He figured Candy might be hating him by now.

Being a cop often meant getting deep into the weeds of the world of records. Prior arrests, yeah, but general information on suspects and witnesses. Getting the word from the streets, which often came through other cops. Research until his eyes nearly fell out of his head. It sure wasn't a matter of walking around wearing a gun and badge like a big man.

Nope. It would have been even tougher if he hadn't had a team.

Candy had no team.

Get her a coffee, maybe suggest a quick lunch. Ask her if she could take a break and join him out at the Castelle house. She might jump at the opportunity by now.

A glance at his watch told him it was nearly noon. Yeah, she could use a break. Besides, he had an ulterior motive. He wanted to see her again.

The bug had bit him.

He found Candy at the back of the office, focused intently on a computer screen. She looked up when he said her name and her eyes refocused.

She spoke. "I suppose I don't have to tell you how much this sucks."

"Nope. Hence my invitation to lunch and maybe a trip to see the Castelles." He put a coffee beside her. "Or you can sit here torturing yourself for the next few hours. I'll come back and help you pick your eyes up off the floor."

That pulled a laugh from her. "Lunch it is." She took the cup and sipped the latte. "Fuel. Or maybe ambrosia."

"Well, then, let's go."

She rose, pulling on her jacket and picking up her cup. "Take me away."

His heart skipped, which it shouldn't have. "Glad to oblige."

Maude's didn't seem very busy for the time of day. They found a booth without any problem, and as they sat, Steve wondered if the murders had caused the emptiness. Were people so nervous they didn't want to come out to lunch? Or so nervous they wanted to keep an eye on their kids? Were kids even going to school?

"Have people gone into hiding since the murders?" he asked her.

"All I know is they're nervous as hell. I'm sure there have been cases of multiple murders here, if for no other reason than that sickos appear everywhere, but I'm not that far into the loop yet."

"If I were a parent, I'd be worried," he admitted.

Then Mavis appeared wanting their orders. Both of them were prompt. This didn't seem like a place you could dither for a while. He wouldn't be surprised if Mavis decided for them.

He went for clogging his arteries again, blaming it on the travel. Or excusing it. A succulent cheeseburger with fries and a side of salad. Candy had apparently given up fighting her appetite, too. No salad, which he was used to women ordering. No grilled chicken. Nope. Steak, corn bread and broccoli.

"Corn bread?" he asked.

She nodded. "Every so often. Love the stuff."

"It's pretty good," he agreed. "I never think of it."

Her answer was dry. "It's rarely on a menu. Besides, I don't like it dry, so I never make it at home."

She dug in happily, as did he. Then she asked, "Anything more that's interesting?"

"My researcher is going to gently sound out her street informants, but she doesn't want to draw attention to any of them."

"I have to admit I'm disappointed in Castelle," Candy admitted. "You'd never guess."

"And maybe that drug stuff is really all in the past. People do recover. But even so, I have to wonder what effect that might have had on their marriage."

"I can't imagine it was good. Maybe they're putting it back together. But the kid. Why would anyone want to torture that child?"

"To send a message. Let him know they've found him. Maybe he thinks this will draw him and Annabelle closer. I can think of a whole lot of motives. Anyway, my producer is hounding me. Work with the damn psychic."

He saw her lips twitch. "Have fun."

"Oh, yeah. Loads of it."

"You don't like psychics?"

Steve shrugged, certain he'd mentioned this before. Or maybe only inside his own head. "I've met a couple that I thought might be genuine. Can't really prove it, of course. Then there are those who walk around giving vague impressions that anyone could provide in the circumstances. Or those who just put on a show to make it look like they're doing something. I'm wondering which kind Ben Wittes is."

She cut another piece of steak. "But you allow the possibility?"

"I've learned not to dismiss anything without proof. I suppose it's possible that some are genuine."

Like ghosts. He just needed some really good proof. Hard proof. The kind he could take to court. How likely was that in this field?

After lunch, Candy ran over to the sheriff's office to check on the progress of her searches. When she came back, they both climbed into her official vehicle.

For once he was agreeable to that when visiting a client. It showed his involvement with the police in case something truly unsavory was going on.

"This search is going to take forever," she told him as she wheeled onto Main Street and drove toward the Castelle home. "I'm astonished how many Ivy Haskells there are. She did turn up in the 1960 census, though. Last time."

He gave a low whistle.

Candy shrugged. "At some point the Census Bureau stopped making names public as far as I can tell. It doesn't really mean much, except it gives me a search bracket. Name changes, divorces, police records, the whole deal."

"There must be a lot out there."

"As I'm discovering. What about you? Anything?"

"More questions at this point. Somebody's going to be facing legal trouble if they're harassing that little girl. Enough said."

Candy spoke slowly. "That drug conviction must have nearly destroyed their marriage."

"I thought of that. A lot here under that Donna Reed facade. Well, I'll find it out."

He always did. People's secrets had been his meat and potatoes as a detective, and that much hadn't changed.

"But why would they want to be on TV, considering the possibilities?"

"Cover," he said flatly. "They get national exposure, and if anything happens to them, it's not going to escape notice. Protection."

She drew a sharp breath. "I hadn't thought of that."

"Most people wouldn't. Under this friendly exterior lies a mind that is used to thinking the unthinkable. The not immediately obvious."

"I have a lot to learn."

"You're on the way," he said as they turned into the Castelles' driveway.

"This is going to be a learning experience."

"I hope not."

THE CASTELLES GREETED them warmly. Viv was out back with Buddy, and Steve and Candy were invited inside.

"Let me run around and check my equipment," Steve said. "Then I'll join you in that coffee."

"Help yourself," Todd answered.

Steve paused. "Anything last night?"

"Not that we were aware of. We were all hunkered down

in our bedroom. As usual. Plus, we didn't want to bother your equipment, like you said."

Steve smiled. "Good job. If I hear footsteps on a tape, I want to know if it was you."

Annabelle laughed. "You may hear the thump-thump-thump of Buddy running around, though."

"I think that would be pretty distinctive." He disappeared in the general direction of the attic stairs.

Candy sat with them at their kitchen table. Like a lot of people, they seemed to prefer it to the more formal living room. It was hard now not to look at them with suspicion, so she turned the conversation in a safer direction.

"You ever consider finishing the attic?" she asked. "From the outside it looks huge."

"It *is* big," Annabelle answered.

"Nice," Todd agreed. "We could put a couple of spacious rooms up there. We've talked about a bigger office. Maybe an extra bedroom. And a bath, for those that don't want to run up and down stairs repeatedly."

Annabelle made a face at him. "I wouldn't be that someone, would I? Anyway, it would lee expensive. We certainly couldn't do the wiring or the plumbing ourselves. But did you get up there, Candy?"

She shook her head. "No, not yet."

"When you do, take a look at the lath. It covers all the walls up to the peak of the roof, and someone stained it at one time. It's a work of art unto itself."

Todd laughed. "It's beautiful all right. Almost a shame to hide any of it."

"Excuses," Annabelle retorted. "Space. We came out here for space."

Candy couldn't help wondering if that had been the real reason.

"Anyway," Annabelle said, "our apartment in the city? Hardly any room. One bedroom, barely big enough for a bed. We had to turn the living room into our office and screen off an area for Vivian to sleep in. Then we had this kitchen that was almost too small to move around in."

"I've seen places like that," Candy said. Mostly in foreign countries where entire families lived in one-room shacks and cooked outside under lean-tos. Many of them probably would have thought the Castelles' apartment was a palace, but she could understand why they didn't.

Steve passed by on his way to the basement.

Annabelle spoke. "I don't know whether I hope he finds something."

"It could be worse," Todd answered.

"Since I heard those sounds, nothing would be worse. Trust me."

Todd slipped an arm around her and squeezed her from the side.

"It's true," she said. "I'd rather have a ghost than wonder if Viv and I are losing our minds."

"You're not," Todd said, giving her another squeeze. "I'm sure of that."

How could he be sure? Candy wondered. Because he knew something? Damn, she hated the suspicions Steve had awakened in her.

But it remained Todd couldn't know, even if it was highly unlikely that both wife and daughter were developing a mental illness at the same time. Or unless he suspected a cause for this that had nothing to do with mental health or ghosts.

Jeez, was this how Steve had to think?

She didn't envy his world at all. She'd lived with suspicion for too long in combat areas. Suspicions about every local she talked to. Sometimes suspicions about members of the local armies. That was some of the baggage she wanted to leave behind. To learn to be trusting again.

Steve returned about twenty minutes later. Conversation

had revolved around exactly what Todd and Annabelle did for their living. Both of them appeared to become excited when they talked about it. Much of it was over Candy's head. 3-D graphics? Like in the movies? She didn't ask.

They also talked briefly about the conventions they had to attend to promote themselves and their work, but mostly to meet fans. The crowds. Candy was sure she would have shrunk in crowds that size.

Then Steve reappeared and joined them at the table, accepting a mug of coffee. "Nothing," he told two inquisitive faces. "But you were right about Buddy. He makes quite a ruckus when he runs."

"He's not at all light-footed," Annabelle said drily. "We always know where he is. So nothing?"

"Not yet. Two things. If you don't mind, I'd like to spend a night in Vivian's room. Listening. Maybe I'll hear something or get a brainstorm. Right now I could use one. The other thing is a psychic. My producer found one, and she's hot to try him out."

Annabelle leaned forward. "I'll try anything if it might help. I just need someone to find out if this is real and, if not, what might explain it. Bring a psychic. Bring the Army. Bring another building inspector." Her eyes teared up. "Anything except make my daughter live with this fear."

"Honey," Todd said. "We'll move."

"Not until we've tried everything," she said fiercely through her tears. "This is our dream. Every dime we have is right here. I want to fight for it."

Candy gave her props for that. A strong woman, determined to stand and fight. Fleeing sure as hell would have been easier.

Todd looked at Steve. "Nothing? Absolutely nothing?"

"Not yet," Steve answered. "One night doesn't mean a damned thing, though."

"Then you'll stay tonight?"

"I said I would. I generally like to do at least several nights by myself. When my crew gets here, I'll repeat it all, but you may want to take our invitation to find a decent motel so you don't have to live with the uproar. If you think spirits are noisy, try a film crew."

That at least made Todd grin. "I can almost imagine."

"Anyway," Steve continued. "Have you done any remodeling since you moved in?"

Annabelle started to shake her head, then stopped. "What do you mean by remodeling? Paint? Wallpaper? Or something bigger?"

"Moving walls? Making holes when you checked the electrical? Things like that. I keep hearing that renovations can disturb the spirits."

"Oh."

The couple exchanged looks.

"Well," Todd said. "I guess we have. I added some track lights in our office. And we had an electrician install more outlets that could handle the needs of our equipment."

Steve nodded. "Anything else?"

"We had some rewiring done, but that was in the barn. Place is a firetrap waiting for a spark. Useless until we can do more about it, but we still need some light in there. A fluorescent lantern wasn't cutting it."

"Great for camping, though," Steve joked. "Well, that sounds like enough to answer audience questions. Have to touch all bases, you know."

Annabelle lifted her head a bit. "You don't believe that renovations could cause this?"

Steve shrugged. "I'm in the business of not believing theories. I'm not sure when last someone actually talked to a ghost about what's bothering them."

Todd snorted. Even Annabelle managed a weak smile.

"That's the point, isn't it?" Steve asked, leaning forward.

"If you want to confirm a preconceived idea about what's happening in this house, I was the wrong guy to choose."

Todd nodded. "That's why we came to you."

"I hope so. The unvarnished truth, if I can find it. That's my way."

Barely two minutes passed before they heard a knock at the front door. At the same time, Vivian burst in through the back door. The air around her and Buddy carried the outside cold.

"I'll get the door," Todd said, as Annabelle leaned forward to hug her daughter and start unzipping her outerwear.

"Chocolate, Mommy."

"You betcha!"

A happy little family, Candy thought. Hard to believe there was something dark behind them.

Then Todd walked in with a scruffy Ben Wittes, who looked as if he could use a shave.

"Ben Wittes," Todd said. "I believe he's expected."

Steve rose and shook the man's hand. As dirty as it looked, Candy didn't envy him.

"Good to see you again," Ben said.

Annabelle turned from the stove, where she was making Viv's hot chocolate, and murmured a greeting. She wasn't happy about this, although she claimed she was willing to try anything to help Vivian.

And Viv herself stared at the man, her eyes huge.

Candy couldn't blame her. Ben looked like something that had crawled from under a rock. When he smiled, the expression wasn't comforting.

Vivian slid off her chair and edged toward her mother.

"What do you want me to do?" Wittes asked Steve.

"Walk through the house with me," Steve said. "Give me your impressions."

Ben nodded. "I'm ready to start. The spirits have been

ramping up since I began driving this way. Guess they have a lot to say."

Candy had trouble keeping a straight face. She waited to hear anything that might stand out from casual conversation. Something with meat on it.

"Do you mind?" Steve asked the Castelles.

"Go for it," Todd said. "No stone unturned."

Except, Candy thought, the one Ben Wittes had crawled out from under.

STEVE TURNED ON one of his recorders and began the walk-through. He wanted one thing, just one thing, that would justify making this man part of his show. If he couldn't get anything but a jumble of impressions anyone could have provided, he'd send the man packing and go to the mat with his producer, Etta Miller. He didn't usually have to fight her, but when he did, he stood his ground until she came around, or they could reach a satisfactory compromise.

But it was fair to give the man a shot at this, especially to placate Etta.

He just hoped someone would clean this guy up before filming. He looked downright disreputable.

He led Ben to the very back of the house, to the Castelles' bedroom. No activity had been reported in there, and it was a good test of Wittes.

"Go ahead," he told the guy, then waited with his recorder on. If the man provided anything useful, he wanted it on tape.

Ben closed his eyes and swayed a bit. Not terribly theatrical, which was good.

"The man is still here," he murmured slowly. "He hangs around all the time, doesn't want to leave."

Steve wanted to question him but waited. That was a pretty general statement, hardly worth paying attention to. Yet.

"He doesn't want to leave," Ben continued. "There are others here. A woman. She's angry."

Again, not much. Again, Steve waited.

Then Ben's eyes snapped open. "Over here," he said, and promptly walked along the hall to Vivian's bedroom.

"Here," he said firmly. "He likes this room. People in here might hear his voice."

That caught Steve's attention. Unless the Castelles had been telling others about this, it might be important. He'd have to ask after Wittes left.

Wittes closed his eyes again, and genuinely looked as if he were listening intently. "A dog senses him. The woman is here, too, still angry but she says nothing. Not that people might hear. She doesn't want to talk."

Ben turned and looked at him. "She was killed here."

All right, Steve felt a little prickle at the base of his neck but refused to give in to it. With the stories that had once floated around this town, the statement was meaningless.

"The woman likes a little girl. She wants to protect the child but doesn't know how."

Finally, Steve broke his silence. "Protect her from what?"

"The shouting man. The mean man."

Ben fell silent once more, appearing to listen intently. "He wants to shout louder because his words aren't being heard."

Not quite true, Steve thought. A voice was being heard, but the words weren't making sense. Or weren't audible enough to be understood.

Ben turned to look at Steve. "He says he didn't do it."

"Didn't do what?"

"Kill anyone."

"Most perps say they didn't do it."

Ben's lip curled upward. "Doesn't matter if you don't believe it. *He* believes it."

Point taken.

Wittes shrugged slightly. "Others are here, but I'm not sure they're attached to this house. They come to me from all over."

Sure. "How do you do this, Ben?"

"They talk to me. Because I can hear them. I'm done. I'm tired. Can I come back tomorrow?"

"I'll see."

As he watched Wittes leave, all Steve kept thinking was that the man had run out of material. What had he done to exhaust himself? Listen to nothing? Or try to act?

Steve made his way back to the kitchen. The first thing he saw was Vivian. She was pale, ignoring the cocoa in front of her.

"What's going on?" he asked her parents.

Annabelle answered. "I don't think she likes that guy. Not that I can blame her. I could smell him across the kitchen."

"Pretty ripe," Steve agreed. "You two ever tell anyone around here about what you're experiencing?"

Two heads shook negatively. "We even told Viv not to mention it at school."

Then Steve squatted beside Viv's chair. "Something wrong, sweetie?"

Her face started to clear and she reached for a spoon to pull out one of the small marshmallows. "Not invisible," she said.

Then she would say no more.

STEVE PROMISED THE Castelles he'd be back later to check his equipment and prepare to spend the night.

"I've got a sleeping bag I can offer," Todd said. "It's going to be chilly whichever room you're in."

But the ride back to town with Candy was silent until they approached the sheriff's office.

He was the first to speak. "Did you notice anything about Vivian while I was out of the room?"

"Only that she looked uneasy. Anyone would look uneasy around that man, especially a child. Nothing else, though. Once he was out of the room she sat at the table for her cocoa."

He nodded, thinking. Ben wouldn't appear to be the friendliest man, but he also didn't appear especially threatening. Still, for a child...

"What she said?" Candy asked. "About not invisible."

"That's bothering me," Steve admitted. "God knows what it meant."

"Did you learn anything useful?"

"Not really. Nothing he couldn't have pieced together from local lore. We'll see what he has to say tomorrow. I just hope I catch something tonight."

"Why?"

"Because I'll take anything that can convince those two parents that their daughter isn't nuts."

"I can agree with that. Well, I need to get back to my computer in the hopes that I can learn something about Ivy Bride. How often do people just vanish?"

"You'd be surprised. It's more common than most people think."

"Sometimes I've wished I could do that."

Candy's comment was nakedly revealing. It jerked his attention back to her, and he wished like hell he knew what to say or do. He offered lamely, "I'm glad you haven't."

"At the moment, so am I. More Wittes tomorrow?"

"It appears so. But I want to do something else."

"What's that."

"I'm bothered by the fact that there's nothing below Vivian's room. I want to take a close look at that foundation."

Oh, yes he did. And he wanted to call Etta and tell her that Wittes wasn't going to look good on screen. Not at all.

If Etta wanted to try to clean him up, let her.

THEY PARTED WAYS at the office, and Candy went back to becoming an online researcher. She supposed she ought to be grateful that she didn't yet have to paw through dusty stacks of files.

To her pleasure, the database had spit out two matches: Ivy H. Bride had married James Flannery. And an Ivy Bride had changed her name to Ivy Cain. Candy made a note to add that to her search.

Hoping there was more, Candy resumed waiting. She didn't want to interrupt the search at this stage. Not yet. She could check on these names when no additional information popped up.

She hoped it would pop up soon, because she'd made up her mind to accompany Steve to the Castelles' house.

Because she wanted to judge for herself exactly what he was doing.

Suspicion kept gnawing at her. The psychic had increased it just by being called in. What if it hadn't been Steve's producer who had introduced Wittes? What if it had been Steve himself?

Then there were all the questions about the Castelles. The whole thing was getting awfully murky.

Chapter Thirteen

Steve was surprised, but not annoyed, when he found Candy parked out in front of his motel room in her official SUV.

Well, well, well, he thought as he joined her. Was she becoming interested? Or just answering her budding cop's instincts that something other than a ghost was going on?

"What did Wittes tell you?" she asked.

"Oh, some stuff about an angry man hanging around and a woman who was mad because she'd been killed."

Candy sighed. "Sounds awfully familiar."

"Yeah. But he gets another bite at the apple tomorrow. If he has no more to add that doesn't fit in with what Tate told us, he's out. As it is, my producer would have to run him through a car wash and a barbershop and buy him new clothes."

"Would she?"

Steve chucked quietly. "She'd have to. Think of audience reactions if he appears looking like he came off skid row." Then he paused. "Guess that's unfair to homeless people."

"It is," she agreed. "Many are vets, to begin with. Then there's the fact you can only sink so low before you have no chance at a job anymore."

Steve knew that to be true. In his job he'd dealt with many homeless people, like one guy who worked six days a week as a dishwasher in a restaurant. Not enough money to get an apartment, but he wasn't at all what people thought of when they thought of the homeless. He'd heard too many stories like that.

"Are you planning to stay all night?" Steve asked her.

"Believe it."

He let it go. He was sure she had her reasons, but equally sure he wouldn't like some of them. Better not to know. Hell, she was probably suspicious of him again. She'd started there, so why wouldn't she finish there?

So much for his sense that she was coming to believe he wasn't running a con. Maybe Wittes had something to do with that. Well, he was wondering if Wittes was a con, too.

Some people, he reminded himself, just wanted the attention.

The Castelles welcomed them pleasantly enough and said the three of them were going to their bedroom for the night.

"No TV," Steve admonished them.

"We get it," Todd replied. "Can one of us at least read to Viv until she falls asleep?"

"Sure," said Steve. "Before it gets really dark, which is soon, I want to check out the foundation around her room. I've got some good light with me, so maybe we'll check out the barn, too."

"Be careful of your footing out there," Todd warned. "The floor is uneven and old."

Then the family disappeared into the back.

"The foundation?" Candy asked.

"Everything. It would make this easier if you'd shine a light from the far side as I go. I want to see if there are any openings at all."

"For rats or mice?" she asked humorously.

"For loose stones that might make a man-sized opening if they were moved."

He could see that she approved. Good. He was no fly-by-night who'd overlook something that obvious.

Then the barn, which could be a good hiding place since the Castelles rarely went out there, if they even had since they bought this land.

Barns. There were lots of spooky stories around them. It would please his fans to see him investigate a derelict outbuilding, not that that was his reason. Nope. He wasn't in the business of skipping over possibilities.

An hour later, the two of them sat on the cold-hardened ground, leaning back against the foundation.

"Something isn't right," Steve said.

"How so? We didn't find any light shining through anywhere."

"And that's what's wrong." He realized that he was sitting on a stone and lifted himself a bit to pull it away. "One stone. I always find it when sleeping in a tent."

She laughed quietly. "Me, too."

"Anyway, as to what's wrong. Does that foundation look like it's sagged anywhere?"

She thought for a minute. "Actually, no."

"Well, it should have, if it's sitting on bare earth. There must be a slab of some kind under that room."

"That tells us what?"

He stared toward the darkened hulk of the barn. "Maybe nothing. I couldn't see anywhere that it was open, and I sure didn't see anything in Viv's room that looked like even the smallest door. Besides, how would anyone get in there without becoming stuck for fear of discovery? I'll have to think about it."

"Yeah. I will, too."

"Anyway, tomorrow the barn." He'd changed his mind about doing it tonight. It was so dark he wasn't sure the few lights would be enough for the close search he wanted.

Even in the darkness he could sense her looking his way. "How could that possibly be involved?"

"I don't know. That's for me to find out. Come with?"

"Sure. I'm starting to enjoy this. What's next?"

That was good news, he thought. In a way it *was* like a treasure hunt.

"Let's go back inside. I'm planning to stay in Viv's room tonight to see if I can hear anything. I'm mostly convinced that some sound is traveling through her wall, either up or down. Or it could be a sound bouncing off the wall. I hope I get to hear it."

"And me?"

"I'd like you in the attic, close to that wall. Maybe you'll catch something." He paused. "I hope I can find something rational tonight, just to put that kid out of her misery."

"Let's go. It's getting cold out here."

"Yeah."

The house was warmer by far, however much he'd been warned that it would be chilly. From the sounds, everyone was asleep now. Good.

"It's going to be cold up there," Steve said.

"Some of the house's heat will get up there. Anyway, I'm dressed for the outdoors."

"I hope you can get comfortable."

But there was nothing he could do about that. Maybe one of the lingering pieces of furniture would help with that.

First, he climbed to the attic to make sure all the equipment was working.

"Since we're listening for sounds, you can keep the lights on. Anyway, the mind tries to fill in the darkness."

"I'm familiar with that."

He supposed she was. Then he headed down to the basement and checked everything. If there were any noises down there, the recorders should catch it.

Then back to Viv's room. He debated whether to lie on the bed, then decided he could sit on the floor with his head against the wall.

Settled against the wall, he listened to a house as quiet as any could be. The heat kicking on, rattling the floor vents just a little. Wind against the windows.

And nothing that sounded remotely like a voice.

He settled in for a long, uncomfortable night.

AT ABOUT FOUR in the morning, he heard it. A faint voice, as if it came from far away. Too faint to make out words, but with the rhythms of speech.

Annoyed that he couldn't just start running upstairs and down, he hoped it wasn't too faint for the recorders to pick up. It shouldn't be.

Then the sound stopped. A few minutes later, Candy came down from the attic.

"Steve," she whispered. "Sorry for deserting my post, but I heard a faint voice."

He stood, bending and twisting to work out the night's stiffness. "Me, too. Well, we know it's there. And now we know it's traveling through a wall. Either we have a wandering spirit or we've got something with a real cause. Let's close down for the night and let the recorders do their work."

"Then?"

"I'm going to think hard about where that sound could be coming from and what could cause it. Because something sure as hell is."

CANDY WAS A bit shaken by having heard the voice. She hadn't expected to hear anything at all. Not a thing. She'd wanted to believe this was a wild-goose chase, even though they needed to help Vivian.

But how could they go to the parents and say that Vivian was hearing something real, but they couldn't solve the problem?

Although, according to Steve, he'd done that before. But

she didn't believe that simply saying it was no threat would make Vivian feel any better. She was too young for that.

As they drove back to town, she glanced at the time. "Too late to try to sleep," she said, although she wanted to desperately.

"Same here. Maybe I'll go to the truck stop and load up on caffeine and an early breakfast."

"Mind if I join you?"

"I'd like that."

And he definitely would. "Your computer still searching?"

"It was when I left the office. Two possibilities. I want more."

"I can sure understand that. Maybe we can brainstorm our problem a bit."

Any excuse, she thought. She was strangely reluctant to leave Steve. Man, this was getting complicated, and about more than the Castelles.

She gave up. Changes were afoot inside her, and she didn't know how to stop them. She was just going to have to live with a hole deep inside when he left town.

The prospect was gloomy.

THE DINER WAS warm enough, but not hot. Long-haul trucks filled the parking lot, growling as drivers let them run. Maybe some were sleeping in their cabs. They might find it easier to drive on dark roads, but sleep made demands, too. Plus, they probably couldn't drive more than a certain number of hours at a stretch by law.

The diner, as well as warm enough, was busy. No doubt this was the time when the business made most of its money. They were surrounded by drivers digging into hearty breakfasts.

Which was exactly what Steve intended to do. Two sides

of ham, for one. Four eggs. Four slices of toast, and something called a cheesy potato casserole.

Candy wasn't far behind in her order. Apparently being up all night made her hungry, too. She spread marmalade on her toast while he was content with the butter.

"Any ideas?" she asked. "We haven't discovered any way that a human could get close enough to that house to make that voice."

"It's bothering you, huh?"

She frowned at her scrambled eggs. "Yeah, it is. I don't believe in woo-woo. That was…"

"Like woo-woo," he agreed. "I'd suggest a speaker of some kind, maybe automatically timed. But I think I'd have found something like that in the basement."

"Or in the wall?"

He shook his head. "I'm finding it hard to believe that a local electrician would have anything to do with that. Besides, they had the work done in their office. No joint wall with Vivian's room."

"That room kind of sticks out into nowhere," she remarked. "For myself I think I'd have used that for an office and given Vivian the office space."

"That's an idea. Maybe I'll suggest it if we can't find an answer." Now he frowned. "I can think of one person who might have put a speaker in a wall, and it's not an electrician."

"Todd."

He sighed and reached for his ham, beginning to slice it into mouth-sized pieces. "I've seen too much, Candy, but this is one I don't want to believe even though I've seen similar situations in the past."

"I hear you." She absolutely did. "Maybe we should have checked the office for the sounds."

"I'm certainly going to get around to it. At this point,

though, I'm more worried about another agent. Now *that* could be a significant physical threat."

"What about a serious talk with Todd about his past?"

"Next on the menu. Maybe before the barn."

Candy nodded. "I think it's time."

Then he shocked her to her very core. "After this is over…"

She looked at him, waiting attentively.

"Man, I can't believe I'm going to be this boorish. Candy, I want you. But even more importantly, I want to get to know you. Really know you. You're like a puzzle box, and I want to turn the key."

She couldn't catch her breath. What was he saying? Sex was one thing, a dangerous thing, especially for women who tended to get emotionally involved. "I'm not a puzzle, Steve."

It was the only objection she could honestly offer.

"I'm not sure I meant it that way. Or maybe you are. But more and more I need to know you better outside this hunt. I'm fascinated."

Nobody had ever claimed to be fascinated by her before. Nor had anyone ever tried to get to know her much beyond the surface.

Her squad had known her as a soldier. They knew how much they could depend on her, what kind of fighter she was, but they'd never really gotten personal. Maybe because when you got to know someone under those circumstances, grief might not be far behind. Besides, the guys had been pretty much superficial with each other. Gab about letters from home, pictures of the kids. Sexual exploits.

Easy-to-share stuff.

Some of them had seemed to grow deeper friendships, but what had really mattered was the brotherhood, and she'd been invited inside it. She had become one of them. But there were plenty of places none of them went, as far as she knew. Self-protection. Like the saying, *Don't get to know the FNGs*. The freaking new guys. Because they were inexperienced, they might be gone soon.

But now here was a guy who wanted to get past that point with her. She hadn't wanted to risk sex with him, but this was an even bigger risk.

She cleared her throat. "You'll be leaving in a couple of weeks."

"I'm talking about hanging around for a while. About building a friendship that can last longer than this job. Just think about it, if you can. If you don't want to…" He shrugged. "I'm a boor and you can just pretend I never said that."

Pretend was the right word for it, because it *would* be pretending. God, what to do now?

She honestly didn't know. All she knew was that with a few words he'd made her ache for a future she'd never believed would happen.

It also meant getting raw and exposed and vulnerable in ways she wasn't sure she could anymore.

"Thank you," she said finally and left it there. For safety's sake.

STEVE WANTED TO kick himself in the butt for pushing her that way. But there seemed to be no way to really get through to Candy that wasn't blunt. All the cards on the table where she could see them. Maybe no more suspicion about what he might want from her.

If she believed him, anyway.

Hell's bells. He'd never wanted to get that close to a woman, but now he did. A fling was one thing. This was no fling he was talking about. He didn't know where it might lead, if it ever happened, but with this woman he wanted to chance it.

After Candy left for the office and he settled on the bed

in his motel room, he dragged his thoughts away from her and tossed around the Castelle case like a ball, one side to the other. Maybe mentally batting it against the wall.

He wanted to shake something out, but he still didn't have enough. He was by no means ready to ascribe all this to paranormal entities, residual energy or anything like that.

Proof. He always demanded it and hated it when he couldn't find any. There had been cases when all he could do was assure people they weren't in any danger. This time he couldn't even do that because of Todd's past.

Usually there was no measurable threat, just people who mainly wanted to be assured they weren't losing their minds. He understood that.

But this was different because of Vivian. There was no evidence that anyone or anything wanted to harm her physically, but that wasn't enough. She was being harmed in another way, a vital way.

Todd was willing to ditch the house and move. Steve would have given him props for that except it was possible that he knew how Annabelle would respond, knowing she wouldn't want to leave.

Or it might be that Todd didn't believe his past could be a threat. Also possible.

But then what? Damn, there were dried peas rattling around in this can somewhere and he needed to find one. Just one, to get him started in a useful direction.

But maybe he was already on that path and just hadn't pulled out the information that would show him.

A bedroom with nothing under it but a foundation and a slab. Sounds he'd heard last night, sounds that Candy had heard, as well. Traveling through that wall as if it were wires to a phone.

He tended to discount the speaker idea, but he wasn't

ready to throw that off the table. Nothing would be discarded until he knew he was clearly on track.

Dena was in an earlier time zone, so he wasn't especially surprised when she called him shortly after seven.

"Nothing on the street so far," she reported. "I'll keep feelers out, but you know these drug operations are pretty strong on secrecy. The Pentagon could learn something from them."

He didn't doubt it, he thought as he walked into the shower. To get anything out of these drug rings you had to plant someone on the inside. Difficult and dangerous. Then you had the problem of cops who fell into the dark side after living that life for so long. They closed up like clams.

First a talk with Todd, he decided. Then the barn. He had become fixated on it. If he could find evidence that someone was hiding in there...

Then what? How would the guy be scaring Vivian?

It was another stone to turn over. He was willing to turn stones over until his fingers were bloody. And then more.

He couldn't stop thinking about Vivian. About that little girl who needed to be rescued from something or someone.

No way was he going to leave her in a lurch.

IT WAS TEN before he phoned Candy, hoping she'd managed to get some sleep.

"Hey," she said.

Her voice didn't sound as if she'd slept much. Well, neither had he, and with another night investigation coming up, they needed to manage a few Zs somehow.

"Anything?" he asked.

"We'll see. I came up with more than a dozen Ivy Brides. Who would have thought the name would be that common. Anyway, more seem to still be popping up, so

I'll let this run a while longer before I start investigating them individually."

He had no problem with that. "Wanna go with me soon?"

"Sure…"

Her voice trailed off. A ruckus sounded in the background and Candy cursed vigorously.

"I gotta go, Steve."

"What's up?"

"A repeat of the other day. Two more."

Now it was his turn to cuss. Two more? Hadn't Wittes said there'd be more?

But his primary reaction was feeling his stomach turn over and his mind kick into detective mode.

"Tell the sheriff my skills are available if he needs them."

"Sure." She disconnected.

God, he hoped she didn't have to go to the scene. Watching the video feed had messed her up enough.

He sat a while thinking about this. Two more murders. Maybe in keeping with the old lore? Tate had quoted the stories as saying there had been four murders.

A week before Halloween. Man, he'd be surprised if any parent let their youngsters go door-to-door.

Which always disappointed kids from what he'd seen. The adventure of trick-or-treating vanished at a big party.

But now he'd have to deal with a frightened, possibly angry, town that had already focused on him, the outsider.

He swore again, torn between the two halves of himself: the cop and the TV host. No way he could do both.

And there was still a little girl who desperately needed help to return to a normal life.

But there were also two double murders, and since there'd been no major release of information on the first two, it was evident that the case hadn't been solved.

He was left wondering for the umpteenth time how humans could do this to each other. Stupid question. If he wondered, Candy could tell him.

Because that woman had seen it with her own eyes.

CANDY TRIED TO stay in the background. Watching the video had been troubling enough, but to have to go live to the scene… Well, she wondered how she'd handle it.

Yeah, she'd seen it in the Army, but that was in the past as much as she could shove it there. This might awaken the absolute worst of her nightmares.

But… She was a cop now. She'd have to face this sooner or later.

She stiffened herself, seeking her backbone. She could do it. She might have to.

Then Gage approached. "I'm a little shorthanded this morning."

Here it came.

"Who found them?" she asked, hoping her voice sounded steady. Or hard. She needed the hardening, and it was growing like ice within her.

"I've got four people out. One of them's sick. Another three left town on vacation. Mainly because I thought we'd be quiet for a while. We were hoping it was someone with a grudge. Nobody expected this to happen again."

"Why would anyone? Who found them?" she asked again.

"A couple of hunters. I expect they're being sick behind some trees."

She might do that, too.

"Candy…"

"I'll go out there." She heard the steel in her own voice. Combat mode was taking over.

"Thanks. If you get out there and feel it's too much, let me know. I can manage somehow."

But why should he? He'd given her this opportunity

when no one else would. She didn't want to fail him. Not on a case as important as this.

"I'll be fine." She hoped. Then she added, "You know Steve Hawks's background. Former detective? He offered to help if you want him."

"I may need everyone I can get my hands on. Tell him he's on standby. This has to stop, and there's only one way."

CANDY DROVE OUT to the site, following her GPS. Her hands were steady on the wheel. The shakes and nausea had vanished for now. For now.

Why should Conard County be immune from the ugliness of people? Her vain hopes had been just that: vain. Now she was in the thick of it, and she knew how to manage. Later, after it was over, she might face other problems.

And she'd deal as she always had. Because she must.

Seeking refuge, she returned her thoughts to the Castelles. She hoped Steve continued his investigation for Vivian's sake. That little girl was still alive, unlike these latest victims. She deserved a kind of priority.

But her mind wouldn't let her off the hook for long. Instead she braced for the coming hours.

STEVE REALLY DIDN'T want to pursue the Castelle case. Not now. His internal tug-of-war was strengthening. Vivian, he reminded himself.

Somehow the Castelles had already heard about the murders. Maybe the grapevine had reached rapid-fire. Regardless of how they'd heard, they were visibly shaken.

Annabelle grabbed him as he came through the door. "You don't think… Vivian?"

"I don't see how these cases could be related." But he wasn't going to dismiss the possibility.

"Todd? I needed to talk to you privately." Might as well get this much out of the way.

"Sure," Todd answered. "Outside."

It was cold as hell out there this morning, but Steve agreed. He didn't want Annabelle or Vivian to hear any of this.

Out back, with Buddy running around like an overgrown demon, he faced Todd. "I need the truth from you, and I need it now."

For the first time Todd looked more than uneasy. He looked frightened.

Steve continued. "I heard about your drug conviction. Cocaine. Rehab."

Todd's nod was jerky. "Yeah. Rehab worked."

"Did it? Honestly? Look, I'm not a cop anymore, but I sure as hell need to know all the possibilities if I'm going to help your daughter."

Todd's gaze slid away. "Yeah, it worked. But maybe what worked more was Annabelle packing to leave and take Vivian with her. That's part of the reason we moved out here, to try to rebuild our marriage. I wasn't sure she'd ever forgive me. I'm still not convinced she has, at least not completely."

"Okay. I wondered. But there's something else." Steve looked at him again.

"Did you leave the city while you owed someone money? Even a small amount." Because drug dealers sometimes made an example for even the smallest sums. Nobody was allowed to cheat them.

"I don't think so. I spent the last two years paying the guy off. It wasn't easy with the interest."

"Did they threaten you? Vivian? Annabelle?"

Todd shook his head. "I was paying them. They never said a word about my family."

Steve wasn't sure about that, even if it hadn't been explicitly stated. He sighed. Maybe this wasn't totally cleared up after all. Steve had needed a time-payment plan. This whole deck would be a lot cleaner if he had paid up front. But the odd thing about cocaine. It was expensive to begin with and as the need grew so did the cost.

"Okay," he said to Todd. "I won't mention it elsewhere."

At last Todd looked relieved. "Thanks."

Don't thank me too soon, he thought as he followed Todd back inside. He still had to recheck all his recording equipment in case he'd missed something.

He wondered if Candy would escape before he went to the barn. He might well need her help.

She'd become his right hand, and now he was glad his crew wasn't here. At this point he didn't need the confusion they'd bring.

But he might not have a show here at all.

And he didn't care.

CANDY WALKED TOWARD the bodies, her stride purposeful. She'd forgotten her qualms and was now focused. As in battle.

Never had she dreamed she'd need that mind-set again.

The area was roped off with crime scene tape. Men in clean suits were scouring the area around it. A weapon. They needed a weapon.

Candy looked at the two teens, a boy and a girl, and seriously doubted a weapon had been used. She knew what those kinds of wounds looked like. Too well.

"Looks like the same thing," Gage said.

She nodded. "They were drugged."

"How can you be sure?"

"I've seen everything any kind of weapon can do, from knives to guns to bombs. Unless you turn them over and find something, I have to conclude they were drugged before they were brought here."

Gage nodded. "The thought had crossed my mind."

"Were they an item?"

"I believe so. I seem to remember them dating."

"Probably. Else why take them both? Any toxicology on the first two?"

"Not yet."

"Hell." She stared, her feelings silenced. "What are you going to do?"

"You mean apart from the investigation? Plant posters and warnings all over town. Take your kids to the party at the high school or keep them home."

"Good idea. I'd assume at this point, though, that the very young kids would be safe."

"But that's not a reliable assumption. I'll get the teens who are staging the party to set a room aside for the little ones. Maybe soften the haunted house. I'm sure they will, under the circumstances."

Candy nodded, using her eyes to seek more information. Then the techs arrived with their yellow numbered markers. Someone called out that he'd found a trail that looked as if the kids had been dragged.

A drag trail. That fit with Candy's idea of drugs. But how? "I hope they'll check stomach contents."

Gage nodded. "That's one thing we can do here."

"But not the toxicology?"

"Not complete enough. There are some things the local hospital can't look for. Not yet anyway. Not enough call for it."

Candy understood, but she sighed anyway. Waiting on information wouldn't prevent another set of murders. They needed to find the killer.

Just as Steve needed to find a perp so he could help Vivian.

STEVE SET ABOUT reviewing all his equipment for any signs that someone had been in this house. Or that a spook had been making noise.

Several hours later he had nothing except the faint sounds coming up the wall that both he and Candy had heard. He didn't want to tell that to the Castelles, because it would only confirm their ideas about the paranormal.

Not yet. He needed more before he fell back on that. Much more than rhythms of speech coming through that wall.

He decided to leave all his equipment in place, then saw Ben Wittes in the driveway. Oh, for God's sake. Like he needed that idiot right now.

But Annabelle let him in anyway. Steve met him in the hallway. "What's up?"

"I told you there'd be more murders. My spirit guide says it's the guy who killed his wife. Talking. Mumbling."

Steve wanted to sigh. Nothing there. Finally he busted the guy's bubble. "You need to tell me something that isn't part of the legends that appear to have been created by local kids years ago. No real murders showed up in police reports back then."

Ben closed his eyes, then snapped them open. "Maybe they didn't find the victims. Or maybe he wasn't strong enough to do it back then. He's strong enough now."

Steve heard a small sound behind him and swung around to see Vivian hiding behind her mother, her face peeping out and looking terrified.

"That does it," he said. "Vivian doesn't want you here. You're fired. And if you come back, no one will let you in this house. You understand?"

Fury flickered across Ben Wittes's face, then vanished.

"If that's the way you want it," he grumbled. "But you'll be sorry if you miss more information."

"You haven't provided one useful thing. If you think you've got something better, then find me in town. Now go."

Steve was surprised at the amount of relief he felt as Wittes disappeared down the driveway.

He turned to look at Annabelle and Vivian.

"Are you sure that was wise?" Annabelle asked.

"He offered nothing that I wasn't able to find out from the old sheriff. Besides—" he squatted and spoke to Vivian "—you didn't like him, did you?"

She shook her head. Then she did something that tore his heart. She put her thumb in her mouth.

"I promise he won't come back."

"Good," Vivian said around her thumb. "Buddy."

Annabelle spoke. "He's out back, honey. Want him inside?"

Buddy came charging in, apparently glad of the warm temperature. Well, yeah. That dog had an awfully short coat. Maybe that was why he'd been running nonstop out there.

Vivian went to the kitchen table, forgetting her thumb. "Chocolate," she said firmly.

Annabelle smiled. "I should take out stock in the instant cocoa business."

"Sounds like a great idea," Steve said cheerfully. "I'm going to take a look at your barn, if that's okay?"

"Go ahead," Annabelle answered.

And where had Todd gone? Steve wondered. Had he just disappeared because Steve had raked up bad memories? Or because he hadn't been honest with the whole story?

Hell, there was no way to know if the guy simply wouldn't tell him.

Frustrated, Steve headed out to the barn. Waste of his time, probably, but no stone left unturned. A major rule of his life.

CANDY RETURNED HOME around seven in the evening. She'd picked up a sandwich for dinner but had no desire to eat it. Habit had made her buy it. Not even habit could make her eat right then.

It was hitting her, she realized. Damn, she had feared this, but there was no way to stop it now. She had been cast back into places she never wanted to go again, and now those memories were swimming with memories of what she had seen today.

More hideous reality. Would she never escape it?

But the wish vanished in the memories. She began to shake. Had to run to vomit. Returned to her kitchen on shaky legs and tried to make coffee but dropped the pot twice and gave up.

Then she collapsed at the table and let the sobbing begin. Tears, so many tears, some of them unshed for so long that they demanded to join the outpouring.

Maybe she was in the wrong job after all. But she recoiled from that idea. Where would she go? What would she do?

She felt trapped in past and present, unable to live with herself, unable to do anything else. She couldn't quit. She wasn't a quitter, and whenever suicide tried to drift through her mind, she tossed it away much more easily than memory.

Those kids. Those poor kids. But how many other kids had she seen die? Eighteen-year-olds wearing the same uniform as hers. Others, as young as ten or twelve in raggedy clothes, dead because they'd been in the wrong place.

Too many kids by far. She couldn't fight it any longer. Memory was taking over and everything else disappeared.

She even smelled gunpowder. Heard explosions and gunfire. She was back in the 'Stan now with more kids riding her shoulders. The weight threatened to crush her.

She hardly heard a familiar voice say, "The door was open…"

Then Steve's strong arms surrounded her tightly. Hanging on to her as if he wanted to stop her fall. But nothing could. Nothing.

One of those big hands stroked her hair but she was hardly aware of it. Lost within herself, she couldn't find a way out.

She continued sobbing.

STEVE SWEPT HER up in his arms when he felt her soften just a bit and carried her to her bed. Then, lying beside her, he felt her soak his shirt with her tears, felt the tremors run through her. Could almost feel the memories that were swamping her.

Though he had some himself that would never leave him, he knew they were nothing like Candy's. If ever he'd wished for a magic wand, he did now.

And he hated wars because they did this to people. All people.

A LONG TIME LATER, Candy's tears dried, and her body stopped shaking. He was relieved when she fell asleep.

He wouldn't leave, though. She was going to wake feeling fragile, and he refused to disturb her sleep.

Sleep was healing, and she needed every bit of it she could get.

He wished he knew if being a cop might eventually desensitize her to memories. Like immersion therapy. Afraid of spiders? Then look at dozens of photos of spiders. Then observe them for real. Maybe eventually let them crawl on you.

But it probably wouldn't, he decided. This wasn't like spiders or anything similar. This was a great gaping wound in her psyche. A little spackle and paint wouldn't patch it.

A grim prospect. He had to hope that time would help her heal. But she'd been doing pretty well so far. She'd landed a job, she appeared to be functioning in it.

Then there was today. He bet she'd gone out to the murder scene this time. Because at her very core she was tough. Tough as steel.

He liked the woman he knew now. But he damn well admired her strength, especially given where she'd been.

She didn't want to see her family for fear of the questions they would ask, worried that they'd see how much she had changed and would start poking around.

Well, that sounded like a good family, the kind he'd like. Someone just needed to suggest to them that they ought to stay away from anything she didn't mention herself.

That thing about feeling responsible for her brother's death really cut at him, though. She didn't deserve to feel that way, and her brother most decidedly didn't deserve it. Give the guy his due for choosing to enlist. Candy hadn't held him at gunpoint.

But how could anyone convince her of that? Guilt didn't yield to logic. Ever.

He closed his eyes, enjoying having her tucked up against him. He wondered if she'd ever open up to him, a prerequisite for any deep relationship, even friendship.

That was a decision she had to make for herself, however. She had to come to trust him enough, and he couldn't see any way to make that happen.

Sleep crept up on him at last, carrying him away into a world of confusing dreams that were half born of the Castelle situation, half born of his concerns for Candy, and the rest, around the edges, about four hideous murders.

Even sleep didn't offer him real escape.

STEVE AWOKE WHILE it was still dark outside, not that it meant much at this time of year, not in these parts anyway.

Candy had slipped away. He could smell soaps and shampoos and feel humidity: a shower. That sounded good to him, too, but pointless. He didn't have a change of clothing.

More important, he wanted to see Candy, to see if she was doing better now.

The aroma of coffee pulled him down the hallway to the kitchen. The pot, still mostly full, issued an invitation. After he filled a mug, he went looking and found Candy seated in the living room, her feet up on a sofa, staring into space.

Keeping quiet, he sat in a chair across from her. She'd speak when she was ready. Or not.

She looked like hell, though. The dark circles under her eyes announced the rough night she'd had.

She spoke at last. "You must need to get to work."

Was that a suggestion that he should leave? If so, he was in no mood to listen. Not when she looked like that. The Castelles could damn well wait a few hours.

He decided to speak, choosing to focus on his work. It seemed like the only safe topic right now.

"I fired the psychic yesterday."

Her gaze found him. "Really? I thought you couldn't."

"I have *some* pull," he answered. "It's *my* show, after all. They give me too much trouble, I walk. Believe me, I know how to walk away."

She nodded wearily. "I guess you do."

Except from her. Stubbornly, he stayed where he was. "You got any time today?"

"All day. Gage told me not to come in. But he didn't tell me not to do my liaising with you."

"So you work anyway." Better for her than thinking about dead kids. Gage was right about that. The man must be pretty good at judging the emotional state of his deputies.

"Yeah," she answered listlessly. "Why'd you fire Wittes?"

"Because he sounds like a rerun of the lore Tate told us about. Nothing new, just a story that may or may not unjustly accuse a man no one even remembers now. Pretty rotten eulogy, if you ask me."

"I agree."

"But he wasn't the only reason. He scared Vivian."

She appeared to be fully reentering the present. "I'm not surprised, Steve. He'd scare any little kid, and some adults."

"No kidding." He sipped his cooling coffee, ignoring the loss of heat. Hers must have reached room temperature by now, but even though he could have refilled their mugs, he decided not to. All that seemed to be pulling her back from the precipice was focusing on something safe... like his ghost hunt.

Ha. Safe? This whole thing was beginning to appear less safe by the hour. His cop senses had gone on full alert.

"I'm not sure those murders aren't related to the Castelle situation." Damn! Bad timing to bring up the killings. Where was his head at? The wrong place. He'd evidently lost some caution in the years since he'd quit his department.

But she didn't withdraw, didn't pull into herself. Her gaze had become clearer. The night's storm seemed to have passed for now.

"You're giving me chills," she remarked. "I need more coffee. Hot this time."

"I could run out and get us lattes, if you want." Much as he didn't want to leave her, he'd have crawled over glass to do just one thing to make her feel that someone cared. To make her feel even a tiny bit better.

It shook him a little to realize he'd seldom cared that much for another person. Willing to give the shirt off his back, but to crawl on glass? Oh, he had it bad.

She smiled slightly. "I'd like that, if you don't mind."

He rose. "I don't mind at all. What about breakfast? I'm sure Maude will dish up something good. Anything in particular?"

"Her home fries. I seem to be craving carbs."

"I'm not surprised." Not at all. That kind of stress, or even shock, required something to pump the blood sugar up.

He pulled on his jacket, not caring how scruffy he probably looked by now. Showering and changing could wait for a better time. He figured he must be breaking the town's speed limit on his way to the diner.

But it was still early, and there were few cars on the road. Maude's seemed to have just opened, and only a handful people sat scattered among the tables.

"I heard," Maude said to him across the counter.

"Yeah. Candy's...well."

Maude nodded. "Ex-soldier, now this. Not what she expected from this job. Load her up?"

"She specifically mentioned your home fries."

Maude frowned, which he was learning to recognize as her smile. "And more," she said decisively. "You, too?"

"Filling the tanks," he agreed.

He left with four foam containers instead of the two he'd expected, and four extralarge lattes. Maude signaled one of the breakfast customers. "Help Steve here out to his car. Don't want them lattes spilling. They're for Candy."

Making it even more clear this was caretaking. The guy she had called over smiled faintly. "You betcha. Gotta take care of that girl."

"Girl?" Maude snorted. "She's done more in her life than you'd ever want to see, Bill. She ain't no *girl.*"

Steve wanted to applaud, but Maude didn't seem like the right woman to applaud. Bill helped him get everything safely stashed in his rental, an achievement with all that coffee. Then Steve was driving back, this time at a sane pace.

It took him three trips, but he put all the bounty on the kitchen table. Candy emerged from the living room and looked at everything. "Did you rob her?"

"Maude made up the order. Was I going to argue? I bet one of her glares could turn me to ash."

That drew an almost natural smile from Candy. She reached first for a coffee and swallowed half of it before at last taking a seat.

Steve, meanwhile, opened the containers, revealing enough fried potatoes to feed a small army, followed by a load of scrambled eggs with a stack of bacon, then generous slices of pineapple with a side of cherries. And finally a container filled with some kind of coffee cake.

"Fit for a king," he remarked as he gathered up utensils and plates. "Dig in."

She finished the first latte, so he pushed a second toward her.

"Want a shot of whiskey in that?"

Her gaze rose to his face. "Do you have any?" She sounded surprised.

"Hell no, but I always thought it would be cool to carry a flask."

Another smile, a small sound that might have been an attempt to laugh. She was taking her first steps toward relaxing. He was delighted to see her reaching for potatoes, fruit and bacon. The eggs didn't seem to interest her, but he could take care of that himself.

She spoke when she'd made a remarkable dent on breakfast. "You have plans for today?"

"Absolutely. Join me, please. I've got more tapes and recordings to run through, and I'm thinking about a second walk-through with my infrared camera. Then there's the barn. I did a quick scan yesterday, but a second pair of eyes would be helpful, if you're willing."

She nodded, eating another slice of pineapple before taking a piece of coffee cake. "That barn keeps drawing your attention. Are you sure you're not obsessed?"

"Who, me? No, it's just that it seems like a good hiding

place. I need to explore it for signs someone might have been hanging around in there."

"Reasonable." She put her fork down. "I've overdone it. I don't think I'll want to eat for a week."

That made him laugh. "You want me to bet on that?"

She looked almost sheepish. "I had a lot of training in *eat when you can because you don't know when you'll get another chance.*"

"I believe it. It's good to see you filling up, though. And I'm catching up."

"Do you work out a lot to keep that figure?"

Well, that was the most personal thing she'd ever said to him. He liked it. "Some. I don't overdo it, though. Doing it for health is one reason. Doing it for show is another."

He cleaned up when they were done, not a difficult task. A few items in the dishwasher, a few leftovers in the fridge.

"Ready to go?" he asked.

Chapter Fourteen

Candy didn't wear her uniform. She sat beside Steve in jeans, a yellow sweater and a quilted jacket. Leather gloves protected her hands.

"What's first?" she asked. "Barn? House?"

"I see clouds on the horizon, so I want to do the barn first, while we still have decent light."

Winter had stolen the last color from the landscape, and the cold ground crunched under their feet as Steve began to pull some industrial-sized flashlights from his trunk.

"Want one?" he asked.

"Oh, come on." She liked his impish smile. Heck, she liked a lot about him, mostly that he hadn't just run last night. She wouldn't have blamed him if he had.

A lot of people couldn't handle her episodes. She'd learned that the hard way, losing friends she'd made since her discharge. She hadn't lost any here yet, but then they hadn't seen her the way Steve had seen her last night. She was just glad she hadn't flown into a rage, something that happened occasionally. Rarely, but it *did* happen.

Steve stuck his head in the house to tell the Castelles what they were doing. Candy half expected Todd to follow them, but he didn't.

"There was more mumbling," Steve said as he joined her on the walk to the barn. "Vivian's still upset."

"She wasn't in her room, was she?"

"No, in the hallway early this morning. On her way to the bathroom."

"Damn. That kid ought to be able to go to the bathroom without terror."

"You'd think."

Light filtered through loose slats in the barn, beams that bounced off enough dust to make them visible.

"Dang," Candy said. "Was it windy last night? What stirred up all this dust?"

Steve simply looked at her and she got the message. No ghost should do that.

A familiar uneasiness began to creep up her spine to her neck. *Hostiles.* Then she caught herself. Overreaction.

Steve spoke. "Let's start toward the back. When we get halfway through, we can climb the ladders to the hayloft and check around."

The loft might be the most dangerous place in this barn if anyone was here.

Candy's backbone was stiffening again. She could feel it. Rising to the demands of the moment. If she'd brought one good thing back from the war, that was it.

The back of the barn wasn't all that interesting. A tack room empty of everything except a ragged halter that at a touch felt too dried out and stiff to ever be used again.

She let go of it, then moved forward with Steve, checking every possible nook, even the decrepit horse stalls. Easy to imagine what this place had once looked like. Filled with horses and hay and other feed. People coming and going. The scent of horses, strangely enough, seemed to linger even after many years.

The loft was still covered with some loose hay. A fire hazard, she thought, but no signs of recent disturbance. Not up here anyway. Then back down and a sweep of the front of the barn. Several times she looked upward because she didn't trust the roof. It sagged too much.

Then her foot snagged on something. A loose board? But when she looked down she saw an old cut.

"Steve? Come take a look at this."

He hurried over, squatting down to peer at the place she indicated with the wide beam of her light.

"That's curious." He straightened and looked around. "My kingdom for some kind of broom."

But Candy was already using her foot to sweep hay and other detritus from the area. The dust in the barn was getting thick. Thick and flammable. She didn't stop and Steve joined her.

Then, with a sweep of his foot, he revealed a large iron ring. He looked at Candy.

"A trapdoor," she said.

Steve stared down again. "It sure looks like one."

He pulled it open, up and back. If they'd expected to find storage, they discovered it empty except for gray boards lining parts of it. Both shined their lights into a dark hole that appeared ten feet deep. The only thing inside it was a handmade ladder, the wood old.

"Weird," Candy said.

"No, look." Excitement crept into Steve's voice. He pointed his light again. "There's a tunnel."

Five minutes later, Steve climbed down into the hole over Candy's strong objections.

"It could collapse on you! Who knows how old this is? Can you trust those ancient boards?"

His expression said he would not be deterred. "You're here to call for help if anything happens. But Candy, this could explain so much. This could be where the voice is coming from."

"I'll allow that, but how do you know someone isn't waiting down there? You could get into all kinds of trouble."

"It's possible, but not likely. If it'll make you feel any

better, we'll sit here listening. If we don't hear anything, I'm going in."

That didn't make her feel one whit better, but she knew when she was running into a brick wall. She gave up arguing. Maybe the boards were strong enough to hold it.

Eventually, Steve refused to wait any longer. "My GPS says the tunnel heads toward the house."

Candy stiffened. God in heaven. Had he found the problem? But then, who might it be? She forced herself to calm down. There was no indication this tunnel ran all the way to the house. Why would it?

Besides, those boards looked too old to have been added recently. Way too old. Maybe there'd been some mining in the past? There were certainly enough old tunnels up on Thunder Mountain to the west.

And now she knew why Steve wore a watch. She hadn't paid it much mind, thinking it was one of those fitness things. Apparently it did more than count his footsteps. GPS. Maybe a compass. Always prepared.

By the beam of her flashlight, and his, she watched him disappear into the dark opening. After a bit, his flashlight diminished, illuminating little from her point of view.

If he went too far, she doubted she'd be able to get him help in time if that tunnel collapsed. Damn, she should never have let him go in alone. Ten or fifteen feet apart might have made one or the other of them much safer, more likely to be able to crawl out for help.

Or not. They might both be sealed in a tomb of tumbling earth and rocks.

Then Steve's head popped out of the tunnel. "There are some fresh boards in here, and something walled off at the end of the tunnel."

"I'm coming in."

"Seems safe enough." He didn't try to dissuade her,

which was good. Hanging around as the protected woman didn't suit her at all.

Moving carefully, she climbed down the old boards, feeling them give a little, but not enough to worry her. These timbers were thick, not simple two-by-fours.

Mining timbers, she thought. An old mine. What good could it be now?

In places she had to crawl, scuffing her knees some despite her jeans. Curiosity drove her forward, following Steve, carrying her own flashlight.

It got dark in a tunnel. Way dark. She was grateful for the beams that stretched a lighted path in front of her.

Steve called out quietly. "There seems to be a wall ahead."

Ten minutes later, they reached the wall he was talking about. She scanned it as he said, "Those are fresh timbers."

She agreed. Water had only just started to darken them.

"Who would...?" She didn't bother to finish the question. Pointless.

Then memory climbed up her throat. "I crawled through tunnels like this in Afghanistan."

His head swiveled to look at her. "You need to get out?"

"No. I made it before, I can do it now. I just wish I had a grenade."

That drew a hollow laugh from him. "I hear you."

Maybe he did. Or her rifle, not that it would make crawling through here any easier. Nah, a grenade.

Unexpectedly, the idea amused her. Some habits died hard, she guessed.

They sat staring at the wall before them.

"It's new," he repeated. "And if my measurements are correct, this may reach under Vivian's bedroom."

She caught her breath. "We've got to get past this. See what's going on."

"Start looking. I'm not too keen on just randomly removing these timbers. If someone is using it, there has to be a way inside."

"Yeah." Candy started running her light around the edges. Good place to begin, she thought. A crumble of dirt from above her head fell and struck her on the back. Her breath nearly stopped in her throat.

But Steve had already rolled on his back, pointing his light upward. "Doesn't seem like much to worry about. A little drying soil. The rest of the timbers look okay."

She wondered about the person or people who had built this tunnel. A lot of work, and those timbers had to be carted in from somewhere else. A heap of determination, but she couldn't imagine the purpose unless somebody had discovered something valuable.

Gold may have washed down from the mountains. Some still did, but not enough to make anyone rich. Silver, too, at times. She'd also seen a lot of tunnels closed off with the radiation trefoil warning. A lot of deadly things were buried deep in the earth, things never meant to be brought above ground in appreciable quantities.

Look at those tailing piles outside the old mining town on Thunder Mountain. To this day, nothing grew on them. She had to wonder what toxic heavy metals were washing down from them into the groundwater, into streams.

Frequent water checks around the town apparently said local water was safe. She wondered, sometimes, if they were accurate.

"Look at this," she said, her gaze suddenly fixing on a narrow line, like a fine cut, finer than the one in the barn floor.

"Damn, your eyes are good."

"Situational awareness," she had briefly. It had never left her.

Steve tapped on it. "It's not that thick."

"I don't see any hinges. Maybe it pulls out?"

He began to test around the edges. He wasn't wearing gloves, so he could feel better. She wasn't ready to ditch her own. It was damn cold down here. Not warmer the way most things underground were, but cold as ice. Her cheeks ached from it.

"There," he said. "A divot, just enough to grip with fingers. You ready?"

"For what? Of course I'm ready. I'm here."

Reaching out, he searched farther. "There we are. A door in this wall."

Her heart had begun to gallop. What were they going to find in there? Nothing good, she suspected.

She reached out to help Steve as he pulled the panel free. Another dark hole greeted them. Light didn't make it look much better.

They crawled in, Steve leading, then he cursed.

"What?"

"I think it's a freaking bomb shelter."

"Wow." She crawled in beside him, scanning the area with her light. Bunks. Water containers. Shelves full of canned foods that had begun to rust. "Another era."

"No kidding. But why an entry out in the barn?"

"Ask the builder," she said drily.

Then everything inside her froze. "Steve? Steve, is that a coffin?"

Steve now saw it, too. Under the bottom bunk. Made roughly of boards like the ones outside. Strangely dust free.

"It looks like one," he agreed. "God. What did we find?"

"Ivy Bride?"

"Ghoulish," he said flatly.

"Don't touch it," she said sharply. "It's time to call for some help."

"Like the sheriff isn't busy enough?"

"It doesn't matter. There are laws against disturbing human remains. You know that, Steve."

He nodded. Of course he knew it. Besides, if there was a body in there, he didn't want to destroy any evidence. Nor would he and Candy learn a thing even if they looked. His detective cap, however, seemed to be pinching his skull.

"Let's go," he said. "We should guard the entry."

Gage arrived twenty minutes later. "You should have called us before you crawled into the tunnel," Gage said when he joined them above ground with four deputies. "Steve, you know better than that."

Steve frowned. "We didn't expect to find anything like that. Dang, Gage, we were just looking for signs that someone might be under Vivian's room making the voices she heard. If that's all we found, we would have still called you. But this?" He shook his head. "Never would have expected it in a million years."

BEN WITTES WATCHED from the distance, the voice in his head growing louder.

They found it. At last.

"What you talkin' about?" Ben demanded of the spirit. "You killed her."

No. I didn't. I just couldn't let go.

Now Ben was truly disturbed. What had he been used for? Why did the spirit want this? What about the angry woman?

"What about the kids killed on the mountain?" Ben demanded of the voice. "You did that."

No.

Just that. *No.* Ben grabbed his head, wanting to crush it with his own hands. He was so confused. So overwhelmed. He couldn't begin to explain it. He just wished it would stop. He didn't want to hear these voices. He didn't *want* to know these things. Why were the spirits tormenting him this way? What had he ever done?

Why had he spent so many nights at the direction of this damn voice sitting down there and talking to that coffin? Singing to it?

To make a dead man happier?

"Go away," Ben said forcefully. "Go now."

The voice laughed. *I'm not done with you yet.*

What the hell did that mean?

Forgetting that he wanted to watch the sheriff uncover all this stuff, he took off running.

Then the voice again. *Find me some more kids.*

No, Ben screamed in his mind. *No!*

He didn't even understand what the spirit meant, but it horrified him.

Wafting up into his terrified brain came memories of waking in the morning covered with dirt. The tunnel? Or something worse?

BY FOUR THAT AFTERNOON, the sheriff's team had pulled the coffin out of its hiding place. Techs crawled everywhere seeking evidence. The bodies on the mountain were going to have to wait awhile.

Steve stood staring into the distance, Candy nearby as she took notes and answered questions.

Two kids. Four now. An old coffin. How could all of this be linked? Because his finely tuned senses told him none of this was coincidence. The voices had been explained, and soon he'd be able to reassure Viv.

But not before this damned coffin was gone. Not until they knew why someone had been sitting down there babysitting that thing.

No true answers until then.

Chapter Fifteen

The last thing Candy and Steve heard about that coffin was that it contained bones. Nothing but bones. Well, Steve thought, that wouldn't reveal much but a medical examiner could find more.

With Halloween two days away, it was sad to see the streets so empty. Local radio had been advising people to take their children to the party at the high school. Posters plastered every light post and flat surface around town.

And not one person had placed a candle in a pumpkin.

The night was growing cold, clouding over with the possibility of snow or rain. An unwelcoming night.

He'd reviewed all the evidence he had from the Castelle house and couldn't even answer their questions about what had happened in the barn. The sheriff's presence had raised plenty of questions for them, but at least they didn't seem to think it could be related in any way to the voices Vivian heard.

Good enough for now.

At nine that night, his cell phone rang. Candy. Her voice sounded as tight as a coiled spring.

"Steve, two more teens have gone missing. We're starting a search on the mountain immediately."

"How long have they been gone?"

"Since shortly after school let out."

Still time, he thought. Still time. "I'm coming, too."

"I'll pick you up."

SHE ROLLED UP in front of the motel, and he was waiting, ready. A heavier jacket this time, gloves, knit cap.

"We've got to find them," she said tensely.

"Alive," he agreed. "At least we've got a general idea of where to look."

Small comfort, she thought. At least these kids hadn't been missing for that long. The others had taken way too long to find. Maybe not this pair.

"Boy and girl?" he asked.

"Yeah. From what I've heard, they decided to walk home from school. Out of town. They both live on ranches, but the houses aren't more than a couple miles from the high school."

"I used to do things like that. It was always fun to be with my girlfriend where no one would bother us."

Candy spoke after a minute or two. "I had a duenna."

He turned on the seat. "Seriously?"

"My family is old-fashioned in some ways. Now that I'm older, I see it differently. Everywhere I went I had protection. My aunt seemed to love it. She visited places she might never have gone otherwise. Heck, at the arcade she got into one of the games. Sometimes I thought I wouldn't be able to pry her away."

"Sounds like a wonderful aunt." Dating must have been difficult, though.

"She was. She always seemed to enjoy watching over me, as if it were a great adventure."

"Maybe for her it was like being a teen again."

"Maybe. I know I chafed at it."

The road had started to climb steeply, then they saw the lights ahead. Flood lamps, flashlights moving through the trees.

Gage stood at a command center, directing the search parties. Radios crackled constantly. Two ambulances stood ready. It looked like half the county had turned out for this one. Just from where Candy stood, she reckoned there were maybe a hundred searchers moving about three feet apart. A good sweep.

She just hoped the teens hadn't been tied up a long distance away.

There was no longer any doubt in anyone's mind what they were looking for. A third case. The first two had set a precedent, but this one would confirm it beyond any doubt.

They had a serial killer.

Two hours later, Candy and Steve heard a faint cry. She took off like a bat out of hell in that direction. Steve dashed after her. Candy's flashlight swept back and forth as she looked out for obstacles or unexpected ravines. He followed suit.

Candy paused, calling out the names of the two students. "Mark? Mabs?"

Again a faint cry, louder this time. A crashing behind them announced that other searchers were on their way. Ten minutes later they reached the two teens, tied to trees facing each other. Cold. Drugged. Only Mabs was awake enough to cry out.

Very soon the medics arrived and survival blankets wrapped the extremely cold pair. A short time later they were carted out of the woods on stretchers.

It was nearly midnight.

On the walk back to the car, Steve said, "I need to get out to the Castelles."

"Why? They must be sleeping by now."

He shook his head. "Candy, someone was in that tunnel. Now six teens have been kidnapped. There's a very strong part of me that can't believe none of this is related. Too much weirdness."

She had to acknowledge that he might be correct. What's more, all the department's activity at the tunnel had ceased when word of the kids' disappearance had reached them. An old coffin containing bones hardly seemed like an emergency.

"I'll go with," she said. Because the feeling had begun to grow in her, as well. A mind that was capable of treating those teens that way was capable of harming Vivian. Urgency rode her as she drove as quickly as she dared toward the Castelles' house.

"Thank God those kids were okay," she remarked. As if they'd ever be okay again. Not after something like that.

Steve's response was short. "They're alive at least."

Consolation, for what it was worth. "You think it could have something to do with Todd's past?"

"I don't know what he might have been withholding. I could hardly threaten him."

Questions plagued her. Drug dealers? She supposed it was possible. Easier to think about than some sicko who'd been walking the streets of this town all his life.

Steve spoke. "Is Candy Serrano your full name?"

What had brought that on? she wondered. "Actually, it's Candela de Serrano."

"That's pretty."

"I've been shortening it since middle school. Candle of the Mountains may have appealed to my parents, but it always seemed like a whole mouthful to me."

"I hope you didn't shorten it because of your heritage. It's beautiful. I just wondered."

Anything to keep from thinking about the danger they might have left behind them at the Castelles'. Never had this drive felt so long.

As soon as they pulled into the driveway, Steve leaped out, running for the front door. Candy, feeling his urgency, pulled her gun belt and service pistol out of her locked trunk and tightened them around her waist. Then she took off after Steve.

She arrived at the door in time to see a harried Todd open it. The instant he spied Steve, he said, "The voice again. And this time I heard it, too."

Damn, Candy thought, her insides tightening. Someone had to be down in that tunnel.

"It sounds like he might be screaming," Todd added. He stepped back, opening the door wide.

"Stay here," Steve said. "Lock the doors."

Todd's eyes widened, his mouth opened, then closed. "What?"

Candy spoke. "Todd, please. Get together and lock up. This might be no ghost at all."

Todd nodded jerkily as if trying to absorb all of it. "That's why the sheriff was out back earlier?"

"It's possible," Steve said. "Just let us check it out."

As they strode toward the barn, Candy said, "I'm calling for backup."

He didn't argue. They were both fairly certain now that there could be a man in that tunnel. Possibly upset about the missing coffin.

Possibly armed. Likely a serious threat if he was involved with those teens.

Candy felt that uneasy prickle again, the sense of impending danger. Like a night patrol, when the enemy could be hard to see even with night vision goggles. Plenty of impenetrable things to hide behind.

This guy had a tunnel. Concealment. No, he couldn't get past them on his way out, or at least she thought he couldn't, unless there was a door they'd missed. But they'd be every bit as trapped as he was.

Glancing at Steve, she decided he was going into his own type of combat mode. Maybe from his street days. There was little light to see by, except what reached them from the house. The clouds had begun to dump sleet.

Thank God they had found those teens before the icy weather had done its work.

They both crept into the barn, aware that any noise they made might be heard below. Impossible to know how much sound the tunnel would deaden.

They found the trapdoor open. They shared a look in the darkness and listened. They heard a voice rambling from deep inside. Not very loud.

"They took you away, my love. I'm so sorry I couldn't stop them."

"Damn," Steve whispered. "I could swear that's Ben Wittes."

"Yeah. I'll go down first."

"But…"

"I'm armed. Quit being a *guy*." She had the feeling that he might have laughed under other circumstances. Regardless, unlike him she had faced situations like this.

She slipped down into the hole, wincing as the nylon of her jacket rubbed against the boards. Loud to her ears, but the voice from down the tunnel didn't stop.

Kneeling, she began to make her way through the tunnel. It dipped down a little just past the entrance, but not enough to cause a problem. There was, however, more detritus on the floor. Rocks, dirt, all the things dislodged by the people who'd recovered the coffin and spent hours logging any evidence they could find.

As her knee hit a sharp rock, she wanted to cuss. Then she heard Steve moving behind her. No light, no light at all so as not to warn their quarry of their approach. Feeling her way along slowed her down, but it didn't matter. She'd crept slower through worse. At least she'd been in this tunnel before.

Then she saw a glimmer of light ahead. It appeared their

quarry had placed the panel over the door, but not fitted it tightly. So maybe the tunnel had amplified his voice?

No, not at all. He was talking and singing loudly now, switching from a lullaby to talk. When he talked he sounded furious, then soothing.

"You're still here," he said. "Sam knows it. Damn those people who took you out of here. Sam wants me to kill them all. And maybe I will." A pause. "I got a gun, Ivy. To make it happen faster."

Hell, Candy thought. She wished she could look over her shoulder and find out if Steve had heard, but it was still so dark in here, despite the little bits of light that worked their way around the panel.

Moving as silently as she could, she unsnapped her holster and drew out her pistol. The faintest click as she released the safety.

A steely, familiar calm settled over her. When she pulled that panel down, she'd have to move fast. Wittes might have that gun he'd mentioned near at hand. She wished she'd taken time to don the body armor that was in the trunk of her car.

Idiotic. But too late.

Candy drew a deep breath, worked her fingers around the edge of the panel and threw it to one side.

"You thought I didn't hear you? Sam knew you were coming."

She stared straight into the barrel of a shotgun.

STEVE SAW THE shotgun over Candy's shoulder. He had enough experience to know what the dispersal of that shot would do to her. He eased forward, trying to figure out how to help. Her pistol was out of his reach. God. He had to find a way.

But experience helped Candy react. She flattened and rolled to one side, out of range.

Startled, Ben tried to follow her with his gun, which gave Steve the opportunity he needed. He launched forward, difficult to do from a prone position, but he managed it, again startling Ben, who didn't seem to know how to handle this.

Ben swung his gun around toward Steve. Candy aimed her pistol and fired, missing Ben.

"You'll never get out of here," Steve growled. "Sheriff's waiting at the head of the tunnel. Don't be stupid and shoot an officer."

Candy, who'd rolled over again with her pistol aimed, ready to shoot, stopped herself.

Steve watched the most amazing thing happen. He saw Ben start to deflate, almost as if he were a balloon. Sagging, shrinking in on himself, looking confused.

The shotgun dropped. Ben stared at it as if he couldn't understand. Then the man looked at them as if seeing them for the first time.

It took only a moment for the two of them to wrestle Ben to the ground. Candy had zip ties on her utility belt, and used them swiftly on Ben's wrists, while Steve crawled into the shelter and moved the shotgun safely away, opening it to remove the load.

"Done," he said. "Now we just have to figure out how to get him out of here."

Candy turned her head to Steve. "What just happened?"

"Darned if I know."

Half an hour later they managed to drag Ben to the tunnel opening. He neither helped nor resisted. Waiting above were Gage and three deputies, Micah Parish, Sarah Ironheart and Guy Redwing.

"Well, I'll be damned," Gage said.

Which pretty much said it all.

Chapter Sixteen

Two nights later, Candy stood inside the gymnasium, watching kids and teens romp, watching parents hand out generous amounts of candy.

Even though Ben Wittes was probably the killer, uneasiness still stalked the area. Besides, it was frigid outside, where the first huge flakes of winter had begun to fall in noticeable quantities. Tomorrow the entire world would be blanketed in a sparkling white coat.

Cleansing, Candy thought.

Steve, who'd come, as well, moved to her side. "Can you talk?"

"Sure." She nodded to Connie Parish, who nodded back. Connie would take over for a little while.

Outside, away from the door, their breath blew white clouds.

"I want to fill you in," he said. They hadn't seen each other since Ben Wittes's arrest.

"I'd like that."

"But I want some info in return."

She smiled into the icy air. "I figured. I can give you at least some."

"Thanks." He rocked on his feet a couple of times. "The Castelles are torn between shock, horror and relief."

"I'd expect that."

"They want to fill in the tunnel. They're going to wait, though, until after we film."

She faced him, surprised. "They still want to do the show?"

"Yup. I'm amazed, too. But Annabelle and Todd said they want the truth out there. To tell people that not everything terrifying is a ghost."

"Um, wow." She thought about that. "But isn't this scarier? Really? Wouldn't it be better for people to worry about ghosts?"

"They don't think so, and neither do my producers. Psychologists will probably be thrilled to be dealing with something besides ghosts."

"Maybe. But what's more terrifying?"

"Not my decision. Consider how many TV shows deal with real murders. People watch them more than they watch ghosts. If that doesn't frighten them, this shouldn't."

He had a point. People were fascinated by true crime stories and didn't have nightmares about them. "Well, you're in line with your principles." Principles she now believed he had.

"Exactly. No lying to the audience. No pretending that something is real when it's not."

"How's Viv doing?"

"They're still promising her the mean man is gone, that he's been arrested by the police. I told her, too. It may take her a while."

Candy felt truly sorry for Vivian. She didn't deserve the terrors that would now probably follow her for a long time. "That's to be expected. That little girl has been scared for nearly a year. Unable to sleep in her own bedroom."

Steve nodded. Snowflakes had begun to collect on his knit cap. "Buddy seems to be relieved, too. No more sessions growling at the wall. I think his reaction is going to do more for Vivian than anything we tell her."

"It probably will."

He tilted his head. "Your turn."

"Well, it gets complicated. We found a sedative in Ben's trunk. The same one used on the teens. We also found clothes in his hamper that are covered with dirt and pine needles. Thing is, he claims not to remember any of it. Sadly, I think he's telling the truth."

"How could that be?" Steve sounded dubious.

"We can't detect any lying. Besides, the first time we mentioned the murders, before they became public knowledge, his face turned a ghastly white. Nobody could fake that drop in blood pressure."

"Unless he was a meditating Buddhist monk anyway. So he killed those kids."

"We've got enough evidence to hold him. We'll get the rest."

"And the body in the coffin?"

She sighed. "It's old. The medical examiner says a female, age around forty. She appears to have been killed in a fall down some stairs."

Steve rocked again on his feet. "So that Bride guy is cleared?"

"Maybe so. Ben is claiming that Sam told him to take care of her, to talk to her and sing to her. He keeps saying that Samuel Bride didn't kill her."

Steve didn't answer for a long time. "How can Ben not remember the murders? And how can he be so sure that Bride didn't kill his wife?"

"I don't know. I really don't. We're beginning to believe there's something loose in his head."

"Maybe." Steve sighed. "Please get the answers. I really don't want to start wondering if that guy is truly psychic."

Despite the circumstances, Candy had to laugh. "I couldn't agree more."

Then Steve smiled at her. "You open for coffee after this shindig winds down?"

Her heart leaped. Oh, this was bad. She ought to tell him no, to start distancing herself. Instead she said, "Yes."

KIDS, STEVE THOUGHT. He got a kick out of watching the youngsters squeal their way through the haunted house that ran along a hallway that opened off the gym.

Candy told him the teens who worked on the party had toned it down so it wouldn't be too scary for the little ones.

And somebody had even found a copy of "Monster Mash" to play, which had kids of every age dancing all around the gym.

But when midnight came, parents had a difficult time trying to round up everyone. Steve remembered the days when he could stay up into the wee hours having a good time. Remembered. He couldn't do that easily anymore.

But at last Candy escaped and he followed her home, wondering if he should go by the truck stop to get coffee and a nibble for them. It would be nicer, he decided, than dumping all that on Candy at this hour.

She was waiting when he arrived, looking wide awake. The evening must have stimulated her. For his part, sleepiness stalked the edges of his mind.

But he needed to spend time with her. Needed to talk with her. Hope was slender, but he had to try. Emotions were welling up in him, beyond his ability to control.

She curled up on her couch beneath a warm throw, sipping coffee and eating a jelly-filled doughnut. "I love these doughnuts," she remarked. "Ever since I was little. I didn't get them very often. My mama and my abuela—that's my grandmother—had a whole bunch of desserts they made, from flan to three-milk cake. Empanadas. All good. Excellent in fact. But not jelly doughnuts."

He hesitated, his own doughnut forgotten. "You don't talk much about your Latin heritage, do you?"

She sighed and shook her head. "It's not a popular topic. Besides, I took enough guff about it when I was in school. It was better in the Army."

Another sign of her growing trust for him. He felt honored. "I don't think you should have to hide it, Candy."

"Maybe I shouldn't have to, but life has taught me otherwise. You know, my family has been in California since it was a Spanish colony. People don't want to know that either. I was frequently told that I should go back to Mexico." She snorted. "My family was there, too, when the state was *part* of Mexico."

"People can be such ignoramuses."

"I doubt many of their school history classes covered the subject. I try to excuse it now, but back then it really hurt."

He didn't answer immediately, seeking the right words. But then there didn't seem to be any but the bald truth. "I've seen it. I've seen a lot of it, and it just seems to keep getting uglier. For indigenous peoples, too. Man, they've been here for at least twenty-five thousand years."

"The world is filled with conveniently short memories."

"Except yours," he said quietly.

Her head raised. "I need to apologize for that night."

"No, you don't. Not ever, not with me. End of discussion."

The jelly filling was gone from her doughnut. He watched her put it aside. "Hey, that's not a cop thing to do!"

She laughed. "Maybe not. How'd that get started anyway?"

"Cops work ridiculous hours and there aren't many places open in the middle of the night. Run in, grab a coffee and a doughnut, then get back on the road. Some places offer it for free."

She lifted a brow. "Isn't that a bribe?"

"No. They never asked anything in return. I always figured they just liked the traffic in their parking lots during those hours."

"Police protection?"

He shook his head. "Police presence for all of four minutes at a time. Like I said, they never asked for a thing, and a dollar cup of coffee and a fifty-cent doughnut hardly classify as a bribe."

"I wouldn't do anything in exchange for that."

"Exactly." He was having a terrible time coming around to what he most wanted to discuss with her. If his hand grew any tighter around his cup of coffee, he was going to crush it.

"Candy?"

"Yeah?" She appeared to have drifted away a little.

"Am I right in thinking you don't want to go back to California?"

"Maybe for a visit eventually. But to stay? I like it a whole lot better here."

"I thought so. So I want to make a proposition."

He had her full attention now. Putting his coffee down, he crossed to sit beside her curled-up legs on the couch. "How would you feel if I came back to visit *you*?"

CANDY CAUGHT HER BREATH. Every cell in her being seemed to be reaching out toward Steve, but she held still. Where was this going? "I wouldn't mind."

"Good." He paused, keeping her dangling somewhere near hope, but also near fear.

God, what was he suggesting?"

"Thing is," he said slowly, "I wasn't kidding when I said I want to know you better. I wasn't kidding when I said I want you. Damn me for a boor if you want."

Her heart was tripping fast now. Heat began to sizzle throughout her body. "You're not a boor."

He compressed his lips for a few seconds, then spoke again. "What I want is a relationship. Hell, I want more than that, but you must need time. But if we build something bigger, it's okay if you don't want to move to California."

Now she could barely breathe. "Why not?"

"My home is there, but I'm almost never there anyway. I could come visit you between programs, between seasons. You don't need to live with me in an empty house for long stretches. Without the job you clearly love, or the friends you're making here."

Now there didn't seem to be any air left in the universe. Her heart and mind had caught on one thing. Live with him? "Steve?"

"I'm a bumbling fool. What I'm trying to say is that I've fallen in love with you, and if you eventually see your way to feeling the same about me, then we can make it work."

It was such a huge prospect that she had trouble absorbing it. A life she'd given up hoping for was now offering her the possibility of it becoming true?

But he'd stayed with her an entire night after her meltdown. He'd never criticized her for it. Instead he'd offered understanding and comfort. Now he wanted to offer her more.

Truth and reality both began to dawn on her, and as they did her heart soared. Honesty caused her to blurt a fact she'd been hiding from herself. "I think I love you, too."

The biggest smile spread across his face. "You've just made me the happiest man alive."

Then, leaning over, he scooped her up into his arms. "Now for the other part of what I want. If you don't mind."

The heat inside her became electric. "Why would I mind? I want you, too."

Then he carried her off to her bed, the first steps on a road to a new future.

She knew she could handle this. She knew she was going to love every minute.

A new day was creeping into the world, and into her heart.

* * * * *

HIS BRAND
OF JUSTICE

DELORES FOSSEN

Chapter One

The moment Marshal Jack Slater brought his truck to a stop in front of the small country house, he drew his gun, threw open the door and raced up the porch steps. He'd already glanced around the road and the sprawling yard to see if there was any immediate danger. If there was, he hadn't spotted anything.

That didn't mean, though, that there wasn't a threat.

And that was why Jack had gotten here as fast as he could, once he'd received the call from the live-in nurse, Lucille Booker. From the instant he'd heard Lucille say "Marshal Slater, there might be a problem" in a breathy voice, Jack had known there was no *might* to it. There was trouble. Lucille had been at this job for three months, and never once had he heard that kind of concern in her voice. No, not just concern.

Fear.

Jack didn't knock. Instead, he flipped up the top of what appeared to be an ordinary doorbell to reveal a panel for the security system beneath it. He punched in the code, which would alert the two women inside that it was him. Only when he heard the clicks that let him know the alarms and locks had been temporarily disarmed did he open the door.

Lucille was there in the foyer, and she had a gun in the white-knuckle grip of her right hand. A gun that Jack had issued to her after making sure that she knew how to use it.

There was no blood on her, thank God. No signs of any injury, and the room showed no indications of a struggle. Everything in the house was neat and tidy, as it usually was.

Lucille was what no one would call petite—another reason Jack had wanted her for this job. Her beefy build, no-fuss choppy brown hair and sharply angled face all gave her the appearance of a woman who knew how to take care of herself. And it was true. In addition to being a nurse with twenty years of experience, Lucille had been an instructor of self-defense classes for women.

"What happened?" Jack asked as he reset the security system. "Where's Caroline?"

An answer to that second question wasn't necessary, though, because he soon saw the blonde in the kitchen. Caroline Moser. Jack cursed, because she was standing there with a butcher knife.

Unlike Lucille, there was nothing beefy about Caroline. She was lean and tall, and the loose pale blue cotton dress she was wearing didn't disguise her willowy body. She had an angel's face, he'd always thought. Like some painting on a museum wall. Once, before things had gone to hell in a handbasket, there'd been a lot of toughness and street smarts beneath those soft, delicate features.

No toughness now, though.

She was way too pale, and she looked way too fragile.

"When Caroline and I were clearing up after lunch, I saw a man," Lucille explained. "A stranger. He was by the pond."

Not good. No one should have been within a quarter of a mile of this place, since it wasn't anywhere on the beaten path. Of course, Jack could say that about lots of properties in the county, which was mainly made up of ranches, farms and small towns. Like Longview Ridge, the place where Jack had been born and raised and where he still lived. This safe house was only about fifteen miles from there—and from him. But it was still far enough away that someone shouldn't have just strolled by here.

"You saw this man, too?" he asked Caroline.

"Just a glimpse." There was plenty of worry and fear in her voice, but there was something else in her jewel-green eyes.

Suspicion.

Jack knew that particular reaction was for him.

She didn't trust him, not completely, anyway, and he'd seen that look plenty of times over the past three months since he'd become her handler in WITSEC. Before that, when she had known who he was, there'd been other emotions…ones that he wished he couldn't remember, either.

Jack wasn't sure why the doubt was there now. Or all the other times he'd visited her here in this safe house over the past weeks. Her doctors had said it was because of the trauma from her injuries and her amnesia. It was hard for her to trust anyone, they'd said, when there were way too many blanks in her mind.

Still, it cut him to the bone.

Of course, there were plenty other things that he should be thinking about right now, things that didn't involve whether she trusted him or not, and Jack went to the kitchen window. That vantage point would give him a good view of not only the pond but also the small barn and pasture.

Other than the two horses that Jack had personally delivered to the place, nothing and no one was out there. However, since Lucille wasn't easily spooked, she must have seen someone.

"You didn't recognize the man?" Jack pressed, glancing back at Lucille.

The nurse shook her head. She put away her gun in the slide holster at the back of her scrubs. "But he had dark hair and was wearing jeans and a black T-shirt. He darted behind the big oak tree when he spotted me."

Darting definitely wasn't a good sign, but Jack was holding out hope that this was just someone who'd strayed onto the property, only to realize that he was trespassing. Too bad the twisting feeling in his gut let him know that wasn't the case.

"I called you right away, just as you told me to do," Lucille added. "And I made sure Caroline stayed away from the windows." Again, that was as Jack had instructed.

Jack made a sound of approval, and while continuing to volley his attention out the window, he reached out to take the knife from Caroline. Her hand went stiff when his fingers brushed over hers. Actually, every part of her seemed to stiffen as her gaze collided with his. Her intense stare held a few long moments before she finally let go of the knife.

"Sorry, Marshal Slater," she muttered. "I'm a little spooked."

Marshal Slater. It wasn't a surprise that she called him that. In fact, it was the only thing Caroline had called him since she'd turned up in Longview Ridge three months ago with that head injury and the amnesia. She said his name with the same edgy suspicion that was in her eyes.

Before the memory loss, she had called him Jack. And

there'd sure as hell been no suspicion then. Only the heat from the scalding hot fire that he no longer saw or felt in any part of her.

I love you, Jack.

Those were the last words Caroline had said to him before she was taken hostage, before this nightmare had begun. Words she'd said when they thought it would be an ordinary, short goodbye. When Jack had thought there'd be plenty of other times for him to say *I love you* right back—and that was why he hadn't said it to her then. Now he might never get the chance.

He was a stranger to her now. He was *Marshal Slater*.

Jack tried not to let that eat away at him, especially since Lucille had insisted on calling him by his title and surname, too. But in Lucille's case, it just sounded as if she'd wanted to remind herself that he was there to protect Caroline and her. Which he was.

"You think it was a false alarm?" Lucille asked, joining him at the window.

Jack lifted his shoulder. "The sensors weren't tripped."

If they had been, Jack would have gotten the alert on his phone. Of course, the guy would have had to get closer to the house for that to happen, since the sensors were arranged around the perimeter of the yard and on the dirt road that led to the house.

There were also some cameras, and Jack fired off a text to his partner, Marshal Teagan Randolph. He asked her to cull out the video feed from all the cameras for the past hour and send it to him ASAP.

"I'll wait around for a while and keep watch," he assured Lucille and Caroline when he was done with the text.

A while was going to mean staying for the night. Or

longer. He didn't intend to take any risks with Caroline, because somewhere in those lost memories in her head was a piece of information he needed as much as the next breath he took.

She knew who'd murdered his father.

The images came. They always did whenever he thought of his dad, Sheriff Buck Slater. Buck had been the law in Longview Ridge, but that had ended one night in a hail of bullets and blood when someone had gunned him down. Caroline was the only person alive who could tell him what'd happened.

Other than the killer, of course.

And Jack suspected he wouldn't be getting any answers from him or her on that. Especially since he had a mile-long suspect list that he hadn't managed to whittle down much since his father's murder a little over a year ago.

He was betting Caroline was eager to uncover those memories, too. Well, maybe she was. She had to want to know what'd happened not just to his father but also to her. She would want to know how she got that head injury. But the doctors had said the amnesia could be a way of protecting herself from a nightmare that was too traumatic for her to face. Still, Jack had to hold on to hope that one day she would push the trauma aside and help him catch a killer.

"I'll make a fresh pot of coffee," Lucille volunteered, and she got busy doing that after she gave Caroline the once-over.

It was the kind of quick exam a nurse would take of her patient, probably to make sure Caroline wasn't on the verge of a panic attack. Jack hadn't witnessed one of the attacks, but he'd heard from Lucille and then Caroline's doctors that she'd had several in the three months that she'd been in WITSEC. It was the reason the US Marshals—and Jack himself—had wanted a nurse to be with her. Normally, when someone was placed in WITSEC, that didn't happen. The person merely started a new life with a new identity and no past.

But nothing about this situation was normal.

Jack had also had to convince his agency that this wouldn't be a conflict of interest for him, that he could do his job as Caroline's handler despite their prior personal relationship. And that it would be all right for him to place her in the local area where he could keep a close eye on her. Maybe some of his fellow marshals did know of his personal interest in the case. But none had doubted that he would do whatever it took to make sure Caroline was not only safe but that she also made a full recovery. Emphasis on the *full*.

When Lucille had moved from the kitchen window, Caroline had came closer to him. But not too close. She always gave him a wide berth, making sure they didn't accidentally bump into each other. Maybe that's why his merely touching her hand earlier had caused every muscle in her body to turn to iron.

"You think that man by the pond came here to kill me?" she asked.

If he hadn't thought that was possible, she wouldn't need to be in WITSEC. But the truth was, he just didn't know. Maybe there was no killer after Caroline, but he wasn't willing to take that chance. Because if there was someone after her, it would likely be the same person who'd murdered his father. The person could want to silence her permanently so she could never reveal his or her identity.

"We don't know who we're dealing with," he settled for saying. He usually gave her a variation of that whenever the subject of her safety came up. Which was often. No need to alarm her and spur one of those panic attacks by spelling out worst-case scenarios. "Was there anything about this man you recognized?"

"No. Like I said, I only got a glimpse." Caroline didn't hesitate, but she did huff. "Has my location been compromised? Will I have to move to another safe house?"

Possibly, but Jack decided to put a softer spin on that. "Let's just wait and see. I'm not going to let anything happen to you." He looked at her as the last of those words were leaving his mouth, and for just a split second he saw something more than distrust on her face.

Anger, maybe?

But it was gone as quickly as it had come.

"I don't know who killed your father," she insisted. The riled expression might be gone, but there was a tinge of agitation in her voice.

Jack glanced at Lucille to see if she had an explanation for this change in Caroline's attitude, and the nurse's mouth tightened a little. "Caroline found some articles on the internet."

Well, hell. That definitely explained it. There were plenty of sites that had gobs of sordid details about his father's shooting. About Deputy Dusty Walters, who'd also died that night, too. And Caroline's name came up often on those sites. Not in a good way, either. The press had had a field day with her because she'd disappeared. There'd been plenty of speculation that had gone along with questions about where she was and what'd happened to her.

Not many people knew the answer to that.

WITSEC had taken care of shielding her identity so that now she lived and worked in this house. In fact, work was the reason she had a laptop in the first place. The Justice Department had created a job for her where she was reviewing witness testimony in cases where no charges had been filed. It was one step above busy work, but obviously it hadn't kept her busy enough.

"Yes, the filters are still on the computer," Lucille assured him.

"I figured out how to get around them," Caroline quickly confessed. "And no, it wasn't something I remembered how to do. I just kept plugging away until I found a web page that the filter didn't catch."

Jack added another "hell." He'd need to tell the doctors about this so they could deal with it during her weekly therapy session. A session that would, ironically, be done online, since Jack had wanted to limit Caroline's visits into San Antonio along with also limiting the number of people who knew the location of the safe house. And he'd managed to do that by limiting that info to his partner, Lucille and his three brothers, who were all lawmen. Jack had wanted them to know in case they needed to make a quick response.

However, even with all the precautions they'd taken, Jack knew that the safe house information could be breached. Their computer filters were more elaborate than the ones on the laptop here, but someone determined to find Caroline could still get around them. A killer definitely fell into the "someone determined" category.

Caroline groaned softly and pushed her shoulder-length blond hair from her face. "I used to have a life. I've read about it," she added in a grumble. "I came from almost nothing. My prostitute mother was killed by a drug dealer when I was eight, and I ended up in foster care." She looked ready to tack on more to that recap of her childhood, but then she stopped, paused. "I got through all of that to get a job working for one of the top criminal profiling experts."

Jack nodded. Yep, all of that was true. She'd had a life, all right, and even though she was alive, she might never get that life back. Would certainly never undo the fallout to her reputation because of the work she'd done with that top expert.

What Caroline hadn't just mentioned in the rundown of her life was her police record. A sealed juvie rap sheet that she wouldn't have been able to access without the prime hacking skills that she'd had before she lost her memory.

This woman with the angel face and almost fragile-looking body had been arrested when she was fifteen for hacking into multiple state records to find the dealer who'd killed her mother. Caroline had then stolen a car, tracked down the man and managed to bash him in the gut with a baseball bat before calling the cops to come and get him. The cops had gone easy on her because of the extenuating circumstances, but she'd still spent some time in juvie lockup.

"I saw a picture of Eric Lang," Caroline went on. She groaned again. "I suppose you know all there is to know about him." But she waved that off. "Of course, you do. You're a marshal. You're Sheriff Buck Slater's son."

Jack stayed quiet, but he knew Eric all right. Eric had been the research assistant for Caroline and her boss/friend Gemma Hanson at the college where the three of them had been working on a new computer program for profiling serial killers. The irony was that Eric himself had been a serial killer, and neither Gemma nor Caroline had picked up on it. Eric had hidden it from the women. From everyone. Then, Eric had nearly killed both Caroline and Gemma when he'd taken them hostage. That was what had sent Jack's father to an abandoned hotel, where he'd been killed.

Gemma had managed to escape that night. Caroline hadn't. Eric had taken her and disappeared into the darkness with her. No one, not even Caroline, was certain what had happened after that, but she'd shown up in Longview Ridge a year later. Because of her amnesia, though, she hadn't been able to tell them what'd happened to her.

"Eric is dead," Jack reminded her. "He was shot and killed three months ago, shortly after you came back to Longview Ridge."

Of course, he'd already told her that, and she had almost certainly read about it in those internet articles, but Jack wanted to spell it out for her that she didn't have to be afraid of Eric. He couldn't come after her again.

"Was I stupid?" she blurted out. Man, the anger had returned with a vengeance, not just in her tone but in her expression. "Was that why I couldn't see a serial killer was working right next to me?"

Jack hated to see her beating herself up like this. "You definitely weren't stupid. I met Eric, too, and I didn't make him for a killer. A lot of people didn't."

That didn't seem to appease her one bit. Her forehead still stayed bunched up, making the scar there even more obvious. A scar that she'd gotten during her captivity. Possibly from Eric, when he'd clubbed her on the head that night she was taken hostage. Of course, until Caroline got back her memory, she wouldn't be able to confirm if that was what had actually happened.

"And what about *us*?" Caroline threw out there.

Lucille's gaze fired to Caroline, then him. Jack didn't know what to make of the question, either. In the past three months, Caroline hadn't asked about them as a couple, but that was because Jack had never stayed around for an actual conversation. He visited twice a week, to check if Caroline's memory had returned. And once Lucille and Caroline assured him that it hadn't, he always left.

Just as Lucille did now.

The nurse must have thought they needed some privacy, because she mumbled something about needing to get something from her bedroom and walked out. Jack hadn't even been sure that Lucille knew Caroline and he had once been lovers.

Had been in love, he mentally corrected.

Jack hadn't talked about that with Lucille or anyone else, for that matter. Still, maybe Lucille had picked up on something or had been doing her own reading about Caroline. That would only be natural, he supposed, since Lucille and Caroline lived under the same roof, and Lucille was partly responsible for Caroline's safety.

"There was something about *us* in the articles you read?" Jack countered.

Best not to blurt out any details that Caroline didn't know or hadn't remembered. That was what the doctors had told him to do anyway. Keep the interaction between them to a minimum so there'd be no risk of planting memories in her head. That way, when she did recall something, it would be because it was a genuine memory. It was another reason he'd need to let her doctors know about this conversation.

When Caroline didn't answer, he looked at her. He saw maybe a flicker of recognition, or something, before she turned away. As she'd done earlier, she waved that off.

Jack would have pressed her for more info, pushing just a little, but his phone dinged, and he saw the file his partner, Teagan, had sent. Lucille must have heard the sound, too, because she hurried back into the kitchen.

"Any problem?" Lucille asked.

"Video from the security cameras." He motioned for her to come closer so she could take a look. When Caroline moved in, too, Jack had to consider which would upset her more: if she saw a would-be killer or if he kept her from seeing one.

He decided to let her watch.

It put them in close contact, with Lucille on one side of him and Caroline on the other. Caroline still didn't touch him, even though her arm was less than an inch from his.

Jack sped up the feed, going through minutes of what the cameras had recorded. Minutes of nothing.

And then there was something.

He slowed down the speed and then paused it when the man came into view. The guy was just as Lucille had described him—dark hair and jeans, and he was indeed by the pond. Too bad the guy was turned away from the camera so that only the side of his face was visible.

The man didn't have a drawn weapon, but Jack didn't like the way he was just standing there. If this was someone who'd just wandered onto the property, he should have been firing glances all around. Or leaving.

Jack touched the screen, moving it frame by frame until he finally got a shot he wanted. The guy turned to face the camera. Jack paused it again, enlarging it so he could run it through facial recognition software.

Caroline gasped. "Oh, God. Jack, I know him."

Shaking her head, she stepped back and pressed her fingers to her mouth. But only for a moment. Caroline's eyes widened when she saw that she'd gotten his complete attention. He could also see that she quickly tried to shut back down to that flat expression she'd worn for the past three months. But it was too late for that.

For that mask.

Because Jack had seen the recognition in her eyes. Better yet, he'd heard it in her voice.

Jack.

"You remembered something?" Lucille quickly asked, maybe not picking up on the sudden slash of tension between her patient and Jack. "Do you really know who that man is?"

Caroline didn't even look at the nurse. She kept her gaze fastened on Jack. Recognition, definitely. And some defiance. She hiked up her chin, and her mouth went into a flat line.

"Yes, I know that man," Caroline said, her stare drilling into Jack. "And I know *you*."

Chapter Two

Caroline's heart had gone to her knees at the exact moment she'd said Jack's name. Mercy, what had she done?

She wanted to take back the last handful of seconds, wanted to fix her expression so that Jack wouldn't see right through her. But she couldn't. The lid was off Pandora's box, and it wasn't going back on. And if that wasn't bad enough, now she had that face on the security video to worry about.

Caroline swallowed hard and looked at Lucille, who immediately took hold of her arm. "You need to sit down," Lucille instructed. "You look like you're about to pass out." She tried to lead Caroline back into the living room, but she held her ground. "Did your memory really come back?" Lucille asked.

"Yes," Caroline managed to say.

Lucille let out a huge breath of relief. Of course, the nurse didn't know how dangerous the man she'd recognized was. She also didn't know something Jack had already figured out.

That she'd regained her memory days ago.

As if celebrating and relieved by the progress, Lucille hugged her. "I'll need to call your doctor. Maybe we can drive out to see him?"

Even though Caroline liked her doctors and she'd had no trouble on the previous trips to San Antonio for her exams, she definitely didn't want a doctor right now.

"No. Could you give me a moment alone with Marshal Slater?" Caroline asked. It probably seemed petty or insulting to Jack that she'd call him by his surname now, but saying *Jack* seemed too, well, intimate.

Considering all the other intimate things they'd done, it would be so easy to slip back into that. After all, she had only told one man that she loved him, and it was the same man who was now glaring at her.

Lucille continued to give her a long, concerned look. "Should I get your meds?"

"No," Caroline repeated. "I'm not going to have a panic attack." She thought that was true, anyway, and even if it wasn't, she couldn't deal with the haze that the meds created in her mind. "I just need a moment with Marshal Slater. It's…personal."

"Oh." Lucille seemed relieved, which meant that maybe she knew or had guessed that Jack and Caroline had once been involved.

Jack knew it too, of course. There was nothing wrong with his memory. Or his glare. He stood there, all lanky and lean, looking more cop than cowboy now—though he was both. He'd come from a long line of Texas cowboys, and it fit him as well as his jeans and his ice-blue shirt.

No ice in his eyes, though. There was so much fire and heat in the depths of all that gray. The color of a dangerous storm cloud ready to shoot some lightning bolts her way. His hair was even darker than that. Midnight black. And right now his clothes, his expression and everything else about him made him seem more than a little dangerous.

Caroline waited until Lucille was out of the room before she said anything else. She turned to Jack, and she answered his question before he could even ask it. "Three days ago. That's when I regained my memory."

Muscles stirred in his jaw, and she doubted his eyes could narrow even more. "Why the hell didn't you tell me?" he asked through clenched teeth.

Oh, he was so not going to like this, and worse, she wasn't going to have time to smooth it over. No time to try to make him understand. "I don't know who killed your father. That's the truth."

"And I'm just to believe that after you've lied to me for three days, or longer?" Jack snarled.

Good point, and Caroline conceded that with a weary sound of agreement. It hadn't been longer, but she doubted she could convince him of that.

"The night Eric Lang kidnapped me, he did injure me," Caroline continued. "He bashed me on the head with his gun." She idly rubbed the scar on her forehead that she'd gotten from that attack. "And when that wasn't enough to render me unconscious, he pumped me full of drugs. Then he hid me and Gemma in one of the rooms of the abandoned hotel, Serenity Inn."

No need for her to get into too many specifics on the location. Jack had almost certainly searched every inch of that old hotel and gone over all the details of the investigation that followed. He knew that Eric had indeed managed to escape with her, and Jack had likely found her blood or some other evidence in that crumbling, smothering room that had once been part of a Victorian mansion.

"Eric didn't kill your father," she went on. "Eric was with me, holding a gun to my bleeding head when I heard the shots. And yes, I know it was the shots that killed your dad, because I also heard Gemma scream. I could hear the chaos that followed." She had to pause and gather her breath. With her breath, though, came the images.

Mercy, the images.

Caroline had to try to rein all of that in. If she had a panic attack, Lucille would force her into taking those meds, and that couldn't happen. She needed to finish what she had to say.

"Eric got away with me," Caroline went on several moments later while Jack stood there and drilled holes in her with his intense stare. "By then, I was barely conscious, but he talked to someone on the phone. A cop or some kind of lawman. And that person helped him escape. I know the caller was in law enforcement because there was a police radio in the background."

She didn't expect Jack to buy that, and even if he did, it still wouldn't justify her withholding the information that she'd regained her memory or the fact that she hadn't trusted him enough to tell him.

"Before I got my memory fully back, before I remembered *us*, I thought the person talking to Eric that night was you," she said. That didn't come out right, so she shook her head. "Or rather, someone you knew, because the other words I heard were 'Longview Ridge Sheriff's Office.' I heard dispatch codes. I thought it could be someone you wouldn't believe would help a serial killer, and that your disbelief would allow him to get to me or someone else."

Now he cursed, and those jaw muscles went to war with each other. "I'm not dirty, and I don't know any marshal or cop who is. I sure as hell wouldn't have helped Eric."

"Maybe not. But someone with a badge did. And I decided that if I wanted to stay alive, I couldn't trust you, the other marshals or anyone in your family."

He opened his mouth as if to blast her with verbal fire, but then he stopped, and it looked as if he'd done some reining in of his emotions, as well. "Yet you let me put you here. You let me come here to visit you."

She lifted her shoulder, tapped her head. "I didn't know, not when I came here. Three days ago, when the memories came, I decided I was safe as long as you and everyone connected to you thought I wasn't a threat. Or as long as you believed that I could eventually tell you who killed your father." Caroline took his phone. "But he's a threat. I don't have to guess about that."

Jack's glare got even worse, and she could tell the last thing he wanted to do was switch subjects. But he was also a lawman, and he'd seen the way she'd reacted to the man. Of course, maybe he thought she had faked that fear, too.

She hadn't.

"His name is Kingston Morris," she continued when Jack didn't say anything else. "And he was friends with Eric. The fact that he's here means he knows where I am and that he could have come here to kill me. Maybe to tidy up loose ends for his old friend."

"Kingston Morris," he repeated, not just once but several times as if testing to see if it rang any bells. "His name didn't come up in the investigation."

"It wouldn't have. I only remember Kingston coming in one time to the office where Eric and I worked."

"The office at the college." There was plenty of skepticism in his voice. "And yet you remembered him after just one meeting."

She shrugged. "He gave me the creeps."

That was an understatement. The guy had made her skin crawl, and because Kingston had seemed to worship Eric, that was the first time Caroline had started to look at Eric in a different light. That was the beginning of her seeing the monster crouched just below the facade he put on as a research assistant. Too bad she hadn't seen it a whole lot sooner. If she had, Jack's dad might be alive. Many others, too.

"If Eric and he were friends, Kingston's name should have come up," Jack concluded.

"Eric had erased all of his contacts. Or rather, he only left contacts and info that he didn't mind being discovered. He just used burner phones for getting in touch with anyone who was important to him."

"And this Kingston was important?" Jack asked while he typed something on his phone. She then heard the swooshes of outgoing texts. Maybe he was reaching out to his marshal friends to do a quick background check on Kingston. She hoped he hadn't mentioned that she'd regained her memory.

She nodded in reply to his question. "After Eric managed to get me away from the abandoned inn, it was Kingston who helped Eric get some money. I heard their phone conversation, too, and Kingston was like a groupie. He idolized Eric, would do anything for him."

This time Jack said a single word of profanity. "And you didn't think you should give this info to someone?" He didn't wait for her to answer. "Even if you didn't trust me, you could have told the cops."

"I didn't know if I could trust them, either." She had to pause again. "And I really did have amnesia until three days ago."

He made a sound that conveyed a whole boatload of doubt.

"I was in a hospital in Mexico," Caroline went on. "I'm not sure how I got there, but I think Eric took me across the border, and then I escaped. Or he could have left me for dead. Someone found me in a ditch and took me to the hospital. I had injuries other than just to my head. Broken bones, and I'd been beaten. There were lots of cuts and bruises on my face."

Jack couldn't dispute any of those injuries, because he had almost certainly seen the report of the medical exam that she'd been given after she returned to Longview Ridge three months ago.

"I didn't see Eric or Kingston after that, and even if I had, I might not have recognized them because of the amnesia," she admitted.

Which meant she'd be dead right now if Eric had seen her.

"After my condition improved in the Mexico hospital, they moved me to a convalescent home because I couldn't use my right hand," she explained. "Because of the head trauma, too. I stayed there until three months ago, when I started regaining pieces of my memory. I still didn't know who I was, but the name Longview Ridge kept repeating in my head."

So had Jack's name. And what she'd said to him kept playing again and again, too. Caroline doubted he would appreciate her mentioning that now, though.

I love you, Jack.

Yes, she'd indeed told him that. After a lazy Sunday morning of sex, he'd gotten the call to go into work, and instead of saying a simple goodbye, she'd said those words aloud. They had just slipped out—as easily as the kiss he had given her only seconds earlier. She'd seen the surprise in his eyes. Maybe the "run for the hills" look. Whichever it was, he hadn't said it back to her.

Everything that came after had happened so fast that Caroline hadn't had time to think about what had been said or unsaid. Unlike the last three days. Plenty of time to think then, and she hadn't liked the conclusion. She'd been wrong to tell him she loved him, even if it had been true.

"If you thought I was such a threat, why did you stay here?" he snapped. "Why didn't you run again as soon as you remembered what had gone on?"

"I stayed so I could try to find out the truth. Like I said, I once had a life, and I want it back. I want to find out what happened that night of your father's murder, and to do that, I have to stay alive."

"And you don't believe I want you alive." It sounded as if that disgusted him. Maybe it did. If he was clean, and she had to pray that he was, then an accusation like that would cut him to the core. But it wasn't Jack who was her biggest worry. It was any and all of the other cops and marshals who would get called into this investigation before this was over.

She opened her mouth just as something flashed through her head. Not a memory. But a really bad thought.

"Gemma," she blurted out. "Oh, God. Kingston could go after Gemma. You have to warn her."

"I already have. I sent Kellan a text to give him a heads-up that there might be a problem with Gemma's safety. *Might*," he emphasized.

Kellan was his brother, the sheriff of Longview Ridge, but he was also Gemma's fiancé. Kellan would protect her, but it twisted at Caroline's insides that she hadn't thought of contacting Gemma the moment she'd seen Kingston's face on the screen. To the best of her knowledge, Gemma hadn't actually met Kingston, but that didn't mean the man wouldn't try to go after her or anyone else who'd been connected to his now dead idol, Eric.

"Just please make sure that no one hurts her," she said.

"Funny that you'd show this much concern for Gemma now. She's your friend and your former boss, but you lied to her, too. Lying by omission is still a lie," he insisted. "Why didn't you tell Gemma that you had regained your memory and suspected that a dirty cop could be part of this?"

"Because I knew she'd tell Kellan," Caroline readily admitted.

"Damn straight Gemma would have, and it would have been the right thing to do."

"Maybe," Caroline muttered, not convinced that it would have indeed been the *right thing*. "But when I came back to town and saw her with Kellan, I knew they were in love. Once I had my memory back, I decided that Kellan must have been a good cop or Gemma wouldn't have those feelings for him. I couldn't take the chance, though, that Kellan would say something to someone whose feelings weren't so *loving*."

"Like me," he snapped.

"No." Frustrated and flustered, Caroline shook her head. "I just couldn't risk anyone knowing—not then, anyway. I can't protect myself. Heck, I can't even shoot straight." She held up her right hand. "Too much damage from the broken bones, and I lost what muscle strength I had." She paused, pushed her hair from her face. "Lucille's been giving me self-defense training. In another month or so, I would have been ready to tell you the truth."

He wouldn't understand the need she had to stay sheltered and protected until she could fend for herself. But then, Jack hadn't been held hostage by a serial killer.

Caroline watched the debate Jack was having with himself, and she wasn't sure if he would hold his ground and continue to stand here and press her for every detail of information in her head, or if he'd continue to be her protector.

The protector won out.

"Lucille," he called out. "Go ahead and get Caroline's and your things packed. Bring only some essentials, one bag each. I need to take you to a new location and will have someone come for the rest of your things later."

Caroline released the breath that she didn't even know she'd been holding. "Please don't bring your brothers in on this," she insisted. "Don't bring anyone else in on it. Not yet."

Jack certainly didn't agree to that, but he did head in the direction of the bedrooms. There were only two of them, hers and Lucille's, and Lucille was in Caroline's room, shoving meds and the laptop into a small duffel bag. Caroline jumped right in to help her.

Jack stood in the doorway, continuing to view the footage from the cameras. "Caroline, did you contact anyone when you did those internet searches?" he asked. Lucille left the room, probably realizing this was a good time for her to get her own things ready.

Caroline supposed that was a necessary question, but it sent a coil of anger through her. "No. I didn't have anyone I could completely trust to contact. Not even Gemma. Because, as I said, she would have told Kellan."

She left it at that, but Jack probably knew that some of those searches would have brought up pictures of Eric's victims. So many of them. Those images would haunt her, too.

"I couldn't access anything about the investigation into your father's murder." Caroline added a change of clothes to the duffel. She was about to ask him if he had any new leads, but his phone dinged before she could.

"Kingston Morris," he read aloud. Obviously, someone had run a background check for him. "Age twenty-four. Address in Dallas. No record. Trust fund baby. His folks own a successful export business." Jack held up Kingston's DMV photo for her to see.

"That's him," she verified. "But he's not in Dallas. He was by the pond about a half hour ago. Maybe you can put out an APB on him—"

"I've already done that." Jack's attention landed on her again. "Still believe I'm trying to kill you?"

"I never believed that," she snapped. "I just thought…" But she waved that off and zipped up the duffel with a hard jerk as if it'd been the cause for the fit of temper she was feeling.

And the frustration, doubt and fear.

"I hate being afraid," she said under her breath. She hadn't meant for Jack to hear that, but judging from the way he huffed and cursed, he had. Worse, he was probably analyzing her now as the shrinks had done after she'd tracked down her mother's killer.

"Then you need to trust me." He didn't say it as a request or plea. It was an order, and he tipped his head to indicate he wanted her on the move.

Jack also drew his gun.

Her pulse hadn't exactly been at a resting pace, but the sight of the weapon jacked it up even more, as it did the hit of adrenaline. It didn't mesh well with that knot already in her stomach.

With a small suitcase gripped in her hand, Lucille joined them in the hall. "How close are you parked to the house?" she asked.

"Close," Jack assured the nurse. "I'll go out first. When I motion for you to leave the house, move fast and get in the truck. Understand?"

The moment Lucille and Caroline nodded, Jack disengaged the security system and went out onto the porch. As he'd done at that kitchen window, he glanced around. So did Caroline, and she wished she had a gun or some other weapon that she could actually use with her still-weak hand. There was no chance of Jack giving her anything like that.

Because he didn't trust her.

She knew plenty about distrust and had spent every waking moment of the past year feeling the same thing. It'd been worse when she hadn't even known who she was. Well, in some ways it had been. Once she'd remembered, the distrust had collided with the fear that someone out there could still want her dead.

Not Jack.

She knew that now. But while she could trust him, she couldn't trust the others who were in his life. Part of her wanted to strike out on her own. But that would involve plenty of risks, too.

Still keeping watch, Jack went down the porch steps and started his truck. He motioned for them to move only after he threw open the passenger-side door.

"Now," he called out.

She and Lucille hurried off the porch, and even though it hadn't been Caroline's intention, she ended up in the middle of the seat, right next to Jack. Since she'd arrived at the safe house she had avoided touching him, but that was impossible now. They were shoulder to shoulder and hip to hip.

Jack immediately hit the accelerator, and while he continued glancing around them, he made a call using the control on his steering wheel. A few seconds later, a woman answered.

"Teagan," Jack said.

Caroline knew that was his partner, Marshal Teagan Randolph. She'd heard Jack give Lucille the marshal's contact info in case there was an emergency and she couldn't reach Jack. That meant he must trust the woman, but Caroline didn't want anyone else brought into this just yet. She was about to tell him that, too, but he cursed before Teagan or she could say anything.

"What's wrong?" Teagan immediately asked.

"We have a tail," Jack spat out. "I'm on the east farm road about twelve miles from Longview Ridge. I need backup right now."

Chapter Three

The moment Jack said someone was following them, Caroline jerked her body around to look out the back window of his truck. She groaned, no doubt seeing exactly what Jack had caught sight of.

A black four-door sedan with a heavily tinted windshield.

The fact that it was a car made it stand out in a place where most folks drove trucks. Maybe a crazed groupie/killer wannabe hadn't gotten the memo on that, and had failed to blend in.

Jack hadn't had a choice about requesting backup. He'd noticed the sedan pulling out of a ranch trail just moments after he had driven past it. Of course, it was possible this wasn't someone after Caroline, that it was just a driver in the wrong place at the wrong time, maybe even someone who'd gotten lost, but Jack couldn't risk not having an extra gun if something bad went down. Or rather, if something *worse* was going down.

The *bad* had already happened.

There was no scenario Jack could come up with that made Kingston Morris showing up just yards from the safe house a good thing. Which was why he should have called for backup even sooner. Unfortunately, Jack had let himself get distracted with Caroline's bombshell. Now that he'd remembered he was a lawman and not her former lover—or the son of a murdered sheriff—he would press her more on why she'd lied. Press her more, too, on the bits of so-called evidence from the night his dad had been killed. For now, Jack just kept an eye on the car behind them.

"Are Caroline and Lucille okay?" Teagan asked. "Are *you* okay?"

"So far." Jack wanted it to stay that way.

"Do you think it's that guy, Kingston Morris, who you asked me to run?" Teagan added.

"Possibly." But the more honest answer would be "Yes." It would be hard to believe it was a coincidence that an Eric groupie to appeared on a security camera and then someone else showed up on this remote stretch of the road.

"There's no immediate threat," Jack added to his partner, "but I want backup in place."

"Understood."

Jack opened his mouth to give Teagan some instructions as to what he needed her to do, but Caroline tugged on his arm to get his attention. At first he thought that was because she'd seen the person behind that dark windshield, but she merely stared at him. No one had ever accused him of having ESP or even being tuned in to nonverbal cues, but he got this one all right.

Caroline didn't want him to mention that she'd gotten her memory back. Since he couldn't see why Teagan would need to know that right at this exact moment, Jack nodded. Obviously Caroline was good with the nonverbal, too, because she blew out a breath of relief.

"I need you to run the plates on a black sedan for me,"

Jack continued with Teagan. He could hear his partner typing away on her keyboard. No doubt arranging for the backup he'd requested. But she could multitask, too, so he rattled off the license plate number to her.

"It's a rental car," Teagan said just moments later. "I'll find out who rented it."

Jack was betting the person who'd done that had used an alias. Well, unless Kingston or the person in the sedan was truly an idiot. That wouldn't make this situation less dangerous, because Jack knew from experience that idiots could kill just as well as smart people. The idiots just didn't tend to get away with it, but that didn't make their victims less dead or instances like this any less lethal.

The seconds seemed to drag before Teagan came back on the line. "Lee Zeller's in the field about twenty miles from you. He's the closest marshal for backup."

Jack kept his speed at a steady pace and considered his options. Zeller wasn't one of them, and he glanced at Caroline to see if she agreed. Judging from the way her forehead creased, she did. Which meant she'd been doing some investigating and had likely hacked her way through the filters in multiple files.

He was getting better at picking up the unspoken stuff.

"Bad choice for backup?" Teagan asked Jack when he didn't respond.

Teagan could read him. She'd been Jack's partner for two years and had read all the files on his father's murder.

Zeller had been involved in an investigation that Jack's father was running at the time he was gunned down. Sex trafficking. Zeller hadn't been a suspect in that case. Heck, there'd been no hints of any wrongdoing on his part, but Jack didn't like the way these particular lines had intersected. Because it would only rattle Caroline even more, he didn't want anyone from his father's investigations playing backup for him.

Well, no one who wasn't family.

That was going to tighten Caroline's forehead, too, and break some rules, but that car behind them certainly wasn't putting her at ease, either. Ditto for Lucille. Both women had turned to watch it again.

"I need to make another call," he told Teagan. "Get me the name on the rental car." Jack hung up and hit the button on his steering wheel.

"Call Kellan," he instructed his phone.

As expected, Caroline whirled back around while shaking her head. Frantically shaking it. There was no need for her to repeat her warning that while she thought she could trust Jack, she didn't feel that way about other cops. Or anyone else with a badge and a police radio who could maybe listen in on their conversation. So, while he waited for the call to his brother to connect, he gave her proof for why she should want Kellan in on this.

Jack sped up.

So did the car behind them.

When he slowed, the sedan followed suit. It let Caroline know that there could be a real threat behind them. Maybe it was Kingston. Maybe hired guns paid for with Kingston's trust fund. It could be someone who wasn't even on their radar, who'd used Kingston as a dupe.

Whatever this was, this situation could get ugly. In fact, the only reason it probably hadn't already was because the driver was waiting until they reached the road leading to Longview Ridge. It was wider and didn't coil around like a rattlesnake. It would be easier to make a move there. Jack was guessing the guy might try to run them off the road or else shoot at them.

Caroline's eyes were already wide, and only grew bigger when she saw how closely the sedan was mirroring their moves. Lucille saw it, too, and she threw her small suitcase on the floor of the truck, no doubt to free up her hands. She drew her gun just as Kellan answered the phone.

"You're on speaker," Jack warned his brother right off. "And I have Caroline and Lucille in the truck with me."

"What happened?" Kellan snapped.

"Kingston Morris, a possible groupie connected to Eric, showed up at the safe house, and now I think he could be following us. And no, you won't find his name in our files. That's because Caroline only told me about him less than a half hour ago. Apparently, Kingston visited Caroline's office while Eric was there, and Kingston made a strong enough impression for her to remember him."

Jack paused to give his brother a second to let that sink in. It sank in quickly.

"She got her memory back," Kellan concluded, and without even taking a breath, he added, "Dad's killer?"

Jack had anticipated that would be the first of his brother's questions. "She claims she doesn't know."

Jack figured the skepticism in his wording was going to piss her off, and it did. But he didn't care. She'd lied to him. And while her lie might not be responsible for the car following them, if he'd known the facts—all of them—he might have been able to pick up Kingston before it even came to this.

Even without having the details spelled out for him, it obviously riled Kellan, too, because he cursed. "Where are you? You need backup?"

"Yes to the backup." Jack gave Kellan his location. "I'm heading to your office, so meet me."

Jack didn't wait for his brother's assurance that he would do just that. No need. Kellan would get there as fast as he could. Maybe it would be fast enough, but Jack didn't like the bad feeling that was slithering its way down his back. That turn with the straighter, wider road was coming up fast.

"You know how I feel involving your brothers in this," Caroline snapped the moment he was off the phone with Kellan. "They could trust fellow cops who are dirty."

"Lesser of two evils," Jack reminded her, and just to prove his point, he slowed down. The sedan kept pace.

She made a sound to indicate she was considering what he'd said, but she didn't argue. Caroline twisted back around to keep watch.

Jack considered just flooring the accelerator and trying to outrace this moron. But that was risky. Curvy roads could lead to accidents, which would in turn make them sitting ducks. Plus, the sedan engine might be souped-up enough that it wouldn't have any trouble catching up with them. Jack wanted to delay the showdown until Kellan was closer.

"Who's Marshal Zeller?" Lucille asked. Her voice was a little shaky. So was she. But she was holding her own and didn't look ready to panic. "Why didn't you want him for backup?"

"Because he could be dirty," Caroline grumbled before Jack could say anything.

As answers went, it was a pretty good one. In her mind, Zeller could indeed be dirty. The jury was still out on that for Jack, but if there'd been any red flags to find, Jack figured he would have found them by now. That was because he'd dug and dug deep. Not just on Zeller but on any-and everyone connected to his father's investigations.

"Zeller headed a sex-trafficking case that popped a little over a year ago," Jack told Lucille. Like the women, he still had his eyes on the sedan. "One that involved some college students. One of those students, Nicola Gunderson, was abducted from a diner in Longview Ridge, and then she turned up dead. That's how my dad got involved. My brother Kellan too, since he was a deputy at the time."

"Oh, yes. I remember." Lucille's voice was a little tight, but Jack knew that wasn't because she had something to hide or even any personal knowledge of the case. However, she did have plenty of knowledge about sex offenses since she'd been a victim of a violent rape fifteen years earlier.

Zeller wasn't the only person Jack had vetted all the way down to ground zero.

Jack hadn't considered Lucille's past a concern, but rather he saw how she responded to it by cultivating her current assets. She'd learned to protect herself and continued her nursing career, and Jack figured that was a bonus skill set when it came to choosing who would be staying with Caroline. Right now, he appreciated that skill set very much, but he hoped he didn't need Lucille to play backup.

"You're taking me to the sheriff's office," Caroline concluded.

Jack couldn't figure out a way to sugarcoat it. "I am."

She sat there, obviously weighing her options as he'd done earlier. She was smart. Smart enough to keep her mouth shut about regaining her memory because she didn't know the snakes from the good guys. And that meant she'd soon figure out that the only choice she had was to go with him to the sheriff's office. That didn't mean she'd like it, though.

Jack had to slow down as he approached the last turn that would take him to town. They were about six miles out now.

Not far.

With Kellan no doubt already en route, it meant he had only a couple more minutes before he could do something about this tail. He wanted to question whoever was behind that wheel. If it was Kingston, he would question him even harder, because maybe he, too, had been at the abandoned hotel the night Jack's father was murdered.

Jack took the turn on the road, and while his attention hadn't strayed from the sedan, he watched it even closer now. Though he soon figured out there was no need for watching, because the driver immediately sped up.

Hell.

Kellan was still nowhere in sight, but Jack got a glimpse of something he sure as heck didn't want to see. The driver's-side window of the sedan lowered. A hand came out. One holding a gun.

"Get down!" Jack shouted to Caroline and Lucille.

Not a second too soon. Because the shot slammed into the truck.

Chapter Four

Caroline ducked down and grabbed on to Lucille to make sure she did the same just as a bullet blasted through the truck's back window. The safety glass shattered, but the pieces that pummeled them had a plastic coating to keep them from being lethal or cutting them to shreds.

The second shot could fall into the lethal category, though.

It slammed into the driver's side of the glass, missing Jack's head by what appeared to be a fraction of an inch.

Fear roared through her, but so did anger. Whoever was doing his—Kingston, maybe—was putting Jack and Lucille in danger, all so he could get to her.

Of course, the flashbacks came. Nightmarish memories of the other attack, the gunfire the night Jack's father had been murdered. Jack was no doubt reliving some bad stuff, as well.

"I can hold the steering wheel so you can return fire," Caroline offered.

With narrowed eyes, he spared her a glance, looking at her as if she'd lost her mind. "You're staying down." And he caught onto her neck to push her lower. "I have no intention of confronting this jerk with Lucille and you in the vehicle. I'll do that later when it's just me and him."

Jack didn't leave any room for argument on that, and he hit the accelerator again just as the shooter sent a third bullet their way. Since Lucille was shaking and mumbling a prayer, Caroline put her arm around the woman to try to comfort her.

Mixed in with the sound of a fourth shot, Caroline heard something else. The howl of a police siren. It gave her a jolt of relief. Then, a wave of more fear. Because this was probably Kellan.

The shots stopped instantly, and behind them was the screech of brakes. When Jack cursed, she risked lifting her head to see what was going on. The shooter had stopped and was turning his car around.

No doubt so he could get away.

Jack pulled to the side of the road, and that was when Caroline looked out of the front of the truck and spotted not one but two cruisers. Two deputies were in one, and they sped past them, heading in pursuit of the gunman. Kellan was driving the second cruiser, and he pulled up next to Jack.

"Is anyone hurt?" Kellan immediately asked, glancing up at the shot-out glass, then his brother. Then, at Caroline. Kellan was probably good at poker, because she couldn't tell what he was thinking other than the obvious concern for his brother and them.

Jack made a quick check of her and Lucille, but his attention didn't stray far from his rearview mirror. Keeping watch for the sedan that had sped away from them.

"We're okay," Jack assured his brother. "I need to get them to the sheriff's office."

Kellan gave a quick nod. "I would have all of you get in the cruiser with me, but the guy might return, and I don't want you out in the open. I'll follow you back and send out another crew of deputies to assist in chasing down that car."

Jack matched his brother's nod and took off. "It'll only take us a couple of minutes to get there," Jack told Lucille and her.

Minutes. Not long before she could be walking into a lion's den. But then, as Jack had said, for her it was the lesser of two evils. She definitely didn't want to hang around, waiting for a gunman.

Those couple of minutes crawled by, and it didn't help that Caroline had broken glass all over her. A reminder of the attack. God, when was this going to end? For over a year she had been fighting for her life, and now she'd apparently brought that fight straight to Jack.

Jack didn't slow down until his truck screeched to a stop in front of the sheriff's office. Kellan must have already called ahead, because another of Jack's brothers, Deputy Owen Slater, was in the open doorway, and he had his gun drawn. As soon as Kellan arrived he took Owen's place, and Owen drove off in the cruiser. No doubt in pursuit of the shooter.

"I called a medic," Kellan said as they all hurried inside. "He'll be here soon." Another of the deputies, Gunnar Pullam, immediately took hold of Lucille's arm. Caroline knew him, and had never gotten any criminal vibes from him, but she still kept her distance.

"Move away from the windows," Jack snapped.

Caroline didn't need a reminder of the danger or another slam of adrenaline, but Jack's words gave her both anyway.

Jack turned to Gunnar. "Do you want to take Lucille to the break room to wait for the medic?" he suggested.

"And after she gets checked out, take her statement," Kellan added.

When Kellan looked at Caroline this time, his face wasn't so poker ready. His mouth was tight, maybe because she hadn't remembered his father's killer. Or perhaps he just thought she hadn't wanted to tell him.

Caroline was certain there was some tightness in her mouth, too. Was she looking into the eyes of a killer? Maybe not. But it was possible that Kellan was covering for one.

With his hand still on her arm, Jack led her across the squad room that was jammed with desks and equipment and took her inside Kellan's office.

"Stay here," he told her and immediately went back out into the squad room, where Kellan waited.

The brothers were only about ten feet away from her, but Jack didn't exactly broadcast what he was saying, keeping his voice barely louder than a whisper. Still, Caroline caught a word here and there. *Three days ago, she said. Dirty cop. You. Yeah, she thinks that.*

The last one caused Kellan to huff and then scowl, but when he glanced over Jack's shoulder at her, the scowl disappeared. The look he gave her riled her to the core. Because it was pity. Kellan thought she was too damaged to think straight. He was dismissing her concerns that a lawman had been the one to help Eric in the attack a year ago.

Jack also glanced back at her, frowned and then mumbled something else to Kellan. She didn't catch a single word of that, but Jack started toward her. Not hurrying, but with every step he took, he kept his eyes on her.

When he reached her, she was about to blast him for spilling all to Kellan, but Jack stopped her with a touch.

He pushed her hair from her face, examining her. Or so she thought until he extracted a blob of the safety glass, then another, from the top of her head.

Dragging in a weary breath, he closed the door, and in the same motion, he turned her to check the back of her hair. "Shake your clothes," he instructed. "Even safety glass can cut if you sit or lean back on it."

Her mouth got tighter, but she shook the dress and glass bits pinged to the tile floor. "You told your brother that I don't trust him," she snapped, "that I think he's a dirty cop involved in his father's murder."

Jack continued to pick off glass bits. "He would have figured it out. He's a lot better at body language than I am."

"You're fine with body language," she grumbled, but Caroline wished she'd kept that to herself.

She whirled around just in time to see him smile that damnable smile, and she wasn't sure if she wanted to throttle him or kiss him. Caroline didn't do either, but it did cause her to freeze.

His next breath wasn't so much one of weariness as it was of relief. The long, lingering look he gave her made her think he was about to touch her again. He didn't. Instead, Jack crammed his hands into the pockets of his jeans.

"If you need to fall apart or cry, go ahead and do it," he offered. "You're shaking," he pointed out before she could insist she didn't intend to do either. She didn't know what she was stewing over more— Jack telling his brother her deep, dark fears or Kellan brushing it off as Jack had done to the glass.

But she was indeed trembling.

Her hands, her mouth. Heck, her legs. She was probably a breath away from both falling apart and crying.

"I nearly got Lucille and you killed," she said, and Caroline cursed her own voice. It was shaking, too.

Jack lifted an eyebrow. "Funny, I thought it was the shooter who nearly killed us."

"The shooter wouldn't have been firing those bullets if it hadn't been for me." She expected him to give her some sugarcoated answer, but she'd obviously forgotten this was Jack.

"That's true." With that hanging in the air, he waited a heartbeat. "And since I'd rather not have any more attempted murders, that means you're going to have to let me help you."

"You mean I'm going to have to trust Kellan," Caroline blurted out. She was feeling a lot less shaky now.

Jack shrugged, took his hand from his pocket so he could tap the badge on his belt. "Every lawman in Texas isn't tainted, and if you dig beneath all the anger, fear and whatever else it is you're feeling, you'll remember that I'm the best shot you've got at keeping us both alive."

He followed that too logical minilecture with a long stare. Jack was obviously waiting for her to come to the only conclusion that she had right now.

"I'm *not* going to trust your brother," she insisted, but left the rest of it unspoken—that she would trust Jack. Again, it was the only choice she had.

He nodded as if they'd just hashed that out with a heated argument. "I'll do whatever it takes to keep you safe." He paused. "Want me to take a bullet for you to prove it?"

Jack didn't wink, but he might as well have, because he was obviously trying to lighten things up. Trying to bring her back down and ease some of the still raw adrenaline. It was working, sort of, since it was something he'd said to her in jest when they'd been lovers. A way of letting her know that he cared that much for her.

"No," she said, drawing out the one-word answer to emphasize it. There was a lot more emotion in her voice than she wanted as she stared at him.

Thinking.

Remembering.

Yes, definitely remembering.

That helped more than his lame attempt at cop humor. His being there helped, too, and despite everything she'd been through—or maybe because of it—Caroline wanted to step right into his arms. Those strong arms with their toned muscles. She wanted to feel the heat, and the comfort that she'd gotten there before. Jack had tugged and pulled at her in a way that no man ever had before.

Or ever would again, she was forced to admit to herself.

Yes, it'd been great sex. The fire between them so hot. The feel of him touching her with those calloused hands. Him, being inside her. She'd felt that, too.

If it'd been just those things, *only those*, she could have pushed it all away. Could have distracted herself with the dark fear that was eating holes in her. But it had been more—way more—and she had to admit that to herself, too.

With those stormy gray eyes locked on hers, he reached up and touched his finger to the center of her forehead. Just a touch, maybe to her scar, the one that Eric had given her when he hit her. Or maybe Jack was trying to ease the tensed muscles there. And despite everything she'd just admitted to herself, Caroline still hadn't been prepared for that touch. For the way his warm breath fell on her. For the look of him.

That face. His eyes. His mouth that had fueled enough fantasies to last her a couple of lifetimes.

"Penny for your thoughts," he drawled. "A dollar for them if you're thinking about sex." The corner of his mouth hitched. Because he knew her thoughts, knew everything she was feeling right now.

Since he was feeling the same thing, Caroline laid her hand on his chest. Over his heart, which she could feel beating to the rhythm of hers.

"Sex won't help," she said, her voice mostly breath.

His slight smile stayed in place. A smile that only he and Mona Lisa could have pulled off. "That depends on the sex."

Jack made her laugh before she could stop herself or remember there was absolutely nothing to laugh about. He hooked his arm around the back of her neck in a casual, easy way, and lowering his head to her, took her laugh with his mouth.

Kissing her.

It was like hot silk sliding through her. Oh, it felt wonderful. That incredible taste. Those clever moves, with seemingly no effort. He made no demands, and yet, also seemed to make the biggest demand of all. Within seconds, he had turned the hot silk to blazing flames.

"It's good to have you back," he whispered against her mouth.

Is it? she wanted to say. She'd brought nothing but trouble with her. But there wasn't time for her question because the door opened, and Kellan stepped in.

Jack moved away from her, but he took his time, which meant Kellan had no trouble seeing Jack's arm around her and their mouths hovering over each other. It didn't make Kellan a happy camper. He scowled at his brother.

"The medic's here to check Caroline," Kellan said, his attention nailed to Jack. "And I just spoke to Kingston on the phone, and he said he'd come in for questioning, to *set some things straight*. He's on his way here right now."

Chapter Five

Jack wanted to curse. Even though he probably should, he didn't regret kissing Caroline. But now he was going to have to listen to Kellan tell him why a kissing regret should be at the top of his list.

And Kellan would be right.

Caroline didn't look so much regretful as she did embarrassed. Nervous, too. That was likely because of the distrust she had for not only Kellan but all the other cops in the building.

"I'll find the medic," she muttered, moving past both Jack and Kellan to hurry away.

Kellan immediately motioned toward Sherry McNeil, one of the deputies at a desk in the squad room. "Keep an eye on her," Kellan said to Sherry, tipping his head in the direction of both Caroline and the ladies' room.

Jack just lifted an eyebrow.

"Caroline lied to you. She waited three days to tell you she'd gotten her memory back," Kellan said, as if that excused the tail he'd just put on her.

"She lied because she doesn't trust me. Not yet."

Kellan made a sound of disagreement. "She looked pretty trusting to me when she was kissing you."

"That was the attraction. It's always been intense between us."

He wouldn't tell his brother that Caroline and he had gone all night their first time together. As if they'd been starved for each other. Hell, they were still starved for each other. If the door had been locked and Kellan hadn't walked in, Jack might have backed Caroline against the wall and taken her then and there.

And she would have let him.

He'd felt that. The way her body had hummed against his. His own body had hummed plenty, too, and Jack knew it wasn't going to be easy to rein in that kind of heat. And he doubted he would be able to count on an interruption to give him the willpower to resist a woman he'd never been able to resist.

"I don't have to tell you this, but I will," Kellan went on a moment later. "Sex could cause you to lose focus."

This was obviously going to be one of the big topics of conversation today. "Lack of sex can do that, too. I haven't been with another woman since Caroline." Jack looked at Kellan then but didn't see even one raised eyebrow. "You don't seem surprised."

"I'm not just a cop, I'm also your big brother. I know you fell hard for her, but she's not the same woman she was a year ago."

"Of course, she's not," Jack snapped. "She was nearly murdered by a serial killer and had amnesia. Hard to come back from that. But Caroline's there. Underneath the tangled mess of memories in her head, she's there."

The sound that Kellan made was still edged with suspicion. "Personally, I like her. There's plenty of toughness beneath that delicate-looking exterior."

Yes, there was, and it was one of the things that had

first attracted Jack to her. But her toughness had some fractures in it now. Thanks to Eric. This latest attack sure wasn't going to help, either.

Jack scrubbed his hand over his face. "I need to figure out how the location of the WITSEC house was breached, and I have to look into those things that Caroline heard the night Dad was killed."

Kellan's jaw tightened. "The police radio transmissions. The mention of this office. The dispatch codes." He glanced around the squad room. "I'll help with that. I trust every person who works for me, but I won't blow off what Caroline told you. That's why I sent Sherry to keep an eye on her. Caroline said the voice on that call to Eric was male, so she should be okay with Sherry watching after her."

Jack sent his brother a silent look of thanks for that.

"The call Caroline heard could have been part of the sick game that Eric was playing," Kellan added after a pause. "Something to throw her off the accomplice who was actually helping him."

That wasn't just possible. It was likely. The trouble would be to convince Caroline of that, and his best shot at doing it was to figure out how Eric could have faked a call like that.

When Jack heard someone clear their throat, he looked to the doorway and saw Tatum Carson, the medic. "Neither of the women has any injuries," Tatum told them, "but if you want me to take them into the hospital for tests, I will."

"No," Lucille and Caroline said in unison. They were behind the medic, and Sherry and Gunnar stood behind them.

Jack looked at both Lucille and Caroline and knew

there'd be no other tests. "Thanks. You can go," he said to Tatum.

With a suit-yourself shrug, the medic gathered his things and headed out.

"Lucille wants to go to her sister's in San Antonio," Gunnar said, stepping up. "I got her statement and her contact info. Her sister doesn't have a car, so Lucille will need a ride. Is it okay for her to go?"

This was touchy jurisdictional territory. The shooting hadn't happened at the WITSEC safe house, which meant technically this was Kellan's case. Jack didn't want to cross any gray lines—when he managed to make an arrest, he needed to have dotted all the i's and crossed all the t's to get a conviction. He also didn't want to step on his brother's toes, so he looked at Kellan, wanting him to respond to Gunnar's question.

"Any chance this shooter will go after Lucille?" Kellan asked Jack.

"Slim to none." Caroline was the target. Jack was certain of that. "But San Antonio PD should be alerted just in case something comes up. That way, they can make sure Lucille is protected."

"She can leave," Kellan said, apparently satisfied with what Jack had just told him. "I can't send Gunnar with her, though, because he's got to testify in court in about an hour. He won't make it back here in time. Sherry, will you drive Lucille and contact SAPD on the way there?"

Sherry nodded, and, as the medic had done, the deputy started to gather her things, too. However, Lucille didn't budge. Instead, she caught onto Caroline's shoulders and looked her straight in the eyes.

"Remember what I taught you," Lucille said.

Caroline nodded. "Open-hand strike to the nose, followed by a hard kick to the groin."

Jack winced, but Lucille smiled, clearly proud of her student. She brushed a kiss on Caroline's cheek, whispered a goodbye and headed out with the deputy.

"Should I take Caroline's statement now?" Gunnar asked.

This was another t-crossing and i-dotting moment. Since Jack had also been on the receiving end of that attack, he couldn't question her. Heck, he shouldn't even be in the room with her during the interview. That meant Caroline was about to be questioned by a male cop whom she maybe didn't trust.

Jack was still mulling over the best way to handle that when he realized the interview and his own mulling were going to have to wait. That was because he saw a now familiar face had stepped into the squad room.

Kingston walked in, and he was wearing the same clothes he'd had on in the security footage. What the footage hadn't captured was the cocky look on his face. It appeared to be a permanent expression.

"Caroline," Kingston purred, his attention going straight to her. "So you're still alive. Too bad that you won't be that way for long."

CAROLINE PULLED BACK her shoulders. Considering Kingston had been friends with a serial killer, she hadn't expected him to look, well, normal, but she also hadn't believed he'd come waltzing into a sheriff's office to dole out what sounded like a threat.

"I'm Kingston Morris," he greeted as if this were a

social call. He thrust out his hand for Jack to shake. "And you're Marshal Slater. Good to meet you."

Jack didn't exchange handshakes, but he gave Kingston a look that could have frozen Hades. He caught onto Kingston, whirled him around and, despite the man's howl of protest, frisked him. No weapon.

"*So you're still alive. Too bad that you won't be that way for long,*" Jack growled, repeating word for word what Kingston had just said. "Along with some other things, you'll want to explain that *now.*"

Kingston was wise enough to drop the cocky smile and the protest over the pat down, but he didn't appear as concerned as he should be, considering that Jack looked ready to tear him limb from limb.

"I said that because of the attack." There wasn't much concern in Kingston's voice, either. *Unflappable* was the word that came to Caroline's mind. "Lots of gossip about it, and from what people are saying, someone wanted to kill Caroline and you."

Now Kingston turned to her, their gazes connecting, and Caroline forced herself not to take a step back. Too bad that he spurred the old memories, and she got a burst of the flashbacks before she could stop them. The pain and the fear. She'd thought she was going to die, and the swarm of emotions that had come with that belief hit her now.

Jack must have noticed or else guessed about the flashbacks, because he moved closer to her, his arm brushing against her. It was surprising and unnerving how just a simple touch from him could soothe her. But Caroline would take it. She definitely didn't want to collapse into a puddle from a panic attack when she needed to confront Kingston.

"You tried to kill Jack and me?" Caroline came out and asked, and she made sure she held eye contact with Kingston.

"No, of course not." It sounded more mocking than genuine, but at least the man started to show some concern when Jack turned on a recorder and began to read him his rights.

"You're arresting me?" Kingston demanded several times while he was Mirandized.

"Any reason I shouldn't?" Jack countered after he'd finished. "You were at Caroline's not long before she was attacked."

Jack didn't add more to that explanation, and Caroline thought she knew why. He was giving Kingston a chance to lie by denying it. If so, that would add weight to his arrest.

However, Kingston shrugged. "Yes, I was there," he readily admitted. "I got a text, giving me the address and saying I should go there."

Jack eased up on the glare to give the man a look of skepticism. Caroline felt the same way, and when Kingston obviously picked up on their disbelief, he huffed and took out his phone. After he'd pulled up a message, he handed Jack his phone.

There it was on the screen. No name of the person who'd sent the message, but there was the address of the safe house, along with the message, Want to get a look at the woman who helped kill your friend Eric Lang? You'll find her here.

"I don't know who sent it, and the number is no longer working," Kingston explained. "My guess is he or she used a disposable cell and deactivated it."

"Or else you used such a phone and sent the message to yourself," Jack quickly countered.

Kingston didn't exactly give him an eye roll, but it was close. "There's no reason for me to do that."

Jack didn't waste any time arguing. "Sure there is. You might think a message like that would get you off the hook. It won't. You were in the vicinity of Caroline's house, and you have a motive to murder her."

"A motive?" Kingston challenged. "You mean because of Eric?" He didn't wait for Jack to confirm or deny that. "I wouldn't kill because of him. Yes, I was intrigued by Eric. He was very interesting and charismatic, but I wouldn't have done his bidding. Besides, he's dead."

Jack leveled his gaze on Kingston. "Yet you acted on what you're saying was an anonymous tip to go to the house of a woman you blame for the death of this interesting and charismatic piece of dirt?"

Kingston opened his mouth, then closed it as if rethinking what he'd been about to say. "I don't blame Caroline for Eric's death." He shifted his attention to Kellan. "I believe you're the one who delivered what eventually became the fatal blow."

"I did," Kellan readily admitted. "I just wish I'd been able to put a bullet in him sooner."

If Kingston had a reaction to that, he didn't show it. Instead, he turned back to Caroline. "Someone wants you dead. The attack proves that. And I think the person who sent me that message thought I'd do the job for him or her."

"Do you want to do the job?" Caroline asked, and thankfully she sounded a lot tougher than she felt. More of those flashbacks bolted through her like lightning, and for just a moment she wished she hadn't recovered those parts of her memory.

Again, Kingston took his time answering. "There's no law against admiring a man like Eric. In his own twisted way, he was a genius. And he kept you alive. That's a key point here. Why would I want to go against him on that? If he didn't kill you, then why should I?"

Caroline didn't have to think long to come up with a reason. A sick one. "Because he's dead, and you might want the thrill of murdering me to honor a man who intrigued you."

"No." Kingston looked her straight in the eyes when he said that. "I wouldn't do that, and I'm not responsible for the attack against you. I merely went to your place out of curiosity."

Caroline wasn't sure she believed that, but the problem would be finding the proof. Maybe they'd get that with the rental car. Jack had asked his brother, Texas Ranger Eli Slater, to assist with locating it, though she was concerned that Kingston had covered his tracks there. Strange, though, that he hadn't done the same track-covering at the safe house. But then maybe he hadn't known there'd be security cameras at the back of the property.

"Did you send Eric money the night he took Caroline hostage?" Jack asked Kingston. Obviously, he intended to press the man on more than just the attack. Of course, anything Jack found out about Kingston could give them more fodder to make an arrest.

"I did," Kingston admitted, "but I didn't know what he'd done. It hadn't hit the news yet that Caroline had been taken hostage, and Eric didn't mention it."

Eric hadn't. Caroline had been there for that entire

call, and not once had Eric said anything about why he needed funds.

"How'd you get him the money?" Jack pressed.

"I gathered the cash. Ten grand. It was all my parents had in their safe. I put it in a bag and left it for Eric on the side of the road where he told me to leave it."

Jack gave Kingston another dose of his lawman's glare. "And you didn't think it was a little strange that a person you knew or at least suspected was a serial killer would ask you for money?"

"No. I didn't know or suspect he was a serial killer," Kingston insisted. "That didn't come out until later, until he escaped with Caroline."

Maybe. But Caroline still wasn't buying it.

"Did you get Eric a car that night, too?" Jack continued.

Caroline had to speak up on this. "No. Eric stole it. Or rather, he had me hot-wire it. It was in the driveway of a house not far from the abandoned inn where your father was killed." She paused, stared at Kingston. "But just because you didn't do that doesn't make you an innocent man."

"No, it doesn't," Kellan agreed before Kingston could respond. "I need to take him to the interview room and get his statement." He didn't invite Jack and her to go with him. No doubt because it would be a conflict of interest since Kingston was a suspect in their attack. Still, Caroline wanted to hear what else the man had to say.

"There's an observation room," Jack told her, and they headed out of the office and toward the hall.

However, they hadn't made it far before the front door opened again. This time, it wasn't a suspect who came in but Gemma. In the blink of an eye, the past months melted away, and Caroline felt the warmth of seeing a dear friend. Even though she figured the flashbacks would soon return, she savored the moment when Gemma rushed to her and pulled her into her arms.

"You're okay?" Gemma muttered.

Caroline nodded. It wasn't the total truth, but she hadn't been physically harmed. That was what Gemma needed to know for now.

When Gemma pulled back, Caroline saw tears in her friend's eyes. Not just from the relief of her not being injured but because her memory had returned. Gemma didn't have to say that aloud for Caroline to know that Kellan had told her.

Jack cleared his throat to get their attention. "I'm going to the observation room. Why don't you two talk in Jack's office?"

Only then did Caroline remember that they were too close to the windows. Not a good idea for either one of them. Caroline hooked her arm around Gemma's waist and got her moving.

"How much have you remembered?" Gemma asked.

"Enough." Caroline didn't say more until they were in the office. "I got my memory back three days ago."

Gemma nodded. Then she sighed. Obviously, her friend didn't understand why Caroline had kept it a secret. Heck, Gemma might not even understand after she'd explained. Still, Caroline had to try.

"Eric made a call to someone the night he took me hostage. I heard a police radio in the background. I heard someone say Longview Ridge. The caller used cop words, including dispatch codes. I know, I know," Caroline added before Gemma could try to explain all of that away. "It doesn't mean Kellan's guilty. But he could be unknowingly shielding a killer because he can't see past his friendships or blind loyalty to the badge."

Much to Caroline's surprise, Gemma didn't dismiss that. "So you think it could be one of Kellan's deputies? Or Jack?"

"Not Jack." Caroline should have at least hesitated a split second. "He might have that badge blindness—" or DNA blindness, she silently added, when it came to his brothers "—but Jack doesn't want me dead."

Gemma was one of the best profilers that she'd ever met, and she turned those profiling eyes on Caroline. And she waited as if she knew Caroline was holding something back.

She was.

Of course, Gemma knew about her history with Jack. Knew all about Jack and her being lovers.

"I kissed Jack," Caroline blurted out, cursing herself. She added some more curse words for Jack, too.

"And you think that was a…wise idea?" Gemma asked as if carefully choosing her words.

"No! Of course, it wasn't. It was the worst idea in the history of bad ideas. Someone's trying to kill me. I don't know who to trust, and I feel ready to unravel. The whole time I'm feeling all of that, I'm thinking how can a man like Jack still want me when I'm like this?" Caroline paused, steadied herself and admitted the truth. "But he did want me. As much as I wanted him."

Gemma sighed and took hold of her shoulders. "You can trust him. And you can trust Kellan, though I don't expect you to just take my word for it."

"I'm sorry I can't take your word for it." Caroline scrubbed her hand over her face. "I really am ready to unravel."

"Yes, I can see that. Just be careful not to unravel in Jack's arms."

That sent Caroline's gaze back to Gemma. "You can't believe Jack would want to hurt me."

"No, I don't, but I think he could hurt you here." She tapped her fingers on Caroline's heart. "Hurt himself, too. Caring this much doesn't always help. Just take things as slow as you can. Keep your mind open." Gemma blinked back more tears, then smiled. "And for Pete's sake, quit aiming your suspicious eyes at the man I love."

Gemma's smile didn't last, though, and Caroline could see the concern return to her friend's expression. Caroline figured she was about to get a lecture about staying safe and cooperating with Kellan and Jack, but Gemma stopped when Jack appeared in the office doorway.

"We have a visitor," Jack said, and judging from his tone, it wasn't someone he especially wanted to see.

Caroline moved closer to him so she could peer over his shoulder, and she saw the tall, lean man making his way toward them. Correction—not just a man, but a marshal.

Marshal Lee Zeller.

The very person that Jack hadn't trusted enough to give them backup when the sedan was following them.

"There was no need for you to come," Jack quickly told Zeller.

But Zeller shook his head. "I need to talk to you," he said. "Because I think I might know who's trying to kill Caroline."

Chapter Six

Until Zeller had said that last sentence, Jack had been about to demand that the marshal get the heck out of there. But that stopped him.

Because I think I might know who's trying to kill Caroline.

Jack put on hold his demand for Zeller to leave and gave the man his full attention. He definitely wanted to hear what Zeller had to say, but he'd take every one of the marshal's words with a grain of salt. That was because underneath it all, Jack didn't trust him.

"I'm listening," Caroline prompted when Zeller didn't add anything else. She sounded steady enough. Maybe even a little riled. But Jack knew her nerves were right there at the surface.

Zeller dragged in a heavy breath, put his hands on his hips and stared at Caroline. "I heard about the breach of security at the WITSEC house and about the attack. Are you okay?"

"Obviously not," Jack answered for her. "Someone's trying to kill her, and you just said you might know who that is. Spill it."

When Zeller shifted his attention back to Jack, the man's eyes were slightly narrowed. Probably because he didn't like Jack's prickly attitude. Tough. Jack wasn't going to ease up until he had some answers.

"Well, it's not me who wants her harmed, if that's what you're thinking," Zeller spat out. "I'm here to help, and maybe then you'll start to trust me again. I wear the same badge you do, remember?"

Zeller had likely said that to try to reassure Caroline that she was in safe hands, but considering what she'd overheard with Eric's phone call, Jack figured it had the opposite effect.

"Lily Terrell," Zeller tossed out there, and he let the name hang in the air.

Jack knew who she was, of course. He knew plenty of the names of people connected to his father's investigation, and Lily was one of them. For that matter, so was Zeller. Zeller and his father had been bumping heads over the sex-trafficking case they had both been looking into around the same time his dad was murdered. Jack still had some niggling doubts that those confrontations with Zeller or the investigation itself had led to his father's death, but what was missing was evidence of that.

"You think Lily Terrell is trying to kill me?" Caroline asked, her tone proving that she could sound just as grouchy as Jack.

Zeller sure didn't jump to say yes. "I think someone in her organization could be responsible," he answered, and Jack didn't think it was his imagination that the man had chosen his words carefully.

It'd been a while since Jack had read anything about Lily, but he could still recall plenty of the details. Lily Terrell was a millionaire heiress from San Antonio. Her organization, New Beginnings, ran a counseling center and residential facility for the girls and women rescued from the sex-trafficking ring that Zeller and Jack's father were investigating.

Jack glanced at Caroline. It was clear from her earlier question that she knew who Lily was. Of course, with her hacking skills, she had likely filled in whatever memory gaps she had.

Jack turned back to Zeller. "You have proof that Lily or someone she knows could be linked to what happened to Caroline?"

"No proof," Zeller readily admitted, "but there's something off at New Beginnings. I've been keeping tabs on it."

Jack could see why Zeller would do that. The killer of Nicola Gunderson, one of the girls who'd been trafficked, had never been identified. With all the leads gone cold, Zeller might believe someone at the facility knew something about it.

"A woman has gone missing from New Beginnings," Zeller went on. "I know that doesn't mean she's dead. She could have just left." He shook his head, grumbling some profanity under his breath. "But what if Lily started that place because she was the one behind the sex-trafficking ring? She could have done that to make sure she could squash any incriminating info that could have come out about her."

Jack wasn't surprised, but he saw Caroline's eyes widen. He'd actually played around with that idea. Call him a first-class cynic, but it made him suspicious when someone like Lily made a grand gesture out of the goodness of their heart. Within hours of the sex-trafficking ring being busted, Lily had come forward with her offer to help the girls.

"Tell me about the missing woman," Jack said to Zeller.

Zeller didn't hesitate. "Her name is Skylar Greer. She'd been a runaway when she was lured into sex trafficking. Skylar was eighteen when she was rescued. She went to New Beginnings because she had no other place to go, and she went missing last month."

"Lily reported it?" Jack asked.

Now there was a pause. "No, she said Skylar just left. Like I said, I've been keeping tabs on the place, and I have someone inside I've been paying for info. A handyman named Bennie Darnell. Bennie claims he heard no talk of the girl wanting to go, but he did overhear Skylar talking about finding out who'd murdered Nicola Gunderson."

Now, that was interesting how it'd circled back to his father and his investigation. Well, it was interesting if it was true.

"Skylar had apparently gotten to know Nicola in the short time she was in the sex-trafficking ring," Zeller went on, "and Skylar wanted justice for her." He shifted his attention to Caroline. "Lily ticks some boxes on the profiling scale when it comes to something like this."

Zeller had obviously assumed that Caroline's memory was clear when it came to her profiling skill set. It was, but Jack didn't like that Zeller had seemed to know that. It made him wonder if Zeller had kept tabs on Caroline, as well.

"What boxes?" Caroline asked.

"For one thing, Lily has a record. Her folks paid plenty of money to make the trouble go away, but she had a fondness for drugs when she was a teenager. She wasted away a good chunk of her trust fund and then fell in with some girls who bilked money out of rich old men."

Caroline lifted her shoulder. "A criminal past doesn't

necessarily mean you'll grow up to run your own sex-trafficking ring."

"No, but I have it on good word that Lily's stayed in touch with her criminal friends."

Still, that was a stretch, and Caroline's huff let Jack know they felt the same way about the information Zeller was giving them. It could be pertinent. *Could be.* Or it could be a smoke screen.

"Lily hasn't been arrested since she was a teenager," Jack reminded Zeller. "Everything indicates that she's not only turned her life around but that she also wants to help others."

But Jack was just playing devil's advocate on that, since Lily's life turnaround could indeed be a facade. From what he'd read, Lily was getting lots of charitable donations from her rich friends for New Beginnings, although she'd pumped in some money of her own. That meant a place like that could merely be a sweet tax shelter for her and nothing more.

"Bennie thinks there's something shady going on there," Zeller continued, "and for now I agree with him. I'll keep digging into Skylar's disappearance. Will do the same for Lily, too, and I'll let you know what I find out."

Jack nodded. He wasn't going to refuse information, but he would darn sure consider the source. A source who could want to get attention off himself and place it onto someone else like Lily.

Zeller snorted, his gaze sliding back and forth between them. "And you're not buying anything I'm saying. You have a different angle on who could be responsible for the attack today?" That question snapped out like a bullwhip.

Jack debated how much he would say, but he knew it wouldn't be long before Zeller heard about the man

Kellan had in the interview room. Besides, if Jack was the one to tell Zeller, then he could watch his reaction.

"Kingston Morris showed up at Caroline's WITSEC house shortly before the attack," Jack explained.

Zeller shrugged. If he recognized Kingston's name, he didn't show any signs of it. Of course, he could be faking his reaction, but Jack hoped that it meant Zeller hadn't extended his "keeping tabs" to background checks like the ones Jack and Teagan had made. If Zeller was clean, Jack didn't mind the marshal knowing what they were up to, but the jury was still out on whether or not Zeller was dirty.

"Kingston was one of Eric's admirers," Jack went on a moment later.

Now Zeller's eyes widened and he cursed. "How the hell did he get the address?"

"To be determined. Kellan is questioning him now."

Zeller belted out more profanity. "The marshals should be doing that. A breach of security at a WITSEC house is our jurisdiction."

"Yeah, but the attack happened on Kellan's turf," Jack quickly reminded him. "Three counts of attempted murder trumps a trespassing charge. Plus, Kingston didn't try to break into the house. He just showed up on the security feed and then left."

Of course, Kingston had perhaps left so he'd be in position to fire those shots at Caroline, Lucille and him, but that was only speculation. Maybe Kellan was getting something from Kingston that would qualify as proof so they could arrest the man.

Zeller checked his watch. "I have to leave and help with a prisoner transport," he grumbled. "But I want to know if Kingston gives you anything."

Jack just lifted an eyebrow and waited for Zeller to tell him why he had a need for that kind of information.

"Caroline's attack could be linked to Nicola Gunderson's murder." Zeller ground out the words, clearly not pleased that he was having to explain himself. "Nicola's killer was never caught, and I want to clear the case along with finding Skylar."

Jack wasn't ruling out that all of those events could be connected, but some of the pieces didn't have obvious fits. Kingston, for one. There was nothing to prove he was involved in the sex trafficking. For that matter, Caroline wasn't connected to it, either. Unless, of course, all of this went back to Eric. Maybe Eric had been working with the sex trafficker, and now the person or people behind that wanted to tie up loose ends. If someone thought Caroline was a loose end, that would be motive for the attack.

Zeller checked his watch again and moved as if to leave, but then he stopped and looked at Caroline. "Did you really get your memory back?"

Jack couldn't tell if that was a good guess or if Zeller had heard that from Teagan.

"Some of it," Caroline said.

As answers went, it was a darn good one. Evasive but also probing, because Jack was pretty sure Caroline was studying Zeller to gauge his reaction. However, Zeller didn't give them a chance to study much of anything. He turned away, heading for the door.

"Good," Zeller told her from over his shoulder. "I'll keep you both posted if I find out anything more about Lily."

Caroline and Jack stood there and watched as he left. "What do you think Zeller really wanted?" she asked.

Despite his bone-weary fatigue and frustration, Jack nearly smiled. He'd forgotten just how sharp Caroline could be and how she tended to think like a cop.

Or a criminal.

"I'm not sure," Jack said, "but it felt like a fishing expedition with some mud throwing for good measure. Don't worry. I don't trust him."

The slight sound she made seemed to be approval, but when she dodged his gaze, Jack stepped in front of her, forcing eye contact. Not very smart, considering the last time he'd done that they'd ended up kissing, but he wanted to see what was going on in the depths of her cool green eyes.

Plenty was going on.

Like him, she was tired and a little unsteady. Riled, too. She'd been through so much already and didn't deserve another attempt to murder her. Worse, Jack couldn't guarantee her that there wouldn't be another attack. Which was why he had to take precautions: losing her again wasn't an option.

He hadn't meant for his gaze to stay locked with hers. Also hadn't meant for the regret about the attack and then the heat to creep into his expression. Of course, with Caroline there was always heat, so it was hard not to have it playing into things. Impossible for her not to pick up on it, either.

"I can't kiss you again," she insisted. Then she huffed. "Well, I could, but I'm asking you to back off. I need room to breathe. Time to think."

Jack immediately stepped back, giving her that space and nearly smiling again when it seemed as if she was disappointed that another kiss hadn't happened. But she was right. They definitely needed some thinking time on this. Better yet, this called for some concentration coupled with plenty of detective work.

He scrubbed his hand over his face, dragged in a breath and started laying out some things. "Kellan should have enough probable cause on Kingston to get a look at his financials. That's a start. Also, I can arrange to have Kingston's friends interviewed just to see how deep his obsession with Eric went."

Caroline nodded. "I can help. Not by hacking into Kingston's bank records," she quickly added when he scowled at her. "But I can call the various research assistants that Gemma and I worked with and see if they remember anyone other than Kingston coming in with Eric. It's possible Kingston had some help if he put this attack together."

True, and searching for that might help Caroline keep her mind off the flashbacks and the panic attacks.

"What about Zeller?" she asked. "Is there any chance you can get into his financials?"

"Slim to none, with what I have on him. Which is nothing." Jack paused. "But he's not the only one who can talk to Lily and others at New Beginnings. Maybe Lily can shed some light on why Zeller has her in his sights for a whole boatload of felonies, including coming after you."

"I'd like to hear what she has to say. And no, I don't recall Eric mentioning anything about the sex trafficking, but he did have contact with a lot of bad people. Stupid, gullible people that he could charm into doing what he wanted," she added. "Look at what Kingston was willing to do for him. Maybe there are others who overlap with Lily, Eric and Kingston."

It was one of those angles that had to be checked out,

but it would also be a big time suck. Jack was worried that time wasn't on Caroline's and his side right now. The person who'd attacked her would almost certainly come after her again.

He was about to suggest they go to the observation room to watch the rest of Kingston's interview, but Jack spotted his brother Eli coming in through the front door. Jack also saw Caroline stiffen, and he didn't have to guess why. She didn't have faith in his Texas Ranger brother because in her mind, Eli could also be connected to that phone call Eric had made a year ago.

Eli made a beeline toward them, glancing first at Jack before his attention lingered a moment on Caroline. Eli lifted an eyebrow. "You got your memory back, but you don't know who killed our father."

It wasn't a question. Nor was it especially sympathetic. But then, Eli wasn't known for his soft touch. His recent engagement had given him a sunnier outlook, but it didn't appear that he was going to spread any of that sunshine Caroline's way.

"I'm sorry," she said. "I wish I did know who killed him, because I would tell you. I also wish that I could trust you, but I don't."

Eli kept his attention on Caroline, studying her, before he shrugged. "Understood. But if you remember anything about me, you know I don't do things half-assed. If I'd actually helped Eric, I wouldn't have let a hostage overhear a conversation I'd had with him. A conversation that could have come back to bite me. That's just an FYI," he added in a growl before he turned back to Jack.

What Eli had said was true. He wasn't the sort to leave stones unturned or loose threads untied. Jack just wished his brother had tried to give Caroline a little more reassurance. She was already spooked, and none of them wanted her slipping into a panic mode.

But Caroline didn't panic. She simply nodded in response to Eli. So maybe that was progress. Soon, though, she'd need to trust all the Slater lawmen because they were her best shot at staying alive.

"I found the rental car," Eli threw out there, causing both Jack and Caroline to turn to him. "It was on an old ranch trail less than a mile from where you were attacked. No one was in it, but the CSIs will go through it."

Good. Finally, there was news that Jack wanted to hear. He hadn't expected the shooter to still be with the vehicle, but maybe the person had left fingerprints or trace evidence behind.

"There's a second set of fresh tire tracks on the trail," Eli went on. "Either the shooter had stashed another vehicle there so he could use it to getaway or else someone was waiting there for them."

A partner. Yeah. Jack had considered that, too, though he was hoping the person was working alone.

"Can we get the model of the second vehicle from the tire tracks?" Jack asked.

"CSI will try, but it's the longest of long shots. They said it was a common tread."

Okay, so they likely wouldn't get much from that. Still, there was another angle on this. "Who rented that sedan?" Jack asked.

"Brad Smith," Eli immediately answered.

It was a common enough name, and judging from Caroline's headshake, it didn't ring any bells for her. Jack took out his phone to start a search on the man.

"Smith reserved the rental car online, but he had a valid credit card in that name," Eli went on. "It was one of those deals where Smith used a code the rental company gave him and used it to get the car from a specific spot on the lot."

"In other words, Smith didn't have face-to-face contact with a clerk," Jack concluded.

Eli confirmed that with a nod. "The rental company has security surveillance cameras in the lot where the vehicles are kept, and they've agreed to turn over the feed to us. They're emailing copies here and to the Ranger lab."

Jack was glad the rental car company was cooperating, but he was betting how this would play out. Smith—or whoever the hell he really was—likely knew there'd be cameras and had probably worn a disguise. Heck, a ball cap could have obscured his face. Still, they'd be able to get height and build, which in turn might give them something they could use against Kingston.

Well, it would if Smith matched Kingston's description.

"There's more," Eli said, and this time his tone had a darker edge to it. He made eye contact with Jack. "I had the Ranger lab do a deep run on all the Brad Smiths in the area, and something *interesting* came up."

"I'm listening," Jack grumbled when Eli hesitated.

And even with that prompt, Eli hesitated some more. A muscle jerked hard in his jaw. "Brad Smith was an alias that came up in an investigation a few years ago. Another sex-trafficking ring that wasn't connected to Dad's case. But according to the file notes, Smith was actually an undercover marshal."

Chapter Seven

Finally. That was Caroline's first reaction to what Jack had just said about Lee Zeller being Brad Smith.

That connection between Zeller and the rental car used in the attack brought together some of the pieces of this puzzle. She hadn't been wrong about overhearing Eric talk with someone in law enforcement. Or at least someone pretending to be in that line of work. But there would have been no pretense needed if Eric's conversation had indeed been with Zeller.

Jack turned to her, the questions all over his face, but Caroline didn't have the answers he wanted.

"No, I don't remember Eric ever mentioning Zeller's name," she volunteered. "But he didn't say any specific name during that phone call."

Plus, she'd been injured and drugged. She didn't want to bring that up now, though, because Jack and his brothers already had enough doubts as to what she'd overheard. She didn't want to add to those doubts and cause them to soften their attitudes about Zeller or any of their other fellow lawmen.

Jack made a sound to indicate he was thinking about this. "If Zeller did help Eric, if they were somehow connected to the sex-trafficking ring, then maybe Zeller thought you'd overheard something to incriminate him."

Maybe, and if so, that could be Zeller's motive to eliminate her. Still, there was something that didn't fit. "Why wouldn't Zeller have eliminated me sooner?" Caroline asked. "Or at least tried to do that? He's a marshal and could have easily gotten the location of the WITSEC house."

"Not easily," Jack insisted. "I'd put the location under several more layers of security, and if someone unauthorized had been poking around the files to find the address, the system should have alerted me."

"Still…" She shook her head. "Zeller probably could have managed it. So why wait to kill me?"

"As long as you didn't have your memory, you weren't a threat." Jack answered that so fast that it let her know he'd already reached that possible conclusion.

"But the timing doesn't fit," Caroline argued. "We were attacked only minutes after you learned I'd regained my memory. How would Zeller have…" She stopped when something occurred to her. "Zeller could have known about the computer searches I've done over the past few days. It wouldn't have been easy for him to do that, but if he'd been *keeping tabs* on me, he could have figured it out."

Both Jack and Eli nodded, causing the realization to settle hard in her stomach. Her searches could have been like loading a gun. Then, Zeller had pulled the trigger.

Well, maybe.

A possible motive was still a long way from proof that he'd committed a crime.

"You're sure when your father was investigating the

sex trafficking that nothing incriminating came up about Zeller?" she asked.

Both Eli and Jack gave her flat looks. Of course, they were sure. They'd likely memorized everything about the case, and it had to eat away at both of them. Here it was their job to bring criminals to justice, and they hadn't been able to do that for their own father.

"It was more of a gut feeling," Jack said. "When Nicola's body turned up and my father had to investigate it, Zeller didn't want him involved. Part of me gets that. The sex ring was his case, but Zeller didn't even want to work with my dad. In fact, he tried everything to exclude him."

Caroline had worked with enough law enforcement officers, so she knew it wasn't unusual for one of them to feel that way and go all territorial. But in this case, it could be a red flag if Zeller hadn't wanted Sheriff Buck Slater digging into anything that would incriminate Zeller himself. However, it was just as possible that Jack and his brothers were being hypercritical. A sort of grabbing at straws in the hope that they could bring their father's killer to justice.

"And then there's Zeller's possible connection to the breach of security at your WITSEC house," Jack went on. "That gave me another bad feeling. Someone texted Kingston that address. Maybe Kingston himself, if he managed to hack into Justice Department files, but it could be someone else."

"Someone like Zeller," Caroline finished for him.

Jack nodded. "That's why I'm having Teagan go through the files to see who accessed that address."

"Maybe you don't trust Jack's partner, either?" Eli asked her after a long pause.

"Eric called a man that night," she quickly pointed

out. But then Caroline had to pause, too. "Of course, that doesn't prove Teagan is clean, but I've got enough trouble without putting her under a microscope."

"Good point," Eli grumbled, and then he tipped his head to the computer on Kellan's desk. "You got access to that?" he asked Jack, checking the time. "If so, the surveillance footage from the car rental company should be ready."

"Yeah, I've got access," Jack said as if still in deep thought. *Troubled* thought, Caroline mentally corrected. Even though Jack didn't fully trust Zeller, it still had to be hard for him to think of a fellow marshal trying to murder them.

Caroline went to the computer when Jack did and she stood behind him, watching him work his way through the password and into Kellan's official emails. The file from the car rental company was there. When he clicked on it, Eli came to his side and all three of them focused on the monitor.

"It was an 8:00 a.m. pickup," Eli said, glancing at the notes on his phone.

Good. That would save them from watching hours of the feed. The timing also fit with something else—Zeller would have had plenty of time to get the car and drive out to Longview Ridge. For that matter, though, Kingston would have, too. Or any other suspect.

She watched as Jack fast-forwarded the images, but then he slowed to a normal speed when the figure came into view. A tall man who walked toward the black four-door sedan. And Caroline groaned at the same moment that Jack and Eli cursed.

The man was wearing a baseball cap, and he had on a bulky dark blue windbreaker with the collar turned up high on his neck. He kept his head down, the camera only getting a good shot of the hat and not the man's face. Worse, the build didn't help, either, because it appeared he'd stuffed things in his pants pockets, which could make him look heavier than he actually was.

Jack rewound the feed and went through it frame by frame until he stopped on the image that gave them a partial view of the guy's chin. Between the high collar and the shadow created by the ball cap, it wasn't very clear.

"That could be either Zeller or Kingston since they're about the same height," Jack grumbled under his breath.

Yes. Or someone either of them could have hired to get the car. "What about the handyman Zeller mentioned?" she asked. "Bennie Darnell. Can you pull up an ID on him?"

Jack didn't point out that it was a long shot. Even though it was. He just tapped into the DMV files and accessed the man's photo and the details listed on his driver's license.

This time, all three of them cursed.

Because Bennie, too, had a similar height and weight to Zeller and Kingston. Not only were they not able to rule anyone out, but now they'd added another potential person of interest.

"Bennie has a record," Jack explained as he went through another database. "He was arrested for drug possession and driving under the influence ten years ago. He's been clean ever since."

Obviously, his record hadn't stopped him from getting a job, and Caroline doubted he'd been hired without some kind of background check. Still, it wouldn't hurt to do a deeper run on him. She was about to suggest that when Jack's phone rang, and she saw Zeller's name on the screen.

Eli must have seen it, too, because he muttered something about getting a cup of coffee, and he headed out of the office. Jack answered the call and put it on speaker.

"You wanted to talk to me?" Zeller snapped the moment he was on the line. He sounded annoyed, and Caroline bet his irritation would only increase after this chat.

Jack didn't waste any time responding. "Who knew about your alias, Brad Smith?"

Now there was some hesitation. "Why?" Zeller demanded.

"Because someone using that name rented the car used in the attack against Caroline and me."

She'd been right about the annoyance, but there was also some anger when Zeller belted out a string of profanities. "Someone's trying to set me up."

"Who knew that was your alias?" Jack pressed, speaking right over Zeller's cursing.

"Hell, anybody with access to our computers," Zeller spat out. "Anybody who came in contact with me when I was on an op and using that name."

"Narrow it down," Jack insisted. "Go through your case files and find someone who intersects with Caroline and me."

"Believe me, I will. Because I didn't have anything to do with that car or the attack. What about security cameras at the rental place?" Zeller quickly tacked on.

"I'm looking at it right now, and I can't rule you out."

"No, but you can sure as hell rule me out because I'm not a dirty marshal. Somebody's setting me up," Zeller repeated. "I want a copy of that surveillance feed. While you're getting that to me, I'll go through the files and get back to you." And with that, Zeller ended the call.

Caroline hadn't expected Zeller to just fess up to renting the car and then hiring someone to shoot at them. No. Even if he was as guilty as sin, Zeller wouldn't cop to anything because he'd know there wasn't any concrete evidence against him.

Not yet, anyway.

"I know the Ranger crime lab will try to enhance the security footage," she said, "but I'd like to have a go at it, too. I might be able to match the jawline to Bennie, Kingston or Zeller."

Jack didn't refuse her help, but he did look her straight in the eyes. A look that likely told him that she was exhausted. She also had a dull, throbbing headache. There'd been no time for her to calm down after the shooting. No chance for her to regain her footing. And the kiss hadn't helped with that. Maybe that was why Jack didn't come to her. Instead, he crammed his hands in the pockets of his jeans.

"As soon as Kellan finishes up with Kingston, we should be able to leave for another safe house," he said.

Her first response was relief. She could get some quiet time and try to level out her nerves. But another concern popped up immediately. For her to get to a safe house, she'd have to leave the sheriff's office and go outside, where their attacker could be lying in wait for them. It was a risk. Then again, she couldn't stay here amid all the badges that she wasn't sure she could trust.

So this was the rock and the hard place.

"Where's the safe house?" she asked.

Jack didn't get a chance to answer her, though, because Eli stepped back into the doorway. "You've got a visitor," Eli said, shifting his gaze to both Jack and her.

Instant alarm went through Caroline. Jack seemed to stiffen with attention. He immediately stepped in front of her.

"Who is it?" Jack pressed.

"Lily Terrell," Eli answered. "She says you'll want to see her because she believes she's a suspect in today's attack."

WELL, JACK HADN'T seen this coming. In fact, he'd thought he was going to have to contact Lily to let her know that he had some questions for her. He'd expected an heiress like that to give him some flak. Instead, here she was, walking straight toward Kellan's office.

Jack closed the laptop and checked to make sure there was nothing that a person of interest shouldn't be seeing. There wasn't. Well, nothing other than Caroline. Jack didn't care for the fact that she was going to have to face yet someone else who may have had a part in the attack.

"She's not armed," Eli told Jack.

Jack appreciated that his brother had frisked the woman, but after getting a good look at her, he figured there weren't many places Lily could have hidden a weapon. She was a tall woman, close to six feet, and she was rail thin. The cobalt blue dress she was wearing clung to every inch of her. No chance of her hiding much in the tiny hand-sized purse she was holding.

"Marshal Slater," she greeted, her voice a sultry drawl. It went well with her cool violet eyes and the auburn hair that tumbled over her shoulders.

She flashed him a smile, extending it to Eli and then to Caroline. "Miss Moser," Lily added.

"How do you know me?" Caroline asked, taking the question right out of Jack's mouth.

"I'm familiar with your work on Crime-Track that you did at the university with Gemma Hanson." Lily's answer was quick and unruffled. Actually, *unruffled* was a good description for the woman herself. If she was bothered by being considered a suspect, she didn't show it.

Caroline had indeed worked on that project, and Jack figured that was common knowledge. The media had hashed and rehashed it after one of the research assistants on the project, Eric Lang, had been uncovered as a serial killer.

"It's work you should continue," Lily added to Caroline a moment later. "It could be very beneficial to law enforcement agencies."

Caroline lifted an eyebrow. "I doubt anyone wants to trust a profiler who worked side by side with a serial killer and didn't know it."

Lily made a sound that could have meant anything and turned back to Jack. "The shooting was on the news," she said. "Details were sketchy, but when I heard your name and Caroline's, I thought it best if I came in."

"And why is that?" Jack had no intention of showing his hand until he found out more about this visit.

"Bennie Darnell is a handyman at New Beginnings, and he told me about Marshal Lee Zeller's *interest* in me. When I heard about the attack on the news, I assumed Zeller would be trying to convince you that I was somehow involved. So I came here to clear my name."

Jack exchanged glances with Caroline and saw that she was just as surprised as he was. Zeller had made it seem as if Bennie was his mole, but obviously the handyman still had some loyalty to his employer. In turn, that called into question any info that Bennie had given Zeller, because maybe Bennie was just the sort who liked to tell people whatever it was they wanted to hear.

"Why exactly does Marshal Zeller have an interest in you?" Jack asked. He tried to keep his tone level, more of a request than a demand, since he was still trying to figure out if Lily was playing some kind of game or if she truly was concerned about making sure her name was clean.

"Because of Skylar Greer." She didn't hesitate, and Lily looked him straight in the eyes when she spoke. Then she dragged in a long breath. "Even though he's never come right out and said it, Marshal Zeller seems to believe I had some part in Skylar leaving New Beginnings. I didn't."

Interesting that Lily had used the word "leaving" when Zeller had described it as a disappearance.

"Why did the woman *leave*?" Jack pressed.

Now she dodged his gaze, but only for a few seconds. "I'm not sure. She didn't speak to me about it, but I assume Skylar felt as if there was some other place she wanted to be. Hopefully, a safe place," she softly added.

Yeah, Jack hoped the same thing, and also wished he could know for sure that the woman was actually alive. "You think Skylar could have gotten lured back into sex trafficking?"

Lily didn't jump to deny that, and she glanced at Caroline. "You both know how hard it is to come back from a traumatic situation. Skylar was a troubled young woman and didn't trust easily. I think it would be very easy for her to slip back into her old ways."

Lily's words were right. So was the concerned expression on her face. But something in her voice and body language didn't ring true for Jack. Or maybe he was just projecting because of the sliver of doubt that Zeller had put in his head.

"Skylar didn't trust you?" Caroline came out and asked.

"Sadly, no," Lily answered.

Again, right tone, but it did nothing to ease that bad feeling. He considered a moment how to deal with this and went with the direct approach.

"I want copies of Skylar's records," Jack insisted.

Lily's expression never changed, and she didn't even pause. "I'm afraid I'll have to insist you get a warrant for that. The privacy of the residents is a top priority for me."

It was the exact answer he'd expected from the woman. Maybe stonewalling. Maybe just trying to be ethical. "I'll get the warrant, and then you'll need to come back in here to give me an official statement."

Lily nodded, but some wariness crept into her eyes. "It sounds as if I'll need my lawyer for that."

"That's probably a good idea." Jack didn't especially want to deal with her lawyer, but he liked that his comment had caused her some tension. He wanted Lily out of her comfort zone, since nervous suspects were more likely to make mistakes.

"We'll get into this more after I have the warrant," Jack continued, and he decided to go with a long shot. "Tell me about your relationship with Eric."

Lily's eyes widened, and she fired nervous glances at Caroline, Eli and him. "There was no relationship." Her voice was clipped now. "I knew Eric only because we were in the same social circles."

"You knew him," Jack emphasized.

Lily's mouth tightened for a moment. "Eric and I rarely spoke and only at parties and such."

But the bottom line was that she had indeed known him, and Jack was fairly certain that hadn't come up in the investigation. Of course, there would have been no reason for it to have. Lily hadn't been a suspect, and there'd been no record of Eric ever contacting her. The only reason Jack had asked her about it was because he was toying with the idea that Eric and Zeller might have had some part in the sex trafficking. They could have teamed up to lure Buck to that inn so Zeller could kill him.

That was a long shot.

However, if Eric and Zeller were connected, then maybe Lily was, too. That could explain why Zeller was so hell-bent on pinning something illegal on her. Maybe he wanted her to be put away so she couldn't expose his own crimes.

"What about Kingston Morris?" Jack went on. "You know him, too?"

Lily's slow nod was as uncertain as the rest of her. "Yes. Again, the same circles, and I knew him slightly more than Eric. How is he involved in this?" she asked.

Jack knew it wouldn't be long before word got out, so he decided to tell Lily so he could see her reaction. "Kingston showed up at Caroline's house. Trespassing," he added. "Her address was protected and wasn't easily accessible. Still, Kingston managed to get it, and shortly afterward, Caroline was attacked."

Lily pressed her hand to her chest as if to steady her heart. "You suspect Kingston of trying to kill her?"

"He's being interviewed now," Jack answered, dodging Lily's direct question, and yeah, Kingston was a suspect all right.

"I see." Some of the color drained from Lily's face. She paused, moistened her lips. "Is it because of Grace Wainwright? Is that how Kingston got Caroline's address?"

Jack glanced at Caroline to see if she recognized the name, but she only shook her head.

"Who's Grace Wainwright?" Jack asked.

Lily opened her mouth, then closed it just as fast. Maybe rethinking what she'd been about to say. "Grace was at New Beginnings. She had gotten caught up in sex trafficking," Lily added. "She also had some family problems that prevented her from going home, and she asked if she could stay there while she straightened out her life. However, before that, she was romantically involved with Kingston."

For someone who was hesitant to share much on Skylar, Lily clearly didn't feel the need to hold back with Grace.

Jack stared at Lily. "And why would Grace have known Caroline's address?"

"Because Grace has excellent computer skills and wasn't always ethical about whose information she accessed. She could have hacked into the files, found Caroline's address and given it to Kingston. Or sold it to him."

Jack didn't have trouble latching on to what Lily hadn't said. "Grace accessed information about you?"

Lily's mouth tightened. "She did. Actually, she managed to steal some funds from my bank account. When I caught her, I told her she had to leave New Beginnings. She did, but I've since heard rumors that she's still using her talents for illegal activities."

He was definitely going to have to question Grace

about that. But if she had indeed managed to get into Justice Department files, then she had to be better than just "excellent" when it came to hacking.

Jack made a mental note to contact Grace ASAP, and then he moved on to the next question he had for Lily. "Why is Zeller so hell-bent about coming after you?"

Lily hesitated, and he saw the pulse kick up on her throat. "I suspect it's because he feels guilty." She stopped, huffed. "Look, I'm guessing you're not going to want to hear anything negative about one of your fellow marshals…"

"Trust me, I want to hear it," Jack insisted.

Lily nodded and made a suit-yourself sound. "From what I've gathered from conversations with some of the girls who came to New Beginnings, I believe Zeller knew Nicola Gunderson and that he talked her into helping him bring down the sex-trafficking ring."

Everything inside Jack went still. He definitely hadn't heard Zeller mention knowing the dead girl, and he was pretty sure that should have come out by now. Especially since it was his father who was investigating her murder.

"I'm not surprised Zeller didn't mention any of this to you," Lily went on. "In fact, I suspect he doesn't want anyone to know that he's the reason that Nicola was murdered."

Chapter Eight

Caroline watched as Jack located Grace's number and tried to call the woman. No answer. But maybe she'd call back soon. And perhaps Grace wouldn't try to avoid them simply because she didn't want to be questioned about her possible involvement in the attack.

Of course, if Grace was indeed avoiding them, it likely wasn't because Lily had warned her. Not enough time for that. It had only been a couple of minutes since she'd left the sheriff's office. Plus, why would Lily have volunteered the woman's name if she was just going to go and warn her?

Jack left Grace a message for her to call him and then tried Zeller again. Even though he hadn't put his phone on speaker, Caroline was close enough that she heard the call to Zeller go straight to voice mail.

Unlike Grace, Zeller was someone who could absolutely be avoiding them.

If what Lily had said was true about Zeller coaxing Nicola into helping him, then the marshal should have already spilled that. Not just to Jack's father but to Jack and his siblings. Zeller definitely needed to answer some questions, and with each new bit of information, Caroline was trusting him less and less.

Jack shook his head in frustration over not getting through to Zeller before he fired off a text to someone, and then he looked at her. Whatever he saw on her face caused his frustration to worsen. "You're exhausted," he concluded. "I'm sorry. I should have already gotten you out of here."

"No, you shouldn't have," she argued. "You needed to be here so you can find the person who tried to kill us."

And while things were still unsettled between them, Caroline knew one thing for certain. She didn't want Jack sending her off with anyone else. Especially anyone else with a badge.

Even though touching him was playing with fire, Caroline risked sliding her hand down his arm. A gesture meant to comfort him, along with getting some comfort for herself. Jack was the only person who could soothe her like this.

Now his eyes flashed with a different emotion. Heat layered over the irritation of the stalled investigation, and soon even the worry seemed to fade away. Apparently, she also had a soothing effect on him, and it was effective if she didn't count the whole arousal thing.

Caroline figured that Jack counted it.

Neither of them had time to act on it, though, because of the approaching footsteps. That sound caused them to move apart, and Jack shook his head as if to clear it before he stepped in front of her. Preparing for a threat. But he relaxed some when Kellan appeared in the doorway. Kingston was right behind him.

"Am I done here now?" Kingston asked. He didn't sound smug or cooperative now, which meant Kellan had grilled him hard. Good. Maybe Kellan had also gotten some info they could use.

"No, you're not done," Jack snapped. He shifted his attention to Kellan. "Lily Terrell came in and chatted with us. She'll be back later with her lawyer for an official interview, but for now she had some interesting theories. One that's connected to Kingston."

Kingston groaned. "Did Lily accuse me of something, too?"

"Do you know Grace Wainwright?" Jack went on, ignoring Kingston's question.

Kingston blinked, clearly surprised by the topic. "Of course, I know her. We were once lovers."

Jack didn't pause even a second. "Did she get you Caroline's address?"

"No." Kingston looked ready to gear up with a more detailed, angrier denial, but then he stopped. "Maybe. But if she did, she didn't tell me she was the one who texted it to me."

No, because that would have incriminated her in a felony. Of course, it was possible Grace had given him the address and that he was covering for her. Caroline figured Jack would be digging deep into the woman's background to try to determine that.

Kellan waited until Jack gave him the go-ahead nod before he turned to Kingston. "You can go, *for now*, but don't leave the state. I'll be bringing you back in when I have more info."

That clearly didn't please Kingston, but he didn't waste any time arguing with them. He turned and hurried out.

"Lily thinks Zeller knew Nicola," Jack told his brother when Kingston was out of earshot. "He might have even talked Nicola into helping him break up the sex-trafficking ring."

The muscles tightened in Kellan's face. "I'll make

some calls and see what I can find out." He glanced away and cursed. "We're not getting answers, just a whole bunch of questions."

"Yeah," Jack agreed, the fatigue now back in his voice. "I've already requested authorization to look into Zeller's computer. That might get us something."

It would, unless Zeller had already wiped the hard drive. Or disposed of it. For someone with the right skills, there were plenty of ways to erase data.

"I also need a warrant to get into the records at New Beginnings," Jack added. "I want to have a look at the file of a woman that Zeller says went missing. But I can wait a little while on that. For now, I need to go ahead and get Caroline out of here. You think you can spare a deputy until morning, or should I see if Teagan can help?"

Kellan glanced at Caroline and then out into the bull-pen. "Since Caroline seems to be more comfortable with female officers, why don't you take Raylene. Caroline knows her."

Yes, she did. Deputy Raylene McNeal. Caroline didn't like putting trust in a person simply because of their gender, but in this case it helped her relax a little. Well, relax about who'd be doing bodyguard duty for her, but her nerves went zinging again when she realized they'd be going back outside.

Kellan stepped into the squad room, motioning for Raylene, and a moment later, the sturdy-looking brunette deputy joined him in the doorway, where Kellan, Jack and she had a whispered conversation. Something that Jack said had Kellan frowning and groaning, but Jack persisted and finished whatever point he was making.

When they'd finished talking, Raylene glanced at Caroline in a gesture that was probably meant to reassure her. Surprisingly, it did. Caroline hated that she needed to be babysat like this, but she wasn't stupid. She'd come close to dying too many times to take unnecessary risks by turning down protection.

"Caroline, Raylene and I will go in a cruiser," Jack explained. "Gunnar will follow as backup but will come back here once he's sure it's safe. Raylene will stay with us."

Raylene nodded. "Just let me get the overnight bag I keep in my locker."

While Kellan spoke to Gunnar, Raylene hurried toward the break room. The deputy didn't take long and was back in under a minute. That was still plenty enough time for Caroline's stomach to start churning with the reminder that the person who'd tried to kill them could be waiting outside.

"Move fast," Jack instructed, and he hooked his arm around Caroline's waist to get her moving.

There were two cruisers parked out front. Raylene and Gunnar went out first, each of them hurrying to get behind the wheel of their respective vehicle. Jack had one last look around before he moved with Caroline, and the moment they were inside the cruiser, Raylene took off with Gunnar following right behind her.

Jack continued to keep watch. So did Caroline. She studied each person on Main Street as if they were a would-be gunman, but no one attempted to fire at them. That still didn't make her relax. She kept her eyes on their surroundings, wishing that she had a gun so she could defend herself if it came down to it.

Raylene drove out of town and onto the rural road that snaked through the countryside. There were no pedestrians here to watch, only miles of woods and pastures, and it didn't take Caroline long to realize where they were going. She whirled toward Jack so fast that her neck popped.

"You're taking me to your family's ranch," she blurted out, and was certain her tone and expression let him know she didn't like that.

"Actually, I'm taking you to my place, but as I'm sure you remember, it's on the ranch."

Oh, yes. She remembered all right. It was the wood-and-stone house where she'd spent many nights with Jack. As his lover. And while it might be more comfortable than standing around at the sheriff's office, it wasn't exactly "safe." Not with all the memories the place held. Specifically memories of Jack and her in bed.

"You can't think going there is a good idea," Caroline said.

He shrugged and continued to keep watch. "I have a security system, and the ranch hands will help guard the place."

Again, that didn't make it safe.

"Are all the repairs done?" Raylene asked him, her gaze briefly meeting Jack's in the rearview mirror.

"They are. The damage wasn't that bad."

Caroline didn't need clarification on the repairs or damage because she'd heard about the *incident* that'd happened at his place. Someone who'd been after Jack's brother, Owen, had rammed his car into the porch. She'd heard bits and pieces about it from Lucille and the media reports she'd accessed, but Caroline figured she hadn't gotten the full story. Wasn't sure she wanted it, either. She had enough bad stuff in her head without adding more.

"Considering that an attack happened so recently at

your place, maybe we should take that as some kind of sign not to go there," Caroline grumbled.

"The attack caused me to beef up security," Jack said as if that answered all of her concerns. It didn't. But then Caroline didn't know anywhere they could go where she wouldn't feel the danger looming over her.

Still…

She had to put her argument on hold for a moment when Raylene pulled to a stop in front of Jack's. Despite those repairs and the security upgrade that he'd mentioned, the place looked exactly the same. It definitely wasn't sprawling like the main house just up the road, where Kellan lived and helped run the family ranch. Jack's place only had three bedrooms and two baths, and was as comfortable-looking and laid-back as the owner.

"Wait here a sec," Jack told her.

He got out and ran to the front door. Caroline watched as he unlocked it and then used his phone to disengage the security system. He also went in, likely to search the place, before he came back out. As they'd done at the sheriff's office, they moved fast, and only after Jack had Raylene and her inside did he motion for Gunnar to leave.

While Jack reset the security alarms, Caroline walked into the living room and glanced around. No changes here, either, and that included the two framed photos of Jack and her on the mantel. In one, he had his arm crooked playfully around her, his mouth pressed to her cheek, while she had a huge grin on her face. The other photo was a shot of Kellan and Gemma standing next to Jack and her, all of them smiling. Obviously, they were taken in much happier times.

"You can take the guest room," Jack told Raylene, and he motioned toward the first room off the hall.

With her overnight bag in hand, Raylene headed in that direction, leaving Caroline with Jack.

"I'll take the couch. You can use my room," he added to Caroline, holding her hand to take her there.

She knew the way, every step of it, and every scent was familiar because it was Jack's. By the time she walked into the bedroom suite, her body was humming with that familiarity. With those memories of what had gone on here. None of the bad stuff. Not here. This was all warmth and pleasure.

He'd kept the same quilt, and Caroline knew the feel of it. The soft cotton that had slid against her skin every time she'd been naked in that bed.

"Afraid to be alone with me?" he asked, coming up behind her.

She shook her head. "Fear isn't the right word for it—"

"You told me you loved me," he interrupted. "That morning before Eric took you, you told me that."

No need for him to clarify which morning, but she didn't like his timing in bringing it up now. "I remember." She cleared her throat so it would have some sound, and had to do it again. Great. Her throat was clogged now, and her breathing wasn't faring much better.

Jack moved in front of her, studying her face. He wasn't frowning, but it was close. "You don't feel the same way about me now."

She wanted to groan. Apparently, he wasn't content with just having her surrounded by old memories of them as a couple. He wanted her to relive it with words, too. And it was working. She felt the slow hum of heat circle around her.

"I'm not sure what I feel," Caroline settled for saying, but it required another throat clearing.

Her answer didn't smooth his near frown. But it was partly true. She didn't know about still being in love. She'd had no time to sort out her feelings, but when it came to Jack, she was certain about plenty of other things. She wanted him more than her next heartbeat. More than she wanted to feel strong and whole again.

And that want was quickly turning into a need.

The silence vibrated between them as he stared at her. It ended when Jack cursed. "I considered offering you no-strings-attached sex. Just to burn off this heat so we could possibly think about something else. *Anything* else. But I can't do that."

Silence fell again, this time because he'd stunned her. "You can't have sex?" And she hated the disappointment in her voice.

A flicker of annoyance, and heat, went through his eyes. "I can't give you the no-strings. The sex is going to happen, but not until you know that it won't be just to satisfy some raw animal urges. *Strings*," he repeated, emphasizing it. "I'll want that I-love-you from you again. Maybe not tonight, but I'll want it soon."

Caroline was about to remind him that he'd never given her those words, but Jack snapped her to him and kissed her. It was hard and rough, not just his mouth but the grip he had on her arms. The roughness was something that Caroline quickly realized made it even better. He wasn't going to treat her like glass. The fragile kind of glass that broke with a careless touch.

He was going to break her in a whole different way. And there'd be nothing careless about it.

Cupping the back of her neck, Jack deepened the kiss. The physical part of it, anyway, since the emotional part was already as deep as it could get. Or so Caroline thought. He proved her wrong when he stopped and eased back enough to stare into her eyes.

There it was. The face that could have been created for an ancient god. The pretty ones who could be both ruthless and very, very desirable. His eyes, dark. That rumpled black hair. Oh, and that scent. Leather and male. It seeped into her, mingling with the heat that his kiss had already flamed.

Jack waited a heartbeat, maybe giving her a chance to change her mind, all the while knowing that she wouldn't do that. Caroline knew it, too.

The next kiss was just a brush of his mouth over hers. Slow and sensual with their breaths mingling. And he looked at her again. Gauging her reaction. She was breathing too fast, and her pulse was at a full gallop. Every inch of her was quivering, waiting, and she didn't want the wait to continue for even a second longer.

She didn't have to.

Jack took her mouth again, and there it was. The raw animal urge that went to full flame and beyond when his hand slid underneath her dress and straight into her panties. Caroline made a gasp of pleasure when he plunged his fingers into her. So much pleasure that his touch would have brought her to a fast climax if he hadn't suddenly stopped.

"No. It won't be that easy," he said, his voice as intense as the look he gave her. Jack reached behind her, shut the door and locked it. "It'll never be that easy between us."

It sounded a little like a threat, and he hooked his arm around her, lifting her as if she weighed nothing. Those strong, corded arms closed around her. He kissed her, hard and deep again, while he took her to his bed.

He practically dumped her on the too-soft mattress that swelled up around her.

When he didn't immediately join her, she reached for him, only to realize that his plan was to stay standing so he could strip off her dress.

Which he did.

Jack sent it flying. Then he got on the bed, his knee landing between her legs. As he loomed over her, she could feel his jeans rub against the inside of her thighs. Could hear the rough rhythm of his breath.

He kissed her breasts through her bra. Again, not gently. Both his hands and his mouth were rough as he yanked off her panties and then her bra. He'd said he hadn't wanted easy, whatever that meant, but he apparently wanted fast.

Good.

Because she wanted that, too. Fast meant she didn't have to think about this. For that to happen, she needed him as naked as he'd just gotten her. Caroline went after the buttons on his shirt, but when he took her nipple into his mouth, the heat roared through her. Fingers to toes and every single place in between. She gave up on the shirt and went after his zipper instead.

Jack didn't stop her when she freed him from his jeans and boxers, but he did stop the maddening kisses. Again, their gazes met. And held. Just as he plunged into her.

Caroline made another of those gasps. Pleasure, yes. Definitely that. Mixed with the brief shock of his hard thrust. Then, even more pleasure. So much more.

This was the animal urge part. His eyes held a need of a different kind, though. The pretty, ruthless god planned to claim what he believed to be already his. To possess her. It frightened her a little to think that he could do just that. Frightened her even more that she wanted him to do it.

It didn't take much. A few more of those deep, plundering strokes inside her, and Caroline couldn't have held back the climax even if she'd wanted to. She didn't. But she refused to go falling over that edge alone.

Knowing exactly how to undo him, she lifted her hips, clamping her knees around him and dragging him harder into her. She let the muscles in her body force him into joining her. Her vision blurred, but still she watched him. And he watched her...while they fell together.

Caroline could feel those strings tightening around her, and while Jack gathered her into his arms and kissed her, she prayed for so many things. That this wouldn't be the mistake she was certain it was. Because those strings weren't just about love and broken hearts. They were about priority and focus.

And those strings could get them both killed.

Chapter Nine

Caroline still slept like a rock. Jack now had proof that it was something about her that hadn't changed. Facedown, arms outstretched and butt naked on his bed, she'd slept all night and then through the beep of his morning alarm. Ditto for staying sacked out during his shower and the phone calls he'd gotten and the ones that he'd made.

While Jack would have liked to let her sleep even longer, he had things to do that couldn't wait. So he poured a huge mug of black coffee that he'd brewed strong enough to the point of being bitter. Just the way Caroline liked it. He added a single ice cube to it to cool it down enough for her to drink it fast—which she would do.

When he went back into the bedroom, he had to push aside the punch of attraction he got from seeing her in his bed. The attraction got another punch when he recalled in perfect detail all the things they'd done there.

Oh, man.

He really needed to figure out a way to deal with what he felt for her so he could do everything possible to keep her out of danger. That had to be his mission now because he couldn't lose her again.

She stirred the moment Jack held the mug near her nose, and then he moved it so her flailing hands wouldn't knock into it and spill it. Yawning and groaning at the same time, she lumbered to a sitting position and groped to take the coffee. Jack kept hold of it, too, until he was certain of her grip.

No sips for her. As expected, she downed several long gulps as if it were the cure for all ills, before she looked up as if just realizing he was there. She smiled until her attention landed on his clothes.

"You're dressed," she said, frowning now.

"Been up for a while." Jack eased down on the bed next to her, but not too close. If he touched her, he'd be toast. "You need to slap me. I forgot to use a condom last night."

"Uh." Caroline repeated that sound, pushed her hair from her face. "I'm on the pill. I started it last month to regulate my periods." She added that last part in a barely audible mumble, and continued, "I haven't been with anyone since, well, just since."

Judging from the way her face flushed, that seemed to embarrass her. Ironic, since she was stark naked.

Something his body had noticed, of course.

Actually, what his body wanted to do was get back in that bed with her and go for another round or two. Not going to happen, though. But the comment that embarrassed her pleased him more than it should have. Which was stupid. Because the reason she hadn't been with anyone else was because she'd been hurt and not because of some unremembered commitment to him.

"Zeller still hasn't returned my calls, but Kellan texted me," Jack explained, forcing his mind back where it belonged, and it darn sure shouldn't be on her breasts. "The warrant came through on the missing girl from New Beginnings, and we have the file. Lily Terrell's coming into the sheriff's office with her lawyer in—" he checked his watch "—about an hour."

"An hour," she repeated, and she sounded a little panicked now.

"I'd like to be there to hear what Lily has to say about those files," Jack went on, "and I don't want you here alone. Raylene's already gone home, but Gunnar's her relief, and he's waiting out front in a cruiser to take us in."

That got Caroline scrambling off the bed and into his bathroom. Gulping down coffee and mumbling, she turned on the shower. What she didn't do was shut the door, so he got even more of the drive-Jack-crazy peep show of her naked body behind the clear glass of the shower stall.

"I had your other things brought over from the WITSEC house," he called out to her. "They're in a suitcase next to the vanity."

While she showered, Jack gathered up what little willpower he had left and went back into the kitchen to finish his own coffee. He then phoned Teagan. It was his second call to her that morning. The first one had been an hour ago, so maybe she had something on how the location of the WITSEC house had been breached.

"You're not going to like what I'm about to tell you," Teagan said the moment she answered, and that caused Jack to groan.

"What happened?" he snapped, trying to steel himself for what would be bad news.

"All the WITSEC files are intact. None of them have been tampered with." She didn't snap at him, but there was irritation in her voice that let him know he might have preferred that to whatever else she was about to tell him. "I think the breach came from the laptop Caroline

was using, the one you had couriered to me. Did you
know she has hacking skills?" Teagan tacked on to that
without even pausing.

"Yeah. One of her many talents," he grumbled. Along
with picking locks, hot-wiring cars and driving him
crazy. "There were filters on that laptop," Jack pointed
out.

"Caroline got past them, and because her skills are
better than ours, it took the geeks all night to find it.
Several of the sites she used to do a search on Eric Lang
had a tracker on them. Something experimental and beyond my skill set to explain. It's called Geo-Trace. It
wouldn't have alerted her, and it was well hidden in the
website codes. But the geeks think that's how someone
found her."

Jack cursed, not just because he was pissed about the
hacking but because this could crush Caroline. This could
put her on the fast track to a panic attack and a guilt trip.
Hell, she'd want to be offering to take a bullet for him
because she would see this as having put him in danger.

"If it works the way the geeks think it does," Teagan
explained, "Geo-Trace would have allowed someone to
track the computer without getting a warrant. And Caroline wouldn't have known about the risk. Like I said,
Geo-Trace is still in the experimental stages. Whoever
put it on the sites was probably looking for her."

And had found her.

"See if the geeks can figure out who put Geo-Trace
on the sites," he suggested. "Maybe try a reverse hacking
maneuver." Ironically, it was something Caroline might
be able to do, but he didn't want to go to her with this
just yet.

"I'll try, but the Geo-Trace program corrupted itself

when our techs tried to examine it. They got portions of it, but it was as if it had an encoded virus to stop someone from digging into it too much."

A fail-safe. One that would have required some serious computer skills. That still didn't convince him to bring this to Caroline. Even if he caught flak for it later, which he was certain he would.

"Don't mention this to Caroline," he added to Teagan.

Teagan rattled off a string of profanities before she said, "You're not going to question her about it?"

"Not right now. I need to ease her into it so that it doesn't send her into a tailspin."

Teagan groaned. "What part of your body are you thinking with right now?"

"Probably the wrong one," he admitted and ended the call just as Caroline hurried into the room.

She was dressed, mostly, but still adjusting the above-the-knee denim skirt and snug red top. Clothes that hugged curves on Caroline that he wished he couldn't see right now.

Yeah, the wrong part of his body was doing the thinking, and that had to stop. With the breach of the WITSEC location, it wasn't a stretch for someone to figure out that she would have gone with him. That was why he hurried when he got her out of the house and into the cruiser. He had to concentrate on who had attacked them and stop the person from coming after them again.

Jack frowned when he looked up at the sky. The iron gray clouds were already moving on, indicating a storm was on the way. He didn't mind bad weather, but he didn't like the idea of it happening when he was trying to get Caroline back and forth from the sheriff's office.

Gunnar flashed Caroline a grin that he seemed to cut

short when Jack scowled at him. He knew that Gunnar didn't have any romantic interest in Caroline. He was just being friendly, but Jack wanted the deputy in concentration mode, too.

"Did they find the shooter?" Caroline asked.

"No. The CSI team processed the car, and all the prints, fibers and trace they collected were sent to the lab. They might find something," Jack tried to assure her.

Since she'd been a criminal profiler and had dealt with investigations for years, Caroline probably knew that was a long shot. Anything collected from a rental car wouldn't necessarily belong to the last person who'd been inside it. Plus, a would-be killer had likely made sure not to leave any evidence behind.

Caroline shifted in the seat and studied him. "Is something wrong? I mean, something other than the obvious?"

There were two kinds of obvious here. The investigation and the personal. Jack had filled her in on everything about the case except for the likelihood that her laptop had been the reason her location was compromised. He still intended to hold off on asking her about that, which left them with the personal. And yes, there were things about that they also hadn't touched on yet.

Since Gunnar was only a few feet away, Jack reminded himself to keep his voice low. "I'm worried I messed up things last night."

Caroline stared at him, her expression flat. "I'm guessing you're not talking about the sex itself but rather the distraction it caused."

He nodded. Neither of them was going to dispute that the sex had been good. Darn good. Heck, they couldn't even try to pretend that it wouldn't happen again. But in this case, there could be a price to pay.

"You're on fragile ground," he said. "I know that. You're recovering from a nightmare that hasn't ended yet." And now he had to pause and figure out how to sort out the jumble of thoughts and emotions going through his mind. It'd been too long without her, and the need had been too much to overcome. "I'm sorry if this is messing with your head."

Her eyebrow rose, and for a moment he saw the flash of humor. Jack almost expected her to make a joke, something along the lines of it hadn't been her head he'd been messing with. But the humor faded as quickly as it had come.

"I suspect it messed with your head, too," she said. "What I don't want it to do is make you feel that you have to shelter me." But Caroline immediately waved that off. "I'm not talking about protective custody here. I'm not stupid. I need that. I need you."

Jack hated that the needing-him part made him feel a lot better than it should have.

She huffed and moved closer, the side of her arm sliding against his chest as she shifted in the seat. Caroline looked him straight in the eyes. "I want you to treat me the way you did in bed," she whispered. "I didn't feel damaged or broken then. And even if I am both of those things, I don't want you to make me feel as if I am. Understand?"

Oh, yeah. He understood all right. It'd been the heat that had caused him to take her hard and fast. No kid gloves. But the bottom line was that while she was healing, she was indeed still broken, and Jack had no intentions of adding to that. It meant he'd walk a fine line between his feelings for her and his need to protect her. Thankfully, he didn't have to get into the details of how he'd manage that, because Gunnar pulled to a stop in front of the sheriff's office.

Caroline's eyes met his again as if she wanted to delay getting out until he gave her some kind of assurance, but Gunnar remedied that, as well, by hurrying to open the door to the building for them. Clearly, the deputy was standing guard and waiting for them to go inside. On Caroline's huff and Jack's sigh of relief, that was exactly what they did.

As he'd done on their previous visit, Jack didn't linger around. He took Caroline past the noise and chatter in the squad room and into Kellan's office. His brother was there at his desk and working on his laptop. Gunnar peeled off from them and went to his desk.

"Lily's already here," Kellan told them, his eyes still on his laptop. "She's in the interview room with her lawyer." He finally looked up from his computer and his attention landed on Jack. Then on Caroline. "You two look…"

"Think carefully about how to finish that," Jack warned him. He wasn't in the mood for another lecture after he'd already gotten a scolding from Teagan.

"You look slightly more relaxed than you did yesterday," Kellan finished after a pause. "It won't last. Lily's not happy about you getting those warrants, so she came in here ranting."

A surprise, since Lily hadn't reached the ranting stage the day before. But then maybe the woman hadn't thought Jack would actually get the warrant.

"Here's the file on Skylar." Kellan turned his laptop in their direction. "There supposedly isn't a hard copy, only the digital one."

Lily was going to have to wait, because Jack wanted a

look at this before he spoke to her. "Anything about the file jump out at you?" Jack asked Kellan as he pulled up Skylar's record.

But before Kellan could even respond, Jack saw an immediate problem. The file was too short. Two pages. The first was an intake form with basic stuff like name, age and next of kin. The next was a record of places the woman had been sent for job interviews.

"There are no reports from counselors or such," Jack concluded.

Kellan made a sound of agreement. "There's nothing about room assignments, day-to-day chores or any interaction with staff." He shook his head in disgust. "I've asked the computer guys at the Ranger lab to go through the files and see if anything was deleted in the past twenty-four hours. If so, we can look into charging Lily with obstruction of justice."

Was Lily really that stupid as to try to hide info from them? Maybe. People did dumb things all the time.

Caroline reached around Jack and typed something on the keyboard while her gaze skirted over the screen. "The file was modified nine hours ago."

That would have been just before the warrant had been served.

"I can't tell if anything was deleted," Caroline went on, "but the file was created a little over a year ago, and that fits the timing for when the woman would have arrived at New Beginnings." She continued to study the screen. "For only two pages, someone certainly spent a lot of time in this file. Over twenty-five hours."

That was too much for simply logging job interviews and background. Still, it wasn't proof of a crime. "Lily's lawyers could maybe say that the file was just left open and that's why the time doesn't jive with the amount of info that'd been entered."

"I want to talk to some of the other women at New Beginnings," Kellan said. "I'll find out if they've had counseling or anything else since they've been staying there. It might help if I also talk to previous residents and find out why Skylar left."

That was a necessary step, one of those drone-work chores that cops had to do in the hope of finding threads they could tug. It could give them something they could use against Lily, but it would take time.

"Does your warrant cover the computers at New Beginnings?" Caroline asked. "Because if so, I could get you what you need this morning so you wouldn't have to wait for the crime lab."

Kellan shook his head. "It only covers the one file." Then he paused. "But I'll see what I can do about getting another warrant so we can search through any-and everything in the damn building."

He took out his phone and stepped to the side to make the call, but he stopped when the front door opened. Kellan's grunt of irritation caused Jack's attention to zoom in that direction.

Zeller walked into the building.

"If you deal with him, I can get started on that warrant," Kellan said, and when Jack nodded, his brother went out into the bullpen to make the call.

"Don't start giving me grief about why I haven't returned your calls," Zeller griped the moment he stepped into Kellan's office. "I've been tied up on an investigation in Austin."

Jack didn't know about any such investigation, but it'd be easy enough to check. Which probably meant Zeller was telling the truth. Or the partial truth anyway. He could have been working a case and avoiding Jack at the same time.

"Tell me about your relationship with Nicola," Jack said.

Since Lily was waiting, it was best not to waste any time getting that out there. Plus, he liked that Zeller was off guard. Judging from the way the man's eyes widened and then narrowed, he'd been first surprised by the demand and then riled. Good. Because Jack was riled, too, that a fellow marshal could have withheld something like this.

"There was no relationship," Zeller spat out.

"But you knew her," Jack countered. "And don't bother to deny it, because I have a witness." That last part wasn't exactly true. He had the speculations of a person of interest—Lily—but sometimes a half-truth got fast results. In this case, it did just that.

Zeller groaned and glanced up at the ceiling as if hoping for some kind of divine guidance. "I spoke to Nicola, that's all," he finally admitted. "She'd had a friend who'd gotten involved in the sex trade."

Jack didn't feel one ounce of joy over Zeller's confession, since it was coming way too late. "How'd you find that out?"

Zeller took a deep breath first. "Nicola's name came up when I was questioning a group of college students about the sex-trafficking case. A lot of names came up," he quickly added, "and I talked to a lot of people. Nicola, included."

"Her name wasn't in any of your reports," Jack reminded him.

"No, because I didn't get anything from her. I swear I

didn't," Zeller snapped when Jack gave him a hard glare. "My conversation with her lasted less than ten minutes, and I realized her friend didn't have anything to do with my investigation. She was just someone who got lured into turning tricks by her sleazy boyfriend."

Jack mentally went through every word of that, and he was sure that Caroline was doing the same. In the squad room, he saw Kellan finish his call and give Jack a thumbs-up. He hoped that meant his brother had gotten the process started for the warrant for the other computer files at New Beginnings.

Jack turned his attention back to Zeller, who was clearly waiting for him to continue. "So, if your meeting with Nicola was all innocent, as you say, why not mention you'd met her once her body had been discovered?"

"At first I didn't remember talking to her. Not until I saw photos of her body." His breath turned into a long sigh. "And then I started feeling guilty, thinking that maybe something I said spurred her to do something dangerous. Like trying to save other girls like her friend."

Jack latched right onto that. "Was that what Nicola was trying to do?"

"I don't know. That's the truth," Zeller added in a hoarse whisper. "Like I said, I had a short conversation with her, one I barely remember, but I guess it's possible she picked up on something that made her put herself in a situation that turned dangerous."

Yes, it was. But then it was just as likely that Nicola had struck out on her own to try to investigate something she should have left to the badges. Of course, in this case, maybe the *badge* was what had gotten her into trouble if she'd inadvertently mentioned something to Zeller that made him believe she was some kind of threat. Perhaps

Nicola had even known something about his involvement in the sex trafficking.

But if so, Jack had no proof of that.

"Look, I feel like dirt over what happened to her," Zeller went on. "She seemed like a good kid, and she was killed. It doesn't matter that I didn't have anything to do with that. She's still dead."

Either Zeller was telling it the way it was, or else he was darn good at putting on an act. If Zeller was feeling guilty, maybe that was the bad vibe Jack was picking up on and it had nothing to do with being dirty.

This time, it was Jack who took a deep breath. "Just cool your heels for a while. I'll need an official statement from you about Nicola, but for now I have to observe another interview."

"Lily," Zeller quickly supplied. "I heard about the warrant to get the file of the missing woman."

Of course, he had. There wasn't much of a chance of keeping a warrant a secret, and Zeller likely had his ear to the ground to hear anything going on with the investigation. Jack couldn't fault him for that. If their positions had been reversed, he would be doing the same thing.

"I want to be in on Lily's interview," Zeller insisted.

"I'm sure you do, but it's not going to happen." Jack considered telling Zeller that he could watch from the observation room, but Caroline would be in there, and Jack didn't want the marshal near her. "I'll ask Kellan to copy you on the report he writes up after he talks to Lily."

Zeller huffed. "We're on the same side here, Jack. I know you don't believe that." He shot Caroline a nasty glance, no doubt to remind her that she was the reason for the mistrust. But Jack had had his doubts about Zeller before Caroline had voiced any.

"You'll get the report if Kellan agrees," Jack emphasized. "That's the best I can do right now."

Obviously, that wasn't enough in Zeller's opinion. He turned on his heels and stormed out. Jack didn't mind the fit of temper. It was better than the alternative of having Zeller linger around and upset Caroline even more. Jack could practically see the jangled nerves all over her face, but he would need to speak to Zeller again. Would need to make it official that Zeller had neglected to mention the conversation he'd had with a woman who had ended up murdered.

When Kellan tipped his head toward the interview room, Jack and Caroline followed him there. Jack intended to leave Caroline in observation while he conducted the interview with Kellan. But before they could even start, Lily came out, with her lawyer trailing right behind her.

"Are you really trying to get a warrant to get into my computer files?" Lily demanded, and she aimed that at Jack. There was fire in her eyes and raw anger in her voice.

"Yes, Kellan and I are," Jack confirmed. He didn't want Lily including Caroline in on the venom.

Lily made a sound of outrage and batted away her lawyer, who tried to whisper something in her ear. "You have no right!" And this time, she directed her anger solely at Jack. "I'm trying to help women who've been violated."

"If that's all you're doing, then having us look at your files shouldn't be a problem." In contrast, Jack kept his voice calm.

Clearly, it was a problem for Lily, because every muscle in her face tightened in rage. "I'll stop you. So help me, I'll stop you."

"Under the circumstances, my client and I need to re-schedule this interview," the lawyer said.

Jack considered nixing any rescheduling, but he re-thought that. Maybe it would be best to speak to Lily after the warrant had come through and they'd done a computer search. That way, they might have some ammu-nition they could use to get her to confess to any wrong-doings going on at New Beginnings. Of course, it was possible for Lily to successfully fight the warrant. That had been known to happen, but if she managed it, that would make her look as if she were hiding something.

"Tomorrow morning," Jack finally said. "Be back here at nine."

That should give them plenty of time to press for the warrant and start searching through the files. He had no idea how many women were actually in the facility or had been there, but the search might take a while.

And it was something Caroline could help them with.

He'd likely run into some protest from Kellan on that, but Jack understood that Caroline needed to be part of this. She should have a hand in helping eliminate the threat to both of them. Besides, Caroline would get through those files a lot faster than Kellan, he or the techs they could get to work on it.

Lily certainly didn't thank Jack for rescheduling. As Zeller had done, she hightailed it out of there, leaving the anger still vibrating in the air.

"I'd better push on that warrant," Kellan muttered, taking out his phone again. As he'd done with the other call, he stepped into the squad room.

"I'm okay," Caroline told Jack before he could even ask. "Really," she added when he gave her a flat look.

She sighed and pushed her hair from her face. "I just want answers. I want the person who attacked us behind bars."

"That's my top priority," he said, though that was one of those half-truths similar to the one he'd told Zeller.

Finding the person responsible and keeping Caroline safe and sane went hand in hand. But Jack knew that once that happened, it wouldn't be the end of things. Caroline still had to recover from the ordeal that Eric had put her through. She'd need time to deal not only with that but also with her feelings for him. And she did have feelings. No doubts about that. But Jack suspected that was the last thing she wanted to sort out right now.

"Sorry I dragged you in here," Jack told her.

Caroline lifted her shoulder. "You didn't get to do the interview, but we still learned some things. Both Lily and Zeller are scared. Maybe they're that way only because of the damage something like this can do to their reputations, but they're scared."

Oh, yeah. And Jack liked that because it could perhaps cause them to make a mistake. It could also make them dangerous. If one of them had indeed run the sex-trafficking ring and murdered Nicola, then there was nothing they'd hesitate to do to cover their tracks.

Because getting caught could lead to the death penalty.

"If Lily tries to delete or hide computer files, we can arrest her," Jack explained. "Ditto if Zeller tries to cover up the unreported contact he had with Nicola."

Of course, neither of those things would be a direct link to the attack, but it could open a door or two. Right now, Jack would settle for a sliver of an opening.

He was about to suggest that Caroline and he go back to his place to work, but before he could say anything, his phone rang. Jack frowned when Unknown Caller popped up on the screen.

Hell, what now?

He hit the answer button, and while hoping that whatever he was about to hear didn't give them another dose of bad news, he put the call on Speaker. "Marshal Jack Slater," he answered.

Jack didn't care much for the long silence that followed, but he finally heard a woman's voice. "Marshal, you've been trying to get in touch with me. I'm Grace Wainwright. I understand you have some questions for me."

Well, he certainly hadn't expected Kingston's friend, and the former resident of New Beginnings, to return his call. Jack had figured he'd have to track her down.

"Yes, I have questions," he verified. "What can you tell me about an attack that took place yesterday near Longview Ridge?"

Since it was a direct question, he thought maybe she would dodge it. She didn't. "Unfortunately, I know more about it than I should." Grace sighed, and it sounded both heavy and weary. "Marshal Slater, there are some things you need to know about Caroline Moser."

Chapter Ten

Caroline couldn't stop the new round of fear and worry that slammed through her when she heard what Grace Wainwright had just said.

There are some things you need to know about Caroline Moser.

She didn't think she had blank spots left in her memory, but it was possible she did. Also possible that this woman was about to give her news that she wouldn't want to hear. Wouldn't want Jack to hear, either. Still, that didn't stop Caroline from moving closer to the phone so that she wouldn't miss a word.

"Where are you?" Jack asked Grace.

It was one of those square-filler questions that lawmen needed to ask. A face-to-face interview was better than one on the phone, and there was the troubling problem of Grace's safety. If she was involved in this—whatever *this* was—then she could be in danger.

"Sorry, but I'd rather keep my location to myself," Grace answered. She didn't sound angry or resentful. In fact, her voice was surprisingly calm.

"That might not be smart," Jack countered. "I could help you."

"Thanks, but I'll manage. I don't exactly trust lawmen and cops."

Caroline couldn't muster up a nod of agreement when Jack shot her a glance.

"By now, I suspect you've talked to Kingston and Lily?" Grace went on.

Jack paused, obviously considering how much to tell Grace. And when to press her on what she intended to tell him about Caroline. "I have. What do they have to do with Caroline and you?"

Grace made a sound, a sort of hollow laugh. "Everything. Or at least, I think everything. It's all balled up together, you see."

"No, I don't see. Spell it out for me," Jack insisted. "What did you want to tell me about Caroline?"

"That she's part of this. Not the crimes. Not the murders. But she's a part of it."

"All right," Jack huffed. "Keep talking. And I'm especially interested in hearing if you helped your old buddy Kingston get to Caroline."

Definitely no laugh this time. "I didn't. Is that what he told you, that I helped him?"

"Kingston said plenty," Jack settled for saying.

Grace gave another heavy sigh. "Well, I didn't give Kingston any information about anyone. Especially not Caroline. She's in WITSEC, which would have meant me hacking into federal files."

Jack lifted an eyebrow. "You aren't good enough to tap those files?" And this time he was obviously goading Grace, probably hoping to spur her into blurting out more than she intended.

"I'm good at digging out data," Grace answered. "I'm sure you've already heard that, but I wouldn't have done something to bring the feds, or you, coming after me. Especially you. You would have hounded me to the ends of the earth to get back at me for going after your woman."

Your woman. So Grace knew about their relationship. Something like that wouldn't have been hard to access, but what wouldn't have been so easy was getting to the depths of Jack's feelings, which would have indeed caused him to go after Grace and bring her to justice. It meant Grace had been thorough when she'd gotten whatever she had on Jack and her.

"How did you know I was in WITSEC?" Caroline asked, knowing that it was going to earn her a scowl from Jack.

It did.

He obviously had wanted her to stay quiet, maybe because he thought Grace wouldn't spill all if she knew someone else was listening, but Caroline had taken a calculated risk. There was a reason Grace had dug into their relationship. Into their situation. And she'd called Jack. Apparently, the woman had something to say.

"Everything pointed to you being in WITSEC," Grace explained. "When the cops found you in Longview Ridge, Eric was still alive. No way would Marshal Slater have risked Eric getting to you again, and with your head injury, WITSEC is the only thing that made sense."

Maybe. But it was possible that Grace had confirmed that by hacking into Justice Department files. Of course, that only led Caroline to yet more questions. Why would Grace have done that? Why was the woman so interested in her?

"I've been looking into Nicola Gunderson's murder," Grace went on before Caroline could press her for more. "And no, I didn't know her, but her murder grabbed my attention." She paused. "I felt sorry for her, that she died that way."

Caroline looked at Jack to see if he believed that last part, but he only shrugged. It was possible what Grace was saying was true. Nicola's death had gotten the attention of a lot of people. An attractive college student who'd been kidnapped and forced into sex trafficking, only to be murdered. Of course, the media hadn't picked up on Zeller's connection to Nicola.

But did Grace know?

Since that would be giving the woman too much information on their conversation with Zeller, Caroline kept it to herself and waited for Grace to continue. She didn't have to wait long.

"After Nicola's murder and Eric's death, I started researching the investigation," Grace explained. "I believe whoever was running the sex trafficking got Eric to kill Nicola."

Caroline felt that hot tightness in her stomach. "Why do you think that?" she snapped. This time the memories came with a hefty dose of anger. Mercy, were they going to have to add another name to Eric's list of murders?

"Because of info I got from hacking into some files. And no, I won't tell you specifically which ones, because if you do manage to find me, I don't want to be arrested for it."

Caroline could see the debate going on in Jack's eyes. No way could he offer Grace immunity, because hacking was a serious crime. Plus, the woman might not even be telling the truth.

"Does the name Skylar Greer mean anything to you?" Grace asked.

That got every bit of Caroline's attention. Jack's, too,

because his eyes widened, then narrowed. "What about her?" Jack countered, obviously keeping his investigative cards close to the chest.

"She was in the sex-trafficking ring, too, and was rescued," Grace went on after a long pause. "Afterward, Skylar started asking questions and was trying to figure out who'd been running the ring."

Caroline didn't think it was much of a stretch that the woman had done that while living at New Beginnings.

"Do you know where Skylar is?" Jack asked.

"No." Grace didn't hesitate before that answer. "But it's possible she's in hiding. I hope she is, anyway. I hope her questions didn't get her killed."

Caroline hoped the same thing, and it twisted away at her to think of the worst-case scenario here. That Skylar may have been murdered by the same person responsible for taking her into the sex-trafficking ring.

Maybe Lily or Zeller.

Heck, maybe even Kingston. Grace had said this was all balled up together, and Kingston was definitely in the mix.

"Do you know if Skylar saw a counselor or therapist while she was at New Beginnings?" Jack pressed, and Caroline knew why. If she had, then that should have been in the file.

"I'm not sure. Maybe," Grace concluded. "She was eager to turn her life around. Eager to find answers, too, and I think it was that search for the truth that maybe landed her in trouble."

Jack gave an impatient huff. "What did Skylar find in that search and how is all of this connected to Caroline?"

"Again, I'm not sure what she found." Grace hesitated. "But I believe whatever Skylar learned, someone wanted her silenced for it. And that leads me back to Caroline. If Eric did kill Nicola at the request of the person running the sex-trafficking ring, then that person might believe Eric told Caroline about it. Eric had her a long time, and he was cocky. He could have bragged to her about it."

Yes, Eric was cocky, but he'd never mentioned Nicola. Of course, that didn't mean anything. Eric had only talked about his murders in a general kind of way. He'd been far more interested in taunting Caroline for not figuring out sooner that he was a serial killer. The taunts had been like an arrow to her heart because they'd been true.

"Do you have any proof to back up what you're saying?" Jack asked Grace.

"None. It's based on conversations and files that no longer exist. Someone wiped them. Someone who almost certainly wanted to cover up their crimes. I'll leave that to you to figure out."

"Obviously, you wanted to help with that or you wouldn't have returned my call," Jack quickly pointed out.

"No, I returned your call to get you off my back. Also to warn you that I believe this all goes back to Caroline and what the killer thinks Eric might have told her. I don't want to be dragged out into the open so I can be silenced."

That was another arrow strike. Maybe Skylar and Nicola had both been killed to protect a killer's identity. A fatal tying up of loose ends. Both Grace and she also could fall into that category, but there was one major difference between them. Grace obviously knew a lot more about this than Caroline did.

"I want you to back off and not try to contact me again," Grace added, and before Jack could say anything, she ended the call.

Cursing, Jack immediately hit Redial to call Grace back. No answer, and Caroline was betting the woman had used a burner cell, so there was no way to trace it.

"She hacked into the New Beginnings files," Caroline concluded, and she got an instant nod of agreement from Jack.

"That's why I need to talk to her again and find out if something was deleted from Skylar's record." He looked at her. "Any chance you can find Grace?"

"I'll try. I don't know her, not personally, but it's possible we brushed up against each other in cyberspace."

Jack's eyes narrowed a little, enough to let her know that he didn't want that "brushing up" to get her into legal hot water.

"I'll be careful," Caroline assured him.

He studied her a moment, then went to her and brushed a kiss on her cheek. Considering the heat that was always there between them, it seemed almost chaste. Something she hadn't thought possible from Jack. He eased back, their gazes connecting and holding for a long time. Too long. Because she saw more than the fire fueled by the attraction; she saw the worry he had for her.

"I'll be careful," she repeated, and this time Caroline was the one who dropped a kiss on his cheek.

He studied her a moment longer as if he wanted to say more, and then he tore his attention from her. "I'll get you a computer."

Jack went into the bullpen and spoke to Gunnar, and a few moments later, the deputy took a laptop from one of the empty desks and handed it to Jack. Jack was on his way back to Kellan's office when Caroline saw the visitor come in.

Kingston.

She was still feeling raw from everything that had already gone on, but she didn't mind going around again with him. Everything she and Jack learned could put them a step closer to catching their attacker, and Caroline was positive that Kingston knew more than he'd told them.

Jack, however, didn't seem as eager to meet with one of their persons of interest, and it was obvious he didn't trust Kingston, because Jack immediately stepped in between Caroline and him. Then Jack passed her the computer, no doubt to free up his hands. Since she wanted to do the same thing, Caroline put the laptop on Kellan's desk.

"I'm here to sign the statement that I gave to your brother," Kingston said. "Somebody called and told me it was ready."

"I did," Gunnar spoke up. "Give me a sec, and I'll get it for you."

Kingston didn't go to the deputy. He stayed put and cast glances at both Jack and her. "I gotta say that the two of you don't make many friends. I was at the diner across the street and saw Lily when she came out. She didn't seem happy."

"She wasn't," Jack verified. In the same breath he added, "What were you doing at the diner?"

"Waiting on a call that the report was ready. There's a storm moving in, and I thought I'd go ahead and drive out here while the weather was still clear." Kingston got that smug look on his face, as if pleased that he'd had a plausible answer.

Gunnar came to the doorway and handed Kingston the report and a pen. "Look that over and let me know if there are any corrections that need to be made."

Kingston nodded and moved as if to step away, but Jack stopped him. "I just had an interesting conversation with someone you know. Grace Wainwright."

Like Jack, Caroline was watching Kingston's face, and she saw it. The flash of concern. "Grace? What did she want? Where is she?"

The last question seemed to only increase his concern. But Caroline didn't know where that particular emotion of his was aimed. Was he worried about an old friend, or did Kingston think Grace had given them info they could use against him?

"She's fine," Jack answered. "Safe."

Caroline figured that last part was wishful thinking on Jack's part, along with being bait to see more of Kingston's reaction.

"Good," Kingston said, but his expression didn't mesh with the response. "I was worried about her. Grace tends to champion causes that can get her into trouble."

Interesting. And Caroline didn't believe it was her imagination that Kingston had thought carefully about how he was going to say that.

"What causes did Grace recently champion?" Jack asked.

Kingston lifted his shoulder. "I don't have anything specific, but that's just the way Grace is."

Jack stared at him. "Nothing specific, huh? Nothing about the woman missing from New Beginnings?"

"Oh, that." Kingston dismissed it with his tone. "Yes, I suppose it's possible Grace would have poked around with that. She would have likely known the woman since they were at New Beginnings together." He lifted the reports. "I'll just find someplace quiet to go over this."

Jack stepped in front of him before he could leave.

"Does Lily have any reason to harm Caroline or want to silence her?" Jack asked.

Kingston huffed and shook his head. "I don't have any details about the sex-trafficking ring. If Lily had a part in that, I don't have proof."

"Any other reason you can think of?" Jack pressed. "Something that's perhaps connected to Eric Lang?"

Again, Kingston shook his head and turned as if to leave, but then he stopped. "Maybe Lily's still upset about the Crime-Track program that Caroline and Gemma were working on."

Of all the things Caroline had thought Kingston might say, that wasn't one of them. "Crime-Track? Why would Lily be upset about that?"

"Lily tried to invest in it," Kingston calmly said.

Jack immediately looked at her as Caroline said, "I don't remember that." And she didn't. She was sure there hadn't been a single conversation about Lily when it came to Crime-Track. Unless she truly had gaps in her memory and this one had slipped through.

"I don't think she advertised her interest in it," Kingston explained, "but she contacted Gemma. Lily wanted to fund the project, but Gemma turned her down. It might have caused some bad blood between them."

Jack took out his phone and handed it to Caroline so she could call Gemma. She went to the other side of Kellan's office while she did that. Not that the distance would give her much privacy, but at least Kingston wouldn't be able to hear her every word.

Caroline scrolled through the contacts, pressed Gemma's number and said a quick prayer of thanks when Gemma answered on the first ring.

"Is everything okay?" Gemma quickly asked. "Was there another attack?"

"No. We're fine," Caroline assured her, and she felt guilty that she'd caused her friend an obvious moment of terror. Not just because of Jack and her but also because the man Gemma loved could have been in the line of fire.

The breath of relief Gemma took was audible. "Sorry. I'm on edge."

Caroline was right there with her. Too bad things would stay that way until they made an arrest. This phone call might help with that.

"I have a question about Crime-Track," Caroline explained. "Did Lily Terrell ever contact you about it?"

"Yes," Gemma answered after a short pause. "She dropped by my office shortly after the project started, before you started working on it."

So that was why Caroline hadn't recalled anything about this. "You didn't want Lily involved with it?"

"No. Because Lily didn't want to merely be involved. She wanted control of the project."

Control? Caroline tried to think of a logical reason for that. Maybe because Lily believed she could use it to help with stopping things like sex trafficking? But that seemed a stretch since the program was being designed to catch killers.

"It was hard to turn down the funding that Lily offered," Gemma added, "but I wanted the data and reports to be as objective as possible. For that to happen, I thought it best if I handled the process. For all the good that did," she muttered.

Maybe Gemma hadn't meant for her to hear that, but she did. And Caroline couldn't even argue with Gemma on that point or try to make her friend feel better. Because Eric had made dupes out of both of them.

"Was Lily angry when you turned down her funding?" Caroline asked.

"Possibly. I mean, she didn't yell or anything, but she also didn't contact me again. Once when I saw her at a party, she didn't even speak to me."

That sounded like anger to Caroline, but she couldn't see it leading to attempted murder. If it had, Lily would have likely gone after Gemma instead of Jack and her.

"You're staying safe, right?" Caroline pressed, just to make sure.

"Of course." Gemma huffed. "Kellan has one of the reserve deputies guarding me, and the ranch hands are on alert."

"Good. Keep it that way."

"What's this all about?" Gemma demanded. "Was Lily involved in the attack?"

"We're not sure. If she is, you'll be one of the first to know. Take care of yourself, Gemma."

When Caroline finished the call and turned back around to hand Jack his phone, she realized Kingston was gone. "I sent him to the interview room so he could read the report," Jack said. "I figured you didn't want him hanging around here."

"I don't." The guy made her extremely uneasy. Of course, any admirer of Eric would. "Did Kingston tell you anything else about Lily?"

Jack shook his head. "Did you get anything from Gemma?"

Caroline put it in a nutshell. "Lily wanted control of the project, and Gemma refused. I'm not sure if it plays into this, though."

He made a sound of agreement. "Hard to see how it would fit. Well, unless Lily thought she could manipulate the program for some kind of vigilante justice or to launch her own illegal spree. Yeah, I know, it's a long shot," he added.

It was, but... "When Crime-Track first started, it was all about gathering data about murders. The idea was to use that data to try to predict when and where other killings would take place and to combine that with profiles to identify possible suspects. It was meant to become a tool for law enforcement, but maybe someone with unlawful intent would want to stop the project in its tracks."

Jack nodded. "And one way for Lily to do that would be to fund it and then crush it."

Yes, but that seemed like an inefficient way to hide her criminal tracks. Still, it was a possible piece that Jack and she could eventually fit into this puzzle of an investigation.

Before Jack could even put his phone away, it rang, and she saw the muscle flicker in his jaw when he looked at the screen.

"It's Teagan," Jack said, and for a moment Caroline thought he was going to put the call on speaker so she could hear any updates on the case. He didn't. And he stepped away from her when he answered.

Combined with the tight jaw and his sudden secretiveness, this couldn't be good. Nor was the fact that he was practically whispering his fast-clipped responses. She heard him say "What?" Then he followed it with some profanity.

The conversation didn't last long. Less than a minute. But Caroline was certain that Jack had just gotten bad news.

"What's wrong?" she demanded the moment he finished the call.

He took his time answering, which only put her more on edge. "Teagan did a scan of the laptop you used at the WITSEC house, and she found a new tracker called Geo-Trace on one of the sites you accessed. A site about Eric Lang."

She listened carefully to each word, processing it and Jack's dark mood that went along with the explanation. "Geo-Trace," she repeated. "It was still in the experimental stage last I checked."

Jack nodded. "It's apparently operational now, and someone put it on that site."

It didn't take her long to fill in the blanks. "And that someone used my search to track me to the location of the house."

He met her eye to eye. "Yes."

Caroline groaned and pressed her fists against each side of her head. "How could I have been so stupid?"

"You didn't know," he simply said, and it was layered with sympathy. Something she didn't want. Didn't deserve. What she'd done was more than just stupid, though. It had nearly gotten them killed. "God, Jack. I'm so sorry."

"Don't," he warned her, and he went to her, pulling her into his arms. "This isn't your fault. It's the fault of the person who put the tracker on the site."

There was something else in his voice now. Anger. And she didn't think it was directed at her—even though it should have been.

Think, she demanded, fighting her way through the emotions that were flooding her mind. *Think*. Had the Geo-Trace been put on the site specifically to find her?

Possibly.

If so, she didn't have to guess why that'd happened. The person wanted her dead, and it almost certainly went back to the night Eric had taken her hostage. Either someone thought Eric had told her something or that she'd overheard or seen it. Something that her attacker wanted to keep hidden, and the way to do that was to silence her permanently. Jack would just be collateral damage.

"There's more," Jack went on. "I asked the computer guys to do a reverse search to try to find out who put Geo-Trace on the site. And they found the source."

The relief came, but it didn't last. That was because Caroline knew that this wasn't good news.

"Zeller," he said, his voice clipped. "Geo-Trace was loaded on the site from Zeller's office computer."

Chapter Eleven

While Jack slogged his way through the list of calls he had to make, he kept his eye on Caroline. She was at a small table that he'd moved into Kellan's office specifically for her, working on the borrowed laptop. Trying to track down Grace.

He also suspected she was trying to deal with her feelings.

Even though she wasn't talking about it, Caroline was probably still burdened with guilt over the whole Geo-Trace problem. And yeah, she was blaming herself. Jack certainly wasn't. He was putting the blame right where it belonged.

On Zeller.

Well, if Zeller was actually responsible, that is. Jack was trying to sort through his own feelings and questions about that.

It would have been incredibly stupid for a marshal to use his computer to install a tracking device like that. Something that could be traced right back to him. So, unless Zeller had gotten careless, it meant someone had perhaps set him up. And that was a question Jack intended to ask Zeller as soon as he arrived.

Jack checked his watch. One o'clock already. Which

meant Zeller should get to the sheriff's office anytime now. Jack hadn't given the man a heads-up on what the visit was about, but it was possible that Zeller had gotten word about what had been found on his computer. It was hard to keep something like that quiet when others in the office would have known that the techs were running checks.

Still, it didn't matter if Zeller knew or if he'd had time to come up with a story to cover his tracks. A face-to-face meeting would allow Jack to look into his eyes and maybe see if he was telling the truth.

Jack gave Caroline another glance before he went into the squad room to refill his coffee. Kellan was there, doing the same, and he'd no doubt take that fresh cup to the interview room where he'd been working for the past couple hours. His choice, not Jack's. Jack had offered to move Caroline and himself into that room, but Kellan had insisted they stay in his office.

"How's she doing?" Kellan asked, tipping his head to Caroline.

She didn't look up at them. She kept her attention nailed to the laptop screen while her fingers seemingly flew over the keyboard. Next to it was the untouched sandwich that Jack had had delivered for her from the diner. Soon, he'd try to coax her again into eating.

Jack didn't sugarcoat the truth when he answered Kellan. "She's not doing that well. Way too much has happened in the past twenty-four hours, and it's a lot to take on."

Kellan gave a grunt of agreement and sipped his coffee. "Does 'way too much' include you two sleeping together?"

Jack nearly snapped that it was none of Kellan's business, but he knew his brother hadn't meant to pry into his personal life. The bottom line was that sex had complicated things. It had made Jack less objective—though he couldn't remember a time when objectivity had played into his feelings for Caroline.

"It does include that," Jack admitted. He rubbed his forehead, where a dull ache throbbed. "I love her and I want to protect her. If you can figure out a way to stay objective about that, I'd like to hear it."

Maybe because Kellan knew that Jack was dealing with as much emotion as Caroline, he wisely held back any judgment or advice. Kellan just patted his brother on the back and headed toward the interview room. Jack went the other direction. He got Caroline a cup of coffee and brought it to her in the office.

"Thanks," she muttered, not looking up at him, but then she stopped, her fingers still poised over the keyboard.

"Problem?" he asked, knowing there were plenty of them. He just hoped there wasn't something new, since they were already grappling with enough.

"There's no sign of Grace. And the phone she used was indeed a burner." Caroline paused long enough to gulp down some coffee. "I put out feelers through old contacts. *Safe* feelers," she emphasized. "I don't want the wrong person finding her, so I only emailed people I trust."

Good. Because they didn't know who the wrong person was—yet. But it was possible that Grace could become a target if she surfaced.

"I also ran a deeper background check on her," Caroline went on. "Unlike some of the other women who were kidnapped and drugged into the sex-trafficking ring, Grace was lured into it through her drug habit.

From everything I'm hearing, she's clean now, but when she was using, she was out of it. Out of it enough to turn tricks to support her habit."

Jack thought about that a moment. "Any idea who got Grace to start turning tricks?"

She shook her head. "Nothing so far, but I think it's important to find that out. Maybe it was one of our suspects, and if so, we could use Grace to tie Zeller, Lily or Kingston to the rest of what's happening."

He was thinking the same thing. But first, they had to find Grace and convince the woman to trust them. Then he'd have to persuade her to tell all and go into protective custody. No easy feat to do that when it was obvious the woman didn't even want to be found.

Jack slid the plate with the sandwich closer to Caroline's hand, and she glanced at it as if seeing it for the first time. Which was probably true. Caroline tended to get wrapped up when she was doing research.

She frowned but took a bite of the ham-and-Swiss that he knew was her favorite. "There's more," Caroline said, chasing the sandwich with coffee. "I did some checking on Geo-Trace—"

He groaned. "Not a good idea. The Justice Department is all over that. Please tell me you didn't hack into their files."

"I didn't." She was quick to assure him of that. "I went through my own sources, and what I got isn't proof. More of the opinion of others like me."

In other words, hackers. Probably many of them with criminal records. Jack didn't groan again, but that was what he wanted to do.

"Geo-Trace could be a fake," Caroline added after she gave him a couple of seconds to rein in his temper.

Jack went still, letting that sink in. Or rather, trying to let that happen. But he had to shake his head. "But Teagan had heard of it, and it was on the computer."

"There's plenty of talk about it," she verified, "but I'm just not finding the proof that someone has perfected it enough to make it do what it's being designed to do—cull out that kind of info from an IP address."

Jack wasn't a computer idiot, but he also knew this was a conversation that could quickly go over his head. "Put that in layman's terms for me."

She nodded, paused again, this time with her forehead bunching up. "Other than the Geo-Trace that you found on my laptop and Zeller's computer, it doesn't show up anywhere else. That's an electronic red flag because you can bet that someone would have used this program if it were actually available."

Yeah, Jack could see that. Stalkers, thieves and other assorted scum would want their hands on it so they could track the physical location of someone simply because they were using a computer with an internet connection.

"I think the Geo-Trace was just a ruse," Caroline went on. "Something designed to make us think my location had been compromised through the laptop."

If so, that meant someone had set Zeller up.

"Yes," Caroline said as if she'd known exactly what he was thinking.

Since Zeller could arrive any minute, Jack shut the office door so that Caroline and he could have the rest of this conversation without the possibility of Zeller coming in on it.

"It doesn't mean Zeller is innocent, though," she continued. "Maybe I'm wrong about Geo-Trace. It could be that he got his hands on a working program. And even if he didn't, he might be going for some kind of reverse psychology. He might want to make himself look innocent by making us believe someone set him up."

That was something he'd need to give more thought, but Jack could see it from that angle. "Perhaps Zeller or someone else put this fake tracer on your computer and his so it would conceal the fact that the WITSEC file on you had actually been hacked. Geo-Trace would be a way of covering up the hacking."

She stayed quiet a moment, obviously giving that some thought. "It's possible. But it would have taken some serious skills to set all of this in motion."

Jack agreed, and that led him to the next question. "Who's capable of doing something like this?" And one name instantly came to mind. "Grace?"

"Maybe. I don't know how good she is. But I've been in touch with some of my old contacts, and one name keeps coming up. Scotty Milford."

Now, that was a familiar name. "If it's the same guy I'm thinking about, he's a criminal informant."

She nodded. "It's the same guy. He got busted a few years ago for cybercrimes, and he's clean-ish."

"Clean-ish?" Jack scowled. Cursed. "Is that like being a little bit pregnant?"

The color actually rose in Caroline's cheeks. Maybe because she was remembering that he hadn't used a condom the night before. He was still kicking himself over that, but the kicks would have to wait. He made a circling motion with his finger for her to continue.

"My contacts are split as to whether or not Scotty is up to his old tricks again," she explained. "He hasn't gotten caught for anything, but he also hasn't been as chatty online as he normally is. Sometimes, being quiet is a way of not letting others know what you're doing."

That was true in the world of law enforcement, too. "You think he could be involved?" he came out and asked.

"Yes," she said without hesitation.

And that was plenty enough for him. Jack took out his phone so he could get Scotty's contact info.

Caroline stood, picking up the notepad she'd been using. "I already have his number. I got it from one of those contacts, but I should be the one to do this. Scotty would be more likely to talk to me about this than a badge."

He didn't have to think long and hard about that. She was right. So he handed her his phone.

"Any chance that your name and number are in Scotty's contacts?" she asked. "Because I don't want 'Marshal Jack Slater' flashing on the screen."

"I haven't talked to him in a while, and I've gotten a new number since then."

With a nod, she pressed in the number from her notepad, put the call on speaker and waited. After three rings, the call went to voice mail. He saw the brief debate she had with herself about what to do, but she left a message.

"Scotty, this is Caroline Moser," she said. "Call me back at this number ASAP. It's important."

Good. Of course, if Scotty did call, Jack would have to pass his phone to Caroline. He didn't want the man hanging up on them before he even got the chance to question him.

Jack saved the number Caroline had dialed to call the man and put it under Scotty's name. He was still in the process of putting his phone away when there was a knock at the door. As he'd done since this whole ordeal with Caroline started, he moved in front of her and made sure it would be easy for him to reach his weapon before he answered it. The person standing there was exactly who Jack had expected it to be.

Zeller.

And surprise, surprise, he wasn't happy.

Jack had riled Zeller so much in the past twenty-four hours that he was going to owe him a huge apology if it turned out that the marshal was innocent. But Jack had no intentions of believing in that innocence just yet.

There was water dripping off Zeller's hair and running down his face, and that caused Jack to glance out the front windows. The storm had moved in all right, and it was pouring.

"I didn't put anything on Caroline's computer that caused the location of her house to be breached," Zeller spat out, though Jack wasn't sure how he could even talk with his jaw muscles that tight.

"Who told you about that?" Jack immediately asked.

Jack hadn't thought it possible, but the muscles tightened even more. "I have friends at the office, and one of them alerted me that you went behind my back and had my computer checked."

"I did," Jack readily admitted. "And as you obviously know, the techs found something. Care to explain how that tracking program got from your laptop to Caroline's?"

Of course, if Caroline's theory was right, a hacker could have made it look as if Zeller's computer had been used. But no way was Jack going to share that with a man who might want them dead.

Zeller opened his mouth as if ready to shout out an argument, but then he stopped and lowered his shaking head. He stayed that way for several long moments before his attention came back to Jack.

"I didn't do this," Zeller said, his voice weary and hoarse now. "I'm being set up, and the person's doing a damn good job of it. I'm being investigated and people are talking. Even when I'm cleared of the computer charges—and I will be—my reputation will be hurt."

In the beginning, it would be. Jack couldn't see a way around that, but a bruised reputation was a small price to pay for getting away with murder. Heck, Zeller could get away with the computer charges, too, because there might not be enough evidence to pin this on him. A lawyer could argue that plenty of other marshals would have had access to his workplace computer.

"It's either Kingston or Lily who's doing this," Zeller went on. "Kingston maybe because he's carrying out some sick beyond-the-grave orders from Eric." He looked at Caroline. "You know that Eric was capable of doing something like that."

She nodded. "Eric was capable of a lot of things, but he liked to taunt. That's not happening here. The tracer on the site was, well, sneaky. And, yes, Eric could have managed to get someone to do that, but he would have wanted me to know that he'd bested me even after he was dead."

Caroline was right, but Jack could mentally play devil's advocate and see this from a different side. Kingston could have done it as an homage to a twisted SOB that he admired. If so, Kingston might not be in the mindset of gloating and taunting.

And that left Lily.

Jack wasn't sure if Lily had the computer skills, but the woman had enough money to hire someone. Plus, setting up Zeller and having him arrested and convicted would definitely get any heat off her.

"You were getting a warrant on the files at New Beginnings," Zeller continued a moment later. "Lily's stonewalling that, and it could be because she's got plenty to hide."

Jack could feel himself scowling. "How did you know about the warrant request?" he asked Zeller.

But Jack immediately waved that off. If Zeller had heard about the computer tracker being linked back to them, then he could have easily heard about the warrant. In fact, he would have taken that as some possible light at the end of a very dark tunnel if they could use that warrant to find anything to incriminate Lily.

Since Zeller had brought it up, Jack took out his phone and texted Teagan to get an update on the warrant. His partner answered right away.

Lily's lawyers are trying to block the warrant, Teagan messaged. They're claiming some of the files have medical info protected under the law. It might take a while to get it all sorted out.

Hell. They didn't have a while. A delay like this could give Lily a chance to destroy any evidence that might be in those files. Jack consoled himself, though, with the thought that a smart person would have already made sure there was nothing incriminating to find.

"Just let the investigation of your computer play out," Jack told Zeller. "If someone planted the tracer to frame you, that will come to light."

He hoped. While Jack still considered Zeller a suspect, he wanted to get to the truth of what was going on.

Zeller's gaze slashed between Caroline and Jack for several moments before the man cursed and walked away.

He didn't storm out this time, and there was a weariness to his posture as he exited the building. Of course, Jack was cynical enough to think that anything Zeller did right now could be fake. Part of the facade to make them believe he was innocent.

Caroline stepped to Jack's side and watched until Zeller was out of sight. "Do you think his computer skills are good enough to pull off planting a tracker on multiple websites?"

Jack had to shake his head. "I'm not sure."

But it was something he could find out. If he could have gone into his office, he would have been able to talk to his fellow marshals, but no way was he going to leave Caroline. Or take her into what she'd consider a lion's den, since she didn't have a whole lot of trust for lawmen. That meant he'd just have to rely on getting that info from Teagan.

On a heavy sigh, Caroline moved back to the table where she'd been working, but she stopped when Jack's phone rang again. Scotty's name was on the screen. Jack hadn't expected the hacker to actually return Caroline's call, but he was glad Scotty had. He handed his phone to Caroline again so she could answer.

"Scotty," she said after she put the call on speaker, but that was all she managed to get out before the man interrupted her.

"I'm in trouble, Caroline." Scotty's words were rushed together, and he sounded scared out of his mind. "You've got to help me. God, Caroline, I think someone's trying to kill me."

Chapter Twelve

Caroline felt the punch of dread go through her. No. Not another attack.

"Where are you?" she managed to ask Scotty. "What's wrong?"

"Someone broke into my house," he blurted out. "I ran out back, but I don't like the timing because the break-in came shortly after you left me that message. Did you set someone on me?"

"No. Of course not." And Caroline hated that he felt she would have done something like that. "Where are you?" she repeated. "Who broke into your house?"

"I don't know who it was. Some guy dressed all in black and wearing a ski mask. I was in my home office when I saw the person on my security cam. Then I spotted the gun he was carrying, and I got out, jumped in my car and drove off. But I think the person is following me."

Definitely not good, and it caused Caroline's heart to pound even harder. Mercy, was it possible that someone had indeed used her to get to Scotty? She'd checked for trackers on the websites she'd used, but it was possible one of her contacts had said the wrong thing to the wrong person.

"Scotty?" Jack said. "I'm Marshal Jack Slater. I need

you to tell me where you are so I can call someone to help you." He paused, maybe to give Scotty time to react to that, but the only thing Caroline could hear was Scotty mumbling. Or maybe he was praying.

"No cops," Scotty insisted. That came through loud and clear.

Caroline wasn't surprised by that. A lot of hackers, even those who were clean, didn't like the law. Plus, she had her own distrust of cops right now. Not just because of Eric's conversation but also because of Zeller possibly being linked to the attack.

Maybe even linked to this.

Sweet heaven. Was it possible that Zeller had used Scotty to plant that tracker on those sites and had now sent someone to eliminate him? Zeller couldn't be doing it himself because there wouldn't have been nearly enough time for him to get to Scotty in San Antonio.

"It's all over the news that someone tried to kill you, that it happened in Longview Ridge," Scotty went on. "Is that where you are now?"

Caroline certainly didn't jump to answer that. Neither did Jack. And there was a reason for that. It was possible that Scotty wasn't alone, that their would-be killer was in the vehicle with him. Then again, Zeller, Kingston and Lily all knew where she was, so it didn't make the risk any greater to reveal her location to Scotty.

"I'm at the sheriff's office here in Longview Ridge," she finally told him.

"Good, because I'm on my way there now."

Jack didn't curse, but that was what he looked like he wanted to do. "Describe the person and the vehicle that's following you so I can get someone out to help you."

Silence from Scotty, for a long time. "No. Don't send

anyone. I don't want to be gunned down or anything. But tell me what's going on. Why is this happening? And I want to hear the answers from Caroline, not you."

Caroline tried to tamp down the whirlwind of thoughts in her head so she could figure out the right thing to say to him. She also tried to steady her breath and her pulse. This wasn't the time for a panic attack.

"I think someone hacked into either WITSEC files or a Justice Department computer," she explained. "Did you do that?"

More silence, and like Jack, Scotty cursed this time, too. "You know I'm not going to admit to that. I could go to jail." But then Scotty paused. "Is that why someone's after me?"

It wasn't exactly a confession, but it was close enough. "Who hired you to do that?" Caroline pressed.

But that only caused Scotty to curse even more. "I need your help, not your questions. You need to get out here now and meet me."

"That's not going to happen," Jack spoke up. "Where are you?"

Caroline could tell from Jack's rough tone that he wanted that location so he could call in some of his fellow lawmen, but Scotty didn't answer. Not his question, anyway.

"No!" Scotty yelled.

And Caroline heard something else. The squeal of brakes. The sound of a collision. She also heard Scotty groan, and there was no mistaking that he was in pain.

"Scotty?" Caroline practically shouted.

She repeated his name over and over again, begging him to respond, but she only got more of those moans.

The seconds dragged by. Seconds where Scotty could be dying.

"How bad are you hurt?" she pressed. "Tell me where you are, and I can get you some help."

Still, no answer, and she couldn't even hear the moans now. Caroline was about to ask Gunnar to try to trace the call, but he spoke before she could say anything.

"We just got a 911 call about a car accident on the east road, just outside town limits," Gunnar said. "A car hit a light pole."

All of her muscles tightened and twisted. Including the ones in her chest. Caroline had to fight just to drag in a breath. Oh, God. Something bad had happened.

"I'm dispatching an ambulance," Gunnar added, "and I'm on the way there."

Gunnar was already heading for the door when Jack went after him. "It's possible there was an armed suspect in pursuit of the driver. It could be dangerous."

Too dangerous to get an ambulance in there, but the cops would clearly have to respond.

"Help me," Scotty finally groaned out. "I'm dying. Help me."

Caroline figured Jack would give her grief over what she was about to demand, but she was going to do it anyway.

"If Scotty's really dying," she whispered, "I need to try to talk to him. He won't talk to you," she added when Jack opened his mouth. "But he might tell me what he did and who hired him to do it."

Oh, Jack definitely didn't like that, but he couldn't argue her point. This might be their best chance at finding out who had tried to kill them. Of course, there was also a good chance they could be put in another dangerous situation.

"I need you to go with us," Jack told Kellan when he came into the bullpen. "I'll explain along the way."

Kellan didn't hesitate. He hurried toward the door, and the four of them raced out to get into the cruiser. The rain had slowed to just a drizzle, but Jack figured it was only a lull. The storm air felt heavy and the clouds looked ready to burst.

Gunnar took the wheel with Kellan in the front seat, and Jack and she got in the back. While Jack filled Kellan in, Caroline kept her attention on Scotty.

"Are you still there?" she asked Scotty. She kept a tight grip on the phone. "How badly are you hurt?"

"Bad," Scotty managed to say through another of those hoarse groans.

"The ambulance will be right behind us," Kellan let her know, and she relayed that info to Scotty. Whether he understood that or not was anyone's guess.

"Scotty, I need you to tell me who hired you to get into the files," Caroline insisted. "It's important."

Nothing. Not even a groan. And the call disconnected, causing Caroline's concern to skyrocket. Because someone could be there with Scotty. Someone who wanted to finish what they'd started.

"Who called in the 911?" she asked Gunnar. She tried Scotty's number again, but he didn't answer. Caroline kept trying and silently cursed her now trembling hands.

"Hank Perez," Gunnar answered. "He said he heard a noise, looked at his window and saw that a little red car had slammed into a utility pole. His house is on the hill just above the road, and there are some trees obstructing the view, but he said he could see the front end of the car bashed in and steam pouring from it."

So Hank hadn't actually witnessed the wreck. "Was there another vehicle, someone following the red car?" Caroline pressed.

"Hank didn't say, but he doesn't have the best eyesight. He's in his mideighties."

Yes, Caroline remembered. During the months before Eric had taken her hostage, she'd seen Hank in town a couple of times. "He uses one of those scooters to get around?"

Gunnar verified that with a nod. Part of her was relieved by that because maybe it meant Hank wouldn't go from his house to the car. She didn't want him getting shot by the person who'd been after Scotty. Of course, that person would be a fool to hang around since he or she would have figured someone would call the cops.

It didn't take them long to get down Main Street and onto the rural road that would lead them to Scotty. Hopefully, before it was too late.

Caroline continued pressing in Scotty's number while she kept watch, and despite the drizzle, she still had no trouble seeing the blue SUV that was coming up the road toward them. Maybe the vehicle that had been chasing Scotty. Gunnar must have thought so, too, because he slowed down a little, and both Jack and Kellan drew their weapons.

When the cruiser passed the SUV, Caroline got a glimpse of the driver inside, and her stomach went to her knees.

"That's Grace Wainwright," Caroline told them at the same moment that Jack's phone rang and Grace's name appeared on the screen.

"Should I go after her?" Gunnar asked.

"No," Jack said, "but call for someone else to do that. I want to question her and find out why she was out here." He answered the call as soon as he'd finished those instructions to Gunnar.

"I didn't do anything to hurt Scotty," Grace volunteered the moment she was on the line. "I was trying to help him, but someone ran him off the road."

"Who?" Jack snapped.

"I don't know." Grace made a sobbing sound. "Is Scotty dead?"

"You tell me," Jack countered.

That only caused the woman to cry even louder. "I didn't see the person who did this to him. But I did see Scotty's car. I drove past because I thought someone was in there with him. Someone trying to kill him. I drove away and called 911."

"There was a second call," Kellan verified in a whisper. He was on the phone with someone, probably dispatch.

"I couldn't help Scotty," Grace went on. "I'm so sorry, but I couldn't help him."

The woman sounded genuine, but Caroline had a ton of questions for her. She was certain Jack did, too, but she didn't get any more info from her because Grace ended the call. Maybe the deputy that Gunnar sent out would be able to intercept her and take her to the sheriff's office. Caroline put that thought on hold, though, when she looked ahead and spotted the red car.

Her breath vanished.

Because the car was practically wrapped around the utility pole. She couldn't imagine Scotty or anyone else surviving that kind of collision.

Gunnar pulled the cruiser to a stop, and he threw open his door. Kellan and Jack did the same.

"Stay here," Jack told her. "Let me check things out before you see him."

He was trying to protect her, to shield her from seeing Scotty. Part of her appreciated that, but if there was any chance Scotty was alive, there might not be much time to talk to him.

But she didn't get a chance to remind Jack of that because of the movement in the ditch.

Caroline caught it from the corner of her eye. Just a glimpse of someone next to the old ranch trail that was across the road from Scotty.

And that someone fired a shot at them.

JACK HAD BEEN so focused on getting to Scotty's car that he hadn't seen the shooter in time.

That was a big mistake.

Because the shot slammed into the back window. Right where Caroline was sitting. There was a bullet-resistant panel over the glass, and it held. The window didn't shatter, but Jack also knew it might not hold up if someone continued to fire straight into it. And that was exactly what happened.

A barrage of bullets came, all blasting into that one area of the window. Jack didn't have time to return fire or even pinpoint the shooter. He scrambled back into the cruiser, catching on to Caroline and pulling her down on the seat. She was already about to hunker down, and she tried to drag him with her.

He couldn't take cover, though, and he didn't close his door. Not with his brother and Gunnar out there. So Jack shifted his position and tried to make sure they were okay. Both Gunnar and Kellan were on the road and were crawling their way back to the cruiser.

Gunnar had also left the door open, and like Jack's, it was on the opposite side from the shooter. It would give Kellan and Gunnar two ways to get back into the vehicle.

Well, maybe.

Jack had to rethink that idea when several of the bullets skittered across the surface of the road. None of the shots hit them, but the gunfire did pin them down. Which was likely what the shooter intended to do, because almost immediately, more bullets blasted into the window before the attacker's aim returned to the area near Kellan and Gunnar. Whoever was pulling the trigger definitely had a target in mind.

And that target was Caroline.

He didn't intend to let this snake shoot her, and that meant he had to do something now to stop it. Jack pushed her down on the floorboard so he could move to the side of the cruiser where so many of those shots were being aimed. Not that he was especially eager to get closer to the bullets, but he needed to get a visual on the shooter. And he got one, all right.

"He's in the ditch," Jack muttered under his breath.

The ditch, he knew, was deep and extended for miles. Worse, there were ranch trails where someone could have—and likely had—hidden a vehicle.

In this case, the trail was littered with trees and thick underbrush. Plenty of places for a gunman to use for escape. Jack didn't want to let things get that far, though. He needed this person, preferably alive, so he could get answers.

Their attacker was low enough, the high banks of the ditch acting as cover, and only the person's head, shoulders and weapon were visible. He was wearing a ski mask. Jack couldn't even be sure the shooter was a male, but whoever it was had to have some backup weapons because he or she wasn't taking time to reload. There were only a few seconds in between each new round of gunfire.

"Scotty," Jack heard Gunnar say, and there was plenty of concern in the deputy's voice.

Jack soon saw why. Scotty's car door creaked open, and the man tumbled out onto the ground. He was alive, thank God. That was the good news. But even from the twenty or so feet of distance between them, Jack could see the blood on his shirt. Scotty was clutching his chest.

"He needs an ambulance," Caroline blurted out, and that was when Jack realized she'd lifted her head up enough to look out his open door and toward Scotty.

Yeah, he did need an ambulance, badly, but unfortunately, that wasn't going to happen as long as there was active gunfire in the area. The EMTs would likely have been able to hear the shots over the police radio, but Kellan had also texted someone, too. He'd requested both backup from the sheriff's office and the ambulance.

The EMTs could stay back until they got the all clear, but whoever was coming for backup would move in to help. Maybe that would happen before the bullets ripped the cruiser apart.

"There's nothing we can do for Scotty right now," Jack told her.

He pushed Caroline right back down on the floor, but he couldn't help but notice her face. There wasn't a drop of color in it, and her breathing was way too fast. Heaven knew what kind of flashbacks this was triggering for her, and it might be too much for her to handle.

She frantically shook her head. "Whoever's doing this wants me. If we make him think I'll come out there, he might leave cover enough for Kellan, Gunnar or you to get off a shot."

So Caroline wasn't near the panic stage after all. That didn't mean she was thinking straight, though. "I'm not going to let you go out there," Jack warned her.

"I agree. I think this person would just gun me down. Maybe he'd do the same to you, too." Her words rushed out with her frantic breaths. "But we have to do something. Maybe I can call out to him to distract him, to make him think I'm coming out? We can't just sit here."

Jack was thinking that sitting there was their safest option. They could wait for backup. Or at least that was what he believed until the direction of the shots changed again. There was a new target for the gunman.

Scotty.

Hell. Jack saw the bullets kick up the dirt around where Scotty had fallen. He couldn't tell if any of the shots had actually hit the man, but it was possible that would happen.

Kellan and Gunnar used the shift in gunfire to barrel into the cruiser. First, his brother. Then, Gunnar, who immediately started the engine. He pulled the cruiser up, blocking Scotty from the gunman's shots.

Good. That was a start. It protected an injured man who didn't appear to be armed. But, of course, the gunman just started firing at the cruiser again. They couldn't just drive away, either, and leave Scotty unprotected.

The bullets continued to blast into the rear window over Caroline's head, but even over the deafening sound, Jack heard something else. A siren. Another cruiser was coming up the road toward them.

And just like that, the gunfire stopped.

Part of Jack was glad that someone was no longer try-ing to kill Caroline, but he knew what the silence meant. The guy was getting away.

"Do you see him?" Jack asked Gunnar and Kellan. He was hoping they had a better vantage point from the front scene, but both shook their heads.

"The shooter's probably using the ditch to put some distance between him and us," Kellan concluded.

Yeah, Jack figured the same thing. "I'm going out there," he said.

That got a loud, quick "No!" from Caroline.

"The gunman could be moving so he can get a shot at Scotty," Jack reminded her.

That didn't exactly stop the protest he saw in her eyes, but she didn't say "No" this time. Instead, she whispered, "Be careful."

He would, but Jack didn't take the time to reassure her. That was because he needed to get aim on the gun-man before he resurfaced and shot Scotty.

Jack got out of the cruiser, and this time he shut his door in case their attacker came out of the ditch with guns blazing. It would be a suicide mission, with three armed lawmen right there and a backup cruiser just seconds away. Still, desperation made people do stupid things.

Hoping to minimize what anyone could label as stu-pid, Jack used the cruiser for cover, running to the front end of it and keeping down. Keeping watch, too. And it didn't take him long to see what he'd been expecting.

The ski-masked shooter.

The gunman peered out from the ditch, and he'd moved all right. The guy was now a good fifteen yards from the cruiser. He pivoted, taking aim at Scotty. Just as Jack took aim at him.

Jack fired first.

Not just one shot but two, and as much as he wanted answers, he went for the kill instead.

And he got it.

The shots Jack fired took the guy down, and even though he was certain he hadn't missed, he hurried to the ditch to make sure. Keeping his gun aimed and ready, he pulled up next to the ditch and saw the man sprawled in the mud and water that'd been left by the rain.

The guy was dead. Jack was sure of it. But there was someone who was hopefully still alive.

"Get the ambulance in here now!" Jack shouted to Kellan and Gunnar. He started running toward Scotty, and he prayed he wasn't too late to save him.

Chapter Thirteen

Dead.

That was the one word that kept repeating in her head, and Caroline didn't think it would go away anytime soon. Nor would the images of seeing Scotty's car smashed into that utility pole.

She hadn't actually seen his body. Jack was responsible for that. He'd insisted on her staying in the cruiser while the backup and ambulance arrived. Caroline hadn't fought him on that since she'd known in her heart that Scotty was already dead.

So was the gunman.

That didn't ease her frayed nerves, though. She would still hear the sound of all those gunshots and remember the terror she'd felt when Jack stepped outside the cruiser. Yes, she would definitely recall all of that with every detail. And more. She'd have to deal with the worry that this didn't put an end to the danger.

Even though they didn't have an ID yet on the gunman, Caroline figured he'd been hired to kill her. Whoever had done the hiring had likely covered their tracks. Maybe there'd been mistakes made and some evidence or a money trail left behind, but the odds were this would go down as another attempt to get to her.

Caroline drew in slow, deep breaths as Raylene's sister, Deputy Clarie McNeal, pulled the cruiser to a stop in front of Jack's house. Jack had spent most of the drive from the sheriff's office on the phone and keeping watch, but now that they'd arrived at their destination, his focus would be on her.

Or at least it would be once they were inside.

Caroline needed the long breaths not only to try to calm herself but also to try to level out the effects of the adrenaline. If she didn't, Jack would see the panic that was just beneath the surface, and it would make him worry even more than he already did. And there was no mistake about it—he was worried.

It was Clarie who got out first, and ducking against the rain that was coming down hard, she ran to the door, unlocked it and did the security check to make sure no one had gotten inside. Then she motioned for Jack and Caroline, and they hurried in.

"No ID on the gunman yet," Jack told Caroline as he locked the door and reset the alarm. "But we should know something soon. And there is some good news. Lily's turning over the files from New Beginnings."

Wiping the rain from her face, Caroline nodded. That was potentially good. Or at least it would be if Lily hadn't managed to erase any useful information.

Going with that whole attempt to make him not worry, Caroline steeled herself and didn't dodge his gaze when he looked at her. A wary gaze that was examining her for any signs of emotional trauma.

"I'm okay," she assured him.

Judging from the burst of sound that he made, no way was he buying that. Apparently, she wasn't as good at steeling herself as she'd hoped.

"All right," Caroline amended, "maybe I'm not okay exactly, but we're alive and unharmed. That's better than the alternative. Better than Scotty got." It would have been more effective if her voice hadn't cracked on Scotty's name.

Jack glanced at Clarie, who was in the kitchen, and he took Caroline by the arm, leading her to his bedroom. He shut the door, turned to her and started whatever he was about to say.

"You can't blame yourself for any of this," he insisted. He crammed his hands into his pockets, and he probably didn't know that he had blood on his jeans. Not his blood, but Scotty's.

"My guess is that Scotty hacked into WITSEC files," Jack went on, "and the person who hired him to do that sent a killer after him today. We got caught up in it."

She couldn't disagree with any part of that; she had already come to the same conclusion. Scotty hadn't deserved to die, but he'd obviously gotten involved with a very dangerous person. Caroline didn't doubt the danger, either, because that same person was likely after her.

"When the cops go through Scotty's files and his home office, they might find something," Jack added. He was clearly trying to soothe her, but she was beginning to think that he needed just as much of that TLC as she did.

Caroline went closer to him. She didn't touch him, though. Not with the powder keg of emotions already in place. Touching him, even for comfort, would fire up heat of a different kind.

"When I left the sheriff's office to go find Scotty, I knew the risk," she said. "But I thought that if we could get answers, it'd be worth it. It would have been," Caroline amended, and she cursed when her voice cracked again.

Jack cursed, too, because despite her facade, she was right on the edge. He did reach for her, and he likely would have triggered that heat by pulling her into his arms. However, he didn't get a chance to do that because his phone rang.

"Grace," Jack grumbled when he looked at the screen.

Caroline definitely hadn't expected a call from the woman, but maybe this was a good sign. Perhaps Grace would be able to tell them what'd happened.

Jack dropped any trace of the TLC when he jabbed the answer button on his phone, and he put it on speaker. "Why the hell were you on that road just yards from where Scotty crashed?" Jack demanded.

Caroline had no trouble hearing Grace's sobs and broken breaths. "Scotty called me. He's dead, isn't he?"

"Yeah, he's dead," Jack snapped. If there'd been an award for good bedside manner, he would have lost bigtime. There wasn't a trace of sympathy in his voice. "Now I want you to tell me who killed him."

"I honestly don't know," Grace answered through another sob. Caroline didn't think either the words or the crying was fake.

Jack didn't approve of that answer, and he showed that by swearing. "You need to go to the sheriff's office in Longview Ridge. As a minimum, you're a witness to a crime, but I'm betting you know a whole lot more than that."

"I don't!" Grace practically shouted. "And I'm not going to the cops. If a dirty lawman is doing this, I'll end up dead, just like Scotty. Maybe like Skylar and Nicola. Caroline might believe in you, but I don't, and personally, I think she's a fool to trust you."

With that, Grace ended the call.

Jack tried to call the woman back, of course, but neither of them was surprised when Grace didn't answer.

After he shoved his phone back in his pocket, his hands went on his hips, and his gaze fired to hers. Oh, the anger was there. A giant ball of it, and he didn't seem to know where to aim all that dangerous energy.

"Do you really think you're a fool to trust me?" Jack demanded.

He seemed to be throwing some kind of emotional gauntlet, and she thought that maybe he wouldn't be happy with any answer she gave him. So Caroline just stood there. Waiting. And watching the rising storm. Outside, the rain was now battering the windows. There was a crack of lightning. Thunder.

But the storm inside Jack seemed even more intense.

He turned away from her, but the temper had him whirling back around just as fast.

"You're an idiot, you know that?" Jack jabbed his index finger at her. He wasn't shouting or touching her, but it was close. "I love you more than I've ever loved anything or anybody. Hell, I love you more than anyone's probably ever loved before. So believe it when I tell you that you can trust me. I wouldn't let a killer get near you. That includes someone in my own gene pool."

Caroline swallowed the lump in her throat. "You just called me an idiot."

He winced and somehow managed to make that expression look hot. "You noticed that, huh? I was hoping all the I-love-yous would gloss that over." His eyes went dark and serious. The color of storm clouds now. *"Believe it,"* he repeated, his voice a hoarse whisper.

She had no doubts—none—that the words came straight from his heart. "I believe it."

And since there'd been enough words, whispers and shouts, Caroline grabbed on to a handful of his shirt, eased him to her and showed him just how much she loved him right back.

With a kiss.

JACK HEARD HIMSELF say Caroline's name. It was more breath than sound, and he felt those tight muscles relax in his arms and chest. The relief came as his cheek pressed to hers with his mouth against her ear.

Of course, there would have been a whole lot more relief if she'd told him she loved him. But he could wait until she was ready. Believing in him was enough for now.

They stayed that way, standing there, for several long moments. He'd just taken her the night before, but the ache was already there as if he'd gone much too long without her. She was no doubt feeling some of that ache because she shifted, finding his mouth, and her kiss already had that hungry edge to it.

Jack understood the hunger.

He'd failed at being gentle with her before, and he could already feel a repeat of that. This time though, it was Caroline who was in the driver's seat, and it didn't seem as if she had *gentle* in mind.

"Your clothes are coming off," she said like an oath.

He wasn't about to argue with that, but he did have to get his eyes uncrossed when her hand slid down into his jeans and over his erection. He could hardly protest the maneuver since he'd done the same to her, but that bold move made him want their clothes off sooner than he'd planned.

Caroline pressed him face-first against the wall, like

a cop making an arrest. "I can't think when you're kissing me," she said. "Your mouth should be classified as an illegal substance."

Jack got just a flash of male pride, which went to hell in a handbasket when she yanked off his holster. That went on the dresser. Not too long after that, his shirt landed on the floor.

Apparently, no area was off-limits for her, because Caroline's mouth went to the back of his neck, trailing down to his shoulders. Jack had never considered those to be parts of him that he wanted kissed, but it added a heap of fuel to the already blazing heat.

When he started to turn, to take her into his arms, she held him in place, using the lower part of her body and pressing him even harder against the wall. He felt her moving around, maneuvering, and then the touching continued.

While she kept up those long, lingering kisses, she slipped her hands around to his chest. Her fingers were as thorough as her mouth, and she traced each muscle to his stomach.

Then, lower.

She didn't slide her hand into his jeans this time. Instead, Caroline unzipped him, pushing both his jeans and the boxers off his hips, and she was damn clever doing it, too. And slow. Inch by slow inch. Her left hand skimmed over his butt while her right one took care of the front.

"Your body should be illegal, too," Caroline said in a breathy whisper that hit against his shoulder.

No time for male pride this time. Her fist slid the entire length of him. Then, that fist got even tighter. Her mouth—and yes, her tongue—continued on his shoulder, making slow circles and those maddening kisses.

Jack gritted his teeth and swallowed a groan. As good as it felt, and it felt damn good, he didn't want to finish things this way. He was about to tell Caroline that when she lowered his jeans and boxers and then used her foot to push them even farther down so that Jack could step out of them. The moment he did that, she took hold of his waist and spun him around.

Finally!

Or so he thought. But she dodged a kiss, stepping back from him. He could see the heat in her eyes. Hell, he could feel it. The air was firing between them like lightning bolts.

While facing him, she took hold of his hips, and walking backward, she led him to the bed. They stepped over his shirt, and that was when he saw her panties on the floor. He wasn't sure when she'd taken those off, maybe right before all that sanity-robbing touching when she'd had him against the wall.

Caroline reversed their positions when they reached the bed, and pushed him onto the mattress. He landed on his back, and before he could even blink, she landed on him, straddling him.

The scalding kiss she gave him nearly had him forgetting that she still had on her clothes. Minus the panties. Jack got a quick reminder of it, though, when he finally got his hands on her, and he felt the barrier of her top and skirt. Her skirt had shifted up, though, so he could at least get one of his hands on her bare butt as he fumbled around to yank off her top.

But Caroline put an end to that, too. She levered up on her knees, and in the same motion, she took hold of him again. And then dropped so that he was inside her.

Jack didn't swallow the groan that time. Hell, it was

possible his heart had skipped a whole bunch of beats. Pleasure roared through him. Caroline made sure that wasn't a solo thing, either. She shifted, riding him, taking everything he was more than willing to give her.

She found the rhythm. The right one that would wring out every drop of this, and just when she had him right at the brink, Jack reached between her legs to touch her, to give her a little boost to take her to climax with him. Before he could do that, though, she hauled him up to a sitting position so they were face-to-face.

The kiss came. It wasn't filled with hungry greed this time. This was gentle. Soft.

And whispering his name, Caroline wrapped her arms around him and finished them together.

Chapter Fourteen

Caroline didn't bother wondering if having sex with Jack was yet another mistake. It probably was. Loss of focus and all that. But she refused to regret what had happened and figured Jack was on the same page with her. He certainly wasn't doing anything to move her off him in the bed. In fact, he looked pleasured and satisfied.

It wouldn't last, though.

No. Not for her cowboy lawman.

Soon, very soon, he'd start to see the problems that this sort of intimacy would cause for the investigation. That didn't mean Jack didn't love her. He did. But clearly in his mind, this would put a little tarnish on his badge and a whole lot more tarnish on his judgment. It had to be hard to think straight when feelings ran this hot and deep for someone in his protective custody.

Hoping to stop his guilt trip before it started, Caroline lifted her head and kissed Jack right on that incredible mouth of his. Rolling off him, she landed on her back next to him.

"Just remember that I'm the one who started this round," she said.

His breathing was still a little uneven when he turned

on his side and looked at her. "I sure didn't do anything to stop you."

"It wouldn't have worked if you'd tried," Caroline assured him. "And that's all the whining we're allowed over this." She gave him another kiss—a quick, almost chaste one—and she forced herself off the bed. "I'm getting dressed so I can start doing computer checks and calls to look for Grace. Besides, Clarie might be wondering where we got off to."

"Clarie's smart," Jack grumbled. "She'll figure it out."

True, which would make it awkward when Jack and she came out of the bedroom and faced the deputy. Still, it had to be done because Clarie was no doubt working on the case, as well. She might not approve of them rolling around in the sack while she did the job.

Since her clothes were scattered everywhere, it meant traipsing around the room naked while she gathered them. Jack watched, of course, as if entertained by the peep show. But then he huffed, got up and started doing the same thing.

Caroline certainly got some entertainment of her own by seeing his incredible body flex and move, and she reminded herself that they wouldn't get any work done if she kept gawking at him.

"You do know we're going to have to do something, well, drastic, to draw our attacker out in the open?" she threw out there, knowing it would get his mind back where it needed to be.

Of course, he wouldn't like that word *drastic*, and Jack expressed that dislike with a scowl. Then a huff, which actually softened his expression. "Look, I know you're upset about Scotty's death, but—"

That was as far as he got with his protest before his

phone rang. His jeans were still on the floor, so Jack had to rummage around to locate it.

Caroline didn't exactly breathe easier when she saw Kellan's name on the screen. That was because he could be calling with more bad news. She hurried to finish dressing in case Jack and she had to do something right away. Jack answered the call, and he put it on speaker.

"We got an ID on the dead gunman," Kellan said the moment he was on the line. "The name's probably not going to mean anything to you. Amos Treadwell. He's got a record and reputation for being a spine cracker for loan sharks and other lowlifes."

So just a hired gun. That did nothing to make her feel better about any of this, because a paid killer could have done just as much damage as the person who'd hired him, or more.

"Please tell me that you can link Treadwell to one of our suspects," Jack told his brother.

"I wish." Kellan sounded disgusted that he hadn't been able to do that. "But the CSIs did get something when they went through his pockets. Treadwell had other targets, and he'd written down the names on what he called his 'to-do list.'"

Caroline felt a fresh coil of fear slide through her. "What names?" she heard herself ask.

Kellan took his time answering, and that let her know she wasn't going to like what he was about to say. "Scotty, Grace, Jack, you and me."

No, she didn't like it, but it wasn't much of a surprise. At least the first four weren't, but she hadn't expected Kellan to be on that list. Obviously, neither had

Jack, because his now tight jaw muscles went to war with each other.

"Why would Treadwell plan to kill you?" Jack demanded.

She had no trouble hearing the long breath that Kellan took before he answered. "The person who hired Treadwell probably thinks Caroline has spilled all by now and that you spilled it to me." Kellan paused, cursed. "The person could go after Gemma, too."

Or anyone else in Jack's family. That could include his partner, friends. The list could go on and on.

"I've put a reserve deputy on Gemma," Kellan added a moment later, "and I'm heading home right now. Eli and Owen are doing the same."

Caroline filled in the blanks on what Kellan *wasn't* saying. He couldn't keep this level of protection going for long. Eli and Owen had jobs to do along with their families to protect. Their attacker could just wait them out. Maybe wait even long enough until their guards were down and then go after them when they didn't expect it.

Mercy.

They had to do something, now, to put an end to it so they could all get on with their lives. Especially Owen and Eli, since their families included babies who needed protecting.

"I've been mulling over a plan," Caroline said.

As she'd expected, her comment caused some concern followed by anger to flash in Jack's eyes. She figured that if she could see Kellan, he'd have a similar expression. That meant she was going to have to do a hard sell to convince them that what she had in mind could work.

Probably.

But she would keep the word *probably* to herself. They'd have enough doubts without her adding more.

"Both of you know we need to do something to go ahead and draw out this person," Caroline continued. "Our attacker seems to believe that I know something. Something that would incriminate him or her. So why not put it out there that I'm remembering more details of what Eric said when he kidnapped me? I could be bait."

That, of course, didn't go over well. Jack cursed and shook his head. Kellan grumbled some of the same profanity.

"Just let me finish," she said, speaking over them. "Word could get out that I'm going to the Serenity Inn to meet with a therapist or counselor. Someone who can help me use the place to recall those final details that will help us figure out who Eric actually called that night and what he said to him or her."

"The killer won't go for that," Jack concluded, but she knew that he'd said that more out of worry for her than any doubt over the workability of the plan.

"He or she will, if word gets out," Caroline argued. "And we can use Grace to do that."

Jack huffed again. "Grace won't even answer her phone."

"No, but I'm pretty sure she'll read a text. We can ask her to leak that I'll be at the Serenity Inn. Tonight," she added, though Caroline cast an uneasy glance at the window. "If Grace is in on the plan to murder us, then she'll get the info to the right person. To the person who wants us dead. If she's innocent, then she can help us with the leak so we can lure out the killer."

The curtains and blinds were closed, but she could hear the rain battering against the glass. It wouldn't exactly be a good night to go to the old, abandoned hotel, but enduring the weather would be the least of their problems.

No huff from Jack this time, but he gave her a very flat look. "Our attacker could just send another hired thug."

Caroline nodded, knowing that was a strong possibility. The proof of that was the now dead gunman.

"We weren't expecting the other attacks," she explained, "but if we know this one is coming, we can be ready for it. Instead of killing any henchman who shows up, we can take him alive. Maybe shoot him with a tranquilizer gun instead of bullets. After we have him, we can make some kind of deal to get him to talk."

Jack certainly didn't jump on that, either, but she was hoping that once he got over his emotional objection, he would see it could work.

"What makes you think you can trust Grace?" Jack demanded. "What if she shows up and tries to kill you?"

"I'm not sure I can trust her, not completely, but that doesn't matter. If it's Grace who comes to the inn, then you can take her into custody and get her to tell you what she knows about Scotty's death." She paused. "But if she gets out the word, then the real killer or his hired gun might show up. It's worth a try."

Judging from the swear words that poured out of him, Jack didn't agree with her. "I don't want you at the inn," he snapped.

Caroline nodded, knowing he would say that. "I don't especially want to be there, either." Not with all the horrible things that had happened to her. There was the possibility of flashbacks. Heck, there was also the risk of a full-blown panic attack that would pretty much put her out of commission in a fight. "But we can't let this danger and the attacks go on."

"She's right about that," Kellan said before Jack could spout what would have almost certainly been more arguments. "It's dangerous for too many people. I can't protect everyone that this snake might target. He or she is desperate. That's obvious. Maybe because we're getting close to finding out what really happened that night Dad was murdered. A plan like this could be the tipping point to get us that truth."

"Yeah, and it could be the tipping point to getting Caroline shot," Jack fired back. But then he groaned.

Caroline went to him, looked him straight in the eyes. "This could end the danger in just a few hours," she reminded him. Then, she played dirty by adding, "We'd be able to get on with our lives."

Of course, Jack was ready for that to happen. Ready for them to be a couple again. To not have to look over their shoulders to make sure a hired gun didn't have them in his sight.

"Option two," she went on when Jack and Kellan didn't say anything. "I leave Longview Ridge. I disappear. Not through WITSEC or any other way that my location can be hacked or traced. And once I'm gone, none of you will be in danger."

Oh, that brought the storm straight back to Jack's narrowed eyes. "No," he said through clenched teeth. "I'm not losing you again."

Once more, it was exactly the answer she'd expected. Kellan voiced a version of the same by just saying, "You can forget doing that."

Caroline hadn't exactly expected them to agree. Nor did she want to leave Jack. But she'd offered it to give them a choice—which really wasn't a choice at all. So maybe now they'd see that her plan of using Grace was the only way to go.

Jack shook his head again. "What if we have Grace leak that you'll be at the inn first thing in the morning with the therapist? That would give us more time to get everything in place and maybe come up with something better." But almost immediately he waved that off. "It'd give the killer more time, too, and that's something we don't want."

"True." Caroline went even closer, until her body was right against his. "Jack, we need to text Grace and set this all up. We need to do this."

Silence was his reply, but despite it, she could practically hear Jack thinking. Trying to figure out a different way. One that didn't involve her. But other than her walking out of his life, he wouldn't be able to come up with anything that didn't put her in the mix.

Because she was at the center of it.

As long as she drew breath, the killer would come. Caroline just wanted that to happen on their terms and not the killer's.

"Well?" Kellan prompted when the silence dragged on.

Jack hesitated several more seconds before he scrubbed his hand over his face. "Okay. Let's get started."

JACK HAD SO many bad feelings about this, and those feelings came at him like a tornado. He didn't know which one he could latch on to and try to fix, because the whole plan was whirling around in his head and twisting up his insides.

The text had gone out to Grace, and the woman had actually responded right away, saying that she was on board with leaking the information, and that she wanted to help catch the person who'd murdered her friend Scotty. The woman assured them that she'd get the fake news to all three of their main suspects: Lily, Kingston and Zeller. That was good if the leak would actually lure out the killer or his hired gun. That was also good if they could trust Grace, but Jack wasn't sure on either of those counts.

Unlike Caroline.

He wasn't certain how she managed it, but she looked confident and as tough as nails. For the first time since she'd gotten back her memory, he didn't see fear in her eyes. Ironic, since this was the time when fear was plenty warranted. Too many unknowns. Too many things to go wrong. And here she could be within an hour of facing down someone who wanted her dead.

She sat across the dining room table from them, listening while Kellan went over the details. She wasn't nibbling on her bottom lip. Her hands weren't trembling. And she even gave Jack a smile when their gazes met.

Oh, man.

He hated putting Caroline in this position, and it was a potentially dangerous position despite Kellan's and his measures to keep her as safe as possible. One of those precautions was for her to wear a Kevlar vest beneath her clothes. Kellan, Clarie and he would, too, but that wasn't going to protect any of them if the killer or hired guns went with shots to the head. That was why once they arrived at the inn, they'd have to move fast to get Caroline inside.

Kellan's phone dinged with a text message, and he gave Jack a nod. "Gunnar says there's still no activity in or around the inn."

That wasn't a surprise, since the killer likely wouldn't

have had time to get there yet. Unlike Gunnar and Deputy Manuel Garcia. Before Jack had even sent Grace the text, Manuel and Gunnar had gone to the inn to make sure it was vacant. That way, the killer couldn't get a jump on them and maybe set explosives or some other kind of trap.

Gunnar and Manuel had searched through each of the dilapidated rooms and around the grounds to make sure there'd be no surprises. After the two deputies had done that, they'd parked their vehicle on a hidden ranch trail where they could keep watch. They were armed with both tranq guns and their service weapons, with the tranquilizers being their first option so they could take the person alive. It wasn't foolproof—someone could still sneak by them on foot, but at least there would be backup nearby in case something went wrong.

And yes, there was a good chance something would indeed go wrong.

Kellan was right about the killer being desperate, and that increased the risk that the person might do something stupid. Stupid enough to try attacking Caroline with lawmen around. Jack didn't know exactly what the killer might do, but they had to be prepared for any-and everything.

At both Caroline's and Jack's insistence, Kellan would be going to his place with Gemma. No way did Jack want this plan to backfire and have the killer go after someone in his family and hold them hostage. That would give the killer plenty of bargaining power to try to get to Caroline.

"Are we ready to do this?" Caroline asked.

Jack couldn't come up with a reason to delay; they had to hurry this along. He wanted Caroline inside the inn before their attacker had a chance to get there first. Of course, if that did happen, then Gunnar would alert them, and Jack could get Caroline out of harm's way while they dealt with the snake that'd made their lives a living hell.

"Be safe," Kellan said, giving them one last look before he headed outside.

Jack didn't waste any time. He grabbed his equipment bag and got Caroline and Clarie out to the cruiser. The rain had slacked up some, but he'd checked the forecast and knew they could get drizzle on and off all night. He doubted that would keep a killer away, but it would make things uncomfortable for Gunnar and Manuel, who were outside in this weather.

"This is your last chance to change your mind," Jack told Caroline the moment they were in the cruiser.

She immediately shook her head. "You know this is something we have to do."

He wasn't sure of that at all. Yes, he was well aware that the threats couldn't continue. Especially since the dead gunman had been planning on going after Kellan and Grace. The person who'd paid him for that could just turn around and hire someone else to carry through on that to-do list.

Clarie drove, and Jack sat with Caroline in the back seat. Even though it was nearly dark now, he continued to keep watch. They'd also had a couple of the ranch hands patrol the road to make sure no one had pulled off or was lying in wait for them.

More precautions.

And Jack took yet one more. He slid a backup weapon from his equipment bag and handed it to Caroline. If he'd seen any indications that she wasn't comfortable with the gun, he would have rethought his offer. But she took it right away.

"Obviously, it's not a tranq gun," he explained, "but you might need it if someone gets past Gunnar and Manuel."

"Thanks," she said. "By the way, I do know how to use it, and Lucille taught me a lot of self-defense moves."

Hell, he prayed it didn't come down to that, and he forced himself to believe that the best-case scenario would happen. That their attacker would rush to the inn and they could catch him or her.

Even though it was only a few miles, it seemed to take an eternity to get to the inn, and Jack's concerns continued to snowball with each passing second. However, he didn't see or hear anything to make him tell Clarie to turn around and go back to the ranch.

When Clarie reached the inn, she pulled up as close as she could to the wide front porch, and Jack leaned down a little so he could look up at the place. Once it had been a mansion. A showcase for someone who'd had lots and lots of money. When the rich owner had passed away, his heirs had turned it into an inn, a business that had ultimately failed, and they'd let it go when they couldn't pay the taxes. So it had stood abandoned, empty and neglected for years. That was why there was definitely nothing welcoming about it now.

"Talk about creepy," Clarie grumbled.

Yeah, that was the right word for it. Most of the windows had been boarded up, and the ones that hadn't been were just dark holes of jagged, broken glass.

The grounds hadn't fared much better with time and lack of care. Once, there'd been gardens, but now it was an overgrown jumble of trees, underbrush and weeds. Some vines coiled out from that tangle and had snaked their way up the brick-and-stone facade.

Caroline was studying the place, too, but Jack figured

it was more than just creepy for her. It was the place of
her own personal nightmares. Where she'd come too darn
close to dying over a year ago, when Eric had kidnapped
her and brought her here.

After Jack gave Clarie a nod, the three of them got out
and hurried up the steps and inside. Nothing was welcoming here, either. Just an empty shell with scarred wood
floors and walls with holes and graffiti.

Broken glass was scattered everywhere, and they
would hopefully use that to their advantage. When Gunnar and Manuel had gone through the place, they'd kicked
up piles of it next to all the doors and the unboarded windows. That way, if an intruder came in, they should be
able to hear when he or she stepped on the shards.

Since the killer was supposed to believe that Caroline
was there to meet a therapist, Jack and Clarie started setting the scene. He stayed right by Caroline's side while
he took out the flashlights. Not for them to carry. No, he
would put these in the foyer and the adjoining room so
it would seem as if that was where they were.

It wouldn't be.

"This way," Jack said, leading Caroline and Clarie
away from the lights.

The plan was to take them to the first room off the
hall behind the winding staircase, but Caroline stopped
and glanced down.

There was a bloodstain on the foyer floor.

Not fresh, thank God.

Nor was it Caroline's.

It belonged to Gemma, who'd also been attacked here
over a year ago. The memory of his father, who had been
murdered that night, gave Jack another sucker punch of
grief. Even though Gemma had survived the attack, see-

ing that bloodstain brought it all back, and he was certain it was even worse for Caroline. She'd nearly been killed that night, too.

Jack pushed that all aside and got them moving to the room where they'd wait this out. It wasn't ideal since it did have a window, but at least this one was boarded up. Plus, if things went to hell in a handbasket, they could move into one of the other dozen or so rooms that fed off the hall.

The three of them stood there a moment so their eyes could adjust to the near darkness. Some of the milky light from the foyer made its way here. Just enough to create some spooky shadows and show dust motes floating like little ghosts around the room.

It was no wonder that some folks called the place haunted and only came here when dares, too much alcohol or both played into the mix.

"There's a blanket in the equipment bag," he told Caroline, knowing she wasn't going to use it. She didn't.

Caroline went to the window with Clarie, each taking a side so they could peer out through the cracks in the boards. Jack took up position by the door so he could see not only the hall but the front door.

And the wait began.

Even though Grace had gotten out the "leak" fast, it didn't mean their attacker had managed to get things ready to come to the inn. But that thought had no sooner crossed his mind when his phone dinged with a text message. A message that had Jack cursing under his breath.

"Gunnar spotted someone on the road," Jack relayed to Caroline and Clarie. "The person's on foot and headed our way."

Chapter Fifteen

Caroline forced herself to breathe normally. Well, as normally as she could manage, considering this was possibly the showdown that she'd been preparing herself for.

And the one that she'd feared.

She wasn't immune to the panic that wanted to explode inside her, but she reminded herself that this was necessary. It would be impossible for her to put the past behind her if she was still dealing with it. And she felt in her gut that the attacks were connected to her past.

Specifically, to Eric.

Either someone thought Eric had spilled secrets to her, or else they were just tying up loose ends that they believed Eric had left behind. Lily and Zeller fit with the first theory. Kingston with the second.

"Did Gunnar spot a man or woman?" Caroline asked Jack. Even though she whispered her question, it practically echoed in the empty room.

"He's not sure." Jack whispered, too, but there was an angry edge to his voice. "Gunnar said he only got a glimpse of someone dressed all in black before the person ducked off the road and into some trees."

There were certainly a lot of trees, and they dotted the landscape all the way from the road to what was left of the old gardens surrounding the inn. Someone could use them for cover, but eventually the attacker would have to come out into the open to make it inside.

Well, maybe.

It was possible to get into the house by crawling through the underbrush at the back, but it would still take some maneuvering.

"You want me to move to one of the front rooms so I can try to see this person?" Clarie asked.

Jack stayed quiet a moment, obviously giving her question some thought. "No. Gunnar and Manuel have good positions. They should be able to see if anyone approaches the inn, and if need be, one of them can move closer to get a better shot with the tranq gun."

Caroline knew it was the *should be* that was eating away at Jack. He wanted absolutes when it came to her safety, but that wasn't going to happen. The best they could do right now was to have a good shot at putting an end to this.

"What kind of range is there on the tranq gun they're using?" Clarie asked a moment later.

"They actually have tranq rifles, and the range on those is supposed to be 210 feet. But Gunnar didn't think it was smart to risk a shot that far out. He'll want closer."

Caroline agreed with that. It wouldn't be like firing an automatic or semiautomatic, and if they missed on the first shot, they'd have to manually reload. That could give the person time to get away. However, Kellan had assured them that Gunnar and Manuel were both good marksmen with steady hands. And if they failed, then they'd go for a nonkill shot with their regular weapons.

There was also a possible problem with the tranq itself. It wouldn't have an instant effect, and it could take several minutes to incapacitate the person. Still, the drug should make it a whole lot harder for their visitor to try to kill them. Plus, as soon as Gunnar or Manuel fired the tranq, they'd move in to apprehend.

"Zeller's stupid if he doesn't smell a trap," Jack muttered just loud enough for Caroline to hear.

That, too, wasn't setting well with him. Jack didn't want to think of a fellow lawman being at the center of this, but it was possible. Zeller had the means and opportunity. He had a possible motive, as well, if he was trying to cover up his involvement in the sex-trafficking ring.

But Jack was right that Zeller should be able to smell a trap.

After all, the marshal had personal knowledge of her case and had almost certainly gone over every record of hers that existed. He might know that there were no other memories for her to recover. However, she was hoping he had enough doubts about her, about what she'd possibly remembered, that he would take the risk of coming here.

Of course, it was just as likely that he could have hired someone to do his dirty work, but she didn't want to think about that now. If Zeller was guilty, he would come, and then Jack could arrest him.

Caroline peeked out through the sliver of space in between the boards and tried to get a glimpse of this possible attacker. Nothing. She could definitely see some trees and vines, but not a person. Listening didn't help, either, because the only things she could clearly hear were the patter of the rain and her own heartbeat in her ears.

Jack's phone dinged again, the sound shooting through the room and nearly causing Caroline to gasp. Clearly, she didn't have her emotions under control as much as she wanted.

"It's from Gunnar," Jack said after giving Caroline a quick look. No doubt to make sure she was still okay. Just because she hadn't gasped out loud, it didn't mean Jack hadn't sensed her nerves. "He got another glimpse of the person, and he's pretty sure it's a woman."

Maybe it was Lily, and if so, it meant she hadn't sent a henchman but planned on doing the job herself. Of course, that didn't mean the woman didn't have hired guns in the area.

"Gunnar couldn't tell if the woman was armed," Jack went on, reading the text. She saw him click the button to set his phone to vibrate, probably so the killer wouldn't be alerted by the sound of any other incoming messages. "But she just ducked into some oaks on the east side of the inn."

Caroline wasn't exactly sure which way east was, but she turned her attention back to the window in case the woman came that way. Behind her, she heard the soft clicks of Jack texting.

"I told Gunnar to try to get closer to the woman so he can take her or get a better shot," Jack explained. "But Manuel's staying in place so he has a bird's-eye view of the house and grounds. This person might be a decoy, and I don't want someone else sneaking up on us."

A decoy would definitely be something their attacker would try. He or she had never come at them head-on and likely wouldn't want to do that now. The person was basically a coward, and that played into the mental profile she'd done. So yes, they needed to expect some kind of trickery or deception, and with the sprawling grounds around the inn, this woman could be drawing their attention while someone—maybe another hired gun—slipped closer to them.

She looked over her shoulder and saw Jack move out of the doorway and glance toward both ends of the hall. He must not have seen or heard anything suspicious, because he stepped back in.

Caroline looked outside again, trying to pick through the darkness and the rain. Willing herself to see something.

And she did.

Thanks to a bolt of lightning, Caroline saw the blur of motion next to one of the massive oaks.

"Did you see that?" Clarie immediately asked.

"I did." And Caroline was almost positive that it was a woman. One who was no longer in sight.

"Clarie, switch places with me for a second," Jack told the deputy, and Clarie immediately hurried across the room to take up position by the door as Jack came to the window.

"She's behind the center tree in that cluster," Caroline explained, motioning in the direction where she'd spotted the person. "I didn't get a look at her face, but I think she's wearing a ski mask."

Which would make sense. Not only would it conceal her identity, but it would make her face less likely to stand out in the darkness. Ditto for the black clothes. If it hadn't been for the lightning, Caroline might have missed the figure.

Jack continued to keep watch. Waiting. And Mother Nature cooperated with another lightning flash. It lit up the area by the trees for just a second. Enough for them to see that no one was there. Either the woman had moved or she had stayed behind cover.

Caroline soon got the answer as to which had happened.

Despite the rain and her own ragged breath, Caroline

heard the sound. So did Jack and Clarie. Their heads whipped up in its direction. It had come not from the trees but rather the back of the inn. And it was something they'd been listening for.

The sound of someone stepping on broken glass.

An intruder was inside the house.

JACK SILENTLY CURSED, bracing himself for a fight.

He'd known all along that it would be possible for someone to get in the house without the deputies or anyone else seeing them, but he had hoped that wouldn't happen. Now that it had, he needed to do something about it.

He motioned for Clarie to switch places with him again and for her and Caroline to stay in place at the window. That would accomplish two things. The women could continue to keep watch in case this intruder was a decoy, and Caroline would keep out of the most probable line of fire.

Because Jack was certain the person who'd just stepped on that glass would soon be heading to the lights in the foyer.

Clarie took out her phone to send a text to Gunnar. It was part of the plan they'd worked out while still back at his house. She would let Gunnar know about the problem, and then either Gunnar or Manuel would move in closer to assist. The other would stay back to watch for anyone else.

Jack didn't move. Not yet. He just stood there, waiting for the next sound, and he didn't have to wait long.

More footsteps.

At first, those footsteps crunched over the broken glass, but then that stopped. It didn't mean the intruder had left or had even quit moving. It only meant the glass was no longer in the path to alert Jack.

Dragging in a long breath, Jack tightened his grip on his gun and leaned slightly out the doorway so they could start the next phase of this trap. After all, they'd lured the killer or a henchman here with the news that Caroline was trying to recover all her memories. It was best if he played along with that for now.

"Just take a deep breath, Caroline," he said, trying to make it seem as genuine as possible. "Try to clear your mind and think about what else you heard in that phone call. What did the caller say to Eric?"

With his lines delivered, he motioned for Caroline to jump into this.

"I'm okay." Caroline's shaky voice definitely didn't mesh with the strong woman who was keeping watch out the window. "And I do think I remember. Yes, I can hear the person speaking…"

She purposely let her words trail off. Also as planned.

Jack listened for more of the footsteps. Nothing. But Clarie gave him the thumbs-up to indicate that one of the deputies was moving closer to the house. Since Jack hadn't heard her phone ding with the message, Clarie had likely silenced it.

"Can you tell if it's a man or woman talking to Eric?" Jack asked to keep his therapy conversation going with Caroline.

Again, she mumbled her response, but she strung it out for a few seconds. Hopefully, the intruder would think she was having some kind of revelation and would get there fast to try to silence her. Jack didn't want this dragging on any longer than necessary, and he could stop the person as soon as she came into view.

"There's someone else out there," Caroline whispered.

Even though her voice had been barely loud enough for him to hear, those words roared through his head. "Is it Gunnar?" he mouthed.

"No. Someone else. I think it's the same woman I saw before. She's still out there by the trees."

So that meant it was a henchman in the house, so maybe the fake therapy conversation with Caroline didn't matter. If this thug had orders to kill, then he wouldn't care what they were saying. Wouldn't care if Caroline remembered anything or not, since the plan was for her to be dead soon.

Jack wasn't going to let that plan happen.

Clarie sent another text. Probably to Gunnar again so she could give him a heads-up. No way did they want the deputy walking into an ambush, since the woman by the tree could gun him down. Of course, Gunnar would be looking for exactly that sort of thing.

Jack finally heard another footstep, closer this time, and he considered doing more of the fake conversation with Caroline. He decided against it, though, in case the intruder could use his voice to pinpoint their location in the house.

Another footstep. Then another. The person was coming closer, and Jack knew it wouldn't be long before the person made it to the foyer. It seemed to him that the intruder was making a beeline toward those flashlights.

"The woman outside is moving," Caroline whispered. "And I see Gunnar."

Jack wasn't sure if that was a good thing or not. Certainly Gunnar had gotten Clarie's warning, but the deputy might not have seen the woman.

Or she might have seen him.

Jack considered having Clarie send Gunnar another warning text, but it was too risky with the intruder this close to them. And the person was indeed close. Even though there were no more footsteps, Jack could hear some kind of movement. Maybe he or she was getting his or her own weapon ready to launch the attack.

It felt as if everything went still. As if everyone and everything were holding their breath. Waiting for something to happen.

And it did.

There was a plinking sound. Something metal had dropped to the floor.

At first, Jack wondered if the intruder had let something slip and fall. Maybe his weapon. But he soon realized that it wasn't an accident.

Jack caught the first scent of the tear gas.

Chapter Sixteen

Caroline had had no trouble hearing the sound of something falling on the old wood floor of the inn. But she didn't know what it was and had no idea what had suddenly put that troubled look on Jack's face.

But she soon found out.

"Tear gas," Clarie managed to say at the exact moment the deputy began coughing.

Almost immediately, Caroline felt her eyes, nose and throat start to burn, and if it truly was tear gas, she figured it wouldn't be long before it basically incapacitated them. It wouldn't knock them unconscious, but they wouldn't be able to fight if they couldn't breathe. If they couldn't see.

And it was quickly getting to that point.

"This way," Jack snapped, and he tipped his head toward the hall. He had his left arm crooked and pressed to his face while he continued to grip his weapon in his right hand.

Both Caroline and Clarie rushed away from the window and toward him. When she looked out into the hall, she saw the wisps of the white fog. Yes, definitely tear gas. And as bad as it was right now, they weren't getting the full impact yet. That fog was rolling their way.

But where was the intruder who'd likely set all of this in motion?

She didn't see any signs of anyone, but it was possible the person had put on a gas mask. If so, he or she could come through that fog after them.

Jack's eyes had to be burning like fire—hers certainly were—but his gaze still slashed all around. A few seconds crawled by, and then he motioned for Clarie and her to follow him. The three of them barreled out into the hall with Jack in front of her and Clarie behind.

They ran fast but didn't go far, only a couple of yards, before Jack ducked into one of the other rooms, and he shut the door behind them. Caroline soon saw why he'd chosen this one. There were no boards on the window, something he'd probably learned from Gunnar and Manuel when they'd done their initial search of the place. No boards would mean both easy access for an intruder and escape for them.

Jack hurried to the window and threw it open. "Keep watch," he said, his voice rough and raw.

Caroline knew there was a good possibility that a would-be killer was waiting for them out there. That could have been part of the plan all along. Get them out so they could be gunned down. But the primal part of her brain was screaming for her to escape from the tear gas and get some fresh air.

Jack went out the window first. The moment his feet were on the ground, he glanced around again. He was looking for anyone who might be there to attack, but in the same motion, he took hold of Caroline's arm. He pulled her out with him, pushing her against the side of the inn. Keeping in front of her to protect her.

She dragged in a long, much-needed breath. Then another. And she blinked hard to clear away the remnants of the tear gas. The rain helped, but her eyes were still stinging and she couldn't see clearly.

Clarie climbed out of the window then, landing on her feet right next to Caroline, but they didn't stay put. Maybe because Jack believed the intruder would be coming to that room, to that window.

Keeping close to the wall, they hurried through the weeds and underbrush. It wasn't easy. The ground was soft from the rain, and Caroline's shoes bogged in the mud while the bushes scraped and poked at her. Still, it was better than being in there with the tear gas.

They ran, weaving in and out of the ground clutter until they were at the edge of the porch that stretched all the way across the front of the inn. They dropped down next to what was left of the porch railing. Not far from the cruiser. But to get to it, they'd have to go out into the open.

"Stay down," Jack whispered to her, and he maneuvered Caroline behind one of the overgrown shrubs while he peered around the corner at the porch. "I don't see anyone," he added.

Good. Maybe they'd get a few minutes to regroup and recover. They desperately needed that, and then maybe they could pinpoint the location of the person who'd gone inside.

As her eyes and mind started to clear, Caroline got a horrible thought. What if the person was already gone? It was possible that he or she had already escaped, maybe because they believed the tear-gas ploy had failed. If so, then Jack and she were right back where they started—without any proof as to who wanted her dead.

"I'll text Gunnar and let him know our location," Clarie whispered, taking out her phone.

While she did that, Caroline got as good of a grip as she could manage on the gun that Jack had given her. Even though her hand was weak, she needed to be able to help if it came down to a fight, and everything inside her said that was exactly what was going to happen.

"Gunnar lost sight of the woman by the trees," Clarie relayed when she got a response to her text. "He's going to look for her while he makes his way here to us."

Caroline welcomed the backup, but she knew it would also pose a big problem. They wouldn't be able to fire if they heard or saw something, because they wouldn't want to risk hitting Gunnar. Plus, this meant Manuel was alone and without backup. The deputy wouldn't be a primary target for the attacker, but he was still at risk.

Jack glanced back at her, their gazes connecting for a moment, and she saw the fear on his face. Not fear for himself but for her. Caroline wished she could do something to assure him that it would be okay, but she wasn't certain it would be.

And that cut to the bone.

Once again, Jack was in trouble because of her.

Maybe she should have just gone off on her own, far away from him. But while that would have been the smart thing to do, it would have crushed both their hearts. She didn't want him hurt, or worse, but at least they were together.

"I'm going to get in the cruiser and drive it over here," Jack said. "I'll get as close as I can. Wait here with Caroline," he added to Clarie.

But Caroline was already shaking her head before he even finished. "You can't go out there. If this person had tear gas, you know he'll have a gun. He'll be watching the cruiser."

Jack didn't disagree with any of that. He couldn't. However, the look he gave her let her know that he was going to do it anyway. Maybe because he felt it was the only option they had.

"We can wait for Gunnar," Caroline tried, though it wasn't much of an argument. They could be attacked before the deputy made it to them, and he had his hands full looking for the woman. If they managed to capture her, it could possibly give them as many answers as catching the person who'd used that tear gas on them.

Jack levered himself up, and he gave her one last look. A dozen things passed between them. A silent conversation that Caroline wished she could have said aloud.

She had so many things to say to him.

"Be careful" was the only thing she managed before he moved away.

Keeping low, Jack left the meager cover of the shrubs and started for the cruiser. Like their trek from the window, it wouldn't be easy. He'd have to deal with the soggy ground along with the rocks and tangled underbrush.

Clarie moved in front of her, protecting her as Jack had done, but Caroline kept her eyes on Jack until he disappeared behind what was left of a hedge. She maneuvered herself up so she could try to see him, and that was when she heard the sound behind her.

Caroline pivoted, bringing up her gun.

But it was already too late.

JACK WAS ONLY a few yards away from the cruiser when the front door of the inn opened and the tear-gas canister came shooting out.

Hell. Not again.

He only got a glimpse of the person who'd launched it, someone wearing black clothes and a mask. But whoever it was immediately stepped back, using the darkness and the white cloud of gas to hide behind.

"Caroline," Jack said on an oath. He couldn't see Clarie or her, but he figured this was some kind of ploy to get to her.

And it could work.

Jack had a fast debate with himself about getting into the cruiser so he could use it to get closer to the women and give them some cover. But with the uneven ground and some large landscape rocks, he could get stuck. If that happened, he might be too late to save them.

Cursing, he turned around and started running to get back to them, but the gas stung at his eyes like acid. Plus, even though he'd only gotten a few whiffs of it, he was already finding it hard to breathe. It had to be a lot worse for Caroline and Clarie. They were right there, next to where the canister had gone off, so they were no doubt getting the brunt of it.

With that thought racing through his head, Jack cut through the same shrubs and weeds he'd just trampled through so he could make his way back to them. He seriously doubted that their attacker had simply tossed that canister just to make them more miserable than they already were. No. This was some kind of ploy—Jack could feel that in his gut.

He could hear the women coughing. That was a good sign because it meant they were alive, but their instincts would be to run. To get as far away from the gas as possible. That would take them out into the open where they could be gunned down, and they wouldn't even be able to see their attacker.

Jack tried to keep watch around him. Hard to do, but he kept pressing. Kept moving. And his heart went to his knees when he reached the side of the porch and didn't see either Caroline or Clarie. They'd moved.

But where?

The weather didn't cooperate as he listened for them. The sky unzipped, the rain pounding down on him, making it hard to hear. It would clear the air, but it wouldn't happen nearly fast enough.

Jack kept running, and he finally heard the coughing again. No sounds of a struggle with a would-be killer, thank God, and he needed to make it to them to keep it that way.

He stayed close to the wall of the inn, but that meant checking each window to make sure he wasn't about to be ambushed when he went past it. He didn't see anyone. That was the good news. The bad news was that Caroline and Clarie had likely moved to the back of the building.

From where the intruder had gotten inside.

The person could be there, waiting.

Caroline and Clarie were armed, he reminded himself, and he hung on to that thought while he kept moving.

Now it was the rain that was stinging his eyes, and somehow the tear gas was still making its way to him. There was some gas coming out of the inn, too, which Jack discovered when he hurried past the window where Clarie, Caroline and he had escaped the first canister. Even though he doubted they would go back inside with that tear-gas fog, he made a quick glimpse inside.

No one.

He could no longer hear any coughing or other sounds

of movement, and he hoped that was a good sign. That Clarie and Caroline had managed to find some clear air and a safe place to take cover.

Jack considered texting Clarie to let her know he was nearby, but he decided against that. If they were hiding from an attacker, he didn't want to give away their location. Besides, Clarie knew that Gunnar was also out here, somewhere, so she wouldn't pull the trigger without making sure it wasn't one of them.

He took another step and cursed when he nearly tripped over something. Not something, Jack quickly realized.

Someone.

It was a woman, and she was in a crumpled heap at his feet.

That sent his heart rate into a gallop, and he felt the cold fear ripple over his skin. No. Please. Not Caroline.

Jack dropped to his knees, and he forced himself to rein in his emotions. At least he tried to do that. It was nearly impossible to think of the woman he loved being hurt. Or worse. To think of her dead.

But it wasn't Caroline.

He could see that once he managed to wipe the rain from his eyes so he could get a better look. It was Clarie. And she was breathing. Thank God for that, but she wasn't okay. There was blood on her head and in her hair, and since there was a metal pipe next to her, Jack assumed that was the weapon that'd been used to assault her.

Where was Caroline?

Jack's gaze fired all around, but he didn't see her, and everything inside him was telling him he had to get to her now. Still, he sent a quick text to Gunnar to let the deputy know Clarie's location and that she needed medical help—fast. He hated leaving her there alone, but whoever had done this to her now had Caroline. Jack was sure of that.

Using his forearm to push aside the sopping wet shrubs, Jack hurried toward the back of the inn. He tried to listen for any sounds she might make. But he heard nothing. That certainly didn't tamp down his fears.

When his phone vibrated with a text message, he glanced down at the screen and saw Gunnar's response. I'm on my way to Clarie now.

Good. That would be one less thing on Jack's mind, but he said a quick prayer that Clarie's injuries wouldn't be critical. With an attacker on the loose, it could be a while before they could get an ambulance in here for her.

Jack pushed through another cluster of overgrown shrubs, and he finally saw the edge of the back porch. The pressure clamped around his heart, though, when there was still no sign of Caroline. Hell. Had the person who'd tossed that tear gas managed to get away with her in tow?

He plowed his way through more of the weeds, and running now, he made it to the porch.

And there she was.

Not alone.

Not safe, either.

Caroline was on the porch, and despite the darkness, Jack could see that the color had drained from her face. With good reason. Because there was someone standing behind her.

Someone with a knife to her throat.

"I'm sorry," Caroline said. There was a trickle of blood

running down the side of her head and more blood on her sleeve. "Because of the tear gas, I didn't see him in time."

Jack pushed aside her apology for something that wasn't her fault, and he focused on the "him" who was holding Caroline. Definitely a man. Jack could tell from his size despite most of his body being concealed. The coward was hiding behind Caroline.

Who was it?

Was it just another hired gun who'd been sent to kill them?

Jack couldn't tell, because the guy was wearing a gas mask. Not for long, though. Using his free hand, he peeled off the mask, tossing it onto the porch, and flashed a smile.

"Hello, Jack," Kingston said. "Caroline and I have been waiting for you."

FROM THE MOMENT Kingston had come out of the shadows and clubbed Clarie on the head, Caroline had known it would come down to this. Kingston wanted her dead, but he hadn't killed her when he'd hit her with the metal pipe because he'd first wanted to use her to lure out Jack. Kingston wouldn't have been able to use a dead woman to get himself in a position to murder both Jack and her.

And it had worked.

Jack had a gun, and to the best of her knowledge, Kingston only had a knife now that he'd discarded the pipe, but Jack wouldn't have a clean shot with Kingston using her as a human shield.

"Is Clarie all right?" she asked, hating that her voice shook when she spoke. She didn't want to give Kingston any more satisfaction from this, and hearing the fear in her voice probably added to his sick enjoyment.

But why was he doing this?

Caroline hoped she could learn that before she got out of this dangerous situation. And she would get out. There were so many lives at risk—Jack, Clarie, Caroline herself and the deputies outside. No way was she just going to let this piece of slime kill them. First, though, she'd need to get away from that knife he was holding. It was sharp—she knew that because he'd already cut her arm to prove that—and now he had it against her jugular.

"Clarie's fine," Jack said before he shifted his attention to Kingston. Jack's eyes narrowed, and his expression was hard as steel. "Let me guess. You're doing some favors for your old friend Eric."

"I am," Kingston readily admitted, and yes, he was enjoying this. He wanted them to know what he was doing and why. "Last year, Eric called me right from this inn while he was holding Caroline, and he asked me to tie up any and all loose ends for him. Ta-da! That's what I'm doing."

She didn't recall that conversation because she'd been drugged, but hearing what Kingston had just said caused the anger to roar through her. Caroline had to force herself not to ram Kingston in the gut with her elbow. They needed more info from him. Because Jack and she had their own loose ends to tie up. Yes, they would stop Kingston and arrest him, but when that happened, he might clam up. They had to know if others were involved in this.

"Kingston hired Scotty to hack into WITSEC and find my location," Caroline said. She didn't have proof of that, but considering the circumstances, that was a good guess. "It wasn't very smart of you to show up at my house, though."

"Of course, it was," Kingston immediately argued. "Me being there, it made me look innocent."

It had. Well, in a way. But Kingston had always been one of their top suspects.

"And after you were done with Scotty, you hired thugs to kill him," Jack said.

Jack moved a little to his left, and Caroline felt the pressure of the blade against her throat. "That's a no-no. Stay put, Marshal, or I cut her before I'm ready."

It turned her stomach to hear him say he was going to kill her no matter what. That made it even more important to draw this out. Because Jack wasn't the only lawman out there. Gunnar and Manuel were here, too. Maybe one of them could get into position to take Kingston out.

"Scotty was a loose end," Kingston went on a moment later. "So is Caroline, but she's been a little slippery when it comes to finishing up things. I thought it would be a nice touch to kill her here. Eric would appreciate that."

"Eric was a manipulative sociopath," Caroline spat out. "The only things he enjoyed were using people and killing. He used you, Kingston."

"Maybe because I wanted to be used."

That was almost certainly the truth. He was as twisted as Eric.

"The person who talked to Eric on the phone that night used cop jargon," she threw out there a moment later.

"Yes, a nice touch. That was Eric's idea. He wanted to play with your head, maybe make you think he was talking to Jack."

That gave her another jolt of anger, and she could see that it'd done the same to Jack. It was too late to punish Eric for that, but they sure as heck could make Kingston pay for his part in it.

She had to pause and gather her breath. "Who else did Eric and you use? Zeller or Lily? How about Grace?"

"None of the above." Again, no hesitation, but Caroline wasn't sure it was true.

Apparently, Jack wasn't convinced of it, either. "You're sure one of them didn't help you?"

"Nope. Me and me alone. Well, other than those two incompetent idiots I hired. Amos Treadwell was supposed to shoot you. He failed. Jessa Monroe was the woman who threw the first tear-gas canister. She panicked and tried to run so I killed her."

Caroline didn't like having another dead body added to this, but she was glad Jessa wasn't around to give her boss any help.

"And that's why I'm doing this myself. Oh, but I did get Scotty to set up Zeller," Kingston added. "You know, by planting that tracking device on his computer. All smoke, I assure you, since Scotty had already hacked in and gotten the address."

Caroline figured Scotty had done all of that for money. Lots of it, which Kingston could have gotten his hands on. Scotty probably hadn't figured the hacking would get him killed.

"And Lily?" Jack pressed. Like her, he must have decided to get all they could from Kingston.

"Nothing to do with me, but I had Scotty do some hacking in her files, too, and she was a naughty girl. Very involved in the sex trafficking. Tell you what. You can have those files for free. Just get them from my computer in my home office. I've got her bank records and some personal emails. There should be enough there for you to convict her of multiple crimes."

"Enough to convict her of murder?" Jack snapped.

"No. Not that." He stopped. "Oh, I see. You think Lily might have murdered that woman, Nicola, and your dad. Nope. Lily scared some woman into disappearing, but she didn't kill anyone."

"Skylar's alive?" Caroline managed to say.

"Alive and in hiding. If Lily had gotten to her, I would have heard about it. And it was Eric who did Nicola. Don't know the full story on that, but their paths crossed."

So, Skylar hadn't been murdered after all, and once Lily was behind bars, Skylar would likely surface. It didn't surprise Caroline that Eric had killed Nicola, but there was a huge piece of this that didn't fit.

"Eric didn't kill Jack's father," she said. "I was with Eric when Buck Slater was gunned down."

Caroline couldn't see Kingston's expression, but she could see Jack. His eyes went dark, and she could feel the dangerous edge whipping off him. And she knew why. Kingston was almost certainly smiling.

Because he'd been the one to kill Jack's father.

"Eric needed a distraction," Kingston said. "He wanted gunfire to draw the attention off him so he could get away."

Her knees nearly buckled. The weight was so heavy on her chest that it felt as if someone was crushing her heart in a tight fist. And despite all of that, Caroline knew what she was feeling was a drop in the bucket compared to Jack. He'd just listened to the man responsible for his father's murder dismiss it as a mere distraction.

Caroline tried to give Jack a steadying look. A silent "calm down" because she didn't want the rage overtaking him so that he charged at Kingston. They just needed more time. Time that maybe she could buy them.

"You can't think you'll get away with this," she said to Kingston.

"Depends on what you mean by getting away with it." She felt his shoulder move in what she thought might be a shrug. The arrogant SOB. "With my lawyers, I doubt very seriously that I'll be declared competent or sane enough to stand trial. And my psychiatric records will prove it."

Records that Kingston had likely doctored. Or else Scotty had done that for him. But Jack and she could try to use his confession to prove otherwise. And even if they couldn't, he would still spend the rest of his life locked up in a mental institution. Not exactly justice, but it would have to do.

Caroline finally saw what she'd been looking for. Gunnar. He crept in behind one of the shrubs near Jack. Kingston must have seen him, too, but he didn't react. Probably because Gunnar didn't have any better angle of a shot than Jack did.

"Once Caroline's dead, there'll be no more loose ends," Kingston announced, and the muscles in his arm and hand tightened. He was going to do it.

Kingston was going to kill her.

Caroline was going to make sure that didn't happen. Gathering her breath, she directed her anger and fear to her voice and let out a vicious shout as she rammed her elbow into Kingston. She dropped her weight, getting her neck away from that knife. She felt it cut her again, on the side of her head, but she ignored that and scrambled away from Kingston.

Jack moved in. As fast and as mean as a snake.

Caroline had managed to get only a few feet away before Jack was on the porch. He kicked away the knife.

And tossed his gun aside.

When Kingston lunged at him, Jack went after the man with his fists, and Jack was a lot better at it than Kingston. He rammed his fist into Kingston's face, causing the man's head to flop back. Jack hit him again. And again. His fists pounding Kingston even as the man dropped to his knees on the porch. Jack might have kept it up, but Caroline touched his shoulder.

"Let Gunnar arrest him," she said, trying to keep her voice as calm as possible.

Caroline wasn't sure that would be enough to get Jack to stop.

But it was.

Jack froze, his fist still poised midair and aimed at Kingston's face. Kingston was crying now, his breath coming out in wet, loud sobs. Jack stared at the man several long moments before he stepped back. Caroline was right there to pull Jack into her arms.

Gunnar rushed forward. The deputy hurried onto the porch and cuffed Kingston, hauling the man to his feet. "Jack, I'll take care of this," Gunnar said, sympathy all over his face. "And I'll get the ambulance out here for Caroline and Clarie."

"I'm fine," Caroline assured him, and she thought that might be true. Kingston had cut her, but it wasn't serious. Even if it had been, she probably wouldn't have admitted it. Not now. For now, she needed to hold Jack and get him through this.

"Kingston killed him," Jack muttered. "He killed him. And he tried to do the same to you."

"He failed," she reminded him, and she eased back so he could see her face. Her eyes. She wanted him to know that she was okay.

Jack shook his head like a man coming out of a trance,

and his attention landed on her arm, then the side of her head. Where he no doubt saw blood.

"You need the EMTs," he insisted.

He snatched up his gun, holstering it, before he jumped down off the porch, pulling her down and into his arms. But he didn't stand her on the ground. Jack started carrying her toward the front of the inn.

"I can walk," she said.

However, she didn't fight him on this. It was something Jack needed, and she soon realized she needed it, too. She dropped her head onto his shoulder and let him soothe her in a way that only Jack could. Yes, there were still plenty of things unresolved, but she took these moments of comfort from him.

When they reached the front of the inn, she was thankful to see Clarie up and moving around. Manuel had brought in the other cruiser, and that was where Gunnar headed with Kingston. Clarie was rubbing her head and pacing in front of the other cruiser while she talked to someone on the phone.

"Don't worry, I'll let the EMTs check me out," Clarie immediately told Jack. "I just wanted to fill in Kellan. He'll meet us at the sheriff's office."

Caroline was exhausted, but she knew the night wasn't over, and she wanted to be there when Kellan booked Kingston. Actually, she wanted to be there for Jack and his brothers.

In the distance, Caroline heard the wail of sirens from the ambulance. But she also heard something else.

A shout.

"You bastard," someone yelled.

Jack immediately stood Caroline on the ground so he

could pivot and draw his gun. But he was too late. The shot blasted through the air.

It took a moment for Caroline to fight through the shock and see what had happened. And then she spotted Grace. The woman was on the side of the front porch, a gun gripped in her hand.

A gun she'd just used to fire the shot.

At Kingston.

Grace hadn't missed, either. The shot had gone straight into Kingston's chest.

"You bastard," Grace repeated, the tears streaming down her face. She dropped her gun, and it clattered onto the porch. "That was for Scotty," she said before she lifted her hands in surrender.

Chapter Seventeen

Jack wasn't sure if it was a good sign that he did not feel anything but relief that Kingston was dead. As a lawman, he knew it would be a more fitting punishment for a killer to live out his life in a cage. But because there'd been the possibility of a mental facility rather than a prison, Jack was having a hard time seeing the man's death as a bad thing.

What was bad was that Grace would have to pay for what she had done. She might be spending the rest of her life in prison, and while that did bother him, Jack knew there'd been nothing he could have done to stop it. He hadn't seen Grace in time because he'd been so focused on getting help for Caroline and Clarie. Still, he wished he could have done something.

"Mentally beating yourself up?" Caroline asked.

Jack stopped his pacing so he could look at her. She was still on the treatment table in the ER while a nurse finished up the three stitches she'd needed for her head. Four more stitches had already been put on her arm. Jack knew the nurse, Mary Ann Colley, and knew she was good at her job. She'd even stitched him up a few times.

Caroline's injuries were minor, he reminded himself, but Jack knew there was nothing minor when it came to

Caroline. For the rest of his life, he'd see Kingston cutting her, and that was yet another reason he wasn't sorry the man was dead.

He nodded in response to her question, causing her to frown. Probably because she didn't believe beating himself up was necessary. But it was. He should have done a better job protecting her.

They'd gotten lucky. Not just with Caroline's injuries but with Clarie's, too. The deputy had also needed stitches and had a concussion, but she was going to make a full recovery and would only end up missing a couple days of work.

It could've been a lot worse. And not just with the injuries. Grace could have hit someone else when she'd been aiming at Kingston. Gunnar had been right there, but thankfully Grace's shot had hit only her intended target.

"Are you okay?" Caroline asked. She reached out, caught his hand and gave it a squeeze.

He knew what she was asking. This wasn't about the injuries now, or the aftermath of dealing with the attack. She wanted to know if Kingston's confession was eating a hole in him. In some ways, it was. The grief was right there at the surface. As fresh as it had been a year ago. But there was another side to this particular coin.

"I needed to know the truth," he settled for saying. "It's the start to dealing with this."

Caroline nodded, and he hated when he saw the tears she was blinking back. She quickly swiped one of them away. "Eric claimed a lot of lives," she whispered. "Kingston's included."

Jack huffed. "Now who's doing some mental beating up?" He got right in her face despite the fact that the nurse was there next to him. "I won't let you blame yourself for anything Eric did. And as for Kingston, he had a choice. He didn't have to do anything for Eric. Kingston did it because he wanted to do it. Hell, he took pleasure in it."

No way could she argue with that. Caroline had been there, with Kingston's knife to her throat, when the man had gloated and bragged. He likely would have turned into a killer even without Eric.

"All done," the nurse finally said. She stepped back from Caroline and took her hand to help her off the table. The woman handed Jack a piece of paper. "That's a script for some pain meds in case she needs it. The pharmacy's closed for the night, but if you give them a call, they'll open for you." She patted his arm. "Take good care of her, Jack. Give her lots of TLC."

Mary Ann added a wink, which meant she probably knew that Caroline and he had started up their relationship again. Heck, everybody in town probably knew. Jack frowned at that, not because of folks knowing, but because he wasn't sure exactly what his relationship was with Caroline.

He loved her, yes, and heck, they'd had sex twice since she'd gotten her memory back, but there hadn't been time to talk of the future and such. No time to do anything except try to hunt down a killer. With that done, Jack figured it was time for Caroline and him to have a long talk.

A talk that would apparently have to wait.

Jack realized that when he led Caroline out of the treatment room and spotted his brothers. All three of them. And they weren't alone. They had their fiancées, significant others and kids with them, too. On the surface, it looked to be an impromptu family reunion, but they were all there to try to deal with the grief of losing a father.

His brother Owen stood from one of the seats where he'd been sitting with his fiancée, Laney. She was holding Owen's toddler daughter, Addie, who was sacked out and totally unaware of the storm they'd all just weathered.

Eli stood with his girlfriend, Ashlyn. He was holding Ashlyn's adopted daughter, Cora. Cora was only a few months old and seemed entertained by all the people milling around.

Kellan was there with Gemma, and it was Gemma who came forward first and pulled Caroline into a gentle hug. She, too, was blinking back tears, and Jack figured Gemma was remembering her own nightmarish past with Eric, when he'd tried to kill her.

"I'm all right," Caroline assured her. Jack didn't know how she managed it, but Caroline even added a smile. One that looked surprisingly genuine.

"Caroline stood up to Kingston," Jack told Gemma. It wasn't pride in his voice. Okay, maybe it was a little of that, but it was mostly relief. It would likely make Caroline feel stronger now that she had done that. She hadn't been a victim tonight.

"I heard." Gemma glanced down at his raw knuckles. "And I heard you got in some punches. Good," she added before Jack could say anything. "I wish we could have all punched him a time or two."

So did Jack, because it had indeed helped to take out some of his grief and pain on his father's killer.

When Gemma stepped to the side, the others swarmed in. There were more hugs, more whispered words of comfort. His brothers and he all shared that silent conversation. A pact and a promise that they would get past this and get on with their lives.

Exactly what their father would have wanted them to do.

"Gunnar took Clarie home about ten minutes ago," Kellan explained. "She's fine, but I wanted her to get some rest."

That sounded like a darn good idea to Jack. He wanted the same for Caroline. "I'll need a vehicle." That was because Caroline and he had come to the hospital in an ambulance.

Kellan nodded. "Figured as much. You'll be taking Caroline to your house?" But Kellan waved that off. "Of course, you will be," his brother added at the same moment Caroline said, "Yes."

Jack looked at her to see if she had any doubts about that. Apparently, she didn't, since she brushed a kiss on his mouth. "Yes," she repeated.

Fighting a smile, Kellan took a key from his pocket. "Take my truck. Gemma and I can get home in one of the cruisers."

Jack thanked him and took the key. On the way to his place, he'd call the pharmacy and get those meds for Caroline. She didn't seem to be hurting, but that might not last. He fully intended to give her the meds and that TLC.

"The San Antonio cops have picked up Lily," Kellan continued a moment later. "The CSIs are going through Kingston's office. They've already found some things. Doctored files and such. She'll be charged with multiple felonies."

Jack knew he should probably care a whole lot more about that, and later he would. He wanted the woman punished for anything wrong she'd done. But for now, he had enough issues to deal with. And speaking of dealing,

one of his current issues came through the door and into
the hospital waiting room.

Zeller.

Hell. Jack hoped this didn't turn into a big blowup.
Caroline didn't need that, and he wanted to get her out
of there so she could rest. Apparently, his family had the
same idea, because they, too, started to file out. All except Kellan. His brother stayed back, maybe because he
thought there'd be some trouble between Zeller and him.
If it was left up to Jack, there wouldn't be.

Jack went to Zeller and met him eye to eye. "I'm
sorry," Jack told him.

Zeller opened his mouth. Clearly, the man had geared
up for some kind of argument, but then he groaned softly
and shook his head. "Everything was pointing to me. I
looked guilty."

"Yeah, because Kingston paid Scotty to set you up."
Jack didn't point out that if Kingston hadn't confessed,
there might still be a dirty smear on Zeller's reputation.
Or at least the questions and gossip.

"How's Grace?" Zeller asked.

Before Jack could answer, Caroline came to his side
and slid her arm around his waist. Showing her support,
no doubt. Jack appreciated it. Heck, he needed it, but he
didn't like that Caroline was going to have to listen to
what would likely turn into a chat about the wrap-up of
this investigation.

"Grace is in custody," Jack told him. "I'm recommend-
ing a psych eval. Her mental state definitely played into
what she did tonight."

Ironic, since Kingston had been planning on using
that card for his own defense. In Grace's case, though,
it might be true. Still, even if she went to prison for the

rest of her life, it had been her choice to pull the trigger. That was something Jack needed to remember.

Zeller nodded. "Good, but don't hold it against me if I say I'm glad that Kingston is dead. He tried to set me up. And he nearly succeeded."

Yeah, he had, and Jack figured there were a lot of people who wouldn't be mourning Kingston's death.

When Zeller stepped away to talk to Kellan, Jack knew that was his cue to get Caroline out of there. Unfortunately, the rain hadn't stopped. It was no longer coming down in buckets, but it was still drizzling.

"Wait here," he told her. "I'll bring Kellan's truck up to the door."

She glanced out the glass doors before turning to him and catching on to his hand. "We can walk. The fresh air and rain will feel good."

No, it probably wouldn't. It would just get them wet—again. But Jack really didn't care. The only thing that mattered right now was that Caroline was safe. And that she wanted him.

He had no trouble figuring that out when she leaned in and kissed him. Long and hard. Just the way he liked his kisses from Caroline. Of course, it stirred the heat. Always did, and when she finally eased back, they were both smiling.

And clearly eager to get home.

Jack grabbed a newspaper from a rack by the door, and he used that to cover their heads as they walked out. Not a mad dash but a slow stroll with Caroline's uninjured arm around his waist. They stopped long enough for another kiss. Then, another. By the time Jack finally got them in Kellan's truck, it felt as if they'd just gone through a round of foreplay. Foreplay that continued when Caroline dragged him back to her.

After he got his eyes uncrossed from the intense heat of it, he winked at her. "Are you just trying to get in my pants?"

"I've been in your pants. It's a nice place to be. In fact, I can say that your pants are the only ones I'll ever want to get into again."

Jack had been about to start the truck, but that stopped him so he could look at her. And kiss her again. "That means you'll have to marry me," he said.

She shook her head. "We don't have to be married for that."

He looked at her, making sure she saw that her answer would mean everything to him. *Everything*.

"Marry me," he insisted. "And don't make me repeat that whole outburst about me loving you more than I've ever loved anything or anybody."

"What if I want it repeated? What if I say it to you this time?" Caroline added before he could speak.

The corner of his mouth lifted, and he could have sworn his heart doubled in size. "I think I'd really like to hear that," he said.

She didn't take her eyes off him. "Believe me when I tell you that I love you. More than anybody else. More than anything. More than I ever thought it possible to love someone. Believe me when I tell you I'll marry you and that I'll spend the rest of my life showing you just how much I love you."

Smiling, Jack kissed her, his words whispering over her lips. "I believe you."

* * * * *

COMING SOON!

We really hope you enjoyed reading this book.
If you're looking for more romance, be sure to
head to the shops when new books are
available on

Thursday 3rd
September

To see which titles are coming soon, please visit
millsandboon.co.uk/nextmonth

LET'S TALK
Romance

For exclusive extracts, competitions
and special offers, find us online:

Get in touch on 01413 063232

MILLS & BOON

THE HEART OF ROMANCE

A ROMANCE FOR EVERY KIND OF READER

MODERN

Prepare to be swept off your feet by sophisticated, sexy and seductive heroes, in some of the world's most glamourous and romantic locations, where power and passion collide.
8 stories per month.

HISTORICAL

Escape with historical heroes from time gone by. Whether your passion is for wicked Regency Rakes, muscled Vikings or rugged Highlanders, awaken the romance of the past.
6 stories per month.

MEDICAL

Set your pulse racing with dedicated, delectable doctors in the high-pressure world of medicine, where emotions run high and passion, comfort and love are the best medicine.
6 stories per month.

True Love

Celebrate true love with tender stories of heartfelt romance, from the rush of falling in love to the joy a new baby can bring, and a focus on the emotional heart of a relationship.
8 stories per month.

Desire

Indulge in secrets and scandal, intense drama and plenty of sizzling hot action with powerful and passionate heroes who have it all: wealth, status, good looks…everything but the right woman.
6 stories per month.

HEROES

Experience all the excitement of a gripping thriller, with an intense romance at its heart. Resourceful, true-to-life women and strong, fearless men face danger and desire - a killer combination!
8 stories per month.

DARE

Sensual love stories featuring smart, sassy heroines you'd want as a best friend, and compelling intense heroes who are worthy of them.
4 stories per month.

To see which titles are coming soon, please visit

millsandboon.co.uk/nextmonth

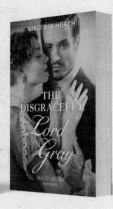

MILLS & BOON
MODERN
Power and Passion

Prepare to be swept off your feet by sophisticated, sexy and seductive heroes, in some of the world's most glamourous and romantic locations, where power and passion collide.

MILLS & BOON

True Love

Romance from the Heart

Celebrate true love with tender stories of heartfelt romance, from the rush of falling in love to the joy a new baby can bring, and a focus on the emotional heart of a relationship.

MILLS & BOON
MEDICAL
Pulse-Racing Passion

Set your pulse racing with dedicated, delectable doctors in the high-pressure world of medicine, where emotions run high and passion, comfort and love are the best medicine.

Eight Medical stories published every month, find them all a

millsandboon.co.uk